DOWN WORLD

DOWN WORLD

Rebecca Phelps

wattpad books **w**

wattpad books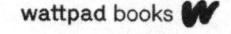

Published in Canada by Wattpad Books, a division of Wattpad Corp.
36 Wellington Street E., Toronto, ON M5E 1C7

www.wattpad.com

First Wattpad Books edition: March 2021

ISBN 978-1-98936-559-5 (Trade Paper original)
ISBN 978-1-98936-560-1 (eBook edition)

Library and Archives Canada Cataloguing in Publication information
is available upon request.

Printed and bound in Canada

1 3 5 7 9 10 8 6 4 2

Cover design by Ysabel Enverga
Cover artwork by © Cosma Andrei via Stocksy and © Joshua Sortino
via Unsplash
Typesetting by Sarah Salomon

For my brother, who was lost, and then found.

PREFACE

So we've decided to leave. All of us, tonight. We'll go as far as the train will take us. John says we have enough money left to buy a place out there, start fresh. And I want to believe him, believe we can put it all behind us. But I'm not so sure. The things we've seen in that dark world, and the things we did there . . .

I would follow John anywhere, and I know that now. And I'll follow him again tonight. I know that too. But the world down below has changed him. Sometimes when I look in his eyes now, when he kisses me, it's like he's not there. He's thinking, and he's planning. He's dark and then he's light. And my deepest fear, if I'm being honest, is that one day he'll just disappear. One day he'll go down and he won't come back. Because I think I know now, I know the truth. Whatever world we found down there, whatever power we discovered, he loves it more than he loves me. More than he loves any of us. He is our leader and our friend, and my only love. And when he goes—because he will go—I know that I will die.

—S

PART ONE

CHAPTER 1

If Robbie were alive, he'd be a senior at this school. That was the thought that struck me when I entered East Township High on that August morning, the first of my sophomore year. I had never set foot in the school before, and I was scared out of my mind. I missed my friends at St. Joe's, the Catholic school the next town over, where I had spent seventh through ninth grades. I missed Robbie. After three years, I still missed him. All the time.

And then there was that stupid little map.

The school had included the map in an orientation packet they'd sent me the week before, but I couldn't make heads or tails of it. East Township, my father had warned me, had originally been built as an army base in the 1940s, and they had intentionally designed it to be confusing. (I guess so Nazis couldn't sneak in and find the top-secret paperwork?) It was full of bricked-up doors, oddly sized rooms, and long twisting hallways that led to nothing.

And the map might as well have been written in hieroglyphics. Everything was color coded, without any indication of what the colors might represent, and not one damn "You are here" in the mix.

The first-period bell rang, and I found myself alone in the hallway next to my empty locker, turning the map in useless circles like a dyslexic juggler, tears stinging behind my eyes.

Pull it together, Marina, I reprimanded myself. *Lost is embarrassing enough. Lost and crying is pathetic.*

I laid the map out on the floor, desperately scanning for some indication of where my math lab might be, when a boy appeared over my head. He and a friend were strolling down the hall like they owned the place, not the least bit concerned that they, too, were apparently late for class.

I didn't notice how cute he was at first: how only one cheek dimpled, or how his shoulder bones made a perfect T with his Adam's apple. I didn't notice that he smelled like lemon-scented laundry detergent and powdered sugar from the doughnut he was eating for breakfast. I was so wrapped up in being lost, and being angry that I was lost, that I didn't notice him at all.

"Where you goin'?" he asked in his low voice, hovering above me. I barely even looked up.

"Nowhere, apparently," I said in frustration, crumpling up the map and throwing it in my locker.

He chuckled, which finally made me look at him. I was shocked to feel my hands go clammy, and I wiped them on my jeans. The boy turned to the friend he had been walking with.

6

"I'll catch you later, man. I gotta help this one out before she burns the place down."

"Later," his friend said.

The boy dipped his head into my locker, so casually it might as well have been his own. "Let's see what we got here, shall we?" He handed me the other half of his doughnut, like we were old friends. Something about him—his voice, maybe, or the flip of his hair—made me feel very safe all of a sudden. Like nothing was a big deal. He uncrumpled the map and spread it out, laughing and shaking his head.

"What's funny?" I asked.

"This map. It makes absolutely zero sense. You can eat that doughnut, by the way. It's my second one today."

I laughed and took a bite. It was weirdly delicious, and I wolfed it down like I'd never had a doughnut before.

"Okay, so first off," he said, conspiring with me over the map, "this makes it look like the math rooms are downstairs. They're upstairs."

"Okay."

"Second, this whole wing over here? It's, like, never used for anything anymore. You don't need that part. So we'll just . . ." He ripped off half the map, balled it up, and threw it on the floor. I smiled, wiping powdered sugar off my mouth as I chewed the last of the doughnut.

"See, now it's manageable."

"Right, of course," I said, like this was our shorthand. Something we had previously agreed on. How is it possible that I felt like I had known this boy my whole life?

He pointed to the number one on the map. "This your first class?"

"Yeah." I nodded. "Math lab."

"You don't have Fitz, do you?"

"I don't know," I said, because I couldn't remember. "Would that be good or bad?"

"Bad. Very bad."

"I think I have White."

"Oh, you're fine, then."

Just then, a very short boy in beige pants and heavy shoes came stomping up to us. "The bell has rung," he said.

"Sorry, dude. Just helping this girl find her class."

"Well, the bell has rung, so she needs a pass. I'll take her to the office."

The doughnut suddenly felt heavy in my stomach. I had no idea who this officious little kid was, but he was ripping me away from my new friend, and getting me in trouble.

"That's okay, dude, we got it covered."

And with that, my new partner in crime grabbed my hand and ran with me down the hall, away from the intruder, who continued to protest even as we turned a corner and started running up a stairwell.

Before I knew it, we were in a sunlit corridor, the walls painted a soothing shade of forest green, and Dimple Cheek pointed to an open door. "Just sneak in quietly and take the first available seat," he said. "You won't get in trouble. People do it all the time."

He handed me the map and started to walk away, turning back to whisper, "Oh, and to get to number two on your map, just head back down these stairs and make a left. You can't miss it."

"Thanks. What's your name?" I asked.

"Brady. Picelli."

"Marina O'Connell," I told him, lingering a moment longer just to watch him leave, and realizing that I was already half in love with Brady Picelli.

o o o

Math lab, as it turns out, is a class dedicated to working on what you've learned in math class. But as this was the first period of the first day, and nobody had actually sat through a math class yet, it was instead a period where everybody broke up into small cliques of friends and gossiped about what they'd done that summer.

I, of course, had no friends at East Township. At least, I didn't think I did. Before my three years at St. Joe's—that is to say, before Robbie's accident made my mother decide to transfer me—I had gone to an elementary school just down the street from here. So at one point, I had probably known a bunch of these kids. But three years is a long time, and I hadn't really kept in touch with anyone.

Across the room, I saw a girl who I was fairly sure was Macy Traper. She had been a willowy little blond thing in the fourth grade, but had now apparently gone Goth. I tried to wave in her direction, but she gave a curt nod and turned back to her friends.

And so I sat alone, doodling in my notebook, my mind wandering to happier times at St. Joe's, where I would often start the day reading under a large elm tree with my friend Lana before first bell. My old school was nestled into a hillside, just outside of town, over where the old estates on "Money Row," as my mother called it, sat rotting into their hundred-year-old foundations. My mother, who had some sort of obsession with anything that she deemed to be wasteful, loved to talk about how, long before the military arrived in the '40s, the town had been formed by a bunch of rich bankers who had made millions by "speculating."

"That's a fancy way of saying 'gambling,'" she had told me.

Gambling was one of my mother's chief deadly sins, especially gambling with other people's hard-earned money, which apparently is a key component to speculating. They used the money to build these hillside estates, sprawling mansions with fifty or sixty or seventy rooms. Every time one banker built a house, his neighbor would have to outdo him. "You have a swimming pool shaped like an egg? I'll build one shaped like the whole hen."

My brother, Robbie, and I snuck into one of them once, the one shaped like a pyramid. It was on a dare from his best friend, Kieren, who had bet us twenty dollars we would be too chicken to spend the night there, since it was haunted by some Egyptian pharaoh whose gold had been stolen from his tomb to make the bricks that lined the gazebo. Or so Kieren said, anyway. You had to take everything Kieren said back then with a *large* grain of salt, as Kieren was the biggest liar in town and everybody knew it.

But still, a dare was a dare, and my brother—at that time a tall and lanky ten-year-old—could never stand to be called chicken. And though I was only eight and scared to spend even one night at a friend's house, I couldn't let the boys think there was anything they could do that I couldn't. If my brother was going, that was good enough for me.

"Don't listen to him," Robbie whispered to me after we'd snuck under a weak spot in the chain-link fence leading to the massive front lawn of the place. "There's no such thing as ghosts. Kieren's full of it." And I laughed to show him I wasn't scared. But I was. All I could think about was how to get out of it, how to convince him we had to go home, arguing that Mom and Dad might check on us and find us missing, which would terrify them.

Robbie could always read my mind. I didn't even have to say it. "We'll just go into one of the bedrooms and I'll take a picture of you sleeping on the floor. That'll be enough. Then we can go home." I must have gasped with relief, because Robbie just laughed at me. He rubbed my head and we crawled in through a broken window into the massive cone-shaped living room of the place. At least, I *think* it was a living room. My memory's a bit fuzzy, and the building was abandoned. It all looked alien to me.

Whatever the room was, we decided it was good enough. I lay down on the empty floor, closing my eyes to a squint, afraid to let Robbie out of my sight. He took the picture with an old camera phone.

"One more to be safe," he said, and snapped another shot with the flash on. I was blinded for a moment, blinking furiously, suddenly overcome with fear.

"Robbie," I called out. "Robbie?"

And then I felt Robbie's hand take mine. "It's okay," he said. "We got it." He pulled me up and guided me back to the window. We ran all the way home. Robbie never let go of my hand.

My breathing intensified even now, as I sat in that first-period math lab, remembering that night. The cool air hitting our faces as we ran, the feel of Robbie's hand in mine. Running and running for our lives.

Kieren never paid us that twenty dollars. We knew he wouldn't, of course. None of us had any money. Our parents couldn't afford allowances. But that was never the point. We had done it, Robbie and I. We had done it together. We were a good team then. It was a great night.

But nothing lasts forever.

The piercing shriek of the bell jolted me out of my seat. I dropped my pencil case, and as I squatted down to pick it up, I could hear Macy and her friends laughing at me. I offered them a weak smile, but they had already dismissed me and were on their way out the door.

I spent the rest of the day looking for Brady. Just hoping to see a friendly face, I guess. And if I'm being totally honest, a *cute* friendly face. But I didn't see him. I did see a couple more kids that I vaguely remembered from the sixth grade, before St. Joe's, when I was still at Sanderson Middle School, but by the time I remembered their names (Jonathan and Casey), it was too late to say hi. It was jarring to see them here, in these strange surroundings and in totally different bodies. It was as though someone had borrowed some faces from a dream I had once and transplanted them onto the necks of complete strangers. I wondered if I looked the same way to them.

When school ended, I headed out front to where the buses waited, but I just couldn't bring myself to get on. I needed some time to think, to be on my own and to feel a breeze in my face.

It was a nice day, the kind of crisp fall weather that used to make me wake up early, excited to get out and see where the day would take me. I crossed the street to start my walk home, and that's when I saw Kieren. I hadn't seen him in years, either, of course, and just like the kids in the hallway, it was like his face was sitting on the wrong body—a tall, broad-shouldered body that bore no resemblance to the skinny kid Robbie and I used to play *Super Mario Kart* with. He looked like his father, who had always scared me just a little bit, with his military haircut and quiet demeanor that often seemed on the verge of exploding.

Kieren just stared at me, and I suppose I just stared back. No one ever told us that we weren't allowed to talk to each other after what happened to Robbie; I think we both just assumed it. There was almost an unspoken rule in our house: we needed an enemy and Kieren was all we had to work with. Kieren, who had been like a second brother to Robbie and me. Who once gave me a penny flattened by a passing train. A penny that I kept in a pocket sewn into my diary, just so my mother wouldn't mistake it for garbage and throw it away.

Kieren blinked twice, as though trying to make out my face in the sunlight. He was holding a skateboard, which he now threw on the sidewalk and hopped onto. He rode away so fast I wondered for a second if I had really seen him. Kieren must be seventeen now, I realized. A senior, like Robbie would have been. So in a year he would be gone for good, and I could go back to thinking of him as a ghost.

The walk home took longer than I had anticipated, the late summer sun still high in the sky. Talk radio wafted from the houses as I passed, with men's and women's voices, tightly wound after too long in each other's company, arguing about unpaid electrical bills or unkempt living rooms.

When I was a kid, most parents were never home during the day. But that was before Proxit Tech closed. Before the hospital lost a key grant, cutting back my father's hours and making him decide it was "a good time" for me to go back to public school. My mother wasn't happy about that, of course. I always knew she had transferred me to St. Joe's to keep me away from Kieren, and he was still around. But even she couldn't ignore the numbers in the bank account.

I walked faster, just wanting to get back to my kitchen and make myself a cup of hot cocoa, watch some cartoons in the TV room, and let my mind turn off for a bit.

As soon as I reached the house, though, I knew that wasn't going to happen. I entered the kitchen through the garage and could tell by the first sight of my mother that she was in one of her moods. I watched her for a solid minute, furiously scrubbing the kitchen tile on her hands and knees, before she paused and looked up, acknowledging my presence.

"Hey," she said, and returned to her work.

It was my cue to keep myself quiet and helpful, to grab a rag and start cleaning with her, so she could know that someone was on her side. That her life wasn't just doing for others, wasn't all a chore. The fifteenth birthday card from my aunt Amalia that had been sitting on the windowsill since January peeked out from under the lid of the garbage can beside her.

I put my backpack down by the door and grabbed a bottle of cleaning solution from beneath the sink. "Here, Mom, let me help you."

"You don't have to. I can do it." This meant it was my turn to say, "I don't mind," or something along those lines. I had made the mistake in the past of taking her words at face value and going up to my room, only to find her eyes red-rimmed and her mouth set in a rigid pout all through dinner. I didn't make that mistake anymore.

I got to work on dusting the windowsills and rubbing down the counters until they shone. I tried to think of something funny and light to say to her—the kind of thing that rolled off

Robbie's tongue so easily, that would always make her laugh—
but nothing came to mind.

"Where's Dad?"

"Got hung up at work."

She didn't stop scrubbing, and so I grabbed my backpack to
leave. "I'm gonna go do my homework."

"Oh," she suddenly said, her mind landing on something that
seemed to surprise her. "I'm sorry. How was your first day?"

"Fine," I said, maybe a bit too robotically.

"Homework already?"

"Yeah, already."

"Jeez."

I could feel the impulse in her to get back to work, as though
she were weighing how long she had to feign interest before she
could be dismissed.

"Okay, I'm gonna get started, then," I said, still standing above
her.

"Okay, honey." She turned back to her scrubbing. "Dinner in
an hour."

"Thanks, Mom." I stood there for a beat, watching her. She
was starting to look thin across the shoulders, and her unruly
hair had all but escaped the overstretched hairband that had
at one point held a ponytail. It was hard to believe that there
was a time when she could have won a Salma Hayek look-alike
contest. That's what she'd looked like when she met my Irish
Catholic dad, while working as a temp at the hospital where he
was a computer tech.

She stopped scrubbing and looked up at me, her eyes momentarily dead before she caught herself and forced a smile.

I forced one back.

I hate her, I thought. *I hate her when she's like this.*

"See you at dinner." I all but ran from the kitchen and took the stairs two at a time, the world turning to a blur until I could be alone in my room.

CHAPTER 2

It was a stupid crush, really. Brady Picelli. The kind of crush that you can't even think about in public because you'll start giggling and everyone will know. But I couldn't shake it. I found myself looking for him every day for the first few months of school, doing a double take when I saw someone with a similar haircut or jacket in a distant hallway. I saw him only twice, both times in school assemblies, but way on the other side of the bleachers. Brady was a senior, so his classes were all in the maroon wing, and mine were in the olive.

I looked for him anyway. Maybe I was just lonely.

I have to admit, I didn't make very many friends in those first few months. The kids who remembered me from elementary school and who knew about Robbie looked at me like I was cursed, if they noticed me at all. Usually people acted like the dead-brother bad luck might rub off on them if they made eye contact.

The others just resented me. Everybody in town knew that the kids from St. Joe's thought they were better than the kids from East Township. Which was true, of course. They really did think that.

Sometimes I'd see my old friends in the hallways and we'd half nod to each other. Holland Pfeffer, who had always been a little pushy, was now a cheerleader with a perma-scowl. She looked down whenever I passed her, and once in the cafeteria, I heard her telling a tall girl in purple glasses about my dead brother, and giggling into her palm.

By the time Christmas vacation came, I had basically given up. I spent the two-week break at home, reading Kurt Vonnegut novels alone in my room, while my father paced the hallway and occasionally asked if "things were cool." Yes, they were, I assured him through the closed door. Though I doubt I was very convincing.

In January I turned sixteen and my dad took me for my driving test. But I hadn't been practicing at all, and I failed the written exam.

"We'll try again next month," he suggested.

"It's fine, Dad."

Honestly, I didn't really want to drive. I had nowhere I needed to be.

And maybe that's why, when I finally did hear Brady's voice coming from the art room sometime in February, I had to stop in the hallway and listen. I had been looking for him for so long, I had started to wonder if I had imagined him. But if I had known what was going to happen next, maybe I would have just kept walking.

Brady sounded angry—that was the first thing I noticed. Or maybe just scared, an oxymoron that didn't coalesce with my idea of the cool guy I had met that first day. If I had to guess, I would have almost said he was pleading with someone. The other voice belonged to a girl—a raspy voice with more than a touch of sadness to it.

Walk, Marina, I told myself. *Don't let him catch you standing here. He'll think you're a stalker.*

But who was I kidding? I wasn't going anywhere, not until I had heard what they were saying. I wasn't eavesdropping, I told myself; just checking to make sure he was okay. I would do the same for any friend.

Only snippets of the conversation came to me. The girl saying, "They'll find me. They'll look for me." Brady then reassuring her, something like, "It's the only way." Or maybe it was, "It's the lonely way." Then a moment later, the girl: "What if they go back to DW?" And Brady: "Then it will be over. And you can come home."

The initials *DW* stuck out to me, because I had seen them before. They were carved into a desk in my social sciences class, deeply etched as though someone had done it with a pocket-knife. I figured they were the initials of someone's ex-boyfriend or something. But then, in the cafeteria, at the edge of the stage, I noticed someone had written in black Sharpie, *Going down, down, down, to DW*. So apparently DW was a place.

The shriek of the bell caught me completely unprepared, and I realized I was alone in the hallway. *Just one more second*, I kept thinking. *Then I'll go to my class on surrealist fiction.* I pressed up against the wall to keep listening.

But then I recognized the thudding feet of the hall monitor

coming my way. I ducked into the nearby handicapped bathroom and waited for what seemed like an eternity before I could clearly hear his footsteps receding.

When I stepped back into the hallway, I realized I could no longer hear Brady and the girl. I whipped around just in time to see them heading for the front of the school, his hand gently resting on her back. She was a tall, thin girl with long brown hair, and despite the circumstances, I couldn't help but feel a crushing jealousy of her—of her long legs and tiny waist. She was a good three inches taller than me and was wearing what appeared to be designer jeans and a fitted suede jacket.

I remained flattened against the wall until they turned the corner.

Okay, I figured. *Now I'll go to class.* But when my feet started moving, it was towards Brady, and the parking lot.

I watched from a window, until I saw them get into a beat-up old Pontiac and drive away. They made a left out of the lot, and then a right onto Clark Street. And since Clark Street dead-ended about a quarter mile from the school, there was only one place they could have been heading: the old train station.

I don't know why I did it. It wasn't like me. I was a good Catholic girl. But it was the last class of the day, and if I went back in now, I'd just get written up.

Maybe I knew in my gut something was wrong, because nothing good ever happened at the train station.

After all, that's where Robbie was killed.

o o o

I hadn't been to the station since Robbie's "accident," which was the word my parents used to describe the night Kieren apparently pushed him in front of the train. The word *accident* always had a certain weight to it whenever they said it—a weight that said, in no uncertain terms, that they believed Kieren had done it on purpose.

Straddling my frozen bike on the sidewalk across from the station, spying on Brady and the girl as they sat in the parked Pontiac talking, I couldn't help but let my eyes drift down the tracks a bit, towards the part where Robbie was hit, and farther down, to the place where Kieren had made me that flattened penny as the commuter train brought workers home from Proxit Tech. That train didn't even run anymore. Since Proxit Tech closed, they shut down the commuter line, and guys like my dad had to start driving to work.

Now only the long-distance lines came through the station: one heading west towards Oregon, I believed, and the other one heading east. I had no idea where that one ended up, but I liked to imagine New York City. They were both dream-chasing trains—the kind you get on when you have no intention of ever coming back.

The station looked abandoned now, the white paint muted and chipping, the weeks-old snow that clung to the roof gray from the exhaust of passing cars. The ivy that adorned the walls had died at some point, and the city had removed all the other plants and trees—I guess because they weren't worth the upkeep. A vending machine had been placed outside, the word TICKETS handwritten across the top.

Brady and the girl finally stepped out of the Pontiac and bought one of those vending-machine tickets. It was hard to tell from where I was standing, but the girl's face looked numb and distant, as though she had been crying for hours. Brady put his arm around her shoulders and she buried her head in his chest.

They stood that way for a long time, and while I knew I should probably go, my feet felt locked in cement. It was like a foreign film. I didn't understand the language, but somehow I couldn't turn it off.

Finally, after about fifteen minutes, the train came. The westbound train. It screeched to a halt and when it pulled away a minute later, only Brady was standing there. I watched him walk to his car and drive away. I had no idea what time it was, but the sky had turned quite dark. If I had to guess, I'd say maybe 4 p.m. It was official. I had cut school.

I wouldn't be able to take the path that ran along the tracks back to my house, as it was probably coated in a sheet of winter ice. I'd have to take the main road, behind Brady. I waited another fifteen minutes, turning my back to the wind and rocking slightly against the chill. Only one car passed.

I couldn't wait anymore. Pretty soon I'd barely be able to see the road, and I wasn't wearing any reflective clothing. I'd have to think up a story to tell my mother about where I'd been after school. I pedaled harder and harder while I thought, the blood rushing through my limbs and finally warming me up. I turned in to my neighborhood of small, identical houses, cold and hungry, anxious to be home.

I wondered where the girl was going to end up, on that train. Did it really go somewhere like Oregon? I imagined her drinking coffee in the rain, my knowledge of Oregon admittedly limited.

It was at this point the headlights first lit up my path, from a car behind me. Someone coming home from work, I figured.

REBECCA PHELPS

I pulled over to the edge of the road to give him room, but he stayed behind me. I turned right onto my street, and the car followed suit, driving slowly. *Too* slowly. As though he didn't want to pass me. As though he was following me.

I biked onto my driveway and fumbled with the keypad that opened the garage door. I didn't dare turn around to see if he was still there. But after the whir of the opening garage door subsided, I could hear it—the faint hum of an engine. A big engine, the kind they put into great old American cars. Like Cadillacs and Broncos. And Pontiacs.

I pulled the bike into the garage. I didn't turn around. I remained frozen there, like a child who thinks that if she keeps her eyes closed, the monsters under her bed won't be able to get her.

A moment later, I heard the tires screech down my road. I looked up in time to see the now-familiar taillights of Brady's car reach the end of my street and then drive away. So he knew I had followed him. And he would obviously be furious with me, prying into his business.

What the hell had I done?

o   o   o

Sitting on the school bus the next morning, staring out at the rain, I felt a great welling emptiness in the pit of my stomach. My palms were damp and I kept forgetting to breathe. I realized I was afraid, terribly afraid for reasons that I couldn't quite put my finger on. Yes, I was afraid that Brady would hate me. But it went deeper than that.

I couldn't get my mind off that girl on the train. She didn't have any luggage. Not even a toothbrush. And she was alone—only slightly older than me, and alone. Did she have any money? How would she eat? Where would she sleep? What was so awful here that she couldn't face it?

I wasn't sitting in my usual place on the bus, and my eyes fell on an etching in the leather of the seat in front of me—*DW I'll never tell.*

"What is DW?" I said aloud. The girl sitting next to me, who was scribbling out the answers on a homework sheet she clearly was supposed to have finished the night before, glanced at me sideways for a second.

"I mean," I stammered, trying to make it seem normal that I was talking to myself, "like, do you know?"

She just shrugged, then slid farther away from me on the seat.

I buried my head, trying to hide inside my hoodie for the rest of the ride.

When we got to school, I kept my head hung low in the universal "I'm not really here" gesture I had picked up since the fall, but I didn't make it far.

A hand grabbed my wrist before I'd gone ten feet and dragged me out of the hallway, through a door I had never noticed before. The hand belonged to Brady, and when I realized this, I could feel a fresh coat of sweat forming in my palms. The anticipation of him screaming at me, demanding to know why I had followed him, was too painful to handle. But at the same time, I couldn't help but think that here we were, ducking into a hidden door and up a short flight of stairs together.

His hand on my wrist was colder than I remembered from that first day when he had led me to class, and he was tugging with no regard for whether or not he might be hurting me, which he

REBECCA PHELPS

was. At the top of the five or six stairs, he opened a door labeled DARKROOM and closed it behind us. The room was, as the sign had promised, quite dark, with only a red light illuminating a bunch of photography equipment and some trays of developing solution. Black-and-white photos hung from clothespins on a line, most of them out of focus.

I was out of breath and shaking. I could barely look him in the eye and instead stared at the ground by his feet.

"Brady, I'm sorry—"

"Be quiet." He looked around the room for a moment, to be sure no one was there, I assumed. He was angry. That much was clear. His breathing was heavy and overly regulated, like he was trying not to scream. "Did you get a good show yesterday?"

"I wasn't—I didn't mean to . . ." I couldn't finish the sentence. I didn't know what to say. I had followed him and spied on him. I had seen something personal, something I clearly wasn't meant to see. There was nothing to say about it. It was a stupid thing to do. "I'm sorry."

"That was none of your business," he almost spat at me.

"I know."

"You don't know. You could get hurt."

"I just wanted to make sure you were okay. I didn't know she was going to get on the train." He glared at me through the darkness in the room, and I knew I was only making things worse.

He sat down on the edge of the table and stared at me for what felt like an eternity. As my vision adjusted, I could see that his deep-set eyes looked haunted and tired. I wondered if he had slept at all. And the thought of him sleeping made me wonder what kind of house he lived in, what kind of bed he slept in. Who were his parents? Were they still together?

"This is serious. You could get hurt," he repeated. "Is that what you want?"

"No." My voice was barely a whisper. "It's okay." I choked back the fear and dared to look at him.

"You can never tell. You have to promise me."

"I won't, I promise."

Secrets. That's what this was all about. That girl on the train held them, and so did Brady. Well, I knew all about secrets. The way my parents never talked about my brother anymore. The way his memory hung over our house, over our kitchen. *I'll never tell*, I thought to myself. And I couldn't figure out right away why the phrase seemed so familiar. And suddenly it came to me—*DW I'll never tell.*

"Is this about DW?" I asked.

He leaped at me then. He was so quick, I didn't even see him leave the table.

Suddenly he was hovering over me. Brady was much taller than I was, and I felt like a child when he stood next to me like this. A child who had done something very, very wrong.

"Don't ever mention that!" he screamed. His hands grasped my upper arms so tightly that his nails clawed into my skin. It hurt, but I didn't want to pull away. His face was inches from mine.

"Okay."

"Ever!"

"Okay." I was scared. Scared of Brady, scared of what I had said.

"It's okay, Brady," came a voice from out of nowhere. A voice belonging to someone neither of us had been aware was in the room. And out of the shadows stepped a face I knew quite well.

Or at least, a face I had once known. The face belonged to Kieren.

Brady, shocked by the sudden intrusion, let go of my arms and seemed to stumble away from me. It was as if the words had hit him with a physical force. His tone changed, and his whole body seemed smaller.

"What are you doing here?"

"Developing film." Kieren nodded behind him. "What are you doing here?"

"She followed me yesterday. She knows."

Kieren turned to me, still cool. His voice had changed so much since I'd last heard it. He sounded almost like a man, his tone creamy and low, dipping at the ends of sentences. I wondered if he had been smoking cigarettes. I knew he was a skateboarder, and that seemed like something a boarder would do. Kieren's mother was a cancer survivor, I remembered. Breast cancer.

There was some secret communication going on between Kieren and Brady—who I hadn't even realized knew each other—that chilled me to the bone.

"Is that true, M? What do you know?" Kieren calling me by my old nickname brought a pang into my throat—a pang of memory and of loss. Only he and my brother had called me M. And no one had done so since the accident.

"Nothing," I insisted, though my voice broke in the middle. "I don't know anything. I just saw the girl get on the train."

"She's going to ask a million questions," insisted Brady.

"I'll handle this," Kieren said, still not showing any emotion. "You should go."

Brady, to my shock, nodded and left the room. What was happening here? Brady taking directions from Kieren struck me as bizarre. The balance of power seemed off somehow. And besides, what were they even talking about? A million questions about what?

"I'll walk you back to class, M."

"Kieren, what is going on here?" It still felt odd to look Kieren in the eyes. It was like both a hundred years and no time at all had passed in the same instant.

"Nothing. He's overreacting. His girlfriend went to visit a friend and didn't tell her parents first."

I nodded. That explanation almost seemed to make sense. *Almost.* Until I started to think about it, and I realized that it left too many questions unanswered. What was DW? Why did she look so scared? And why did Brady? But something deep down told me that I shouldn't let on to Kieren that I had any doubts about his story. Something was going on here, something that I wasn't supposed to know about. *You could get hurt.* That's what Brady had said. Hurt by what?

"That's all you need to know, okay?" Kieren was already grabbing his bag from a nearby table. "Come on."

I hesitated for a moment. I didn't know why at first, but then I realized it was because I was still a little afraid of Kieren. Afraid that my parents would find out I was talking to him. Afraid that he could hurt me. Because of Robbie. Because of what he had done to Robbie.

Kieren put one hand on the door handle and reached out the other for mine. "Let's go, M."

I swallowed hard in order to find my voice. "I can walk by myself."

He eyed me for a moment, and the darkness in the room obscured his expression just enough that I couldn't read it at all. Maybe I was being ridiculous. Maybe everything my parents had told me about Kieren, about what had happened that night, was a lie. But maybe it wasn't.

He stepped out of the way and I walked past him. I almost tripped down the stairs and didn't feel normal again until I was back in the bustling hallway, all alone in the oblivious crowd.

CHAPTER 3

I was twelve years old when Robbie died. He was fourteen.

That year, Robbie and Kieren would always wait for me after school so we could bike to meet our dads at the train station. I always got a little rush of excitement when I saw them by the bike rack, like they were springing me out of jail.

We felt like royalty then. The coffee-cart girl smiled when she saw us. All Robbie had to do was tell her she was pretty, and she'd blush and toss us some Werther's candies. All the girls loved Robbie, even if they were too old for him. He had a way of noticing details about you, of really looking at you, that made you feel like you were the only person in the world.

Kieren was the opposite. He barely spoke at that time, but when he did, it was usually to say something that he had considered quite carefully. I didn't understand Kieren for a long time.

REBECCA PHELPS

I thought he just didn't like me, or that he thought he was too good to hang out with Robbie's little sister. He would tease me at times, laughing at the way I held a fork or correcting me when I thought eBay was an actual place. How was I supposed to know what eBay was? I was just a kid.

But over time I began to realize that Kieren thought of me as one of their gang—and it's always okay to tease someone in your gang. He expected me to do it back, and probably didn't understand why I never did. He would be surprisingly kind, then quiet again. He liked a girl at school, I think, but he wouldn't talk about her when I was around. One rainy day, he and Robbie taught me how to play poker. We used matchbooks for the ante, and every time I lost, which was every time, they'd each take turns giving me half their matchbooks so I could keep playing. And when we biked to the train station, they wouldn't let me cross the street without them. They knew I didn't like Werther's candies, so they stole me some M&M's by shaking the vending machine when no one was looking.

I had known Kieren since I was seven, but that was the year he really started to feel like a second brother to me. A second protector. Kieren would pull the skateboard out of his backpack and show off on the railing of the stairway. Robbie and I would laugh and eat our candy.

I can't remember the first time I noticed that they acted differently when other boys from their class would show up at the station. It was so subtle at first. But soon it became clear—the way they stood, making a little imaginary circle that didn't include me; skating over to the other side of the parking lot, where only boys hung out. I would watch them, pretending not to care.

I played a game with myself where I would hold an M&M

in my mouth for as long as I could, daring myself not to bite down. Sucking away till all the flavor had dissolved. Watching that endless train track, looking for the first microscopic dot of Dad's train to appear on the horizon. Shivering a bit as the days got shorter and colder.

Someday I'll leave this town, I would think. *I'll live in the city. With a bead curtain dividing the kitchen from the living room.*

Soon Kieren and Robbie just headed straight over to the other boys. There was no pretense of spending any time with me. They'd still pick me up so we could bike over together, but that was it. No more skateboard stunts. No more stolen candy. I told myself I didn't care. I'd bring a library book and read. Who wanted to hang out with a bunch of stupid boys?

I'll paint the bathroom fire-engine red.

Once or twice, despite myself, I'd glance over there, just to see what stupid things they were doing. And a couple of times I caught Kieren staring back. I'd quickly look away. He couldn't catch me caring. Couldn't make me cry.

Fall turned to winter. It was getting dark by the time we got to the tracks, and the boys started gathering closer to the station, where the heat and the light from inside would spill out onto the platform. Some of them would smoke. Once I saw Robbie do it, too, but I didn't say anything. I wasn't a rat.

One day Robbie stayed home sick from school. I stood alone on the platform, shivering a bit from the cold. I couldn't believe how dark it was already. I was hungry and bored.

Kieren and the other boys were gathered nearby. I couldn't quite make out what they were saying, but I could tell from their tone that they were talking about me. One of the boys was laughing. I turned up my collar, pretended not to hear them.

"Hey, dweeb," one of them called. My heart froze. "Why are you always alone?"

I rocked a bit, my heart racing.

"Where are your friends?"

I held my breath. I knew Kieren was with them. I knew he would shut that boy up in a second. I couldn't wait to hear him do it. Maybe he'd even hit the kid. I got a little rush thinking about the fistfight that was about to break out, all because of me.

"Where are your friends, dweeb? Don't you have any?"

This boy was relentless. I waited and waited for Kieren to say something. But nothing came. Had Kieren gone home? I didn't dare turn around to look. I couldn't confront this boy head-on. I knew I wasn't strong enough. Where was Kieren? Why wasn't he saying anything?

"She doesn't have any." I knew the voice immediately. It was Kieren. "She's just a weird kid. Come on, let's wait inside."

I choked back a lump in my throat as they went into the station. My heart was thumping, breaking. I must have been wrong. That couldn't have been Kieren. It must have been some other boy who sounded like him. I slowly turned and looked over my shoulder. They were inside, laughing and shaking the vending machine. And Kieren was there. He turned and caught my eyes. And I realized that tears were streaming down my cheeks. I couldn't let him see me cry. Couldn't let him have that satisfaction.

I jumped on my bike and started pedaling down the path along the tracks, pumping my legs as hard as I could. I pedaled and pedaled. It was dark by then and there were no lights on the path.

I heard a voice behind me, but I didn't slow down.

"M!" Kieren shouted. I could hear the clinking of his bike chain. I kept pedaling. But he was faster and stronger than me, two years older. He caught up pretty quickly and cut me off, so I had to stop.

"What do you want?" I screamed.

"I'm sorry, okay?" he stammered. He sat on his bike and stared at me.

"I'm going home."

"You're not supposed to bike here by yourself. I'll go with you."

"I don't want you to go with me!" I wasn't crying anymore. I was angry.

Kieren got off his bike. "I'm sorry, M."

I stayed where I was but flinched away from him, like he was made of acid.

"You just—you can't hang around the station anymore, okay?"

"You can't tell me what to do," I insisted.

"Yes, I can. Your brother hasn't told you this, because he doesn't want to hurt your feelings, but you—you just need to get your own friends."

I stood still, wanting to cry again. What was he talking about? He was my friend.

"Friends your age, you know? Like, maybe girlfriends."

I shook my head. I was being kicked out of the gang. What had I done wrong? "But you're my friends."

"We can't be your only friends, M. You're a little girl. You need to hang out with other little girls."

The ground beneath our feet began to tremble. I looked to the horizon and saw the bright headlight of the train growing larger and larger. As the train got closer, the wind picked up. I clutched my jacket tighter around me. I wished more than ever that I could magically appear back at the station, that I could be there when my father stepped onto the platform so I could throw myself into his waiting arms. But it was too late to get back.

Kieren had stopped talking. The approaching train made it impossible to hear anything. The whole earth seemed to be crumbling with its arrival. Kieren and I watched it getting closer and closer.

Suddenly, without warning, Kieren leaped for the tracks. I had no idea what he was doing. I screamed his name, but I knew he couldn't hear me. He pulled something out of his pocket and quickly placed it on the rail. I don't know why he thought it was so important to put it there, why he risked his life to do it. But then again, maybe he didn't think about it too much. Kieren could be impulsive like that. It was impossible to know what he was thinking half the time.

The train whizzed by us, barely missing his hand as he pulled back. He came and stood next to me again as it passed. I looked in the windows for my father's face, but all I could see was a blur.

Once the train had passed and the vibrations were dying down, it was just Kieren and me again, standing in the eerie quiet and darkness.

He walked up to the track and retrieved what he had put there—a penny, now flattened.

"Here. This is to keep you safe."

"You're crazy," I said. "You're completely crazy."

I hopped on my bike and rode home as fast as I could. I was suddenly terrified. Terrified of the train, of Kieren and his dangerous act. Terrified of being out after dark. I pedaled so hard my sides ached. I pedaled and pedaled until I was safe in my kitchen. And it wasn't until I was standing over the sink, catching my breath, that I took the penny and held it, feeling its sharp edges cut into my palm like a knife.

o o o

The accident happened at the end of May. There were two weeks left of school, and I was looking forward to our summer vacation. There's a little town in Indiana where they have a lot of lakes. My dad was planning for us to take a trip there. We were going to rent a cabin and go fishing. It sounded extraordinarily boring, I have to admit, but I was going to bring a lot of books and sit by the water and read. And my dad said there was a river there where everybody went inner tubing. Hundreds of people went floating down the river, listening to music and talking and laughing.

And then the phone call came.

I was in the kitchen eating a piece of chocolate cake after dinner, thinking about those inner tubes and picturing my body stretched out across that warm dark rubber, gently flowing down a river. The thought made me so happy.

Robbie hadn't come home that night for dinner, which had become more and more of a common occurrence. My mom was worried. My dad was angry. I was the only one at the table, and I was seriously considering getting a second piece of cake.

At first I didn't think anything of the phone call. My mom's voice filtered into the room, a series of tense little vowel sounds. I had become accustomed to hearing her voice grow tense more and more often since Robbie started ditching dinner.

My mother's voice went silent. Soon there was a strange sound that at first I couldn't understand. I thought a wild animal had come into the house. But it wasn't an animal. It was my mother. It was my mother wailing. And I knew immediately that only one thing could be that wrong.

I couldn't breathe. I couldn't see. I was afraid I might pass out, but I couldn't move from the table. Time stood still. I heard a clock ticking. My throat closed around a little lump of chocolate cake, and the overly sweet taste of it dripping down with each gulp nauseated me. I tried to breathe. I was going to be sick. I closed my eyes and tried to breathe.

Before I knew it, my mother and father were sitting in front of me. I hadn't moved from the table. My mother sat, rocking her body. My father put his large hand on her back. I had never seen him cry.

They said there had been an accident. They said Robbie wasn't coming home.

I tried to breathe.

The train. The accident involved the train. The train came. They were on their skateboards.

"He was with that boy," I remember my mother saying. She spat out the word like it was poison. "He was with that horrible little boy." And saying it made her body shake again, made the tears start up again. I heard her wheezing, gasping for air.

The horrible boy must be Kieren, I realized. Was Kieren dead too? I didn't dare ask.

We sat in silence for a moment. I wondered if I'd ever leave that table. I started bargaining with God—just let this moment be over. Just end this moment, and let my body disappear.

I stared at the table, at that stupid little plate of chocolate cake. My tears pooled around its rim, carrying away the little black crumbs, like inner tubes floating down a river.

CHAPTER 4

Piper McMahon. That was her name. And she had been missing for over a week. It was all over the local news. Flyers displaying her beautiful face, her flowing brown hair, had sprung up on every bare wall in the school. In the picture, she was wearing the same tan suede jacket she had been wearing when I saw her with Brady in the hallway.

Her parents were devastated, naturally. A mob of reporters camped out in front of their house. They appeared on TV at night, begging viewers for any information. Her mother's eyeliner formed black tears that streamed all the way down to her chin.

And then the principal called an assembly. It started like all assemblies—long trains of kids lining up in their classrooms and shuffling down the hall like human tributaries converging into a reluctant river.

REBECCA PHELPS

But there were no cheerleaders. No pom-poms. Only the school principal, a slight woman of Middle Eastern descent with bouncy black hair named Miss Farghasian. She looked somber. She looked like she had been crying.

Piper McMahon was last seen on a Tuesday.

And the rest of the words came out of the principal's slight mouth, booming from her little body with a shocking amount of volume. Piper McMahon. She was seventeen. She was on the homecoming court. She loved The Smiths. She was missing.

I looked over at the part of the bleachers where upperclassmen sat. The rest of the homecoming court looked destroyed. The girls caught their breath. Some of their boyfriends comforted them. Some just sat and stared at the floor.

Piper McMahon was a straight-A student.

Outside the tall window, the bare branches of the trees seemed to shiver, defenseless against the descending chill. My fingers clenched my jeans at the knees. I thought of my mother. I thought of our kitchen. The seat at our table that had been my brother's.

And then I saw Brady.

Has anyone seen Piper McMahon?

Brady's eyes pleaded with me, his lips curled into an almost painful circle, like he was about to speak. And I could hear the words he was saying to me, floating soundlessly from his eyes to mine: *Please don't say anything. I can explain. Just wait.*

My body felt ready to explode, my heartbeat battering my rib cage. What was I supposed to do? Brady's eyes continued to plead, and all I could think of was Piper McMahon, alone on a train headed west. Piper McMahon without so much as a toothbrush. What was she running from? Did Piper want to be found? Would she want me to speak up?

The shuffling of feet around me made me realize we had been dismissed. I sprang from my seat and ran as fast as I could out of the room. I'm sure I attracted more than a couple strange looks, and I'm pretty sure I could hear my homeroom teacher telling me to come back, but I couldn't stop my feet.

I ran from the packed auditorium towards the temporarily empty school, and I quickly found myself completely lost in the labyrinthine hallways. This was a part of the building I didn't know, and like the rest of the school, it made no sense whatsoever. Doors leading to half-finished hallways, windowless rooms that all looked completely identical. I ran farther until something looked familiar: blue lockers. I knew the blue section. And I knew what I would find there.

The door to the darkroom was in front of me. I ran up the stairs and into the blissful, quiet red light. The photographs were gone, and the room was empty and still. I quickly looked in the shadows for Kieren, who was not there. It struck me as funny that once you've seen a person in a certain place, you expect to see them there every time.

I needed a moment to think. Well, my decision was clear, wasn't it? I mean, I had to tell Piper's parents. They were terrified. They didn't know where their daughter was, or if she was even alive. I knew all too well that fear, that moment between knowing something is wrong and knowing just how wrong it is. That endless gulf of pain before the words confirm your worst fear—gone forever. He is gone forever.

What was I thinking about?

Piper McMahon.

I was going to tell Piper McMahon's parents that she got on a train. I was going to betray Brady, and he would hate me for it.

But so what? What allegiance did I have to Brady, anyway? Did I owe him loyalty? Friendship? No, it was the hope of more than that which had made me feel a devotion to him. A silly little crush on an older boy who would graduate in a few months and be gone forever.

Gone forever.

Could I sacrifice Piper McMahon for a crush?

I suddenly hated Piper McMahon. I hated her for getting on that stupid train. I hated her suede jacket. I hated her parents, crying on the news, and the cheerleaders who missed her so much.

Why did she get on the train?

I shuffled over to the tables that held the various baths for the photographic negatives. They all sat empty, their slightly tinted liquids reflecting my image in the red light that hung above them. Without warning, the pools started to undulate, ever so slightly, and the obscure girl reflected in their waters lost all form, her outline blurring into nothing. Swallowed by the dark water.

Dark water. "DW I'll never tell," I said to no one. "This is about DW."

The baths had been disturbed by footsteps on the stairwell leading up to the door. Someone was coming for me.

I looked quickly for a place to hide, but it was too late. That was just as well. The time for hiding was over. I turned to face the door.

Brady came in, out of breath. He had clearly been searching everywhere he could think of since the assembly let out, and when he saw me, the look of fear was quickly replaced with relief. But then a darkness came over his eyes. He closed the door behind him.

"You need to tell me what DW is. Now. Or I'll go to the principal." I couldn't believe the assertiveness of my own voice. I sounded so confident, so grown-up. I wondered if he could see that my hands were trembling.

Brady nodded and came closer, and I immediately felt my stomach betray that newfound confidence by tensing up with his proximity. I willed my cheeks not to blush. And yet, there he was, not two feet away from me. And my face got hot, and I could only hope that in the darkness he didn't see it.

"I mean it." But this time it didn't sound as strong as before. And I realized, hearing the waver in my voice, that it wasn't just his nearness that was making me nervous. I was terrified of DW, a force so powerful it had made a girl disappear.

"I was trying," Brady began, his body slumping next to me against the table, "to keep you out of it."

I stood next to him, his warm flannel shirt so close I could feel it brush my arm. And I knew that whatever it was he was going to tell me would change everything.

"I don't know why," he continued. "There was something about you, in the hallway that first day. You reminded me of . . . someone."

"Piper." And he nodded. Despite myself, I couldn't help but be flattered. I reminded him of beautiful, missing Piper McMahon.

"She used to get lost every day in this school. I drew her a map, but she couldn't understand it. So I would just take her to class and tell her to wait for me after. One day she didn't wait."

I nodded.

"We were freshmen then. A little younger than you, I guess. Feels like a million years ago."

"You're not that much older than me." I realized immediately that it was a stupid thing to say. Brady swallowed and took a deep breath. He hadn't seemed to hear me.

"It was Piper who found it," he went on. "She didn't wait for me. And she got lost. And then she found it."

"DW?"

Brady looked at me a long moment. As my eyes adjusted to the faint light, I could just make out the intensity of his gaze.

"Do you really want to know?"

o   o   o

Before it was a high school, as my father had told me, East Township High was an army base called Fort Pryman Shard. Dad's grandfather, like all men back in the early '40s when it was built, had been a young kid from a nearby farm, recruited to go and fight in World War II.

The fort was considered a great thing for the town, and for the whole county, really. Ever since the prospectors from the fancy houses on the other side of town, or "Money Row," as my mother called it, had abandoned the place during the Great Depression, times had been tough. Now there was industry, manufacturing, all kinds of jobs for men and women, and all for the most noble reason of all—to defeat the Nazis. The way my father told it, the fate of humanity rested on the shoulders of our forefathers. And they had been very successful.

But nothing lasts forever.

When the war ended, the army sealed up the parts of the complex that were intended for top-secret purposes and connected the rest of the scattered buildings with a twisted network of hallways, forming a makeshift high school for all the screaming babies who had been left behind by the departing soldiers. The result was a building that was not quite useful for any one purpose, and which gave the overall effect of a web spun by a disoriented spider. But as far as the army was concerned, it was good enough.

The women found ways to pay their mounting bills. It was well known that beneath the fading paint of Groussman's Pharmacy, across the street from the train station, was a sign advertising DANCE HALL GIRLS. Robbie was the one who'd shown me that. I can't remember when. I was probably about seven. I laughed, because I could tell it was supposed to be funny or shocking. But I had no idea what a dance hall girl was.

The basement of Fort Pryman Shard became a boiler room for East Township High School. And it was one of the darkest, eeriest, and quietest places I had ever seen. If I hadn't had Brady's hand to hold, I never would have made it down the stairs.

It took a moment to adjust to the lack of sound. I couldn't remember when I had experienced quiet like that before. It hurt my ears. I could feel my eardrums straining for some vibration to latch on to, and finding none, they seemed to beat against my ear canals in protest.

Brady kept holding my hand. "Just let yourself adjust to it for a second."

As my pupils grew accustomed to the light, or rather the lack of it, I began to make out some figures. The enormous shell of what must have been the old boiler sat in the corner, clearly having been abandoned years ago with the invention of gas-powered heat. Nearby, worktables were covered with all sorts of objects, from hammers and wrenches to old textbooks.

"What is this place?" I asked.

"It's just where they store stuff."

"What does this have to do with Piper?" There was no other way to put it—this room was creepy. I shivered, although I didn't feel cold. But rather, there was some feeling worse than cold seeping down my back. This place was wrong. And I knew deep in my gut that I wasn't supposed to be in here. I couldn't help but think about how Piper McMahon had come down here alone.

Brady clutched my hand a little tighter. "You can go back if you want."

The way he softened his voice as he said it made me realize that he meant the words not as a challenge, but as a gentle reminder that it wasn't too late for me to forget about all this and go back to my life upstairs. My life without Brady.

I shook my head, although I doubted he could see it. "No."

After all, if I went back upstairs, nothing would be any different. I'd still have the dilemma of what to do about Piper. I'd still have that haunting image of her on the train. I'd still have the voices of her parents on the news each night, begging me—me—to tell them where she was.

"I'm not leaving until you tell me why we're here."

"Okay," he said, his body seeming to tense up and collapse a bit all at once. "It's through here."

We walked farther into the room, past the machinery. In front of us lay a dark, heavy door. Brady walked with the familiarity of someone traversing his own living room, and I wondered how many times he had been down here in the three years since Piper had found it.

Brady reached for a key hidden on top of the door frame and jammed it into the lock of the door. He jiggled it a bit and twisted it left and right until we heard a click.

"Someone made this in woodshop," he explained. "It doesn't fit perfectly." I looked down and saw that the key was made out of wood. Then Brady pushed his full body weight into the door until it finally budged with a reluctant creak.

I held my breath as the door moved aside, clearing my view of . . . a hallway. Of course. What else would there be in this twisted place but yet another hallway? The long corridor was only slightly illuminated by some high-up storm windows that seemed to be caked in decades' worth of leaves and dirt. But the light that remained was enough to show that this was a typical East Township walkway, changing course midpath, twisting one way and then the other as though it had been built to avoid hitting the trees in some imaginary forest. Only one thing set it apart. Along the wall on the right side, somebody had scrawled in black magic marker: *Down down down.*

Doorways along the hallway had long since been stripped of their doors, revealing that behind them lay nothing but brick walls. This was a common sight around the school. The story was that either the doorways had been intended to lead to rooms that never got built, or else Dr. Frankenstein's laboratory was back there somewhere. In either event, the brick walls were probably a good thing.

Finally, we reached one last doorway at the end of the hall. But this one had a door—a very common-looking door with a metal handle. When Brady pushed it open and flipped a switch on the wall, the view that greeted us immediately struck me as absurd. The room could have been my science lab.

It was clean and tidy with very little dust on anything. The tables had workstations, complete with microscopes and Bunsen burners. Lab coats hung neatly on little pegs along one wall, next to a giant blackboard covered with various equations and diagrams in faded white chalk, which spanned its length. It was all gibberish to me—lots of little circles and numbers. The only thing that seemed clear was a drawing near the middle of the board which showed a small circle being bombarded from all sides by long arrows; it looked like the sun being attacked by its own rays.

The room was timeless. It had no computers, but other than that, there was nothing to distinguish it from the rest of the schoolrooms. Yet there was one thing in it that made no sense to me, because I couldn't for the life of me figure out what it was doing there.

It was a tent. A very small army-green tent that almost looked like a mock-up of what a real tent would be. It was maybe three square feet, but taller than Brady.

Brady motioned to it.

I got angry then. "Brady, what is this? Is this a game or something? I'm not going to keep going in circles . . ."

"Just go in. I promise, that's the end of it."

I looked down at our hands, still entwined. He let go of me then, and I felt like a sinking ship whose life raft had just come untethered. One thought made my legs move—*Piper McMahon was not afraid.*

I walked over to the tent, took a deep breath, and pulled back the flaps.

Inside was a hole in the ground, nothing more. And a closer inspection of that hole revealed a spiral staircase, twisting its way even farther into the earth.

My heart was thumping. How much farther down could I go? Where would it end? Down, down, down—into the world below. And suddenly I knew. I knew what DW stood for. It was Down World. How many kids knew about this? How many had been through this science lab, into this tent?

I descended until my feet hit solid ground, and a slight purplish light emanated around me, almost magically. I took a few steps forward, gulping back a bitter taste in my mouth. And then I saw the doors.

There were three of them, all standing equally before me. And they each had a wooden sign hanging on them, letters burned into the wood, the words taunting me with their innocent simplicity: Yesterday, Today, Tomorrow.

I became aware that Brady was standing on the spiral stairway behind me.

"Only the middle one works," he said, referring to the door marked Today.

"What do you mean?"

"The others are just brick walls."

I looked to Brady to see if he was teasing me, but he was staring with a deadly seriousness at the doors. So I decided to check for myself.

I opened the door marked Yesterday, and found, sure enough, that only a solid brick wall lay behind it.

"I told you. Kids have tried to pry the bricks out before, see if there's anything behind them. But there's nothing. Just more brick wall."

The wall had a tiny little slit on the upper right corner that looked like an eyehole. I lurched up onto my tiptoes to peer into it, but could only see darkness beyond.

"The one marked Tomorrow is the same thing," Brady explained.

I stepped back, closed the door to Yesterday, and turned to face Brady.

"Okay, so what about this one?" I asked, nodding my head towards Today and trying to sound less freaked out than I was actually feeling.

For all I knew, this was some sort of new-kid hazing. I had heard about these things. A roomful of cheerleaders was probably waiting behind the middle door to steal my backpack or spray paint *loser* on my forehead. I became acutely aware that this was a test. And Brady must be in on it.

"It's okay. I didn't believe it either. Nobody does. That's why we all went through the door. Deep down, you don't think anything's really going to happen."

"There's nothing behind that door," I insisted. "This is a stupid joke. It's not funny."

"It's not a joke, Marina. But if you want, I'll take you back upstairs. You don't have to go in." His voice shifted as he started to get more and more excited. "Come on, take my hand. Let me take you back up. This was a mistake. Come on."

The urgency in his voice only made me more curious. And before I could form another thought, I walked straight ahead and opened up the door marked Today. But then Brady was gone. I held my breath and was momentarily blinded by a bright yellow light, accompanied by an intense heat. Then that quickly went away. As the light faded, I became aware of a wonderful smell. I would know this smell anywhere, because there's nothing like it in the world. It was bacon frying in my mother's kitchen.

And before I knew what was happening, my mother appeared before me, standing in front of the grill, turning the bacon with her red-handled tongs. I walked up to her, and with every step, more of my kitchen appeared before me, behind me, all around me. It was like walking into a painting that was still being created. One moment, there was nothing to my left—just light. But slowly, the longer I stood there, the details appeared and became cemented in reality.

A laugh came booming from the kitchen table, suddenly sitting in its usual place by the window. The laugh belonged to my father. He was reading the Sunday paper, complete with colorful comic strips. I looked down and saw that I was in my pajamas, my bare feet pressed against the brown laminate tile that my father had laid when we moved into this house.

Soon all the puzzle pieces came into stark light, the whole house embracing me with an aura of warmth and security. But there was something wrong. There was a feeling in this room that I hadn't felt in my house for years. My mother's shoulders seemed too relaxed. My father's laugh a bit too sincere.

I realized I hadn't seen them this way since—well, not for years.

They were happy.

And then I knew. I knew what this room was. My head turned slowly back towards the kitchen table. A knot formed in my mouth, and I started hyperventilating with excitement. Because I knew what I would find there. And for a moment, everything seemed right in the world.

There he was. There was Robbie. He was at the table next to my father. He looked about seventeen years old, the age that he would have been. He was tall, his head several inches higher than my dad's. He was eating an enormous plateful of eggs. He always had such an appetite. My parents used to joke that he'd eat them out of house and home.

House and home. Robbie was at our table. Robbie was alive and eating eggs at the table.

"Have a seat," said my mother, and her voice was simple and buoyant in a way I hadn't heard in ages. "You better grab some eggs before they're gone!"

My father laughed, but my brother just grunted. He started piling more eggs onto his plate—a game we used to play. Hurry, hurry, hurry. Grab it before it's gone.

And I wanted so badly to go sit at that table. To fight my brother for the last bit of eggs. To eat that delicious bacon. To hear my father laugh.

No. It's a lie, I reminded myself. *Robbie is dead. This is a lie. It's a trap.*

I reached out and grabbed the first thing my hands could feel, an egg timer my mom kept on the counter. It felt real enough. I twisted the dial and could hear it ticking. *Tick tick tick.* The sound was real, the knob turning in my hand like in real life. But I knew it was a lie. And the knowledge made it ugly. The knowledge made it all seem ridiculous.

I pushed the images away from me, and like a painting left out in the rain, the colors and the shapes began to melt and swirl. My brother's face blurred around the edges, and soon I couldn't make it out anymore. I stepped backwards. I kept going farther and farther from my kitchen, the sight melting away and being replaced once again by that yellow light. Soon I backed into a wall. No, it wasn't a wall. It was a door. I turned around, twisted the knob in my hand, and walked through it.

I was back in that dark little room below the school. Brady had slumped down against the wall, his head in his hands. He was waiting for me.

I took a moment to catch my breath. What had just happened? An illusion? A dream?

"Is it real?" I asked Brady.

"Do you want it to be?"

I realized I was still holding the egg timer in my suddenly clammy palm, its slight ticking echoing in my ears with the intensity of a telltale heart. Brady didn't seem to notice, however, his eyes remaining focused on mine.

I slid the timer into my pocket, still trying to process that I had brought it back with me from the other side. I had to go home. I had to see if it was really missing from my mother's kitchen. I started backing away from Brady.

"Marina," Brady said, quite calm. "About Piper . . ."

"What about her?" I asked, still backing away.

"You can't tell anyone about her. If you do, it'll lead back to this place. And if people find out about this place . . . if the world finds out . . ."

"Brady, you're scaring me."

"She'll come back on her own. I know she will. I know Piper."

The egg timer was still ticking, and it seemed to be growing louder. I felt dizzy, the sound echoing around me. I realized that I could still smell bacon on my shirt. I scooped up the timer and dropped it in my backpack, trying to hide it away.

"I have to go home," I almost whispered.

"Marina, promise me . . ."

I didn't want to hear it. I kept climbing, up the stairs, out of that little tent and through the science lab. I ran and ran, down the hallway and away from that terrible dark little boiler room. I wouldn't stop until I was back up in the school, and then out of the school, through the front door, onto my bike, and home again.

The final bell rang as I was emerging from the boiler-room door, so I easily lost myself in the gathering crowd of people. I weaved in and out of their heavy backpacks and overstuffed coats.

"Where you goin', Marina?" called a girl I recognized from my chemistry class. Christy or Kirsty. I turned quickly to find her in the crowd and waved. She looked concerned.

"I—I gotta go," was all I could muster before running off again.

"You okay?" she called after me as I ran.

I pretended not to hear her. I had to get home again. I had to see if it was gone from the kitchen.

I brought back an egg timer, I thought.

What did Piper McMahon bring back?

CHAPTER 5

I pedaled so hard the chain on my bike started to rattle and I was afraid it would fall off. I slowed down a bit, not wanting to be delayed by anything. But then my mind would start to race again and my feet would pump even harder, and soon the chain would be rattling again.

The farther I got from the school, the more the whole thing felt like a dark and twisted dream. That room hadn't been real. Of course it hadn't.

Robbie and I had seen a magic show once with my parents, one with all sorts of classic illusions—making a bunny disappear; sawing a woman in half. On the drive home, I think Robbie could tell how freaked out I was. I kept imagining the sword slicing through the woman's body and the look on her face while the magician did it—she was smiling. So obviously it wasn't real. Right?

"It wasn't real, you know," Robbie had whispered into my ear on the drive home. My parents were talking quietly in the front seat. "He didn't really saw her in half."

"Well, I know that," I said. But I didn't, really. I saw the sword go through the box. I saw the man pull the box apart into two sections. That woman's body was ripped in two. Her feet still dangled out of the end. I knew it was a trick, of course. But I didn't see how it could be.

"How does it work?"

"Mirrors."

"What about them?"

"They just use mirrors. Everybody knows that." Robbie turned back to the window.

And I realized that he didn't really know the answer either. He knew mirrors were involved, but he didn't understand *how* any more than I did.

Still, the answer satisfied me. She wasn't ripped in two. Because mirrors. That was all I really needed to know.

Once again, Robbie had made everything seem all right.

I was still thinking about that magic trick when I pulled my bike into the driveway and dropped it off to the side of the garage so I could run into the house.

My mother was sitting at the kitchen table, her pen hovering over a half-written shopping list. She had her head resting in one hand and she looked even more tired than usual. She seemed shocked to see me.

"Hey. You're home early."

"School let out," I said, probably a little too enthusiastically. I tried to dial the volume down a notch. "I'm just gonna get a snack."

"Okay." My mom turned back to her list. The great thing about having a depressed parent was that they didn't notice too much.

I gulped down a deep breath and searched the counter for the egg timer, fully expecting to find it there, just like normal. And yet . . .

"Where's the egg timer?"

"Hmm?" my mother grunted while writing something on her list.

"Isn't there usually an egg timer here? Where's the egg timer?"

"Do you need to time something?" my mother asked, still disinterested. "Use the app on your phone."

"I—I need it for school. What happened to it? It's usually right here. Did it . . ." I could barely finish the sentence. I had to gulp down some spit and start over. "Did it disappear?"

I could feel my cheeks getting hot. The room started to spin. I looked over at the stovetop, the very place where my mother had been making bacon just a short while before. I could still smell it if I closed my eyes.

"Of course not. It's right . . ." My mother examined the counter. "Um, it should be right there. Look behind the flour."

I looked behind the flour, and behind the sugar. Soon I was furiously pushing aside everything on the counter, but it wasn't there.

"Did you find it?"

I clutched my backpack to my chest. And there it was—*tick tick tick*. The only egg timer in this kitchen was the one I had brought from school.

"Found it," I stated flatly, inhaling a sharp gulp of air. "Excuse me. I'll go do my homework."

I ran upstairs as fast as my legs could carry me and sat on my bed. *Okay, don't panic*, I thought. *There has to be an explanation.*

And then it hit me.

Kieren.

Kieren knew. Of course he did. It was Kieren in the darkroom. And something that hadn't made any sense at the time seemed to come to light. Kieren had told Brady to leave, and Brady had. Brady's just a soldier in this thing. It was Kieren who pulled the strings. It was Kieren who was in charge.

The idea of Kieren as a master manipulator made perfect sense to me. He'd manipulated Robbie, hadn't he? He'd taken Robbie to the train station that night.

That horrible little boy. That's what my mother had called him.

What if she was right? Kieren had made Robbie disappear, and now Piper McMahon. Maybe Kieren was a monster after all.

No, stop, I told myself. *Don't think that.* I walked over to my chest of drawers, took out my old childhood diary, and removed the flattened penny from the sewn-in pocket in the back, where it had lain all these years. I stroked it between my fingers, feeling its sharp edges.

This will protect you, Kieren had said to me. He was my protector, not my enemy.

One thing was clear: whatever was going on, whatever was happening under the high school, and whatever it was that had made Piper McMahon get on that train, Kieren must have known all about it.

I put the penny into my pocket, and I immediately felt better. Like those kids at my old Catholic middle school who carried

St. Anthony around with them and were convinced they would never lose anything as a result, I resolved to always keep the penny with me, to feel that much closer to the safety it was meant to provide.

And then I knew what I had to do.

o o o

The wind swirled my hair into my face, strands getting trapped in my mouth, as I stood at the dilapidated train station the following afternoon. I watched the track, overgrown with weeds, winding its way towards the endless nothing that lay past the borders of this town.

I watched one lone dying flower poking out through the cracks in the sidewalk, swaying in the wind, and I reviewed my list of questions: How does DW work? Is it real? Why was Robbie in my kitchen? And what about the egg timer? And Piper?

I suddenly knew that even if Kieren got the note I'd left in his locker—which was a big *if*, since I didn't even know if he was at school today—and even if he came to meet me here like I'd asked, he wouldn't simply tell me the answers to these questions. A girl had disappeared because of these questions. Kieren had threatened Brady over them. I needed a better plan.

I fought away the chill as I stood there, and started pacing back and forth down the station platform to keep my blood flowing. To a stranger, it must have looked like I was waiting for a train. And for a brief moment, I wished that I were.

"M."

I whipped around with a gasp.

Kieren looked so different these days, it always took me a

moment to recognize him. He really had gotten so tall. And his nose was somehow different—longer. Stronger, I guess. His lips were the same, though: tight and raised a bit on the right side, as though his mouth were asking a question. We both turned to watch the train tracks. Habit, I guess. We knew no train was coming.

"The pavement's all cracked," I said, not knowing where to begin.

"Yeah."

I sniffled then, and realized my nose was running. I wiped it on my sleeve.

"You're cold. Let's go in," Kieren said.

"It's locked."

"Oh. Right."

We stared at the tracks. This was it—it was time to ask him. But now that I had him here, there were a million questions I realized I wanted answered more than the ones about DW. I started to feel light-headed. Being here with Kieren, it was like we had been transported into the past. It was like I could reach into a hole and pull out my memories. Hold them one more time. When I swallowed, I could taste M&M's.

This was a mistake.

"I know you have questions, M." I was glad he was talking, so I didn't have to. "I don't know what I can tell you."

"You know about DW—I mean, Down World?"

"Yes."

"And you know that Robbie is alive down there?

His chin set into a locked position as he wrestled with a thought. "How do you know that?" he finally asked. "What did you do, M?"

I swallowed hard. I didn't want to get Brady in trouble, but I was tired of lying. I needed to know the truth, and I needed it now.

"Brady took me to the boiler room."

"I'll kill him . . ."

"Robbie was there, Kieren. Robbie was in my kitchen."

"Look, M, here's the thing with DW. You have to understand that it's not real. It's just, like, a movie or something. A movie with a different ending than the one we're in."

"Okay. What does that mean?"

"It means the boy you saw isn't really Robbie. Or at least, not the one we knew. He's another version of him. One that doesn't belong to us."

I shook my head, not understanding. "He looked real to me. And I was real too. My mother told me to sit and eat."

"That's because as soon as you crossed over, she saw you as the Down World version of her daughter. That's how it works. That way, you never run into the other you or anything like that."

"Okay. But then what happens to the other version of me?"

"You're one and the same for a minute. And she reappears when you leave."

"What if I don't leave?"

"You have to leave. You can only stay down there for a few minutes."

"Or what?" I asked. Everything he told me was just raising more questions.

"Enough. That's all you need to know," he said in a very final kind of way. I was annoying him, but I wanted to know more. "Just be careful if you choose to go see that Robbie."

"You visit him there?"

"No." It was such a short and definite answer, and the coldness of it hit me like a slap. Kieren was staring ahead, not at me. All his warmth seemed to have faded away. "Like I told you, the kid you saw isn't real."

I paced for a moment, trying to collect my breath, my thoughts. But I knew already what I was thinking. "But if he came up here? Would he be real if he came up here?"

"You can't take anything out of DW," he began before I'd even finished, as though it were a fact he had resigned himself to long before.

"I did."

Kieren looked at me, and the look in his eyes could only be described as sheer terror. "What have you done?"

"I brought back an egg timer." I lost my breath for a moment, but collected myself to keep going. "I had it in my hand . . ."

"Where is it?" Kieren suddenly demanded. His eyes grew wide and his mouth clenched. Was he afraid?

"It—it's in my room."

"We have to go get it. Now! We have to put it back."

"Why?"

"Now, M! Grab your bike."

"Kieren, it's just a timer," I insisted. What was going on here? Why was Kieren so afraid?

"M, you can't take anything out of DW," he repeated.

"Why not?"

"Because . . . ," he began, grabbing my frozen bike off the rack and handing it to me. He took his skateboard out of his backpack. "Because then you'll owe them something."

He started guiding me towards the bike path then, and my heart froze. *Then I'd owe* who *something?*

CHAPTER 6

Two weeks went by and there was still no word of Piper McMahon. Two weeks of sad cheerleaders walking by, of her "Missing" posters starting to fray around the edges, of the evening news moving on to other stories.

I hadn't talked to Kieren since the day he took the egg timer from me to put back on the other side of the Today door. He had followed me to the end of my street after we'd met up at the train station, careful to stay far enough away that my mother would never see him from our front window. Once I returned with the timer, he had grabbed it and shoved it in his backpack.

"I'll clean up your mess this time," he had warned me, "but not again. You understand?"

I asked him then if the Today door always led to my kitchen. He said it didn't; that there was no way of knowing where you

REBECCA PHELPS

would end up once you walked through. But as long as the timer was somewhere on the other side, it wouldn't affect us anymore.

I could only nod sadly, painfully aware of how coldly he was treating me. I had wanted to ask him more about the portals, of course, but he rode away before I got the chance.

That felt like a lifetime ago, I realized now as I walked the halls.

Several times a day, my mind would drift to Piper McMahon's mother. I had never met her, but I knew who she was. I knew what she must have been feeling every day. I knew that moment when she would wake up in the night, and for just a moment she could dismiss it all as a bad dream. Until she remembered that it wasn't.

In those two weeks, I watched my own mother start to lose her mind. I would come home and find her scouring the internet for a word, a hint, anything she could track down about what had happened to Piper McMahon. It was like she had made Piper into Robbie, and maybe if she could find Piper, then Robbie wouldn't be . . .

I was a monster. I knew where Piper was—or, at least, I knew where she had gone. And I wasn't saying anything because Brady had begged me not to. Brady insisted that she would be back, that everything would be okay. Brady made one thing clear—whatever DW was, whatever power it held, it was a million times worse than the suffering of Piper McMahon's parents.

But was he right? How long was I supposed to wait?

I started averting my eyes every time I had to pass the door to the boiler room. It almost felt like walking past a roomful of ghosts. Like walking past my brother and pretending I couldn't see him. I knew what Kieren had told me: that the Robbie I saw wasn't real, that you can't take things out of DW. But I couldn't stop thinking about what I had seen behind the Today door. Robbie had been just feet away from me, eating those eggs at the kitchen table. If I had taken a couple of steps towards him, I could have touched him.

He had been as close to my hand as . . . as the egg timer.

Things couldn't go on this way. I would need more answers.

I had seen Brady only a handful of times, always walking dead-eyed down a distant hallway. People still avoided looking at me. That girl Christy from chem class—for her name, it turned out, was indeed Christy and not Kirsty—was the only one who was nice to me. We had started sitting together at lunch, and using our free period to study in the east stairwell. She was smart and talkative, and a gifted singer who would sometimes belt out her math answers to the tune of a Broadway melody. A whiz at social media, she had a YouTube channel that had reached ten thousand followers—all strangers—by the time she was twelve. Soon, these study sessions were the only thing getting me through the day.

The rest of the time, I was usually alone. Sometimes it would get to me. I started to feel like I was the ghost. I worried that I was going insane, that I would end up like my mother after a bad day of missing Robbie, cleaning the kitchen on her knees, furiously scrubbing at imaginary stains.

Piper hadn't come back like Brady said she would. And before I went to the police, I knew there was one more question I had to ask him.

o o o

REBECCA PHELPS

Brady's car was parked in front of a large redbrick apartment building. It didn't take much to find him, since the old-fashioned White Pages at the bottom of our kitchen utility drawer told me there was only one Picelli in town.

I rode my bike up to the end of the street, which I had never been down before. It wasn't an ugly building, but being set as it was at a slight distance from all the other apartments, down near the end of the road, with only a service station and a car wash across the street to provide a view, it struck me as a deeply depressing place to live.

I parked my bike and walked up to the entryway, my heart beating faster as I went inside. I was suddenly kicking myself for coming here, for this whole stupid plan. But I knew I had to give Brady a chance before I went to Piper's parents.

Picelli. There it was in the building directory. I rolled my neck a bit and let out an exhale, and then I pushed the little button next to his name. The door buzzed immediately and I went upstairs.

The man who opened the door to Brady's apartment was about thirty-five years old. He looked vaguely like Brady—same wavy dark hair—but I couldn't figure out their relationship. He was much too young to be his father, seemed too old to be a brother.

"I'm his cousin," he said when he saw me staring.

"Oh." I offered a weak smile.

The cousin went back to the couch, where he had been playing a video game. "He's in his room," he called out over his shoulder. He gave a slight nod of his head towards a closed door near the kitchen, and then forgot I existed.

It was a small place. There only seemed to be two

bedrooms—the one Brady was apparently in and another one across the hall. Glancing into the slightly open door of the other room, I saw an unmade bed and a bunch of clothes on the floor. A poster for some sort of band was on the wall. I didn't recognize the band—a bunch of guys wearing black. That must be the cousin's room, I figured. So if Brady's in there and his cousin's in here . . . where did Brady's parents sleep?

I knocked on the door with as much confidence as I could muster.

"Yeah," I heard Brady reply. It was clear he thought it was his cousin knocking, but I couldn't find my voice to tell him otherwise. I nudged the door open instead and poked my head in, only to find Brady on his bed, reading a book with no shirt on.

"I'm sorry, I'm sorry," I stammered.

"Oh jeez," he said, getting up and looking for a shirt to put on. "Hold on."

"I'm sorry, I would have called. I didn't know, um, the number."

"Let me just . . . hold on."

I didn't know where to look, so I stared at the floor while he put on a sweatshirt. The awkwardness of it made us both start to laugh.

"What are you doing here?" he asked. His tone wasn't cruel, just curious.

"I needed to ask you something."

"Yeah, sure. Okay." He looked out the window, from which the whirring of the car wash filled the room with constant sound. "Do you want to sit down?" He pushed some clothes off a wooden chair by a desk and offered it to me. My eyes wandered to the unmade bed as I crossed the room, then darted away again.

"I used to smoke," Brady said, out of nowhere, as he sat on the edge of that bed. "Stupid habit, don't start. I mean that."

"Okay."

"It was just something to try to look cool, you know? My friends would come over and sit where you are, and I'd smoke and blow it out this window."

I nodded, letting him talk. It was nice to hear his voice.

"When you walked in, my first thought was to reach for a pack." He laughed again. "But I don't smoke anymore."

"When did you stop?"

"Um, probably about two years ago. My dad, he has a bad lung. Lifelong smoker. So . . . stupid habit."

"Where is your dad?" I asked, although I knew it was none of my business.

"Up north. He's been working on a salmon boat since December. He'll be back next month."

"Oh." I struggled for something else to say. "You live with your cousin?"

"Jack. Yeah. He's a good guy. Works at the station across the street."

It felt weirdly grown-up, discussing other people based on what they did for a living. Was this how adults talked?

I had a million more things I wanted to know about Brady's life, but I didn't want to pry too much. Mostly I wondered where Brady's mom was. Somehow I knew, however, that that was a question I shouldn't ask.

"Did you tell anyone?" he asked now, before I could speak.

"Tell anyone?"

"That I took you down."

"Oh," I nodded. "Just Kieren."

He laughed, shaking his head. "That figures."

"What does that mean?"

"Nothing."

"I mean, I thought since he already knew about it, and—"

"It's fine," he cut me off. "I can handle Kieren."

I swallowed down a sudden rush of apprehension. Brady didn't say anything else; he just sat examining me like I was a math problem he didn't know how to solve. "Brady, I have to ask you something," I repeated.

He nodded. He reached for his jeans' pocket, probably looking for that imaginary cigarette pack again but, remembering that it wasn't there, he put his hands on his knees.

"What did Piper bring back from DW?"

He looked up at me. A smile cracked across his lips. "You're so smart. You figured it out right away, didn't you?"

"Well?"

Brady turned away from me a bit, fiddling with his sheets. It seemed like he wasn't going to say anything. After a few silent moments, I grew afraid he might ask me to leave.

"Her parents," he finally said, so softly I had to lean in to make sure I had heard him.

"What?"

"She brought her parents back. Her DW parents."

"Why?" was all I could think of to ask. "What happened to her real parents?"

Brady stared at his feet for a moment.

I ducked my head a bit to try to meet his eyes. "Brady? Look at me."

He did, and as always, I had to catch my breath for a moment. But I was feeling brave, and I wanted answers. "No more secrets."

He nodded, still looking at me. "No more secrets."

He got up and paced the room for a second. "Six months ago . . . ," he started, "there was an accident."

"Okay."

"Piper's parents were killed. They were up in the mountains last August. Camping trip. They were hit by a car and went off a ravine. Piper crawled out before the car exploded."

I shook my head. "No," I said, trying to wrap my head around it. "I saw them on the news."

"They died in the ravine," he said slowly, as though trying to help me understand. "And Piper, she went into Today. She found her DW parents in their room and she took them out."

"So the people on the news . . . ?"

"They're not real," he said. "They're from DW."

"But they were crying on the news."

"Yeah," Brady said. "Piper said they told her they wanted to go home, back through the boiler room. Back to their own daughter, who lives on the other side."

I didn't know what to say. My mind was reeling, thinking of those people I had seen on TV. How could they be from the other side?

"She begged them to stay. She said she'd hurt herself if they left. That's why they were crying. They're afraid she's done something to herself."

I took a deep breath, imagining how terrified those people must be, living on the wrong side of reality and worried about both versions of their daughter, Piper.

"But they can't stay here. Can they?" I asked, secretly thinking of my brother.

"No. Being on the wrong side makes everything unstable. It creates a void on the other side, and that's when things start to fall apart. Buildings appear and disappear. People get hurt. And the longer you stay on the wrong side, the worse it gets. At first, just things that are close to the void are affected, which is why Piper and her parents were the only ones to see it. But after a while, it spreads."

"What are you talking about?"

"There's this thing, right? It's like energy. It's like . . . the *balance* of energy. When the balance is off, everything starts to cave in on itself. One day, Piper was walking to school and the sidewalk changed to a dirt road. One day the trees became a wooden fence."

"Why?"

"Because she was seeing pieces of another reality. When the balance is off, the worlds can cross. That's why you can't take things out."

"Oh my God."

"She knew she had to put them back. Before it was too late."

"But she didn't do it," I realized. "She got on the train instead. Why? Where does it go?"

Brady considered the question for a moment. "Oregon," he finally answered.

I was surprised to hear that I had been right about the train's destination this whole time.

"What's in Oregon?"

"There's this group of people. They live in a little town outside of Portland. They call themselves the Mystics. And that's where Piper went. To ask them."

"Ask them what?"

"You know what."

"I don't!" I insisted. "I have no idea."

"If there's a way," he stated calmly, "to take people out and keep them."

I stared at him, and I felt my mouth suddenly go dry. Piper McMahon may have found the answer I'd been looking for since I'd gone into DW.

"And what did she find out?"

"I don't know."

"What do you mean you don't know? Haven't you talked to her?"

"Of course."

"And?"

Brady got up then and stared out the window. The dull humming of the car wash seemed almost to be taunting us, adding a hint of the mundane to his story.

"She stopped answering her phone two weeks ago," he finally admitted.

I stared at his back, trying to process this bit of news. Piper had truly disappeared. Or at least, she didn't want Brady to know where she was.

"I'm sure she's called her parents—or, her DW parents, whatever. We'll ask them."

Brady chuckled, shook his head.

"Why not?"

"They're gone, Marina. I went to their house last night. It's empty. They must have gone home, snuck into the boiler room at night."

So that was that, then. Obviously Piper hadn't solved the mystery of how to keep people from DW on our side. If she had, her parents wouldn't have left.

I felt like the universe was ripping my brother away from me all over again, and I couldn't think of anyone else to ask for help. Unless . . . unless these Mystics could help somehow.

"It wasn't supposed to be like this," he continued. "You know where Boulder is? In Colorado?"

I shrugged. I had never heard of it.

"It's at the foot of the Rockies. The university is there. Piper and I were supposed to move there after school ends in June."

It was painful to think of Brady and Piper living together in a little apartment somewhere, just like the one I had imagined, in some beautiful college town at the foot of a mountain—it was too perfect.

"She would take classes at the college and I'd get a job. I've helped Jack out at the garage a lot. I could do something like that."

"Yeah," I agreed. "That sounds nice." I suddenly felt overwhelmed by emotion. I felt like the world was spinning without me.

Brady must have heard the defeat in my voice. He knelt down by my chair, so close I could smell the sweetness of his laundry detergent. But I knew he was thinking of someone else.

"I should go," I said.

"Yeah."

I stood and headed for the door. "It'll be okay," I said before leaving. "You'll see her again. I know you will."

He only laughed in response, quietly and without a hint of joy. He was still kneeling on the floor by my empty chair. "You even sound like her."

I let myself out of the apartment, suddenly missing my brother more than ever.

REBECCA PHELPS

CHAPTER 7

I stood in front of the door to Today, dumbfounded, my eyes blinking in disbelief.

There was nothing but a brick wall, just like the other two doors. I quickly glanced behind Yesterday and Tomorrow, to see if they had changed as well. But they were all the same now. A thick brick wall, with only a tiny slit of an eyehole to confirm that no magical portal lay beyond. Only darkness.

DW was gone.

And with it went any hope I had of ever seeing that magical version of my brother again.

Suddenly I could hear footsteps in the science room above, and I froze. It was late on a Friday afternoon. The school was open only because spring basketball had started, and so the gym door was unlocked. Nobody was supposed to be in the rest of the school. I had been sure the coast would be clear.

And yet the footsteps grew closer. I tried to find a way to hide, but there was nowhere to go. The only way out of this little waiting area was to go back up the spiral staircase. The footsteps began to descend, and there was nothing I could do but steel myself to face whomever it was that was coming.

I was actually relieved to see that it was Kieren, an ironic reaction considering how many years I had spent being afraid of him. He didn't seem surprised to find me there, and approached me with a steady but serious look on his face.

Kieren looked sad and too old for his tall, slightly skinny body. The light had gone out of his eyes, and it finally hit me that maybe that was the reason I found it so hard to look at him—not because of what he had done, but because all I could see in his face was the shadow of the friend that I had lost.

Kieren went over to the Today door and peeked inside, closing it only a moment later. "So it's true," he said with a sigh. He leaned his forehead against the door, as though gathering his thoughts. It seemed to take him a moment to remember I was there.

"What were you doing down here anyway, M?"

"I wanted to see Robbie," I admitted. "I know I'm not allowed to take him out, but I can see him, can't I?"

Kieren and I used to talk to each other so honestly, so easily. I wanted to see if any of that still remained between us.

He chuckled. "You haven't changed. It's my fault for telling you to stay out. Should have known you'd just do the opposite."

"You don't know me that well."

"Sure I do. I do know you, M," he added, locking his eyes on mine.

REBECCA PHELPS

"What happened to the door?" I could hear some of the confidence in my voice fading a bit.

"I told you, there are consequences."

I must have looked confused, so he went on.

"Things change. Sometimes they disappear. You can't take things out of DW. You take out something small, like the egg timer, and there are small changes. But you take out something big . . ."

"Like Piper McMahon's parents," I finished his thought.

"You know about that?"

"It's okay. Brady thinks they crossed back over, so everything should be fine again."

"The damage is already done, though, isn't it?"

Kieren looked angry suddenly, as though I were rubbing it in his face that I knew so much about this whole thing, despite all his efforts to keep me out of it. "Come on, M," he said. "You need to get out of here." He grabbed my arm and started leading me back up the stairs.

"But Brady said . . ."

"I said come on!"

I stopped in my tracks and pulled my arm away. "Stop ordering me around, Kieren!"

"Be quiet, M."

"No! You never went to visit him. Because you don't miss him. But what do I expect, anyway?"

"Just stop talking!"

"You're the one who pushed him in front of that train in the first place."

"Stop!" Kieren slammed his palm over my mouth to stop me, and though I don't think he meant to do it, the force of his hand pushed my whole body back against the wall. I gulped with shock.

Kieren immediately pulled his hand away, and the look of surprise in his eyes made me think maybe he had scared himself more than me.

"I'm sorry," he said. "I'm so sorry."

He backed away a step and we both caught our breath. I tried to regulate my inhales so I wouldn't cry. It hadn't hurt. It had just scared me.

"I didn't mean to do that." He was also breathing very hard, almost as though he were trying not to cry himself. "I really didn't mean it, M."

"I'm okay," I said, despite the fact that the tears were starting to fall down my cheeks.

He reached out to wipe them off and I instinctively flinched away from him, more aggressively than I had intended.

"I just wanted to get you out of here."

"I'm okay." It was a relief to see how upset he was. It made me realize that somewhere in this strange body before me, maybe my friend was still hiding.

"I would never hurt you."

"I know that," I told him, controlling the tears now. Feeling emboldened by his remorse, by how vulnerable he suddenly seemed to me, I took Kieren's hand. He looked down at our hands and held onto mine so tightly I was afraid he might cut off the blood supply. "Talk to me," I said, trying to catch his eye. But he kept looking at our hands.

"Brady told you about Piper?"

"It wasn't his fault. Don't get mad at him. I made him tell me."

"Of course," he said, nodding as if to himself. "You like him."

I broke away from him then, feeling the blush fill my cheeks despite myself. "What? No, I don't," I insisted weakly.

"And so you're glad Piper hasn't come back."

"Of course not. Do you think I'm a monster?"

"No," he said, looking at me again. "You think I am."

I shook my head, but I couldn't deny it. A monster is exactly what I had been told Kieren was for the past three years.

"I'll tell you more," he continued. "But not here. Someone else might be coming. Let's get our bikes. I'll take you home."

We walked together down the corridor and up through the boiler room, sneaking out of the gym entrance past a group of sweaty basketball players who were taking a short break by the water fountain. We didn't say anything to each other the whole time, and yet I felt like we had broken through something. The silence between us seemed comforting, not strained.

Out back, I saw his old Schwinn locked up next to my bike, so they sat side by side. I realized he must have gone home after school and then come back. It was the first time I'd seen him on something other than his skateboard, and I wondered if Kieren had come back here only to look for me. Or had he come for the same reason I had? Maybe he did visit Robbie after all.

I didn't ask, though. If the answer was yes, I had a feeling he'd tell me in time. We biked alongside each other, able to cut through a nearby park now that the warm spring air had thawed the last of the winter ice. A bloom of pink petals rained down from a row of cherry blossoms, forming a pink sea that lined the path back to my house.

Finally, we got to the end of my street, the same place where he had stopped the last time. We pulled over, our legs straddling our bikes. He stared in the direction of my house. "I can't go any closer," he said.

"I know."

"She still hates me." I knew he meant my mother. It wasn't a question, it was a statement, as though he had been in my house over the past few years and knew it to be a fact.

"She hates everything," I told him, and hearing the words out loud, they sounded very cold and perhaps a little too dramatic. But they were true.

He nodded, still looking at the house. "If she ever hurts you, you come and tell me."

"She's not like that. She just . . . she's sad. I hear her sometimes . . ." It was hard to talk about my mother, but it occurred to me that I had never had the opportunity to tell anyone what it was like to live with her. No one had ever asked. "I hear her in the bathroom crying. Sometimes she just closes her bedroom door. She doesn't come out. I want to knock. But I don't."

"I do care," Kieren said then. "About Robbie. Of course I care."

"I know you do. I shouldn't have said that."

"I've been trying, M, to find a way. A way to get him out of there, but for good."

The shock must have taken over my face.

"There's a group of us. We've been working on it for a long time. Piper was part of the group. But she acted alone and screwed everything up. We weren't ready yet."

"I'm in," I said. I didn't even think. "Whatever it is, I'm in."

Kieren stole one more glance at my house and started to turn his bike around. "You know the pyramid house? On the other side of town."

"Of course I know it," I said with a laugh. "You dared Robbie and me to spend the night in it once, remember? What about it?"

"Tell you later," he said, and then hopped up onto his seat.

"Tell me what later?" I asked. He didn't hear me, though. He had already ridden away.

o o o

The next morning, I was licking the last bit of whipped cream off a stack of blueberry pancakes at Pat's Diner, my parents both chewing absentmindedly on either side of me, when a woman I didn't know approached us, staring intently at my mother. She was about Mom's age, but she somehow seemed younger. Maybe it was the flowing white dress or the long, braided hair falling halfway down her back.

"Rain?" she asked, as she approached the table. She said it like it was a name.

My mother's eyes opened wide for a moment, then darted back down to the table. She straightened herself up and seemed to shuffle for a moment, so visibly uncomfortable that my dad and I couldn't help but exchange a glance of concern.

"Ana," my mother said, revealing her own name. "It's Ana."

The woman seemed confused for a moment, but nodded when she took in me and my father—some hidden conversation they were having right in front of us.

"Ana. Of course." Then she offered my mother a smile that seemed so completely genuine and warm, there was no doubt in my mind that she had not confused my mom with someone else.

"I'm Sage," she said to my father, when no introduction came from my mother. Another weird name. My father stood up and shook her hand, and when he did, a bracelet full of little blue beads rattled on her ample wrist.

"Steve," my father responded, and my mother seemed to snap to life upon hearing his name.

"Sorry," my mother said, shaking off whatever thought was clouding over her brain at the moment. "Sage, this is my husband. My daughter, Marina. You remember."

"Marina," Sage exclaimed. "My, my, my, look at you. I met you once, but you wouldn't remember. You were very young."

Dad looked to Mom then, clearly waiting for an explanation that wasn't coming.

"Jesus, she looks just like you, Rai—Ana." She turned to me then, her big, warm hand enveloping mine. "You look like your mother, did you know that?"

I shook my head, because I didn't really know what the appropriate response was. I did have my mother's Mexican coloring and brown hair, but my father's Irish eyes. Honestly, considering the tired, defeated look my mother usually had these days, I didn't really consider her comment a compliment.

"Such a beauty," Sage continued.

"Sage and I grew up together," my mother offered. It was an awkward addition to the conversation, however, not betraying a hint of warmth. Instead my mother seemed caught, as though Sage might reveal secrets about her that I wasn't supposed to know.

"Won't you sit down?" my father asked.

My mother waited a beat too long before seconding the offer. "Yes, please sit down."

"We have to be going, thank you." Sage nodded over her shoulder to a man at the counter who could have only been with her, judging by his all-white clothes and the string of beads hanging around his neck. "We're just in town for a couple of days."

My mother's eyes flickered to the man with a flash of recognition and a half-hearted smile, but then she looked away again, back to Sage. "Your mom still live here?"

"No, she passed," Sage said, the calm in her voice not wavering for a moment, as though she had come to peace with the fact.

"I'm sorry to hear that," my mother said, and I could tell it was true. "She was very warm."

"Yes, she was," Sage agreed. "George and I wanted to see the old grounds."

"They're gone," my mother offered, a bit too quickly. My mother looked again at the man by the counter, who offered a sad smile of recognition, but made no move to approach her.

"Yeah, so I saw. Just a gas station now, huh?"

My mother nodded. "And some fast food places."

My father put his hand on my back then, almost in a protective way, and I wondered what he was protecting me from. What were the old grounds? And who was Rain?

"Well, I guess that's it, then," Sage concluded, and for the first time a bit of sadness crossed over her face. "The end of the road."

My mother nodded. She offered the woman another half smile. "I should go say hi to George," she said, as though it had just occurred to her.

"He's not feeling well. Maybe next time."

My mother nodded and settled back into her seat, somehow chastened. "Tell him I hope he feels better," she said so quietly I almost didn't hear her.

Sage smiled and nodded, causing all her jewelry to jangle around her.

"It was good to see you, Sage."

"You too, Rain." Sage caught herself, a beat too late. "Sorry . . . Ana." She turned to me then and smiled. "Such a beauty."

Sage walked away, the little beads on her wrist rattling and a scent of some kind of exotic oil trailing behind her, and we all watched as she and George left the restaurant.

The walk back to our house from Pat's Diner was typically awkward. My father whistled an old tune that I recognized from an album he used to play, and my mother pretended to smile whenever she caught my eyes.

"Lana's gonna come over later, okay?" I asked.

"Of course," they said in unison, but they were both distracted.

The rest of the day, I tried to put the lady from the diner out of my mind. Christy and my friend Lana from St. Joe's came over, and we painted each other's nails and talked and watched old romantic comedies from the '80s. Lana had a boyfriend, she told us. Christy had been promoted to first violin in the school band. I was happy for Lana. I was happy for Christy. But my mind kept drifting.

Had my mother been living a double life all these years? What else about her past didn't I know? My friends kept talking, but I didn't hear a word they said. My mind was fixated on one thought:

Is her name really Rain?

My mom came into my room late that night after the girls had left and sat on the edge of my bed, something she hadn't done in a long time.

"Did you have fun with your friends?" she asked. She looked so beautiful in the light from under my door, her hair pulled back and a soft black sweater on. Little blue earrings I hadn't seen her wear in years were dangling from her earlobes, and I think she was even wearing lip gloss. I wondered if she and Dad were having a little date or something.

"Yes," I said. But I couldn't help thinking about how far away from the other girls I had felt all night, like there had been a wall between us. Maybe that wall was Robbie, or DW. There were so many things that didn't get said in this house. Which was why what my mother said next surprised me so much.

"I know how hard it's been for you, Marina. I know you've been alone. And I'm so sorry."

"It's not your fault." I had understood for a long time that my mother was depressed, and that there was nothing she could do about it.

"It is and it isn't. We all make choices. But I want you to know how much I love you, how proud I am of you."

The tears started to sting behind my eyes. I couldn't remember the last time she had said something like that to me.

"You've done everything right," she continued. "And I know how strong you are. Stronger than you realize."

I took her hand, and she clutched mine with both hands.

"You are my warrior," she said. She kissed me on the forehead and said it again. "You are my warrior."

"I love you, Mom."

She nodded. "I love you, too, Marina." She smiled at me before she left the room.

It was the last thing I remember her saying to me.

In the morning, she was gone.

CHAPTER 8

At first, my father and I assumed Mom had gone to visit Robbie's grave. She would sometimes do that without telling anyone, just to be alone there for a while. But after several hours, when she hadn't come home, we called the cemetery. They hadn't seen her.

My dad made a few phone calls. Neighbors stopped by. People came and went. And the day grew long and hours passed. Soon it was getting dark. There was no word of her.

You are my warrior, she had told me. *What did that mean, Mom? Did you think I was strong enough to live without you? Did you just leave?*

A police officer came by after dark to tell us they believed she had been spotted. A man had seen someone walking on the train tracks near the station late the night before, after my mother had said good night to me. The woman on the tracks matched my mother's description. According to the officer, the woman had been standing in the middle of the tracks, as though waiting for the train to come hit her. The witness screamed for her to get off the tracks, but apparently she said she couldn't. She insisted that she had to wait for the train, then shouted something else that the man couldn't make sense of. So he called the police. But by the time they arrived, the woman on the tracks had left.

"We suspected . . . ," the officer paused, eyeing me before deciding whether to continue, "perhaps attempted suicide."

I could feel, rather than hear, my father inhale by my side. The air in the room became quite stiff, oppressive even.

"We searched but couldn't find her. We can't be sure it was your wife." The officer was a middle-aged man, wide around the middle, with more hair on his knuckles than on his head. He couldn't look my father in the eye, and instead talked to his chin.

"And then about an hour ago, we get a call from the high school. Security guard was reviewing some footage this morning and he caught a woman sneaking in through a back window in the middle of the night. No record of her leaving, however. We've searched the school, but we can't find any trace of her."

"You think it was her?" my father asked, and I couldn't gauge from his voice whether he found any of this surprising. It was like he was made of steel.

"We need you to come look at the footage, sir. To verify it."

My father nodded, his hand on my back. I remembered how he had put his hand on my mother's back while they were telling me about Robbie's accident.

I love you, too, my mother had told me.

"You can do it in the morning, if you'd like," the officer

continued, twirling his wedding ring around his fat finger, where it tangled with his knuckle hair.

"I'll come now," my dad answered, turning to me. "You'll be okay for a bit?"

"Yes, Daddy."

He kissed my forehead, and they both stood up and turned to leave the room. But before they could make it very far, I stood up myself.

"Sir?" I asked.

"Yes?" the officer responded.

"The man who saw her on the tracks . . ."

"You mean the witness?"

"The witness, yeah. He said the woman on the tracks said something that didn't make sense. What was it?"

The officer glanced at my dad, as if looking for permission to respond. But my dad was already lost in his own mind.

"She was raving," the officer said, shaking his head. "Something like, 'It's on the tracks. It happens on the tracks.'"

o o o

It took me about fifteen minutes to bike down the path to the train station, after sneaking down the stairs at one in the morning and carrying my bike from the garage, through the kitchen, and out the back so as to not wake my dad by opening the garage door. He hadn't been able to confirm much at the police station. The surveillance footage had looked like her, but it was blurry enough that he couldn't be sure. He had come home about an hour after leaving, his shoulders slumped, and kissed me good night.

A light rain fell on my head now, which I tried to cover with a hoodie that blew off the moment I started pedaling. Soon the rain soaked my hair and made my jeans stick to my ankles. I kept pedaling anyway, even as the denim against my skin felt like icy fingers pulling my knees in the opposite direction.

The first bolt of lightning came as I approached the train station and threw my bike down on the pavement. I started walking along the track. Looking for what, I had no idea.

I felt like a complete fool. I became aware suddenly of how cold I was, shivering, my teeth chattering. There was nothing on these tracks but cold rain. I was empty and numb, so I decided to head back to my bike. But first, I took one last long look down the length of the tracks, as far as I could see through the dark swirling images that danced in the rain.

And that's when I saw the figure.

It was far in the distance, maybe a hundred feet down the tracks, down in the part where the accident had happened. For just a second, seeing the silhouette against the gray splattering rain, I felt like maybe it was him—Robbie. Like somehow he had escaped and had come to find me. I ran towards him.

But, of course, it wasn't him. And not until I was a few feet away, the silver curtain of rain the only thing between us, did I see that it was Kieren.

He was examining the tracks, as though looking for something, walking with his head down. He didn't see me approach.

"Kieren!" I called.

He looked up, startled. "Go home, M."

"What are you looking for?" I asked, my voice cracking a bit.

"Nothing."

My lips were quivering from the cold and I could feel my whole body tremble.

He threw up his hands, frustrated. "Come on," he said. "You're freezing. Let's get you inside."

"How did you know to come here?"

"Inside," was all he said. He took my arm and guided me back down the tracks.

We didn't speak as I picked up my bike and started pushing it. Kieren lived a block from the station, and I didn't realize he was taking me to his house until we were at the door.

"Around the back," he said, taking my bike and leaving it under an eave as we walked around the side of the house to a sliding glass door that led to the downstairs rec room.

The rec room was just as I remembered it from years before, the same posters on the wall of some basketball players I didn't know from the '80s. The posters, I assumed, belonged to Mr. Protsky, Kieren's dad, and I realized in that moment what a great disappointment it must have been to him that his son had no interest in sports.

I came into the room, still trembling. The weakness in my legs wouldn't go away.

"Jesus, M, why'd you bike to the station in the rain?"

"It was only driz-driz-drizz . . ."

"It's okay, don't talk."

Kieren took off his sweatshirt, glued as it was to his body, and then he came and helped me with mine. I was too cold to be self-conscious about it at that point. He reached down to feel my shoes and socks.

"Your feet are soaked. Okay, wait here. I'm gonna get you some sweats and a T-shirt. Take those shoes off."

I started to untie my shoes, but my fingers were numb. My teeth were chattering so loudly, I couldn't hear anything but the *clackety-clack* of them hitting against each other.

Kieren came back in, wearing dry clothes himself and with some things for me, and saw how helpless I was. "Here," he said, reaching down to help me with my shoes. "Your pants are drenched. You need to change."

"T-t-turn around," I said.

"It's fine, M. I've seen you in a bathing suit, like, a million times."

"I was ni-ni-ni-nine."

He just laughed and turned around. "I'm not looking," he promised. I changed my clothes as quickly as possible while the feeling returned to my fingers. When I was done, I sat on the couch.

There was a laundry area in the corner, and Kieren went and threw my things in the dryer.

I found a throw blanket next to the sofa and wrapped myself in it. I was already starting to feel sleepy, but I knew I had to head back home as soon as the rain stopped. I couldn't still be gone when my dad woke up in the morning. All he needed was one more scare.

"Feeling better?" Kieren asked when he came back over to the couch. I nodded. I couldn't help but stare at Kieren's face as he sat down next to me. His eyelashes were the same as I remembered, and so was the way his hairline came down a bit over his right eye.

He laughed then. I don't know why. Maybe just the awkwardness of being so close. "I can't leave you alone for a second, can I?"

"Why were you on the tracks?" I asked. He didn't respond. "Kieren, please."

"I just . . . I go there sometimes."

"Why?"

He shrugged, looked at his feet.

"It's how I feel close to him," he said, so softly I could barely hear him. "It's like, some people visit graves. I visit where he died. It's stupid, I know."

"It's not stupid."

"He's not at his grave," Kieren said. "I feel like . . . like he's somewhere else."

I had to admit that I felt the same way about Robbie. But still, the coincidence that Kieren was on the tracks after what had happened with my mother, after what she had apparently shouted, just seemed a bit too convenient. What more did Kieren know? What wasn't he telling me?

"Do you promise there's no other reason?" I asked. "You said you were working on taking Robbie out. Is that why you were there?"

"No, that's not it. When I know more about that, I'll tell you."

I started to protest, but then he looked me in the eyes and took my hand. "Promise."

I nodded, feeling hopeless.

"We've done all we can for now, M."

I thought of Robbie, and all the times we had played together in this very room. The endless games of Candyland; the time Kieren had taught us five-card draw, something he had picked up from an old movie he wasn't supposed to watch.

The tears came hot and full, plopping down on the sweatshirt Kieren had just given me. I couldn't stop them, and I didn't try. "My mom is gone," I said. "She's been missing since last night, and I have no idea where she went."

I couldn't tell if Kieren was surprised by this statement, or if maybe he had already known somehow. He pulled me to him, and held me so tightly my ribcage strained under the pressure of his arms.

I felt Kieren's lips on my forehead as he whispered things I couldn't understand. Words that fell around me like the raindrops that still splattered against the roof. "It'll be okay," he said. "I'll fix it." I looked up at him, and his lips landed on mine for just a moment, before he seemed to catch himself and sit back a bit.

I was struck by the irony of it: my first kiss happened at the worst moment of my life.

"Why don't you sleep?" he asked. "It's still raining. You're tired."

"I have to get home. My dad will be worried."

"Sleep," Kieren insisted, helping me lie back and covering me with the throw blanket. "I'll wake you before dawn. Promise."

My eyes didn't need any more encouragement than that to close. I felt the rough corduroy of the couch hit my cheek as Kieren stood and turned down the light. I could feel the warmth of his body fade away from me, like a train pulling out of a station.

CHAPTER 9

Weeks passed, and she didn't return. My father and I fell into a pattern, trying to do "normal" things like eat dinner, do the dishes, fold laundry. At first, we talked about her all the time, like she was just out at the grocery store. "When Mom comes back . . ." "When you talk to your mother again . . ."

Then we didn't talk about her at all.

Sometimes I'd wake up in the night, trying to feel her presence in the world. I knew she wasn't dead. Was she in DW? If so, how did she get in there? Was she looking for Robbie? Would she come back if she didn't find him?

The questions had begun to drive me insane. I would pace in my room at night, touching things to be sure that they were solid. That they hadn't disappeared.

Late May came, and the seniors graduated. Christy and I watched the ceremony from the back of the auditorium.

"Could you help me with something?" I asked Christy in a whisper.

"Sure," she answered, her eyes on the stage.

"There's this summer camp upstate. I read about it online."

Christy glanced over to me for a moment, then back to the seniors. There was a hunger in her eyes, watching them, like she couldn't wait for it to be her turn. Christy and I had that in common.

"It's just two weeks," I continued.

"Okay," she said, clearly not knowing where I was going with this. "Are you—do you want to go there?"

"No. But I need my father to think I have."

Brady made his way to accept his diploma, followed by Kieren, and we stopped talking to watch them. I couldn't help but feel proud of them both, standing onstage in their caps and gowns as the rest of the seniors filed in beside them.

But then an odd hush fell over the room. One name had been conspicuously absent from the roll call.

"We'll now have a moment of silence for Piper McMahon," said Miss Farghasian, and a ripping sound of grief caught in her throat at the name.

The silence was accompanied by much weeping throughout the auditorium. Whispers ensued, everyone adding their two cents to whatever the latest rumors were about Piper's whereabouts ("She went to have a baby in Ireland" was the most common theory), and then more silence.

Almost four months had passed and no new information had been given. Some people assumed she was dead.

Brady kept his eyes downcast, neither crying nor showing any other visible emotion. He looked tired, and seemed to realize that many of the eyes were falling on him. One of the rumors that had briefly circulated had been very unflattering to him, all but accusing him of her murder. But like all rumors, it eventually faded into air.

"She wasn't that pretty. She just had a good body," I heard Holland Pfeffer whisper behind me. The girl next to her responded with a stifled, "Oh my God, stop. You're the worst."

"Why summer camp?" Christy whispered to me, while Miss Farghasian walked to center stage to give what I'm sure she considered to be a Very Important Speech.

"I want to go to Oregon. It's a long story, but I think there are people there who know something . . . about my brother, Robbie."

"And your dad won't let you go?"

I thought about it for a second. "I haven't asked him."

"You know," she started, "your dad is cool. You're lucky like that." I could tell she was referencing her own parental situation with that last dig. Christy's mother had been the first woman in her family to go to college, and she had let Christy know at an early age that she expected her to follow suit. She'd basically been planning Christy's life out since birth.

"If you asked him . . . ," Christy continued.

"If I asked, I know what he would say," I responded, having already had this conversation with myself eighteen times. "He would either say no, that it's time to move on and let Robbie go. Or he would decide to go without me because I'm too young to possibly understand. Trust me, I've been hearing it my whole life. It's just two weeks. I'll be fine."

REBECCA PHELPS

She nodded, needing no more convincing. "What do you want me to do?"

"Help me make up some stationery from the summer camp, for a letter saying that I've gotten some scholarship or something and that I can go for free."

"You're crazy," she said, laughing.

"I know."

Miss Farghasian droned on about the bright future that lay ahead for all the graduates, which everyone in the room knew wasn't exactly true. Probably only about half the kids up there were going to college. And we all knew which half. The other half, the one Brady belonged to, well . . .

"Okay," Christy said. "What's their website? I'll copy their letterhead and paste it on an acceptance letter. You'll have to buy some nice paper to print it on."

I stole one last look at Brady on the stage in his gown and mortar as we stood with everyone else to applaud the graduates.

"Thanks, Christy," I said. She followed my eyeline to Brady. I had told her, of course, about my pathetic crush on him.

"You know," she said, "he really is pretty cute."

I could only laugh in response, certain that I was blushing.

o o o

I went out to my dad's garage workshop a week after the graduation and watched him work. This was something we used to do all the time—switching motherboards and fiddling with wires. But it had been a while.

"Is there something I could do to help?" I asked.

"Sure, kiddo. Um, bring me that big piece there." He pointed to a metal box with a million wires coming out of it. "We're swapping out the hard drives, but first we have to trick them into thinking they're compatible."

"They're not?" I asked, only half understanding what he was talking about.

"Not exactly."

We worked in silence for a bit, and it was nice to be doing something normal with my dad again. Nice to take a break from not talking about Mom.

"Thanks for letting me go, Dad. To the summer camp." The "acceptance letter" had arrived the day before, thanks to Christy.

"Aw, it'll be good for you," he answered, and I could tell by his tone that he'd already given it a bit of thought and this was the conclusion he'd come to. "You need to get out of here for a bit. This can't be good for you, this thing with your mom."

I nodded. So that's what we were going to call my mom disappearing, huh? A "thing."

"I'm just in the middle of a project at work, or else I'd drive you—"

"That's okay," I quickly interrupted. "It'll be fun to take the bus up with Christy and her mom." Christy and I had already planned this whole thing out in detail, complete with fake email addresses for the camp. As far as he knew, Christy and I were going to the camp together. Her mom was taking the bus up with us and would come pick us up when the camp ended.

I suddenly felt an enormous cramp in my stomach, and I realized it was nerves. And maybe a little guilt. I never wanted to be someone who lied, especially to my dad. And for a brief moment, it occurred to me to just tell him the truth. Maybe I was wrong about him. Maybe he would let me go, or even go with me.

"This kind of a situation," he began, his eyes still intent on his work, his fingers rigorously plucking out wires one by one, "it's not good for a kid."

I nodded. Someday, I knew, my dad and I would talk about this part of our lives. We would talk honestly. And I would tell him about Oregon. Maybe I'd even tell him about Down World. And the other version of Robbie. Assuming, of course, that someday I would understand it myself.

Later that night, after my dad had gone to sleep, I went into my bedroom to get ready for bed. I soon heard a rapping on my window.

I opened the window and looked out, and saw Kieren standing in the street with his bike behind him. He was actually tossing pebbles at the window, like something out of a cheesy old movie.

I raised my hands in a silent question. *What is it?* I mouthed. Even though my father was surely sound asleep across the hall, I was afraid to make any noise.

Kieren nodded over his shoulder, beckoning me to come down.

I slinked down the stairs and went out through the kitchen door, knowing that my father would never hear that from his room, even if he were conscious. Kieren and I walked several feet down the street before I spoke.

"What are you doing?" I asked.

"I've been texting you. Don't you ever check your phone?"

I took my phone out of my pocket and saw that it was dead. "Sorry."

"We're having a meeting at the pyramid house. Come on, let's go," Kieren said, yanking on my arm.

"The pyramid house? Wait, my dad . . ."

"Is he awake?"

"No, but . . . okay, but I have to be back in an hour."

"No problem. Get your bike."

Kieren pedaled hard, like there was some urgency in getting there. I had to pump my legs hard to keep up. It was a mild night. Summer had officially begun, and even though it was probably close to midnight, the air was still somehow illuminated.

When we reached the large, pyramid-shaped abandoned house, Kieren helped me hoist myself up to the window and enter the cavernous living room. There was still no furniture in the place, just as there hadn't been when Robbie and I snuck in years before. But I didn't have time to dwell on the memory, because even though there was no furniture, the room was not empty.

The meeting was already in progress.

Kieren's friend Scott, a boy I distinctly remembered as one of the kids who used to tease me at the train station, was talking in a frustrated tone. There were two other guys I recognized from the old days at the train station, but I didn't remember their names. And standing next to them, listening, stood Brady.

Kieren and I approached the group together, and I could see Brady looking at us as we stood there, side by side. He seemed a bit flustered, and then looked away.

"What is she doing here?" Brady asked no one in particular.

"We need her," Kieren answered. "Robbie was her brother, after all."

"That doesn't matter. We're not doing that!"

"You don't get to decide, Brady," Kieren shouted. I had clearly walked into a fight that had begun earlier. "We already talked about this."

"That was before."

"I say we call it off too," Scott answered, and one of the other boys grumbled some sort of agreement.

"Then go home, I don't care," said Kieren. But his tone betrayed that he cared very much. "We don't need you. M and I can do it by ourselves." Kieren took my hand, and suddenly I was his partner in crime. Except I had no understanding of what the crime was, exactly.

Brady watched Kieren take my hand, and he shook his head. "I'm out," he said. "I'm going home."

"Wait, stop," I demanded, pulling my hand away from Kieren. "Just everybody stop right now."

I took a moment to gather my thoughts as everyone reluctantly quieted down.

"Will somebody please tell me what you're talking about?"

"I will," Brady said. "Your boyfriend wants to go into DW, find Robbie, and take him out—"

"What are you talking about? You know you can't take anyone out," I began, flinching momentarily at the word *boyfriend*. "Piper's parents . . ."

"Take him out through the train portal," Brady said, completing his earlier sentence.

"I'm telling you, it'll work," Kieren said.

"You'll both be hit by the train!" Brady insisted.

"He's right," another boy chimed in.

"Okay, enough!" I cut in. "What the hell is the train portal?"

Kieren and Brady exchanged a look. "Sit down, M," Kieren began. "I have to tell you something."

o o o

We sat around in a circle. I made a point of not sitting near Kieren or Brady. I wanted to be by myself.

"The night that it happened . . . the night Robbie died . . . ," Kieren began, finding his voice as he talked.

I took a deep breath. So now we were going to talk about Robbie. Okay.

"We were down at the train station. We were just messing around on our boards."

I instinctively put my hand over my heart as he talked. Oh God, this was it. I was going to hear the story of how my brother died. The story that I had been sheltered from for almost four years. This was the moment I had been waiting for, and I didn't know if I was strong enough to hear it.

"We had worked our way down the track a bit, popping wheelies over the rails. It's stupid. I know it is," he added, as though hearing the protests in my mind. "We were kids."

"Go on," I said, steeling myself for what was to come.

"The train came," he said, his voice growing softer, but still continuing.

The hot tears burned my cheeks, but I was ready to hear this.

Kieren's voice broke, and he started to cry, something I didn't know he could do. "I thought he would jump."

One of his friends put his hand on Kieren's back, but Kieren didn't seem to notice.

"At the last minute, when the train came, there was this flash. This flash of light. You know the light I mean, you all do. The yellow light. And right before the train . . . hit him, I swear I saw it."

"Saw what?" I asked, my voice barely a whisper.

"Robbie . . . disappeared."

I gasped, and thought I might collapse. I put my fingers on my temples and tried to breathe. Was it possible?

I felt an arm around me and realized Brady had come over to sit beside me. But I felt like I was floating away. Did Robbie go through a portal that night?

"They never found the body . . . ," Kieren continued.

"They said it was . . . that there was nothing left," I told him, repeating the story I had been told for years. Robbie's burial was ceremonial. The casket was empty. I was told it was because there was nothing left to bury.

"I didn't understand what had happened until I got to the high school the next year. And I heard about DW. The first time I went down to the Today door, and saw that flash of light, I realized what had happened to Robbie that day on the train tracks."

I nodded, still thinking of my brother's empty shoes, found by the tracks that night.

"Robbie went through a portal," Kieren continued. "There's some sort of portal on the train track. I've tried to go through it a million times, but it's not there. I think maybe it's only there when the train comes. And I think Robbie is stuck inside it . . ."

"Stop," I demanded. "When you say 'Robbie is stuck inside it,' do you mean . . . you mean DW Robbie?"

"No, M. That's what I'm trying to tell you. I mean *real* Robbie. Real Robbie is in DW. He's not dead. He was never dead. And if I just get into that train portal and pull him back out . . ."

"You'll be hit by the train," I answered, repeating what Brady had said. "If you pull him out when the train is coming . . . Brady's right, it won't work."

"But what if it could?" Kieren asked. "What if there was a way?"

"Piper's parents threw off the balance of energy," I muttered, repeating what Brady had told me. "Because people from one side can't stay on the other."

"Because Piper's parents were never supposed to be here in the first place!" Kieren shouted. "But Robbie is."

"Why did he do it?" I asked.

"What's that?"

"Robbie wasn't stupid. He wasn't reckless. Why would he be on the track when the train was coming? It doesn't make any sense."

Kieren didn't say anything at first. He just hung his head. I could see the tears falling off his face onto his shoes, and he clearly didn't want his friends to notice. But we were all staring at him. There was no hiding it.

I thought about Kieren, about the way we had been when we were kids. I looked around me at the beautiful old pyramid house, the one he had dared us to spend a night in. He was always daring us to do things. Everything was a joke then.

"I didn't push him," Kieren said to his shoes. "I swear I didn't."

"I know that," I told him, voicing what I had always known, despite what my mother had believed. Kieren would never have pushed Robbie in front of a train. But then something occurred to me, and I knew it to be true as soon as I thought of it. "But you dared him, didn't you?"

Kieren continued looking down.

"You dared him to go onto the tracks. Was it a game? Were you playing chicken?" I was getting angry.

Kieren was crying hard. "I thought he would jump," he said so softly I could barely hear it. And then he repeated, "I thought he would jump."

I wasn't even angry anymore. I was just done with all these boys.

"I was an idiot," he said, finally looking up at me. "I'm sorry, M."

I wiped the tears off my cheeks. "My mom wasn't trying to kill herself," I realized. "She was trying to follow Robbie."

My mother grew up in this town. Did she know about the portals? Was it possible that she had always known Robbie wasn't dead, and had kept it from us for over three years? How could she do that to my father? To me?

I followed the thought one step further, imagining my mother, in her little blue earrings, looking for that magical spot on the train tracks. "But she couldn't find it," I said, mostly to myself, just as Kieren hadn't been able to find it. The only piece I couldn't fit into the puzzle was why she had gone to the high school. And if the doors were still sealed, then why didn't she ever come back out?

A respectful moment of silence followed, everyone lost in their own thoughts.

"I have to tell my dad," I said, standing up decisively.

"No." It was Scott who spoke, but he wasn't looking at me. He was looking at Kieren. "She can't do that. This is why I told you not to bring her here. She's going to tell everyone."

"Shut up, Scott," Brady said.

"Screw you, Brady. This isn't a game. What do you think happens when this stupid kid blabs to everyone that there's a portal on the train track? You think we can keep this quiet after that?"

I looked around at the sea of unsympathetic faces.

"We can make it right," Kieren said. "We don't need to tell anyone, M. Your mother will come back when she can't find Robbie and she'll see that we've already saved him. He's not dead. He's just trapped in there. We can get him out." The more Kieren talked, the more excited he got about his own idea.

"You've done enough," I said. I wasn't leaving this up to Kieren. "Here's what's going to happen now," I continued, looking straight at Scott. "In one week, I'm going to Oregon. I've already told my dad I'm going to a camp up north. It's all arranged."

Everyone in the circle froze.

"You're going to the Mystics?" Brady asked.

I softened my tone, realizing that this was a sore spot for him. "Yes. I need to find out what Piper couldn't—if there's a way to take people out for good." Brady nodded slowly, his jaw muscles tensing.

"You can't go," Kieren began. "M, think for a second. You can't travel by yourself. You're only sixteen. You'll get caught and they'll call your dad."

I was taken aback by this. Of course, he was right. Someone would call the cops on me for sure. I wasn't one of those sixteen-year-olds who could pass herself off as eighteen. At five foot four, I was only about a hundred and five pounds, still waiting to fill out. If anything, I looked younger than my age.

"I'll go with her," Brady said, standing up next to me. "I can say she's my kid sister, that we're going to visit an aunt or something."

"Absolutely not," Kieren said firmly. "I'll go."

"I don't want you to go," I said to Kieren. I knew it would hurt him, but I didn't care. I needed some space from him. I knew he had been a stupid kid when he dared my brother to stay on the train tracks, but I still blamed him. I didn't think I would ever stop blaming him.

"How would you go, Kieren? What would your parents say?" Brady countered.

Kieren had no response to this. He clearly realized the same thing. He had no excuse to leave town.

"But it's no problem for me," Brady continued. "I was planning on going there anyway to see if I could find Piper. And besides, there's no one here to wonder where I've gone."

I knew he said it to justify his argument, not to fish for sympathy. But it couldn't help but sound pitiful coming out of his mouth. Again, I wondered what had happened to his mother, and when his father was coming back from Alaska or wherever he was.

Even Kieren had to admit that the plan was perfect. But I was secretly terrified inside. Was this really happening? Was I going to Oregon with Brady? How would that even work? Where would we sleep? How would we find the Mystics? And what if they couldn't help us?

When Piper McMahon traveled west, she probably would have killed to have Brady with her. I should feel lucky. But somehow, knowing he was going just made it seem more real, more overwhelming.

"It's settled, then," I said. "We leave next Sunday."

I looked down at the group, all sitting on the floor. No one had any objections, even Kieren. I looked over at Brady, and he nodded. "Next Sunday," he agreed.

The meeting was over. Everyone started to get up and mill about. But I didn't have anything more to say. I turned and walked over to the window, climbed out, got on my bike, and pedaled home as fast as I could.

I didn't know how this would end. And I was scared out of my mind. But I knew one thing for sure: if there was a way to get my brother out of DW, I was going to find it. The truth was coming out, and I wouldn't stop until I knew all of it.

PART TWO

CHAPTER 10

The following Sunday was unseasonably hot for June. Even at 8 a.m., as I hauled my suitcase down the stairs and onto the driveway to wait for my dad to take me to the bus depot, the air was thick with an early-morning fog that made my hair stick to my forehead.

"Ready, kiddo?" he asked as he came out the front door behind me, searching his pockets for something.

"Yup," I answered over my shoulder. The car was already idling in front of the house. When I closed the trunk, my dad handed me an English muffin with a scrambled egg stuffed inside. He had clearly been up for a while. "Thanks."

"You know, the project at work isn't that urgent. Why don't I take the day off and drive you up to the camp? You could even drive for a bit of it. You need more practice."

"Dad, I told you, you don't have to do that. Everyone's taking the bus." My palms were sweating. The lies were starting to flow from my mouth so naturally. I hated this. I felt like I was already a million miles away from my dad, from our house, from the family we'd once had. "It's only two weeks."

"Yeah, yeah," he agreed, a little too quickly. "Well, get in. Let's not be late."

We drove to the bus depot in silence, and I stared out the window at our passing town as though I might never see it again.

"Call me," he said quietly as we pulled up to the parking lot of the depot, "if you need anything."

"We're not allowed to use our cell phones," I reminded him. Christy had planned out the communications. She said that cell phones are traceable, and that if my dad checked the phone record, he might see where I was calling from. So my cell phone needed to stay off for the entire trip. Instead, she set up an email from the "camp administration," requesting that all correspondence be sent that way.

I realized, as my dad took my suitcase out of the trunk, that part of the reason for the knot in my stomach was simply the precariousness of the plan. I was banking on my dad being too distracted about my mother's disappearance to notice any of the holes in the story. And so far, it had worked perfectly.

I got out to join him behind the car as he placed my suitcase on the curb. Several people were waiting in various stages of boredom. My heart was beating out of my chest, but I knew I needed to look like I had it together, at least until my father drove off.

"Did you want me to wait with you?" he asked.

"You'll be late for work," I responded, ready with my answer immediately.

"Yeah." He nodded sadly.

"Will you be okay, Dad?"

"Yeah, yeah. I'll be fine. Don't you worry about me, kiddo. You just have a good time."

A good time. The idea of it seemed ridiculous, even cruel.

I threw myself into my dad's arms then, and I waited for the sting of tears to burn behind my eyes, but it never came. Why was that? I had never been away from my dad for two weeks before.

I stood and watched him get into the car and drive away, waiting until his little Honda became nothing more than a speck of tan color at the red light of the intersection outside of the parking lot. And then the light turned green and he disappeared around the curve. I let out a huge sigh, and felt my body shake with nerves.

A full five minutes went by before Brady showed up in his old muscle car and popped the trunk. I started hauling my suitcase over. Brady jumped out to help me, but I was already picking it up.

"I got it," I said, and he stood back a bit. I got into the passenger side and put on my seat belt.

Brady got back in and sat next to me. He must have been able to tell that I was scared. I knew I was shaking, and I couldn't stop.

"You nervous?"

I could only nod.

"Listen," he said, his tone gentler than I had ever heard it. "I've been thinking. Do you want me to go without you?"

My head whipped towards him.

"It's not a problem. If they can help, I'll call and let you know. But there's no reason for you to make this whole trip."

"This was my idea."

"I know that. But you're just . . . you're so young, Marina. Maybe you shouldn't be going so far . . ."

"I'm going," I said, my decision final. "Don't worry, I won't be in your way."

"That's not what I meant and you know it."

We sat for another minute, neither of us saying a thing.

"I can't stay here, Brady," I said, fully realizing it was true as I uttered it. "I have to see for myself. I lost my brother. And then my mom."

Brady nodded.

"Would you be able to just sit here and do nothing? Knowing that Piper might be stuck in DW somewhere, and only you can save her?"

"Of course not."

"Then let's go."

There was nothing more to say. Brady put the car into gear and we drove over to the train station, where he parked and then hid the ignition key under the floor mat.

"Don't lock the door," he told me. "My cousin's coming to get the car later."

"Cool." I nodded, hoping nobody would steal it.

I had over eight hundred dollars in cash that I had taken out of my savings account, mostly from old babysitting money and birthday gifts from grandparents. My dad had given me another one hundred dollars before I left, for "incidentals." I gave almost half the total to Brady for the round-trip ticket, and I prayed that the remainder would be enough for the room in the hostel and some food.

Kieren had been right, of course: I never could have made

this trip on my own. Brady and I approached the station to buy the tickets from the vending machine, only to find that in the mornings the machine was locked up, and there was a real person inside to sell them. It was a surly old man in suspenders who looked me over, a young girl in a T-shirt and Keds with a suitcase next to her, and then looked at Brady.

"She's my kid sister," Brady explained. "We're going to visit our aunt."

The man looked back at me and I offered a weak smile, trying to be convincing though my stomach was still in knots and my mouth seemed wired shut.

But the man seemed to believe us, because he sold us the tickets. Brady picked up my suitcase and carried it to the platform. He had only a large backpack on, and I suddenly felt ridiculous for having packed so much. I tried to look up the weather in Portland before leaving, but the report said to expect everything from driving rain to bright sun, and I couldn't figure out how to pack for that.

Standing on that familiar platform, I realized there was only one thing I hadn't done at this train station, and that was actually wait for a train. My eyes couldn't help but wander down the tracks, to the place where my father's work train used to pull in. Farther down the track, deeply set against the horizon, was the place where Kieren had made me the lucky penny, which, as always, I carried now in my pocket. Somewhere in between was where Robbie had disappeared.

Brady had his headphones in, and his eyes down, and looked like every other teenager in the world—a blurred face under a hoodie. And even though he was standing right next to me, I felt completely alone. The heat had only grown worse since early morning, and I felt an uncomfortable stickiness under my arms and inside my shoes.

That's when Kieren appeared, walking up with his eyes averted as though trying to make sure no one was watching him.

Brady didn't notice at first, lost as he was in his own thoughts.

"Hey," Kieren said to me.

"Hi. What are you doing here?"

"Just came to make sure you got off okay." He nodded to Brady, who took out his earphones.

"Hey, man," Brady said.

"Do you mind if I talk to her for a sec?" Kieren asked Brady. I couldn't help but feel like property being passed between the two of them.

"It's up to her," Brady replied, echoing my thoughts.

Kieren looked at me for a response, and my eyes flickered to Brady and the still-empty train tracks for a moment.

"If you've come to talk me out of it . . . ," I began.

"No, no, nothing like that," Kieren insisted. "Please."

We stepped away from Brady a bit, and sat on the bench by the station where we had probably sat together dozens of times before. But now there was the wall between us.

"I wanted to give you something," he said, reaching into his pocket.

"Another lucky penny?" I asked, sounding crueler than I had intended.

Kieren laughed. "Not this time."

He brought out a little bag of M&M's and handed it to me, and I couldn't help but laugh, remembering all the times he had given me the same gift before.

"You steal them from the vending machine?"

He smiled. "I paid for them."

I opened up the bag and popped a little candy into my mouth, feeling the sweet, familiar zing of sugar melting onto my tongue. I offered him one, but he shook his head.

"They're for you," he insisted. "I wanted to thank you, M. For going."

"I'm not doing it for you."

"I know that. And I understand why you didn't want me to go with you."

"It made more sense for Brady to do it. He's eighteen. He can buy the tickets and stuff. And like he said, he was going anyway."

Kieren nodded, and his eyes seemed to search mine for a trace of emotion when I talked about Brady.

I was feeling a million emotions in that moment, but they were all about Kieren. Memories of the past, thoughts of the present. Ideas about what our friendship had meant, and what kind of a future we could ever hope to have. If Robbie came back, could we put it all behind us? If Robbie was here, could we be friends again? Could we be more? And what if Robbie never came back?

It was as if Kieren could read my mind. He took my hand, and I let him. We both sat, staring at our hands, our fingers intertwining.

"If there's a way to get him out," Kieren began, "you call and you tell me. And if it means . . ."

"Kieren?"

"If somebody has to take his place . . . if that's what they say it takes, to balance the energy again, then I'll do it. I want you to know that."

"That won't happen."

"But if it does," he said. "And somebody else needs to go in . . ."

"Stop it," I said, no longer able to even entertain the idea of it. This is what I had been afraid of. I knew Kieren was feeling desperate, and I knew what kinds of crazy thoughts were in his mind. "I'm not going to let you do that."

"But then you'll have him back," he said, looking right into my eyes with such complete sincerity that it was scaring me to my bones. "And then . . . and then you can forgive me."

I held his gaze for another moment, but then I had to look away. It was too much. That's what Kieren had wanted all this time. That was why he had been obsessed with DW, with getting Robbie out. All this was to get me to forgive him, something I had tried to do so many times, but always failed.

The train pulled into the station with such force that it made wind swoosh down the platform, blowing my hair into my eyes. It was the first relief I had felt all day from the oppressive heat, and I wished I could sit there and feel it on the back of my neck for a while longer. But the train stopped and the doors opened.

Brady walked up and nodded that it was time to go.

"I'm coming," I assured him. Brady carried my suitcase. I turned back to Kieren, who stood up, still holding my hand.

"Will you text me when you get there?" Kieren asked.

"Yes," I said, but then I remembered about my phone. "I have to leave my phone off. But I'll text you from Brady's phone when we know something."

I started to walk away, following Brady onto the train, but then stopped and ran back to Kieren at the last minute. I threw myself into his arms for one last hug. "Don't do anything stupid," I whispered to him.

He held me for a moment, like he had done in his rec room.

"Promise me."

"I promise," he whispered back. His hand swept a piece of hair off my cheek, and I had time for one more look into his deeply sad eyes before running to meet Brady on the train. We made it on just in time, with the doors closing right behind us.

Brady and I took our seats, and I stared out the large picture windows, at Kieren standing alone on the platform. And as the train pulled out of the station, and his figure grew smaller and smaller, I was struck by the crazy cycles of life.

I had become the girl on the train.

o o o

Brady was polite but withdrawn the whole ride. I stared transfixed out the window, watching as we wound through forests I had never seen, towns I didn't know existed, and miles and miles of the nothingness that lay between them. Every now and then, when I saw something completely new, I would tug on his sleeve to get his attention. And he would look for a moment and smile at me, before turning back to his phone or a book he was reading.

Up and down the train, I saw only children and myself staring out the windows. The adults were busy, like Brady. And I realized that maybe in some ways I was still one of the children, and Brady had already crossed over to the other side of whatever it was that happened when you no longer stared out windows, wondering who was out there.

For lunch, I pulled out a couple of granola bars, and Brady shared some PB&J sandwiches he had thought to pack. That was it for the food. I had wanted to bring a bunch of canned soup and stuff, but couldn't figure out how to get it into my suitcase without my father noticing.

By the time the train pulled into the station, I guessed it was about 10 p.m. I was hungry again and very tired. Brady offered to carry my suitcase for me, but I refused. I had to show him that I wasn't completely incompetent.

He used his phone to guide us to the hostel, which was thankfully only a few blocks away. Again, I stood back from the counter while he explained to the teenage boy who worked there that I was his kid sister, and he had reserved us two beds. I started to get goosebumps when he said it. I had never stayed in a hostel before and didn't really understand if the beds were going to be in the same room or not. But as it turned out, this hostel was more like a military barrack. Each large room had four bunk beds in it, and boys and girls stayed in different wings, with a common room full of computers and vending machines between them.

We stopped briefly in the common room so I could email my dad from the private account Christy had set up and tell him that I had gotten to camp fine and was sleeping on the top of a bunk bed shared with another nice girl. I then emailed Christy to tell her we were okay.

Brady and I got a couple of Cup Noodles out of the vending machine and stood silently while they heated in the microwave. When we sat down to eat, I guess he could tell I was nervous. I really had no idea where I was, and no real clear plan for the next day. We had some vague directions of where to find the Mystics, but we didn't even know what they looked like. I should have been panicking, but I think I was too tired.

"You okay?" Brady asked, watching me stare at my noodles.

"What if we don't find them?"

"We will," he answered a little too quickly, as though he had already been asking himself the same question.

"And what if they can't help?"

He nodded and ate his noodles. "Then we'll think of something else."

When we split up to go to our own wings and find our beds, I felt like I was being pulled apart from my conjoined twin. I realized that the only reason I had been keeping it together was because Brady had been next to me. And now I would be completely alone for the rest of the night.

Well, not completely.

I walked into the room and nodded at the half dozen other girls already in there. Only one nodded back, and then looked back at her phone. All but two of them were doing the same thing, and those two seemed to be engaged in a very private conversation. I ducked into the bathroom to brush my teeth, and then climbed up onto the top of the one bed that didn't seem to be taken. The light was still on, and the girls were still talking, but I didn't care. I was grateful that a wave of exhaustion was taking over me, wiping my mind clear of the million thoughts and fears that had been plaguing me. My last thought was that I had forgotten to text Kieren. I opened my eyes momentarily, but then shut them again. I fell into a deep sleep, and dreamed I was standing alone in a cold and empty field.

When my eyes opened in the morning, it took me a full second to remember where I was, and I almost rolled right out of the bunk. I climbed down, a harsh early-morning light coming through the windows, and tried not to wake the other girls as I grabbed my suitcase and slunk into the bathroom. I changed my clothes quietly in the stall, my suitcase at my feet, and brushed my teeth at the sink. I thought about taking a shower but didn't want to leave my suitcase unattended while I did it, and I didn't have any shower shoes.

In the common room, I ate another Cup Noodles while I waited for Brady, and sat down at the computer. Each guest was allowed twenty minutes of free internet. I checked my email, both my real account and the one that Christy had set up. The only reply was from her, and it was simply a line of emojis showing happy and excited faces. There was nothing from my dad.

I suddenly thought of Brady, who seemed so comfortable traveling alone. I had asked him the night before if he wanted to email his dad, but he said he was still in Alaska on the salmon boat and couldn't get emails.

I decided to look up the Alaskan salmon boats to see where his dad might be. Maybe I could surprise him with it when he woke up, letting him know that I'd found his dad's boat. It would be nice to wake him up with some good news.

I typed *Alaskan salmon boating* into the search window, and several fishing sites came up. But as I started to skim through them, I noticed they all began with the same piece of information: salmon fishing is a summer thing. The season starts in May and it's over by fall. After that, most of the fishermen come back home until the following season.

But that didn't make any sense. Brady told me his dad had been on a boat since December. So either Brady's dad was lying about what he was doing and where he was living, or Brady was lying about it in order to cover for him. But why?

I didn't have time to finish the thought, as Brady walked into the room. I immediately closed the search window and tried to

REBECCA PHELPS

act natural as he poured himself a cup of coffee and came to sit at the table next to me.

"You gonna eat anything?" I asked.

"I can't eat in the mornings," he said. "Got a bad stomach."

I finished my cup of soup and Brady finished his coffee. A light drizzle had begun to fall outside the window.

"Can I use your phone for a second?"

He handed it over and I found Kieren's number. I really didn't know what to say to him, but I wanted him to know we were okay. So I just typed: *We're here. All is well.* I waited to hear the little swooshing sound that meant it had gone through and then handed the phone back.

"You ready?" he asked.

I nodded, not exactly sure what it was I was supposed to be ready for. "Where do we go?"

"I'll tell you on the bus."

We walked along the sidewalk to a bus stop and waited with a bunch of morning commuters. I tried to act natural, to look like I belonged there, though my paranoid brain was convinced everyone could see right through me.

"How far?" I whispered.

He showed me the map on his phone. "Just a few miles. We'll take the bridge over the river and then keep heading down a little bit."

I stood anxiously, clutching my suitcase, and Brady must have noticed how scared I looked. He put his hand on my back and whispered to me, "It's okay."

I took a deep breath and nodded, mostly for his benefit. The bus came, and we took our seats in a back row.

"So you know the science lab?" he began once we were seated.

I was still getting my bearings and almost didn't hear him. "What's that?"

"The lab behind the boiler room," he continued, still speaking quite softly. I kept my head bowed near his so I could hear him.

"Yeah."

"Piper found these notebooks that the Mystics left behind. Most of it was scientific equations that we didn't really understand. It was pretty advanced. But there were pages and pages of notes too. Ideas about what made DW, about the balance of power."

"Like you were telling me? About . . ." I looked around to make sure we weren't being overheard. "About the sidewalk turning into a fence or something."

He nodded. "One of the books was somebody's journal. It didn't have a lot of useful information in it, just a lot of personal stuff. But the last page was interesting."

"What did it say?"

Brady reached into his pocket and pulled out a well-worn piece of yellowed paper. He unfolded it and handed it to me.

"See for yourself."

The handwriting seemed to belong to a woman, judging by the roundness of the cursive letters. The penmanship was perfect. The paper felt very light, like it had been folded dozens of times and might disintegrate in my hands. I held it very carefully and had to squint a bit to make out the slightly faded text. My jaw dropped as I realized what it was about, and I reread the ending twice:

Whatever world we found down there, whatever power we discovered, he loves it more than he loves

REBECCA PHELPS

me. More than he loves any of us. He is our leader and our friend, and my only love. And when he goes, because he will go, I know that I will die.

—S

I thought that was the end of it, until I flipped the page over and found a postscript.

But in the meantime . . . I hear there's an old hotel about an hour out of Portland, in a little town called Preston. And that's where we'll be, searching for absolution. We wanted to be Mystical. We wanted to be free. What fools we were. I am so sorry.

There was no more. "What does she mean? What did they do down there that was so terrible?"

Brady shook his head and shrugged. "I should tell you that Piper is not the only one who went to look for them."

I waited for him to continue.

"There was another guy named Adam who went a few years ago to ask them about all this. He was obsessed with DW, wanted to learn everything about it. How to navigate it."

"And what did he find out?"

"He never came back," Brady admitted. "And then Piper went and . . ."

"And she didn't come back either. What are you saying? That we won't come back? That once we go there . . ."

"No. No, that won't happen. Listen to me," he commanded, looking me in the eye. But Brady never needed to remind me to listen to him. He always had my attention. "We're gonna stay together the whole time, you and I. And after we talk to them, we're going to leave right away."

I nodded, agreeing completely.

"I don't know anything about these people. They sound a little crazy to me. So you stay by my side and let me talk, okay? We'll be fine."

And with that, Brady sat back against his seat and looked forward, the conversation over. I felt a chill run up and down my arms. What had I gotten myself into? Did the woman who wrote that diary really have any answers? I started breathing heavily and tried to steel myself against a wave of panic.

Brady noticed my breathing, and he put his arm around me. I let myself fall into his side, relieved for the warmth he provided and grateful he was there.

"We'll be fine," he repeated. And as always, I believed him.

The bus let us out in front of a little bench with a tiny, inconspicuous sign over it reading WELCOME TO PRESTON. Only two other women got off at the same time as us, and they started walking away down the long road. We were alone, staring at a one-block business district that looked like it hadn't been touched since the 1950s. A small pharmacy, a diner, a shoe store that advertised *Cobbler Inside*. I didn't know there still were cobblers, and it almost seemed like a movie set instead of a real town.

And right smack in the middle of it was the tallest building, maybe five stories high, with a sign at the top that simply said: HOTEL.

"This is it," Brady said. "Piper texted me a picture of it before she . . . when she got here."

We approached the building and I looked for a front door, but

Brady stopped me and pointed his finger to a small alley along the side.

"Around back," he whispered. "That's what Piper said."

I nodded, and we made our way around the building and down the long narrow alley, with me still lugging my heavy suitcase. An alley cat ran past us and I nearly leaped out of my shoes. Brady laughed at me, and I could only laugh with him.

The back of the building was nothing special. A little courtyard contained an old couch and a mishmash of overly abused lawn chairs, most of which no longer had seats. A handful of planters contained nothing but dead plants or dirt.

There was one door, and it had no handle. I looked to Brady, who looked back at me and shrugged. He walked up and knocked.

"Just a minute!" came a cheerful woman's voice. I was suddenly struck by the idea that we were in the completely wrong place. We needed to run while we could. But it was too late.

The door opened and the woman before us stood digging through an old leather purse. "Hold on, I'm looking for fifty cents for a tip. I know I've got it somewhere."

She was wearing the same white flowing blouse and skirt she'd had on when I had first met her at Pat's Diner, and she smelled the same, like some sort of bitter cooking oil.

"Hello, Sage," I said.

Sage blinked several times, as if trying to make my shape out against the sun. She looked left and right, seeming not to notice Brady by my side. "Oh God," she said. "What has she done?"

CHAPTER 11

"You'll have to excuse the mess!" Sage said as she cleared two cats and some half-full Tupperware containers off a couch in a large room that looked like it was the hotel's office. "We don't get a lot of visitors."

"It's a hotel," Brady said, pointing out the obvious, which made me chuckle.

"Yes." She seemed to realize the confusion immediately. "Oh, but people come in through the front, of course. And to be honest with you, we don't get a lot of guests at the hotel either. This isn't the hip part of town. Sit, sit."

Brady and I slowly did as we were told, sitting gently on the old couch. I snuck a quick look to be sure I wasn't landing on anything gross, but other than some stray cat hair, it seemed safe enough.

"We did have guests, when we started. There was a botanical garden near here. People would stay for that. But then some billionaire bought it and made it into his own backyard. Oh, well. He does open it to the, um . . ."

She was cleaning obsessively the whole time she was talking, and no matter how frantic her actions, it didn't seem to be making things any better. She ducked out of the room for a moment with an armful of trash, and Brady and I sat still on the couch, not sure if we were meant to follow her.

The building was clearly very old. I would guess a hundred years or so. It still had some pieces here and there—an old chandelier hanging from the ceiling, some iron wall sconces—that were both beautiful and eerie, if completely out of place with her decorations of cat toys and incense sticks.

" . . . to the public," she said as she walked back into the room, arms empty, finishing her earlier thought.

"What's that?" Brady asked.

"The billionaire."

"Sage, we need to ask you . . . ," I began.

A knock at the door sprung her out of her seat. "Pizza!" she all but shouted, and continued to talk as she walked back out the door. "You must be hungry. There's plenty to share. Let me just grab my purse . . ." Her voice faded as she turned the corner, without any indication that she was actually going to stop talking.

Brady turned to me. "How did you know her name?"

"She's an old friend of my mother's. I met her at Pat's Diner the day that . . ." I gasped slightly as my mind galloped ahead to the next thought. "The day that my mother disappeared."

"Did you know Sage was one of the Mystics?"

"No, of course not." I started to get out of my seat, trying to figure out what Sage and my mother's disappearance had to do with each other.

"It's okay," Brady said, pushing me gently back down. "We'll get to the bottom of it."

We could hear Sage returning, still talking. Her voice reminded me of the jangling blue bracelet she had been wearing when I'd first met her: constantly in motion.

"I hope you like pepperoni," she said as she came back into the room, opening up the box. I looked at Brady, whose eyes were on the pizza, and I realized he was probably starving. I nudged him lightly, realizing that we'd both think more clearly with some food in our stomachs. He grabbed a piece and started wolfing it down. Sage laughed. "Ah, young people. I forgot how you eat."

Brady laughed too. "Sorry," he muttered through a full mouth.

"No, it's nice, it's nice," Sage continued. "I just need to save a couple pieces for John. He always eats a big lunch. If he eats after five, he gets heartburn. Should I order another?"

"John?" I asked, and Brady wiped his mouth with a napkin and leaned in a bit. I could have sworn the man she'd been with at the diner had a different name.

"My husband," Sage continued. "Do you want juice? I have juice."

"Sage," I began, looking to Brady for support. I pointed subtly to my pocket, where I had the diary page, and he nodded. "Is this yours?"

"Well, what's this?" she asked, taking the letter, her voice still jolly and a bit distracted. "Hold on, let me grab my . . ." The sentence simply trailed off as she stood and started pushing things around on a desk. While her back was to us, Brady turned to me.

"When you met her, what did she say to your mom?" he whispered.

I looked over at Sage, whose back was still turned, although she had finally stopped talking. "I don't know. They talked about something called 'the old grounds.' I didn't know what that meant."

At this point, we noticed that Sage was still quiet. She was standing at her desk, facing away, holding up a pair of reading glasses with only one stem as she read the diary page. I heard her sniffle, and I stood up.

"Where did you . . . ," she began, but once again, she let the sentence die.

"Sage?" I asked as I approached her.

"Where did you find this?"

"Behind the boiler room," I said.

She nodded and finally turned to face us. She had been crying, and made quite a show out of wiping her eyes and grabbing her purse to dig through it for a tissue.

"I haven't seen this in a long time. I have to find . . ."

"You wrote it?" I asked again.

She stopped messing around with her purse then and simply leaned against the desk. "I was probably your age," she said. "How old are you?"

"Sixteen."

"Ah," she nodded. "I was a bit older than you, then. Your mother and I were seventeen—it was senior year of high school."

I stiffened a bit when she mentioned my mother, and I became aware that Brady had stood up beside me.

"You two have been behind the boiler room?" she confirmed, and we both nodded. "And you've been down?"

Brady put his hand on my back in the same protective gesture my father always used, and I suddenly felt like a child who was supposed to remain silent while the grown-ups talked. "Yes."

She chuckled then. "And we thought we were being so smart. We thought when they blocked off all the old science rooms, that it would be over. We should have known. Now you're showing up in droves . . ."

"In droves?" Brady asked. "Was there someone besides Piper?"

"Just a boy named Adam. But he's . . . he's different."

"Different how?" Brady asked.

"It doesn't matter," Sage said, distracted again.

"I think it does," Brady insisted. "I knew Adam. He was a senior when I was a freshman. Do you know where he is, Sage?"

"No."

"Do you know where Piper is?"

Sage looked at Brady, almost as if seeing him for the first time. "I get it," she said. "You're the boyfriend." She turned to me. "And the two of you thought if you came here, I could help you find her."

"Can you?" I asked.

"No, sweetheart," she said, turning kind once again. "Piper was here, but she . . . well, she went down. I tried to talk her out of it, but once you cross the River Styx . . ."

"What are you talking about?" I demanded. "Down the river?"

"Sorry," she laughed, shaking her head. "That's what we used to call it. What do you kids call it now? Down World? That's cute."

"So you do know about the portals?" I asked.

"Yes. We discovered them."

"Who's we?"

"Me. John. And a few of our friends."

"You mean my mother, don't you? Has my mother known about the portals this whole time?"

Sage hesitated only a moment, and then seemed to realize that by hesitating, she had already confirmed it. "Your mother was the first one in."

"And what about my brother, Robbie? Does she know that Robbie is in there?"

"Yes, she knows. She wrote to me right after it happened."

"Why?"

Sage looked to Brady, unsure if she should continue.

"He knows everything," I assured her. "Just tell me."

"To see if we could find a way to get him out."

I felt a great exhale expel itself from my lungs, as though under the strain of this information, they could no longer perform their function. "That's why you were in town that day. At the diner."

"Yes. We . . . we had been trying to find the answer for three years. I wanted to tell her to her face. It's not the kind of thing you say over the phone—"

"But you barely said anything at the diner. Just something about the old grounds."

"That was a code. To meet me at the grounds that night."

I nodded, replaying the conversation in my head. That explained why my mother had been acting so strange that day, why she had left that evening. She must have been going to meet Sage before going to the tracks. "What did you say to her that night?"

Sage started stuffing the letter into a drawer, suddenly quite distracted. "You'll really need to ask your mother about that, dear. I can't—I really shouldn't . . ."

"I can't ask my mother about it."

"Why are you two here?" she asked. She was rummaging in her desk. "You shouldn't be here. Did your mother send you?"

"My mother can't do anything," I told her. Her face froze and a panic set into her eyes. I swear I could see her lips curling as she stood before me. "She's gone. The day she saw you. She had some sort of mental break. Someone spotted her on the tracks, but then she disappeared."

"No."

"They said she was trying to kill herself. But she wasn't, was she? She was trying to follow Robbie. It didn't work, though, because then she went into the high school. And now . . . now she's missing."

"No, that's not—that's not right. That's not what she was supposed to do."

I turned to Brady, as if to confirm that he had heard her. He stepped before me. "What *was* she supposed to do?" he asked.

Sage sat down behind her desk, as if she were suddenly too weak to stand. "Nothing," she said. "There was nothing to do. The answer to her question—about whether there's a way to get Robbie out—the answer is no."

o o o

I don't know how long I sat behind the hotel, shifting uncomfortably in one of those lawn chairs with only half a seat. It could have been ten minutes or an hour; my mind was at once racing with information and yet muddled with all the parts I still didn't understand. I had been convinced that Sage would know where my mother had gone. But now I could see that she didn't.

All that I knew was my mother had been lying to me, and to my dad, for the past three years. She'd known Robbie was in Down World. She'd known that in some universe, in some way, he was still alive. I suppose a more gracious way to think about it is that she was burdened with a secret she couldn't share. "My son's not dead—he got sucked into a train portal and he's trapped in another dimension" isn't exactly the kind of thing you can just drop at the next PTA meeting.

And maybe she was holding out hope the whole time that her old friend Sage would discover the secret way of rescuing Robbie. And when that last shred of hope fell through, she did something desperate—whatever that was. I could hardly blame her. The absence of Robbie in our house had been making us all feel desperate for years. Our family without Robbie was like an old blanket that had been sewn together using one thread, and it was being slowly unraveled as that thread was pulled out until nothing would be left.

"Okay," Brady said, entering the courtyard and pulling up a chair, only to fall right through the bottom as he attempted to sit on it.

I couldn't help but laugh, and I was surprised that anything could make me do that. Brady buried his head in a silent chuckle, trying to extricate himself from the remains of the chair.

"You like that?" he asked. "Thank you, folks. I'll be here all day."

He looked around and grabbed a planter, caked in dry mud and full of the dying remains of what used to be some sort of plant. He picked the whole thing up, shook it until all the debris fell out, and placed it gently upside down by my side so he could sit on it.

"Let's see if my ass falls through this one too."

I laughed again. I couldn't tell if he was doing this for my benefit, or if Brady just had a way of finding the lighter side of things.

"Okay, so here's what I was going to say. You ready?"

"Yes."

"This woman's a nut job. This hotel is creepy and the pizza here sucks. I say we get back on the train and head home, go into DW, and find them ourselves."

"How? The brick walls," I reminded him.

"There must be a way to open them. We'll get some TNT and blow them if we have to."

I thought about that for a moment. What were the portals beneath the school anyway? They were doorways, like passwords to open a computer program. The doorway itself didn't matter, only the program that you were accessing.

"No, it wouldn't work."

"Why not?" he asked, clearly growing frustrated.

"Blowing the door won't make the world behind it suddenly appear," I said. "We need to find out why the brick walls appeared, and somehow undo it."

"That one's on you, kiddo," he said. "I'm getting lost here."

I laughed again. Nobody called me *kiddo* except my dad.

"I want to talk to John," I realized. "I want to ask him. Sage doesn't know everything."

"What makes you think John will?"

"Just the way she described him in her journal. That she was afraid he might disappear someday. He was obsessed with it. And he's older now. So maybe after all this time, he's figured out some things."

Brady nodded.

"Are you with me?" I asked. "Because if you want to go . . ."

"I'm with you," Brady said, his tone softening. "Of course I'm with you."

We were sitting close together again, conspiring in whispers like we had in his room that day. But then he pulled away.

"Besides, it's the only way I'll find Piper." He stood and offered me a hand to help me up.

"All right, then. I guess we should invite ourselves to dinner or something."

"Okay," Brady agreed, guiding me over to the hotel again, "but remember, if John eats after five, he gets heartburn."

I laughed again. "I'll bring him a celery stick," I said, indicating the garden plot beside us marked CELERY, but containing nothing but weeds and dirt. Brady cracked up as we walked back inside.

We searched the whole ground floor for Sage, who had apparently disappeared.

"Hello?" I called as we made our way from room to room. As Brady had pointed out, this place was indeed "creepy." The whole building was very old and looked somehow frozen in time from the Old West. The carpet and the wallpaper both used the same dark red and brown colors, designed in swirls, which, while clean, had been dulled and darkened by the years.

There was a front desk with an old-fashioned register and an actual rotary phone hanging from the wall. It smelled like burned coffee and I looked around for where it might be coming from.

"Do you feel like we're in an episode of *Scooby-Doo*?" Brady asked.

"Totally," I agreed. "And they would have gotten away with it too..."

"... if it hadn't been for those darn kids."

It was then that we heard the music drifting down from upstairs. It was a bluesy kind of music, and it reminded me of something my grandpa would listen to—a woman with a high voice singing on what sounded like an old record player. Floorboards creaked overhead. The hotel was so old that every time someone moved above you, you could trace their every step simply by listening to the creaks.

I pointed to the sound and started walking up the wide staircase that curved behind the front desk, covered in that same threadbare burgundy carpet. Brady followed.

The second floor looked like a typical hotel floor, with long dark hallways leading to maybe a half dozen doors in either direction. We heard someone humming to herself from one of the rooms with a propped-open door, and I could tell it was Sage, probably doing some cleaning. That must have been the source of the footsteps we'd heard, but not of the old-fashioned music. That came from farther up the stairs. I glanced at Brady, who nodded towards the music.

With each passing floor, the music grew louder, but we had not yet reached its source. Each of the next three floors looked exactly the same, and there was no indication that any guest was staying in any of the rooms. In fact, judging by the generally dank smell of old cigarettes and mildew, I would guess that no one had stayed here in decades.

Around the next bend, the staircase narrowed and was met at the top by a door. It was notable, since it looked like the front door of a house, complete with knocker, and had clearly been installed by the hotel's owners. The door was slightly ajar and the music was pounding out of it, accompanied by the tapping of a foot keeping rhythm inside.

I looked to Brady, who gave me a shrug and nodded towards the door. I smiled and nodded in agreement. I took a second to collect myself and then banged the knocker a couple of times.

I wasn't prepared for how loud it would be. It echoed like we were standing at the rim of the Grand Canyon. I flinched, and Brady moved to edge himself in front of me in a protective way, until we could see who answered.

"Is that them, Sage?" came a man's voice. "I thought you said they left."

Brady seemed to think about it for a second, debating whether to respond or just push the door open. "It . . . it's us, sir," he called.

After a brief moment, the music turned off and the silence from behind the door was startling. "Well . . . ," the man finally said. "Are you coming in or what?"

Brady positioned his body to block mine even more as he pushed the door open. I couldn't really see anything but his back when I heard him gasp at the sight before us.

"What? What is it?" I asked, all but pushing him out of the way. I came around him and saw the last thing I had been expecting.

The top floor of the hotel had been completely gutted. They had knocked out all the walls, removing every room, and leaving nothing but a few support posts here and there. The hideous carpet had been replaced with hardwood floors, highly polished and bolted together with what looked like flattened black railway ties. What remained was one enormous loft, clearly decorated by Sage, with sitting areas here and there peppered with ornate throw pillows, white billowy sheets separating a bedroom area from a dining area, and wisps of yellow sunlight streaming in across a coffee table that looked like it had been handmade using one enormous piece of wood from a giant tree. And a glimpse to my right revealed a large bathroom area, the only part of the whole place with a door, painted fire-engine red.

Sage and John lived in my dream apartment. It was like they had read my mind. Or maybe I had read theirs. It was so beautiful I suddenly wanted to cry.

John was sitting at a workbench. He had a magnifying glass strapped to his forehead and seemed to be painting little figurines under a lamp. It seemed like an odd pastime for a man who looked about forty, but judging from the collection of little warriors and knights before him, he had been at it for quite a while.

"Well, don't leave the door open," John ordered.

"Sorry," Brady said immediately and closed the door behind us. It sealed with a resounding thud, which made me swallow back a tinge of fear. "We're sorry to disturb you."

"Well, I already told her I can't help you," John said, muttering so quietly I almost couldn't make him out. He didn't stop painting the whole time, and didn't look up at us once.

Brady seemed to be weighing the situation, figuring out how to approach this man. "Nice work there," he finally said. "May I?"

John muttered some sort of approval under his breath. And so Brady walked across the great expanse of floor and approached the table, picking up a figurine. "Great detail," he finally said.

"I sell them," John responded. "There's a shop in town. The kids here love them."

"Oh, yeah?"

I quietly walked a bit closer so I could hear them, taking in the artwork on the walls as I passed—a hodgepodge of cultures and images, ranging from a bust of a Greek woman to a picture of a Japanese geisha putting on makeup to a tableau of African women doing laundry in a river.

"That's awesome," Brady added. "You know, my dad owns a shop like that where we're from. He would love this stuff. Maybe I could buy a few pieces for him?"

I listened, a bit dumbfounded. Brady had said it so naturally that anyone listening would never doubt it was true. For a moment I wondered if it was. Maybe his dad *did* own a shop somewhere, and the fishing-boat story had been the lie.

"Suit yourself," John said, still not looking up.

"Sir, the reason we're here . . . ," Brady began.

"I can't help you get your girlfriend back," John interrupted him, having obviously already talked to Sage about this.

"It's very important, though, sir," Brady kept going. "If you could help me talk to her. If you could tell us how to find her . . . ," and here he paused for a second and glanced at me, "or find Marina's mom . . ."

"If I knew how to find someone down there, do you think I'd be here painting hobbits for the rest of my life?"

"You must know more than you're saying," Brady insisted. "I mean, you invented it."

"I didn't invent it!" John suddenly exploded, standing up from his chair. "I didn't do that. *They* did that. It's not my fault!"

"Okay, okay," Brady said, backing down.

"You think I wanted to lose everyone and everything to that pit? You think I chose this? I warned them."

"I believe you," Brady said, but it was too late to stop the torrent of words from John.

"I warned them and nobody would listen to me."

"John, stop," came a voice from behind me. We turned around and saw Sage standing in the open doorway. She was still holding the attachment to a vacuum cleaner. "Don't do this. They're just kids."

"Why is this always my fault?" John asked.

"It's not your fault, honey," she said, clearly having been down this road with him before. "Sit down."

John did as he was told and sat back down at his worktable. But he took the magnifying lens off his head. He rubbed his hair absentmindedly while he continued to mutter to himself.

"Sage," I began. "Can you please tell us what he's talking about?"

Sage came into the room a bit and put down the vacuum attachment. "Well . . . ," she began, stretching out her back and sighing. "How well do you understand nuclear fission?"

Brady and I looked at each other with the same blank faces.

This was going to be a long afternoon.

o o o

We sat on the floor on some of those beautifully knit throw pillows around the coffee table. The afternoon sun was still high in the sky and the loft had turned quite warm. John opened a couple of windows and turned on some ceiling fans, creating a nice breeze that stirred the curtains and made the whole place feel like it should be in a design catalog.

"So when you explode an atom," Sage began, "and stop me if you already know this, I don't want to bore you . . ."

Brady and I both shook our heads.

" . . . you release an extraordinary amount of energy." Sage looked to John, who was at his worktable, actively ignoring us. She poured us each a cup of tea from a large pot with a bamboo handle. "Do either of you take sugar?" She offered us a little spoonful of some large yellowish grains, about the size of ants.

"Yes, please." Our response, in unison.

"Imagine," she continued, "dropping a grain of sugar into, say, a pot of tea." She took the lid off the teapot and, while the steam billowed past her, she took one of those large sugar grains into her hand and dropped it into the tea. It landed with a plunk.

"Did you see it?"

"It fell in," I replied.

"Not the sugar," she continued. "That's just the dead weight. I mean the energy. Look closer."

Brady and I leaned in a bit closer, until the steam from the tea was tickling the tiny hairs at the top of my forehead. I didn't see what she was talking about, but leaning over the dark liquid like that made me think of something. It reminded me of the darkroom at the school, of that time I was hiding out up there, and I knew someone was coming up the stairs because of the vibrations in the little pool of developing solution.

"Do you mean the vibrations?" I asked.

"Smart girl," she answered. "When you disturb a flat pool, you set off a series of waves, emanating out from the drop point. They're in the teapot now, even if you can't see them. And where do they end?"

Brady sat back a bit. "They end when they hit the pot."

"If they're in a pot, they do," she agreed. "Now imagine there is no pot. The pool is infinite. Where do they end?"

I looked to Brady, who was shaking his head and smiling a bit to himself. He was clearly done with this lady and her weird metaphors. "I don't know."

"They don't end," I realized. "They go on forever."

Sage smiled at me. "That's right."

"So what?" I asked. "What does that have to do with nuclear fission?"

"The pool is time," she explained. "And yes, it goes on forever. And the sugar grain, in this scenario, was the explosion of the atom. But now imagine that there isn't just one plane of time and space. There's the plane that we live on, of course, which is like the surface of this table."

We all looked at the flat surface of the beautiful table, the one that looked like it had been carved from a single tree.

"But there are also infinite planes. Above us, below us. Infinite tables."

"I don't understand," I said.

"The other planes contain the other existences," Sage said. "The ones that *might have been* if you had been born a second later, if you never existed, if you hadn't . . ."

" . . . had an accident," I finished her thought, finally beginning to understand where she was going with all this.

"We aren't supposed to know about those planes. They are parallel, they're never meant to intersect. But when an atom is split . . . Have you seen a mushroom cloud?"

"Of course," Brady said, the stiffness in his body reflecting a growing impatience with this whole conversation.

"It doesn't just go out in a flat circle, does it? It goes everywhere, up, down. The waves of the energy explosion, they start to blur together the different planes."

"But we never split an atom in our town," I said, not sure what any of this had to do with the portals under the school. "Wasn't that New Mexico or something?"

"That's where they tested the bomb," Sage explained. "But they first split the atom in *that school*. Of course, it wasn't a school then, was it?"

"This is stupid," said Brady, whose body suddenly burst up from the floor. He paced tensely over to the window.

I watched Brady as he stood by the open window, looking down on the town below. I wasn't sure why this was upsetting him so much, but I needed to hear more.

"I wish it were," Sage insisted. "The closer you go to the time of the explosion, the less you can see its effects. The waves haven't had a chance yet to make much of a difference, to blur the planes too much. But over time, as the waves travel farther and farther, as they grow smaller and more intimate, well, then you can see it. Then things that shouldn't exist together begin to do just that. And when you travel to another plane, you can see what might have been. Yesterday isn't so bad. When you enter Today, things may seem normal, but they're not. And Tomorrow—Tomorrow is the one you have to be really careful of."

"You're the one who labeled the doors," I realized. "Yesterday, Today, Tomorrow. That was you."

Sage smiled. "No, that was your mother."

"But the doors all worked?" Brady asked.

"What do you mean?"

"They're brick walls," Brady said, clearly exasperated. "All the doors, just brick walls inside."

"All of them?" she asked. It was clearly news to her. "Oh, dear. Did you hear that, John?" she called out. "All of them now."

"Mmm," John responded. "Probably for the best," he added a moment later.

"It isn't for the best," I countered. "People are still trapped down there. My brother and Piper. Maybe my mom too." Sage nodded as I spoke, unmoved.

I looked to Brady, who still stared out the window.

"Let's go," he said suddenly, turning to me. He reached out his hand as he walked over, and I couldn't help but stand to take it. "She's crazy," he whispered to me, taking my hand with more force than I had anticipated.

"I wish I were," Sage said, having overheard him. I was deeply embarrassed that we had offended her, and couldn't figure out what had upset Brady so much. We were almost to the door when Sage stood up and said one more thing.

"Marina, there's something else. It's about the portal on the tracks."

It was as though she had pulled me back with a string. I yanked my hand away from Brady's. We both turned back to face her.

"We discovered that portal before we left the town. It's why we left."

I stared at her for a moment, a million emotions bubbling up.

"Your mother always suspected that Robbie had fallen into it. Right after the accident, she was going to try to follow him. But she knew there'd be consequences. She might miss the window and be hit by the train. Even if she could find the portal, who's to say she wouldn't be stuck in there with your brother forever? None of us had ever been in the train portal before. At that time, we didn't even know how it worked. But one thing that seemed very clear was that you couldn't just back out of it like you could

REBECCA PHELPS

with the other portals. And if she did get stuck, she'd never see you again."

"She stayed for me?" I asked, and my voice sounded high and tinny in my ears. All this time she could have been with Robbie. But she stayed for me.

"And so she asked us if we could find a way . . . a better way, that is, to save him."

"But you said the answer was no. How could you be sure?"

"Because what we did find . . ." Sage trailed off again. I'd never met someone so distractible; it was like trying to have a conversation while loud music was blaring. "What we did find was not good, Marina."

I readied myself for whatever she was about to tell me. Brady had put his hand back on my lower spine, and I suddenly realized what he had been so upset about. He knew bad news was coming. He sensed it somehow. And he was trying to protect me.

"You have to understand," Sage continued, "the train portal is different. Because the crossover is so violent, the moment so fleeting . . . That portal is unstable. It doesn't just take you to another plane, it takes you to *all* the planes. It doesn't blur the lines, it whirls them around. It's constantly in motion. Do you know about the balance between the dimensions?"

"Yes," I nodded, remembering how Brady had explained it to me.

"Small imbalances cause small disruptions. But an imbalance in the train portal . . ."

Sage turned to John, almost as though she couldn't bring herself to say whatever was next.

John put down his tools and sighed. He looked at Brady, not at me.

"The brother—Robbie, is it?" John asked. Something about his voice seemed disingenuous, and I got the feeling he knew exactly what my brother's name was.

Brady nodded.

"He can't stay in there. He's the reason it's all falling apart now, the reason the cracks are showing. He's probably the reason that brick wall appeared over the door. He's been in there a few years, right? So it's becoming noticeable."

"Okay," Brady said. "But you said you didn't know how to find anyone down there, and besides, the portal that actually worked is bricked up, so what do you want to do?"

"I said I didn't know how to find Piper, because when you go in through a regular portal, you could end up anywhere, on any plane. There's no way of knowing where to look. But the train portal . . ."

John seemed to lose his train of thought, and I was losing patience. I turned to Sage. "Please help us," I implored. "Sage, what do we do?"

"Your brother has to come out," Sage said, and something about her tone reminded me of doctors on TV shows telling the family that someone has died on the operating table.

"You just said there's no way," Brady said with a sigh, exasperated. "Make up your minds."

"There's no way . . . ," John began. His eyes shifted to me for a moment, and then back to Brady. "There's no way to take him out alive."

The room turned quiet, and his words echoed against the wooden floor.

"Someone will need to go into the train portal," John explained, "find him, and push him back out." He paused, still eyeing Brady. "You understand what I'm saying, son?"

I could hear a loud hissing sound, a buzzing in my ears, and it took me a moment to realize it was my own breathing. My head was spinning. And I felt nothing but relief as Brady put his arm around my waist and practically carried me out of that room, slamming the door behind us.

We were almost down the stairs to the lobby when Sage caught up with us.

"Wait," she implored. "Don't go yet. Please wait."

I could feel my breath still straining to regulate, my body gulping down short bursts of air, as though my lungs couldn't decide if they were too full or too empty.

"She needs to lie down," I heard Sage say. "I've made up a couple rooms." The words seemed to be drifting to me through a wind tunnel. The lights went all dark and I realized I was passing out.

CHAPTER 12

I woke up in a strange place and felt a moment of panic, just as I had in the hostel that morning, before remembering where I was.

The sky outside the window was starting to dim, and with the long summer days, I figured that must have made it around 8 p.m. Somewhere in the distance, children were running and squealing. Grasshoppers were singing in chorus. I sat up slowly and took in a painting across from the bed. In it, an old man and a young girl were rowing in a small boat across a sea. The man was looking down at the girl lovingly, but she, straining to pull the enormous oar in front of her, looked directly out of the painting, as though imploring the viewer for help.

I was still staring transfixed into her small eyes, feeling trapped in my place, when I heard Brady's warm voice nearby.

"Hello, sleepyhead," he said. He was sitting in a chair by the window, his figure obscured in shadow, with only the glow from his cell phone illuminating his face.

"Hi," I said. "What happened?"

"You passed out."

I let out a snort. "You're kidding." I sat up a bit and realized I wasn't wearing my shoes. "Well, that's embarrassing."

"Why?"

"It's just so damsel-in-distress of me."

He laughed. "It was a lot to take in. I was feeling a little light-headed myself."

"So what do we do now?"

"We get out of here," he answered. "They didn't tell us anything we didn't already know."

"Are you kidding? They told us everything! About the planes and that whole atom-bomb thing."

"They don't know how to find Piper, and they don't know how to get Robbie out alive."

"Because there is no way."

"As far as they know. Think about it, Marina. These guys created this mess twenty years ago, right? Then they sneak out of town to some random hotel where they can hide out for the rest of their lives. Why? Because they don't know how to control the thing that they found. They don't really understand it, any more than we do. So why should we believe them when they say there's no way to take him out? They could be wrong."

I nodded, wanting desperately to believe that Brady's logic made sense, that this wasn't just wishful thinking. "Okay."

"There's one thing I don't get," Brady said.

"What's that?"

"Piper never came back to town. She would have called me. But that woman Sage said she went into DW."

"Right."

"How? When? Is there another portal we don't know about?"

"She probably went in down by the lake," I said, opening up my suitcase, which someone had left at the foot of the bed.

"What?"

I stopped in my tracks. I had no idea why I had said that, but I suddenly knew beyond a doubt that there was a lake down a path behind the hotel, and that somewhere down there was a portal. I looked up at Brady. "Come with me."

We snuck out of our room, glad that Sage and John didn't seem to be anywhere around, and then tiptoed downstairs, through the lobby, and into that run-down courtyard with the broken lawn furniture. I looked around, having the craziest déjà vu of my life. Images of the hotel, the smell of the burned coffee, the way the light danced into Sage and John's apartment—I felt like I was remembering it from a million years ago. The trees and vegetation were completely overgrown behind the building, but somehow it seemed that if I could pull away a couple of branches . . .

I climbed over some weeds and parted the very tall cattails blocking my path, my feet getting muddy in the swamp-like water. Brady followed behind me, not speaking. A few steps more revealed that there was indeed a path winding its way down into the woods. I stared at it in disbelief.

"How did you know?" Brady asked.

"Brady, I think I've been here before." I turned and looked over his head at the top of the hotel, poking up above the high branches. At the highest windows, I could make out the billowy white curtains of Sage and John's apartment. I thought of the red painted bathroom, the little coffee table by the window. The apartment of my dreams.

"Why didn't you say so?"

"I didn't remember," I insisted. "It was so long ago. But I know I've been here. I've been in that apartment. And down this path . . ." I turned to look down the windy pathway, which widened and firmed up a bit as it went along. "There's a lake."

We walked in step with each other, side by side. It took about fifteen minutes to make our way down the gentle slope of the hillside, winding ever deeper into the darkening woods. I knew making our way back would be difficult, as it would be completely black by then. But I didn't want to wait until morning.

We reached the lake as the sun was setting behind it in a brilliant puddle of orange and red. An evening breeze was picking up, offering some relief from the sticky heat of summer, and even though I was sure we'd be eaten alive by mosquitoes, I didn't care. It was a breathtakingly beautiful sight, oddly familiar. I turned to my left, looking for the boathouse that I was sure I would find. But it wasn't there.

"Look for a boathouse," I instructed Brady, and we both scanned the horizon in different directions.

"There." Brady pointed to our right.

We walked the couple hundred feet down the shore of the lake to the little hut, discovering that its one little door was padlocked shut.

"If only we knew how to pick locks," I said.

"I do," Brady responded, reaching for a stone near our feet. He picked it up and pushed me behind him a bit. Before I could protest, he hurled the stone through the window, and the glass smashed with a resounding echo.

"Are you crazy?"

"Did you want to go ask your old friends at the hotel for a key?"

Brady cleared the remaining glass shards with his shoe, then knelt down and cupped his hands to boost me up.

"Why do I get the feeling you've done this before?"

He smiled and shrugged. "I never said I was a saint."

"Oh, I already figured that out," I said, stepping up into his hand and climbing gently through the windowpane, landing with a thud on the other side. I turned to help him climb through after me.

It was a tiny little hut, full of bait cans and fishing tackle. And against one wall was what appeared to be a metal scaffold covered with a large white tarp.

I took a deep breath. Brady seemed to sense my apprehension, and he stepped forward, pulling the tarp down over the frame so it landed near our feet. Underneath, there were three stacked fishing boats. There didn't seem to be anything odd about it.

I stood and shook my head. We were missing something. I looked up and down, searching the tiny one-room structure. I crouched down and looked under the scaffolding frame, but there was nothing but a concrete floor below it.

"I'm sorry," I said to Brady. "I could have sworn."

"Do you remember anything else from when you were little?"

"I don't know." I searched my brain, trying to elicit memories that had been buried for so long. "There were other people. Adults. And I was with my mother." I walked over to the broken window and stood, staring out at the melting sunset beyond the tranquil water.

Brady came and stood beside me. "It's pretty, anyway."

"Yeah," I agreed. The water was growing dark as the sun sank lower. And it looked at once so familiar and so new. My mind was racing in circles, and I couldn't seem to nail it down. But then a thought occurred to me.

"What did Sage say?" I asked. "You drop a stone into a lake . . . an infinite lake . . ."

"Yeah?"

"They were swimming," I remembered, my head swirling with images. My mother by my side. She was in a white bathing suit. She was worried. And she said something, something that had stuck with me over the years, but I could never place where I had heard it. "They won't come out."

"Who won't?"

"That's what my mother said. She said, 'They won't come out.' They were swimming in the lake."

That seemed to be all the information Brady needed. The next thing I knew, he was leaping out of the window. He ran over to the lake and peered into the darkening waters. "Come on!"

I watched as he kicked off his shoes and took off his T-shirt.

"Are you serious?"

"You want to know, don't you?" he shouted, already making his way into the water.

I had to find a trash can to turn over and place by the window so I could climb back out, and by the time I reached the shore, Brady had already dived in, wearing nothing but his shorts. I stood there frozen. Sure, a guy could go swimming in his shorts. They're basically swim trunks. What's the difference? But what was I supposed to wear?

Brady's head disappeared under the water for a moment, long enough that my mind began to turn to dark thoughts of him not coming back up. I raced closer to where the water lapped the gravel, my shoes getting wet, looking for him. He popped up maybe twenty feet away and waved me in.

"You have to see this," he said, before gulping down a huge breath and going under again. He was gone before I could even ask him what he'd seen.

"Fine," I said to myself, quickly pulling off my Keds and jeans. I threw my clothes away from the water and ran in, diving head-first when I felt the water reach my thighs.

It was exhilarating. In the humidity of summer, I had spent the day covered in a film of sweat. But with the cool water surrounding me, I finally felt a bit of relief.

I swam over to where I had seen Brady's head pop up and looked around for him. I took a deep gulp, preparing to go down and look for him, when he sprang up right next to me.

"Gotcha!" he shouted, quickly tickling my sides and pulling away before I could catch him.

I couldn't help but squeal when he did it. "What are you doing?"

"Sorry," he laughed, though he clearly wasn't. Brady never seemed to stay in one mood for too long. Even today, with the stress of being here, with the knowledge that Piper was still in DW somewhere, he found reasons to laugh. I realized that maybe the reason I had fallen so hard for him was because everyone else I knew seemed to drag invisible chains behind them at all times. While Brady did a couple of backflips in the water, I thought of Kieren and his sad eyes, of my mother and her secrets.

"What did you find?" I asked as he swam around me.

"I don't know. Some sort of box. You ready?"

I nodded.

"Take a deep breath," he instructed, and I did as I was told. He did the same, and we both dove down as far as we could.

Beneath our feet at the lake floor was indeed a wooden box, barely visible in the fading light. I paddled against the water with all my might to reach it, grabbing on to the edge of it in order to secure myself once down there. Brady had beat me there by a second, and he held up a finger and then pointed to a handle on the top of the box. He grabbed it and yanked. The lid came up. The inside was so dark that I couldn't make anything out, but Brady took his hand and reached in anyway. Right before I ran out of breath and had to go back up, I saw a split second of telltale bright light. It was a portal.

I shot back up through the water, my head bursting through the surface, and gulped in a deep breath. My heart was racing. How on earth did a portal get out here? Did they build it? How? And my next thought, of course, was that if they'd split an atom in this lake, then the whole thing was probably radioactive. Were we both going to get cancer swimming in it?

Brady appeared next to me, but it was getting so dark, he was just a silhouette against the horizon.

"How?"

"I don't know," he replied. "But it's there."

We bobbed in the water for a bit, inching our way closer together so we could make out each other's faces. The singing of the crickets was echoing in my ears, and tiny little water bugs were dancing on the surface around us. I knew we needed to go in, but at the same time, I wanted to stay here with Brady forever.

"At least now we know how she went in," I offered.

He nodded, staring at me.

"Should we follow her?"

Brady looked around a bit, as if taking in the light. "Not tonight," he decided. "It's late. And you haven't eaten anything. Let's do it tomorrow, okay?"

I nodded, although I wasn't sure he could even make out my head in this light. "Yes."

Without even thinking about it, I leaned over and kissed him, our legs bumping into each other as we paddled in the dark water. Brady put his hand on my face, but I couldn't tell if he meant to pull me in or push me away. It was almost like his hand needed to touch me to be sure that I existed. I pulled back a bit and searched his expression for some reaction, good or bad. But in the sinking light, all I saw was my own reflection in his deep brown eyes.

"We should get in," was all he said.

Humiliation rushed over me. So he was just being polite after all. He didn't want me. I had concocted this whole connection in my head, and now I had made a complete fool of myself. I swam away as quickly as I could and raced up onto the shore, grabbing my jeans and my shoes.

I walked quickly down the path, still in my underwear, though it was so dark I couldn't see more than a foot in front of me. I stepped into my pants once my legs were dry enough and threw on my shoes, all by feel alone. There didn't seem to be any moon tonight, and I started cursing myself for the stupidity of starting out on this expedition so late. Somewhere in the gulf behind me I could hear Brady calling out for me to wait for him, but I couldn't.

It occurred to me after a bit that he was intentionally staying

REBECCA PHELPS

several feet behind me on the walk back, like a parent following a hysterical child who needed some time to cool down. There was something so condescendingly protective about it that I couldn't help but hate him for it. I wanted to run away from this whole thing so badly, but for the first time in my life, I felt I no longer had the dream apartment to fantasize about. Realizing that all this time, my fantasy had been nothing but a fading memory of Sage's place, something I must have seen once as a child, somehow corrupted it. It was like it had been stolen from me, along with my mother and my brother and the million other things I had lost since.

I hated Sage, her sweetly kind voice talking down to me like I was a wounded bird she'd found in the street. And now Brady was treating me the same way. I didn't need Brady, I didn't need Sage, and I hated that stupid hotel with its never-ending stench of burned coffee.

I was crying, of course. I was crying out of frustration as I walked. And I desperately didn't want Brady to hear it and feel even sorrier for me.

Somewhere from that stupid safe distance behind me, I heard Brady call my name one more time. It was like hearing a gun go off. I ran with all my might the rest of the way, tripping several times on hidden rocks and branches, each time catching myself at the last minute before I fell. I didn't stop running until I was back in the lobby of the hotel, running past Sage, who was knitting on an old musty chair and clearly waiting for us. I sprinted up the stairs and into the room where I had been sleeping before, and I slammed the door behind me.

o   o   o

I was coming out of the shower a bit later that night, after I had calmed down and my anger had been replaced by waves of embarrassment coming back to taunt me every few minutes.

To drown it out, I turned on the old TV, which I quickly discovered only got two channels, both of which were obscured by static and wavy lines. I turned it off and thought of emailing my dad, but the only internet around here seemed to be on Brady's phone. This was completely hopeless.

I heard a knock on the door and I ignored it. It was a gentle knock, almost too polite. It was like even the knock was condescending to me.

"I'm sleeping," I finally said, hoping that would be the end of it.

"I brought you a sandwich," came Sage's sweet and light voice. "Should I leave the tray?"

I sighed. There was really no excuse to be so rude to Sage. She had been trying to help us since we got here. She was letting us stay in these empty hotel rooms for free. And I was, I had to admit, completely starving.

I got up and opened the door as slightly as possible, mortified that Brady might be there. When I saw that he wasn't, I quickly let her in and closed the door behind her.

Sage came and sat on the edge of my bed while I devoured the sandwich and the two little cookies that she had placed next to it.

"When I was your age," she began, though I was only half listening to her as I chewed, "I had the biggest crush on John. Oh my God, I was in love with him."

I looked at her, certain my cheeks were turning red. Great, so she knew. Did Brady tell her, or had she guessed?

"He thought of me as just a friend, of course. He only had eyes for one girl."

"Yeah, who was that?" I asked, sounding snarkier than I had intended.

Sage smiled at me, a question appearing in her eyes. "Your mother, of course. You didn't know?"

I gulped down a bit of sandwich and took a long drink of water. I shook my head. "Obviously, I don't know anything about her. Do I?"

Sage nodded and bowed her head for a moment, almost as if to give me some space. "What do you want to know?"

"She brought me here, didn't she? I've been here before."

Sage nodded. "I think you were four. Your brother didn't come—he stayed with your father. It was just a short visit."

"Nothing is *just* anything with you people. Why did she really come?"

"You're a quick one. I'm gonna have to watch out for you!"

"Tell me, then."

"Okay," she said, almost to herself. "Okay."

She stood up and paced for a bit. "So twenty years ago, when we were your age, your mother and John discovered the first portals. The ones under the school. Your mother was the real genius of the operation. She experimented with every portal. She's the one who realized that the three doors under the old science lab all had different properties. That one seemed to go to an alternate plane of the past, and another of the present, and the third of the future. And so she made the signs. She was obsessed with trying to control it. To figure out how to go to a specific time and place, not just end up somewhere random."

"And?"

"She couldn't figure it out. We tried stepping in the exact same place as the time before, concentrating on where we wanted to end up. Nothing worked, though. So it became part of the game. Which plane will we end up in this time? We all followed John and your mother because they were the popular couple, and we all wanted to be wherever they were. All of us. Jenny and Dave first. And then George. George probably would have followed me anywhere. I know that now."

"Who's George?"

"Oh, you met him. In the diner when I first saw you. Remember?"

I nodded, remembering the man in the white clothes who waited by the counter when Sage came over to our table. And I remembered the distant look in his eyes, like he had just woken up from a deep sleep.

"We were able to keep the secret for quite a while, more than a year. We developed rituals around it. Out on the old grounds—there were these old carnival grounds that had been built in the forties for military kids. Fun houses and swings. It was all made to look like a little Nordic village. By the nineties, when we were teenagers, it wasn't used for much. The company that had run it went out of business and the town used it on occasion for holidays. At night it was empty.

"We would go there before going down into the portals, late at night, and we would hold a little ceremony, blessing our journey."

I smiled, trying to imagine my mother as a part of that group, how beautiful she must have been then.

"I know it probably sounds strange to you, that we were on our own so much. You have to understand, things were very different then. No one locked their doors. Kids were expected to take care of themselves quite a bit."

I nodded. "And then?"

"And then spring came and we all graduated. But nobody wanted to leave. Our parents couldn't understand why none of us wanted to go away to college. Dave's dad threw him out, called him a bum. He and Jenny got an apartment outside of town.

"John started to warn us that we had to be more careful. That we needed it too much, like a drug. He was right, of course. It can become an obsession. Our eyes would be glassed over during the day, wired open at night. We found ourselves unable to talk about anything else. Unable to enjoy anything that didn't happen when we were inside one of the doors, finding a new plane. Taking risks we wouldn't take above ground."

"What kind of risks?"

She nodded, seeming to weigh the question, or maybe unsure how to answer it.

"The different planes, they're like galaxies. Nobody knows how many there are. Billions, maybe. Maybe more. And it started to become clear that you could do whatever you wanted in these planes. Probability told us we'd never end up in the same one twice, so there were no consequences.

"We started to steal things from the different planes, try on new personalities, crash in empty houses. Dave cheated on Jenny, figuring she would never find out anyway. But she did."

"How?"

"Because I told her," Sage said, a sardonic smile on her face. "He'd cheated with me."

"That's terrible," I uttered, without really thinking. "I'm sorry, it's just . . ."

"No, you're right. We did terrible things. When you believe there are no consequences, you start making incredibly selfish decisions. And we were all going down that rabbit hole. It was corrupting us, splitting us up. I'm not proud of it.

"Jenny was furious. She wanted to leave. And then John said it was getting too dangerous, and we all had to leave, immediately. It was like the moon had fallen out of the sky.

"I demanded to know why. I wasn't ready to go. And then John told us. He and your mother had discovered the train portal. It was an accident, of course. They were biking along the track when your mother noticed a squirrel run in front of the train. And she could have sworn she saw that flash of light. You know the one?"

I nodded, flinching at the thought of the train hitting the squirrel, and thinking of my brother.

"They experimented with it for a while, trying to find it and realizing, of course, as you have, that it only exists for a split second when the train is passing. But while they stood waiting, searching, that's when they noticed. The planes shifted. Buildings disappeared. For a moment, the track itself was gone, and they were in the middle of a great farmland. And then the track was back, and the rest of the city around it. But the colors were somehow off, they said. Like they were home, but somehow still in Down World. They waited until the next train passed to see if the flash happened again. But instead, something else happened. The squirrel leaped back out in front of the train and was immediately struck and killed by it.

"When the train had finished going past, the little body of the squirrel was there, crushed. And everything went back to normal.

"But we knew, all of us, that something had shifted. Things were getting too real, too scary. John had some money a grandmother had left him. He used it to buy this hotel after he found it at the back of an old real-estate flyer. It was going to be a fresh beginning. We were going to move on."

"But you didn't, did you?"

"You have to understand," Sage began, her eyes imploring me. "You try. Every day you try. You try to be good. You try not to think about it. You try to remember what it was like before you knew. And we all pretended for a long while. For the first year we all lived out here together, congratulating ourselves on how well we were doing. But then it would creep in again. Someone would mention another dimension at dinner or wear a bracelet I knew they had stolen from another plane.

"It was too much for your mom, and she left John. She went back home, said she missed her parents. She was done with the portals, done with us. It was her way of moving on, by leaving us. We were nineteen then."

"And you took her place."

"I had always been in love with John. I guess a part of me was always waiting for her to leave.

"So your mother met your father, got married, had your brother and you. And then one day, maybe five years later, she showed up here with you by her side. 'Just a visit,' they told me.

"I didn't know it, but John and your mother had been talking on the phone."

My face must have revealed my shock, or maybe it revealed that I didn't believe her.

"It wasn't an affair. Don't worry. Just old friends. Talking about old times. But John had asked her to bring something.

She refused at first. They fought about it. And he told her if she did this one last thing, it would be the end. The real end."

"What did she bring?"

"It's a kind of a key," Sage said. "One that John had built years before. No one knew about it but Rain. Sorry, Ana."

"A key that builds a portal?" I asked. It was getting very late and we had been talking for so long that despite myself, I felt my eyelids growing heavy. It was all so much, too much to take in. All these things my mother had done. It was like she was talking about a person I had never met.

"A key that builds a portal," Sage conceded. "I thought John was done with all that. I thought he had moved on, away from the world down below, away from your mother. But I was wrong. And when I saw what she had brought, I knew. I knew that it would never be over. Not for us. And I suppose I also knew that John would never love me the way he had loved your mother."

"Where are Dave and Jenny?" I asked, thinking of that magical door lurking beneath the surface of the lake, and imagining it swallowing them whole. *They won't come out.*

"They left years ago. I don't know where they are. Now it's late," Sage said, taking away my dinner tray. "Get some sleep."

She stood and turned off my bedside lamp, revealing how dark the nights were here in the middle of nowhere. Slowly a bit of starlight started to glow through the drawn curtains, and I was looking at it as I finally acquiesced to the sleep that my body seemed to crave.

As Sage tiptoed out of the room, one last question escaped my lips. "Is her name really Rain?"

But she was already gone.

REBECCA PHELPS

CHAPTER 13

I woke before dawn, engulfed in blackness. The quiet was deafening, and I had no idea what time it was. Maybe 3 a.m., maybe 4 a.m. I tried to relax my body and go back to sleep, but then I heard a soft rapping on the door. Was that what had woken me up? Did I hear it in my dream?

Another round of rapping came, accompanied by Brady's voice, whispering with an urgency that made me forget for a moment that I was too embarrassed to talk to him.

I stood to open the door, growing worried about what could possibly be so important that he would wake me up so early for it. I cracked it open, the bright light of the hallway making me squint. I still wasn't entirely awake and I could feel myself shrinking away from the world outside.

"I have to come in."

I was glad to close the door behind us, shutting out the harsh lights and bringing him into the safe space of the quiet room. But he immediately turned on a lamp.

"What's going on?" I asked, waking up even more as the look on his face confirmed that something was indeed quite wrong.

"You got a phone call," he said, holding up his cell phone.

"Okay." My mind was racing. Nobody knew to reach me on Brady's cell phone. I rubbed my eyes, the thoughts processing all at once. "Who?"

"Your dad. I didn't answer. He didn't leave a message. But I saw your home number come up on the ID."

"What?"

"I'm sorry, Marina. I didn't know what to do."

"How did he . . ."

"He must have traced the source of the emails. Or, I don't know, would your friend Christy have told him?"

I caught my breath, thinking very clearly now. Brady was right—there were only a handful of options. One was that he had traced the emails. My dad was a genius when it came to computers, but I was pretty sure even he wouldn't have the technology to do something like that. But the police would. Oh God, were the police involved?

"Christy wouldn't have told him," I said, talking more to myself than to Brady.

"Even if there were an emergency?"

I looked at Brady, and I had never seen him so worried. "What emergency?"

"Your mother?"

"Kieren would have called if she were back."

"What if he doesn't know?"

"Just stop!" I shouted. "I'm sorry, but please stop. I have to think."

I started to pace, and Brady sat down on the edge of the desk, staring at his phone again as though somewhere inside of it all the answers lay hiding.

Brady's phone beeped. I ran over to look at it.

It was a text from my dad: *I know where you are.*

I grabbed the phone out of his hands and stared at it while Brady leaned over my shoulder.

Another text came a second later: *Stay there. I'm on my way, crossing the Oregon border now.*

Brady muttered something under his breath that I didn't catch. My eyes were fixed on the phone, and the message that seemed too awful to be true.

My heart sank. If my dad came here to take me home, then that would be the end of it. We had officially failed. And I had humiliated myself in front of Brady. And for what?

"It's over," I said. "It's all over. We lose."

Brady looked up from his phone. "What do you mean, 'we lose'?"

"Well, we failed, didn't we? We didn't save anybody. My dad will be here in the morning to take me home, and that'll be the end of it. I just made everything worse."

"That's not true. Listen, things couldn't be any worse than they were before. And when we get back home, we can try the doors again. I'm sure they'll work this time—"

"Stop!" I shouted, surprised by my own anger.

"What?"

"Just stop making things up, Brady! God, you lie about everything. I'm not a child and I'm not an idiot. So stop."

I could tell I had really hurt him, and I immediately regretted it. But I couldn't help myself. I had never felt so frustrated.

Brady stood, and I was afraid he was going to leave. "What do I lie about?"

I sighed, wondering if I really wanted to do this with him, if it was even worth it. "Nothing."

"No, say it."

"Okay." I turned to face him. "Your dad is not in Alaska. Is he?"

Brady stared at me like I had stabbed him with a knife.

"Good night," he said, turning to leave.

"You can't do it, can you? You can't be honest with me."

"What do you want?" he asked, turning to me.

"I want you to tell me the truth, just once."

"I came here to help you."

I could tell he was getting angry, so I tried softening my tone. "Then help me. Don't make me do this alone."

"When have you been alone, Marina? I've been with you the whole time."

"In the lake," I reminded him. "You wanted to kiss me back, I know you did."

He didn't say anything, looking down at his feet.

"Why didn't you? Because of Piper?"

"Of course because of Piper," he said, still not looking at me.

"She left you, Brady," I reminded him. I took a step towards him, trying to catch his eyes, to get him to acknowledge me.

"That doesn't mean anything," he said, still addressing his feet.

"It means everything."

"Your mom left you. Did you stop loving her because of it?"

The words stung, and I backed away a bit, seeing a flash of

regret in his eyes. He took a step towards me, but I kept inching away.

I walked back to the window, where the slightest trace of blue morning light was starting to divide the blackness. It was eerie and quite beautiful, like staring out at the surface of the moon.

Brady stepped a bit closer, and his voice was calm. "I don't know where my dad is, Marina. Okay? He *was* in Alaska for a while. And then he was in jail for a while. And for all I know, he's in Alaska again now. I don't know and I don't really care. He wasn't a very good guy when he was here."

I turned to look at him from the window and nodded to let him know it was okay to go on. That I would never judge him.

"I don't have a mom. She left him when I was three. Then she died when I was ten."

"Oh my God." My hand reflexively covered my heart, as if to protect it somehow.

"It's okay. It really is. I'm not sad. I'm fine."

"It's not okay."

"No, it's not okay," he agreed. "You're right. It sucks. But what I mean is that *I'm* okay. Do you understand the difference?"

I nodded, wondering if I could have survived a childhood like that.

"I don't have parents. I have my cousin. I have my friends . . ." He paused for a moment. "And I have Piper."

I nodded, finally understanding what he had been trying to tell me. And I realized how incredibly selfish I had been, trying to get him to leave Piper, when she was really all he had. And for what? So he could be with me instead? No wonder everyone had been treating me like a child. I had been acting like one.

"Okay," I said, making my decision right then and there.

"Okay what?"

"Okay, let's go then."

He shook his head, not sure what I meant.

"We came here to rescue them, didn't we?" I asked. "My dad will be here in a few hours. If we go now, we'll be back before he even arrives."

I looked back out the window, towards the breaking light and the shadow of the trees, slowly emerging into form, which held the trail to the lake. "Let's go find them."

o o o

We ran hand in hand down the trail, the forest around us becoming clearer and clearer with every step as the light began to flood down through the treetops. It was the opposite experience of the night before, which had been clouded in darkness. With every step, I could feel the urgency of the lake calling to us. I had no idea what kind of portal was under there, or where it would lead. Would we be back in our town? Would I be in my kitchen again, like I had been before? And most importantly, would Robbie be there again, or had I gone too far away from him?

We reached the lake, kicked our shoes off, and dove in wearing our clothes. Wherever we ended up, I hoped it was as warm there as it had been here, because we didn't bring anything to change into.

We swam out a bit to where Brady had found the hidden doorway the night before. Sunlight was beginning to brim over the trees, washing the lake in a blurry gray. Brady took a deep inhale and I followed suit. And then we both went down. Brady

REBECCA PHELPS

hoisted the trapdoor open and we stared at the blackness inside for a beat before diving in together.

The flash of light passed and we were in darkness. And it wasn't until I opened my mouth to breathe that I realized we were still underwater. It was terrifying, to be in the dark with water filling my mouth. Were we still in the lake? Were we at the bottom of the ocean? Dear God, would we drown here? I reached for Brady's arm, and within seconds, my eyes adjusted and a stream of light shot through, illuminating Brady's face.

He pointed to his own air bubbles, indicating that they were floating downwards. We had become completely turned around in the whirl of water. My mind quickly adjusted to the reality that up was now down, and we followed the bubbles like a shot out of the water. I broke through the surface, gasping in a huge gulp of air. I had never felt so grateful to inhale.

Brady popped up next to me and we surveyed the world before us.

We were in the lake, exactly in the spot we had been before.

"It didn't work," Brady concluded, and for a second I agreed with him.

But then I noticed the light. The light was different, the sun high in the sky. In fact, everything seemed brighter. The birds were singing from the shore.

"Yes, it did." My eyes caught a wisp of something then, a small plume of white smoke. It was coming from the little boathouse. Why would a boathouse have a chimney? I pointed it out to Brady as we both paddled on the surface, and he nodded.

We came up on shore, seeing that on this plane, our shoes were not there. I struggled to remain brave as we approached the boathouse. This was the portal Piper had gone through. So it was possible that she was nearby at that very moment. I wondered if that thought had occurred to Brady.

The window of the boathouse was not broken on this side. As we approached, we could smell something cooking. I was reminded of the first time I'd gone into DW, and the distinct smell of bacon that had immediately filled my nose. And for a moment, I was certain of it—I had found my mother.

I almost tripped over my own feet running to the window. My eyes took a second to adjust to the darker light within, but when they did, I saw that I had been wrong. In fact, I had been wrong about everything.

This wasn't a boathouse. At least, not on this plane.

It was a small cottage. And inside, a man was leaning over a small metal griddle in the fireplace making breakfast. The boats were gone, replaced by a small, neatly made bed. The only other contents of the place were a small table and a rocking chair by another window with a perfectly folded blanket lying over it. Whoever this man was, this was his home. And I wondered how long he had lived here.

The man's back seemed to freeze, and suddenly he whipped towards us, grabbing a shotgun from above the mantel and pointing it directly at my face.

I gasped. It took a moment to register what I was looking at, and that it was real and this wasn't a movie.

Brady's reflexes kicked in faster than mine, and before I knew it, he was pushing me to the ground. I landed on my hip, the sharp blow reverberating up my side and making me realize that we were in very real danger. I looked up and saw Brady still standing facing the window frame above my head.

Brady's eyes were locked on the man, and he slowly raised his hands.

"It's okay," Brady said. "It's okay, don't shoot."

"What do you want?" the man asked.

"Sorry," Brady said, his voice trembling. "We didn't know anyone lived here. We'll be on our way, okay?"

I watched from the ground, too scared to move, wanting to grab Brady and drag him away from there, away from danger. After what felt like an eternity, I saw Brady bring his arms down and take a deep breath. The man must have lowered the gun.

"Who was that with you?" the man almost shouted. "Stand up, girl. Let me see you."

"She's nobody, sir," Brady insisted, keeping me pressed down with his foot. "We're really sorry we bothered you. We're going now, okay?"

But I could hear the man approaching and had no idea what I was supposed to do. Would he get angrier if I stayed ducked down? Should I do what he asked?

The decision was made for me when the man stuck his head out of the window and looked down at me. I knew his face, but from where?

"Jesus," the man said. "It's you."

I tried desperately to place him, feeling that I had seen him recently.

"You look exactly like your mother."

And that's when it all came back to me. He had been the man in the diner when we'd first met Sage, the one she had mentioned. His deep-set, haunted eyes were the same. And my mind flooded with questions. How long had he lived here? And why?

"I know you," I told him. "You're Sage's friend."

"George."

"Yes, from high school. Right? She told me about you." I was feeling more confident as I stood up next to Brady. This man was an old friend of my mother's. He would never hurt me. "And you know my mother."

"Go back," he simply said. "Go back into the lake. You can't stay here."

Brady and I stared at him, neither one of us willing to go without finding out more.

This man remembered me from the diner. That meant he was the real George. "You're not from DW. What are you doing here?"

But that's when we heard the dinging sound, like a small bell on a bicycle. A man was whistling. Looking back at the path, no one was yet visible. But another dinging followed, and it seemed like more than one person.

"Damn it," George said. "Now look what you've done."

Brady and I both instinctively took a step back to examine the path, looking for the bikes.

"No, no," George whispered. "Get in here." He practically pulled Brady in through the window, then leaned over and pulled me in behind him. Once inside the warm little cabin, the man quickly ushered us away from the window.

He led us towards the back of the room and shoved us into a closet, pulling the accordion-style curtain closed in front of our faces. Brady and I both stood in shock, standing with our backs pressed against the man's musty clothes. There were no more than a couple of inches to move in, and a hanger was stabbing me in the back. I started shifting some of the clothes over to make more room for myself, but Brady grabbed my arm to stop me.

"Wait," he whispered. "Don't."

We heard the footsteps enter the cabin then. As I had suspected, there were at least two sets of men's boots stomping into the room, mere feet away from us. One of the men greeted George in a pleasant tone, but with words that I couldn't make out.

George responded in a boisterous voice that completely negated the sad, quiet man he had been a moment before. They talked for a couple of minutes before I realized they weren't speaking English. I couldn't place the language, but George seemed to be fluent.

Brady held his ear to the curtain, and even though I knew he couldn't understand them, he seemed to be listening to their tones to try to figure out what they were talking about.

The longer they talked, the more nervous I became. Who were these men that were so dangerous we had to hide in a closet while they were here? We heard forks scraping against plates as they talked, and it was clear they were eating the breakfast.

Every now and then, a phrase in English would pop up: "More coffee?" "No problem." And very often, simply, "Okay." But then they would go back to the other language and I would be lost again.

My eyes scanned the closet, adjusting to the dimmed light. An open shoebox of photos sat on a shelf along the wall, and I leaned over as quietly as possible to try to make out the images on the top picture. It was an old Polaroid, and I recognized the outline of my mother's face.

I flipped through a few more and realized I knew some of the images. They were pictures of a group of people lounging by the lake. My mother had some of the same photos in an old album in her room. I had seen them years before but had never thought much of them. These must have been her friends once. I saw a picture of my mother and John laughing. George was in the background, watching Sage with hungry eyes.

The sound of shuffling boots made my heart freeze. I sensed Brady stiffening next to me, clearly thinking the same thing: What would we do if they opened the closet? His hand reached back towards me in a protective motion, as if he could hide me completely behind his arm.

But the shuffling of boots did not head in our direction. The men exchanged some words, all seeming very cordial. And soon the sound of their heavy feet made its way outside, where the little bells on their bikes were again happily dinging. The crunching of the dirt beneath the wheels grew fainter as the bikes receded, and I felt my breath begin to regulate again.

Brady leaned in a bit closer and whispered to me, "It's okay, they're gone."

I nodded. Several seconds went by, and I wasn't sure if we were supposed to come out or not. Finally George appeared, opening the closet door.

"Now you need to go."

"Who were those men?" I asked, looking around now that the light was streaming back into the closet. I stole one last glance at the stack of pictures, and saw that the one on top was definitely of my mother. We came out into the tiny room, and George went on as though I hadn't said anything.

"Just make sure they're not watching," he said. "Act like you're going for a swim, and when you're sure the coast is clear, dive down and go back to the other side."

"The other side?" I repeated breathlessly, realizing something about the portal we had just gone through. "George, does the lake portal only lead to here? Not to any other dimensions?"

"That's right. Now go."

"And this is the one my mother and John built, right?"

George was momentarily distracted from his task of kicking us out. "How did you know that?"

But I didn't want to take the time to answer him. "Why did they build this particular place? Who were those men, George? And why do you live here?"

He sighed deeply, looking like all the air was seeping out of him. "You'd have to ask your mother what she was thinking, because I've never been able to understand it. I guess this is the world she and John wanted." His sad eyes crinkled in the light of the doorway, his face set in rigid stone.

Brady leaned forward. "Don't you throw off the balance by living here?"

George shrugged. "I don't disturb anything or change anything. I keep to myself." He sighed deeply, deciding whether to continue. "Near as I can tell, you can stay in another dimension for up to a week or so. There's no exact science to it. I stay for four or five days at a time, then head back up. After that . . ."

"Go on," I all but demanded.

"If you and your other self diverge too much from each other, it can be too late to go back."

I choked back an aching fear from his words. *Robbie's been down for over four years now.*

And my mother . . . and Piper. Dear God, was it too late already?

But then another pressing question escaped my lips: "Why come down here at all?" George's body language was growing more and more tense with my delays, but I needed the answers.

He finally nodded towards the woods where the strange men had ridden off. "They don't know about the portal. I'd like it to stay that way. I can keep an eye on it from here."

Brady started to lead me off, but I had one more question I needed to ask. "Wait . . ." I pushed Brady back gently. "You know what's happened to my mother, don't you?"

George turned to Brady, as all the adults seemed to do when they were done with me. "Take her back. It's not safe here. You understand me?"

"I understand you, sir," Brady said, and I couldn't tell if he was being polite in order to placate this man who had greeted us earlier with a shotgun, or if he was just stalling for time while figuring out what we should do next.

"We haven't even looked," I protested.

"Let's head back," Brady said, addressing me but keeping eye contact with George. "We can talk about it on the other side, once we're safe."

Something in Brady's eyes told me that I was supposed to simply say yes. Had he noticed something I hadn't? Was he trying to tell me something?

I nodded and we walked slowly through the room towards the door, past the dirty plates sitting on the little table.

George watched us from the door frame as we headed for the lake, making sure we didn't stop. As we walked out of his earshot, I whispered to Brady, "What are you doing?"

"We can't stay down here, Marina. There's something wrong about it."

"Do you mean those men who were talking? Did you understand what they were saying?"

Brady kept walking slowly, his hand grasping my upper arm, and I was reminded of the time I had seen him in the school hallway, holding on to Piper that way. Leading her away from danger, or so he'd thought.

I broke away from his grip and started to run. I didn't dare look behind me to see if George was still watching, but even if he was, I was sure I could outrun him. He was old and out of shape. Brady could catch me, of course, but I had a feeling he would run with me. Either way, I wasn't going back through the lake portal empty-handed.

I had made it inside the lip of the forest trail when Brady ran up behind me and grabbed me by the shoulder.

"Wait, wait, wait," he said as he slowed us down.

"Do you want to find Piper or don't you?"

"I don't think . . . ," he began, looking around. "I don't think this is a safe portal."

I stared at him, seeing how scared he looked. What was I missing here?

"Hello, children," came a man's voice from behind us in the woods.

We spun around and realized that both of the men from the cabin were standing about eight feet away from us, holding their bikes.

Brady stepped in front of me again. He chuckled, trying, apparently, to act casual. "Hello," he replied.

"What are you two talking about?" the first man asked. I was shocked that he had no accent whatsoever.

"My sister . . . ," Brady began, nodding to me. "She wants to go to the movies, but I told our mom we'd be home."

I was frozen. The men were wearing identical outfits—shorts

with neatly pressed blue T-shirts and sparkling white sneakers. They even had baseball caps on, but they didn't have any logo. It was like they had read in a book somewhere how to dress like an American, and had tried to emulate it, missing something along the way.

"Sorry if we're disturbing you," Brady continued.

"Oh, you're not disturbing us," the first man continued. "I'm just not quite sure why you're lying."

A moment of silence ensued in which all of us seemed to stare at each other, waiting for someone to make the first move.

"Why don't you come back with us?" the first man asked. "We can call your mother from the hotel. She must be worried about you."

I silently weighed our options and realized that we didn't have any. We couldn't go back through the lake portal. They would be watching. And there was no point in trying to run back to George's. We had already been spotted. There was nothing he could do for us now.

Going back to the hotel did seem like our safest bet. Maybe the DW versions of Sage and John could help. Maybe we could escape from there when no one was looking.

I reached out and took Brady's hand, squeezing slightly to reassure him. "Okay."

We all walked back at a steady clip, the men pushing their bicycles. Along the way, they occasionally made what was clearly intended to be polite conversation. They talked about the weather and asked if we were hungry.

We both simply grunted and smiled, not sure what to say. Who were these men? Brady never let go of my hand. I kept telling myself that soon enough we'd be able to sneak away and run back to the lake.

We broke through the woods at the end of the path and when I saw the hotel, it was all I could do not to gasp.

It was completely transformed. Gone was the dilapidated little garden plot with the broken lawn furniture. In its place was a sleek patio with clean white lounge chairs. Several guests were sunbathing on the chairs, all looking like movie stars from the golden age of Hollywood. The women, with their hair piled high on their heads, wore retro bathing suits and large dark sunglasses. The men also looked very tan, and also somehow out of date. Their hair was all parted on the side, the swim shorts coming up too high on their waists. Was this some kind of theme party?

To our right I noticed a lap pool where the garden had been. A man did a rigorous backstroke down its length.

The two men parked their bikes next to a gurgling fountain, not bothering to lock them, and led us into the hotel through the back, which was now two large double doors leading directly into the lobby.

I had never seen anything like this place. A large atrium with trees and even more fountains sat in the middle, and dozens of people milled about, checking in at the very sleek front desk. Actual bellboys were tagging luggage. Again, everyone seemed to be dressed like they were attending a 1950s costume party.

I looked down at the highly polished tile beneath my feet, wondering what had happened to that hideous dark red carpet.

"And who are these two?" a woman asked as she approached. On hearing her voice, my body clenched as though it had been hit by a car.

I looked up and saw her standing there, her hair up in a bouffant style like all the other women. She was wearing a bright red suit, matching her perfectly applied lipstick. She looked young and she looked beautiful, like a telenovela star. And she looked right through me, not recognizing me for a second.

My mother had never been prettier.

CHAPTER 14

I felt frozen in time as I stared at my mother, my brain not able to process how she was standing before me, and half expecting her to take me into her arms. I waited and waited. But it never happened.

"Are you children lost?" she asked.

I felt the tears start to sting behind my eyes. She really didn't know me. How was this possible?

Sage said that the different planes of DW are simply alternate existences—a world in which you hadn't had an accident, or had been born in a different city. Was this the plane where I didn't exist at all? Was this the version of herself that my mother had really always wanted to be?

"Brady," I whispered, turning to him. I didn't think I could stand this for one more moment, to be in her presence, to feel the coldness coming off her.

"We were hoping to use your phone, ma'am," Brady said, polite and calm. He had no idea who she was, of course.

The two men in the baseball caps were still standing next to us, and the first one—the one who had done all the talking—spoke softly to my mother. Once again, the words were not in English. This time, standing right next to him, I could recognize it as Russian.

My mother laughed and responded in perfect Russian, a language she did not speak a word of on our plane.

The man leaned in and kissed her on the cheek, his lips lingering a beat longer than necessary, and I was repulsed by the certainty that this weird man with the bicycle was probably my mother's boyfriend down here.

He and the other man walked off, and we were left alone with my mother in the bustling hotel.

"Come along," she said. "You may use the phone in the office."

She led us behind the huge front desk, nodding to incoming guests and stopping briefly to say something in Russian to one of the clerks. The clerk nodded and handed her some mail to take with her. My mother was clearly in some kind of position of power at the hotel now. It seemed like maybe she even owned it.

The office she was referring to was not the little room where Sage had given us pizza when we first arrived. Instead, a large polished suite, which seemed to include the space where that room had been, waited for us through a door behind the front desk. All I could think when I saw it was that everything looked so sleek. Lots of highly polished marble and gold fixtures. The only things that remained from the previous incarnation of this hotel were the original chandelier and those ornate sconces, both of which now seemed perfectly in place.

We heard water run in a small bathroom in one corner of the office as my mother led us to a sofa where we could sit. We looked up to see a very clean-cut man in a suit and tie emerge, wiping his hands with a small towel. It took me a couple of seconds to recognize the man as John.

"What do we have here?" John asked.

"They were babes lost in a wood, apparently," my mother replied. Then she turned to Brady. "You can use the phone on the coffee table."

We looked at the neatly organized table before us and saw Sage's old rotary phone, with an actual cord coming out of the back. Brady picked up the receiver. Even if I had wanted to try to call a real person down here, the only phone number I had memorized was my father's. Who would Brady call?

John put his towel back in the bathroom and approached my mother, who was neatly slicing open the mail envelopes with an ornate bone-handled letter opener.

"They're probably just hungry, you know," he said privately to my mother, but loud enough that we could hear.

"This isn't a soup kitchen."

John gave her a look.

My mother temporarily let her hands, still holding envelopes and the small opener, fall to her sides in an exasperated motion.

"All right, dear," he said. "I'll be back in time for dinner." He, too, gave her a kiss on the cheek and left.

Brady began to dial next to me, and my back tensed, waiting to see who would pick up, if anybody. After a moment, he put the receiver back down.

"Nobody home," he said to my mother, who was reading her mail. "Thank you for your hospitality. We'll be going." And he stood up, his hand on my back to indicate that I should follow.

"I'll have Alexei show you out," my mother replied, not looking up.

"Oh, we know the way . . . ," Brady started, but my mother had already pressed a button on some sort of old-fashioned intercom box sitting on her desk.

Alexei, the first man with the bicycle, must have been right outside the door, because he came in immediately. He cleared his throat, waiting for us.

Brady gently pressed on my back, clearly anxious to go. But I couldn't bear the thought of leaving my mother here. Even if she wasn't real, even if she didn't know me, I couldn't help but think that I may never see her again.

Is this the way I would always remember her?

I stopped before we reached the door and turned to her. I couldn't help myself. She didn't even look up from her mail. She looked like a character from one of those black-and-white movies. Impossibly beautiful and impossibly cold.

"Mom?" I asked.

Brady froze by my side, and I could see his head turning from my mother's face to my own, probably seeing the strong resemblance.

My mother, however, didn't flinch. I needed her to look up. I needed her to recognize me. It wasn't possible that any plane could exist in this universe in which a mother wouldn't recognize her own daughter. Something would have to register with her.

She looked up at me finally, her mouth twisted into something I could only describe as disgust. She shook her head, as though I had screamed an obscenity in church.

186   REBECCA PHELPS

"Don't come back here," was all she said. "The lake is for hotel guests only."

And with that, she looked back down at her mail, and Alexei led us out of the room and through the lobby. My mind had gone completely numb. Where were we? Were we in the past? Was it really the 1950s here? I knew it was possible to go to other times in these portals, I just had never seen it.

But if this was the '50s, why was a version of my mother living here? And a version of John? How did these people get transported to another time?

I was processing all these thoughts, with Brady walking next to me, when I heard him take in a deep breath, almost like a gasp. He kept time behind Alexei, trying not to give anything away, but his eyes were transfixed by what he saw before him.

I followed his sight line to a spot slightly above the main entrance to the hotel as we were about to walk out the front door. Nothing seemed odd at first. Just an American flag, and next to it, an enormous portrait of a man with a strange appearance. He was probably in his seventies, but his hair had been dyed jet black and his skin seemed to be painted tan, unsuccessful attempts to make him look much younger. Beneath his portrait, in gold letters, were the words: God Bless Our Leader.

Beneath that, the words were repeated in what looked like Russian.

o o o

Alexei walked us through the front gate of the hotel, for there was now a gate to walk through. Everything about the street had changed. This small town was now clearly a resort destination.

All the mom-and-pop stores that had lined the walkway up and down from the hotel were gone, with towering elm trees and a few boutiques taking their place. The street looked newly paved and fancy old cars were zooming by, their radios blaring jazz and bebop.

We were standing on the sidewalk outside the gate, taking it all in.

"The hotel has a strict policy on trespassing," Alexei said. "If we see you here again, we'll have to call the authorities."

Brady nodded, clearly waiting for him to leave.

"And tell your friends too," Alexei added, before heading back inside.

"Yes, sir," Brady responded, already turning me away from the hotel to lead me down the sidewalk. "Just walk."

"Where are we, Brady?"

"I don't know," he replied, keeping his voice low and nodding to passersby, clearly trying to blend in. But we were still barefoot and wearing our modern clothes. Everyone stared at us, not looking confused so much as annoyed that we were on their street.

"But is it still modern times?"

"I said I don't know," Brady continued, walking faster and pushing me from behind.

A well-dressed couple passed us, and I could hear the woman whisper to the man, "Why doesn't the city do something about them?"

"Just ignore them," the man replied as they hurried past us. I spun my head to watch them go, and saw the woman looking over her shoulder at me, her brow furrowed in repulsion.

My mind raced, desperately trying to put together the pieces. We passed a newsstand.

"Wait a second," I said. I could feel Brady's frustration that I had stopped us, but I had to see the newspaper.

When I did, my heart sank. "Oh my God."

We weren't in the past, or the future either. We were right here, right now. The paper was called *The Lakeside Charter*, and it had today's date on it.

"Don't read it if you're not going to buy it," the man guarding the newsstand barked at me. I stepped away from the papers. Brady hadn't said a word; he just stood next to me. "You kids need to get back to your part of town. You'll get arrested here."

"Sorry, sir," Brady said, again being curt and polite. He clearly wanted to get us away from this place, and I couldn't blame him. I let Brady take my hand, and we walked as quickly as we could down the street and away from the commercial area. Soon the fancy buildings and the palm trees gave way to some more-run-down old shops and small houses. The neatly mowed lawns slowly became overgrown with weeds and dried-out bushes. And all the fancy cars were nowhere to be seen. Other people who looked like us began to appear, wearing torn old T-shirts and jeans with no shoes. Nobody seemed to notice us anymore, or care that we were there.

"Over there," Brady said, pointing to a small diner on the corner. "We can talk in there."

We walked in and saw the place was nearly deserted. Only one booth was occupied, by an old lady who was clinging to a cup of coffee, her eyes lost in a maze of thoughts. As we headed to the back and found a booth, I couldn't seem to take my eyes off her. Why did she look so hopelessly sad?

Brady led us into the farthest corner and pulled me deep into the middle of the booth before scanning the room. Immediately, a waitress appeared. She seemed to be about our age and, like us, was not wearing any shoes.

"Do you have any money?" she asked.

For a moment, I was completely confused. Was she a waitress or someone who had come in here to beg? But she was holding menus in her hand.

"Of course," Brady answered.

"I have to see it." She looked over her shoulder quickly to see if she was being watched, and leaned in a bit closer. "I'm sorry, they make me ask."

I froze for a moment, thinking of my suitcase still sitting in the hotel room. In it, the rest of my money was tucked into a hidden pocket sewn into the lining. The only thing close to money I had on me was the flattened penny Kieren had given me.

Brady made a slight show of checking his pockets, but I knew he must have realized what I was already thinking—it didn't matter because the money here was certainly different. He took his hand out again, empty. "Sorry, you got us. We'll go."

"Wait," she said, again looking over her shoulder. When she seemed confident that the coast was clear, she looked at me and then at him. "Are you a part of it?" she asked, her tone suddenly anxious.

"Part of it?" I asked.

She seemed to think for a second. Then she asked us a question in Russian.

We both shrugged.

The girl seemed to give up on us then, and stood back up, her voice returning to its droll monotone. "I can bring you coffee, but that's it. Then you have to go."

She walked away before we could respond.

Brady leaned in towards me, his face almost touching mine. "It's not real. Look at me."

I looked up at him, trying to find some comfort in his being near me. But I still found myself shaking.

"It's not real. We're going home."

"It's real to her," I said, nodding to the waitress.

"That's not our problem," he quickly countered. "We're sneaking back to the lake tonight and going home."

"How, Brady? You heard what they said."

"There's got to be a way. We'll find it."

The waitress came back with the coffees and Brady sat back immediately, as though he had been caught passing notes in class.

"She looked right through me," I said, picturing my mother's cold eyes. "She didn't even know me."

"That woman is not your mother."

I stared at my coffee, wanting desperately to go back home. What had I done? Why did I bring us here?

"Did you hear me?"

I could only nod. I looked out the window at the desolate street. A few more people shuffled past, all tired and barefoot. Whatever money was in this world, it was clearly all concentrated among those at the hotel.

I thought of the hotel, and John in his nice suit, and my mind raced back to what Sage had told me.

"John wanted this," I said out loud.

"What?"

"Sage told me that John built this portal. He asked my mother to bring him some sort of key, and he used it to build a doorway to this place."

Brady glanced around at the hellscape surrounding us. "Maybe he didn't know it would be like this."

"Or maybe he made it like this on purpose."

But Brady just shook his head, not letting the words land. "How?"

I thought about it, trying to imagine the day John first came through his new portal into this flip side of his reality. What would be the first thing he'd do? "The Yesterday door."

"You think he changed something in the past?" Brady asked, still incredulous.

"It's the only way this world could be so different—it was set on a different path a long time ago."

"Why, though? Why make it like this?"

"Look at it," I insisted. "He's got everything here. Money, a successful hotel . . ." I paused, imagining the monogrammed hand towel he'd used to dry his hands. "And my mother, of course. That's really all he wanted."

"The John we met wasn't evil, Marina. He's just a weirdo who likes to paint action figures."

"You just described every serial killer," I couldn't help but observe, which made Brady chuckle into the back of his hand.

I took the thought one step further. *A weirdo who likes action figures.* Did he like other toys too? "Maybe it's like a game to him. Like cosplay. When things get too boring up there"—I nodded towards the sky, but Brady knew what I meant—"he can dip down here for a bit, take over this dark, powerful version of himself. Pretend he's a captain of industry or whatever the hell that dude was."

Brady nodded slightly, but his eyes were fixed somewhere on

the table. "It's hard to believe he would make all these people live like this . . . just for a game."

"You don't know what's in people's hearts," I said.

It's not real. They do it with mirrors. My brother's voice kept echoing in my mind. If the John in the hotel was the version of himself he always wanted to be, then was that cold woman with the red lips a reflection of my mother? Was this what she had been hiding in her heart the whole time?

"Don't lose hope," Brady said. "This place is a mistake. I'm going to get you back home." He grabbed my hand then, and I could see something shifting inside of him. "Let's go."

He all but dragged me out of the booth. We stood up and were about to walk away when he took a dollar out of his pocket. "Here. I don't know if this works here, but it's something." He threw it on the table and led me outside. The old lady in her booth didn't notice us as we zipped past.

We were already down the street when the waitress popped out of the diner behind us.

"Wait!" she called.

We turned and saw her holding up the dollar bill. She seemed to examine us both then, taking in our clothes and looking into our eyes. She approached slowly, like a tiger sizing up its prey. "What's the capital of France?"

I couldn't help but laugh. What was she talking about? I looked to Brady, who also seemed to get a chuckle out of the question.

"Um, Paris?" he asked rhetorically.

She nodded and walked the rest of the way up to us, handing Brady back his dollar.

"There is no France," she said. "You're from the other side."

I felt a ball drop into my stomach. We had been caught. I

didn't even want to think about what happened to people here who were caught doing something wrong. I tugged on Brady's hand, ready to make a run for it.

"It's okay. I'm part of it." She quickly turned her wrist over, showing us three dime-length scars on the inside of her lower arm. It looked like she had cut herself on purpose, and I realized it must be some sort of code.

A couple walked by, and even though they looked somehow preoccupied, just like the woman in the booth, the waitress's body stiffened and she looked to the ground, not speaking until they were past.

"We meet here at midnight. Hide that," she said, referring to the dollar. "Don't let them see it."

Brady quickly stuffed the bill back into his pocket.

"You should go to the school until then. Walk to Mason Street and make a right. You'll see it at the end."

"Okay," Brady said. "Won't they notice two kids they've never seen before going to school?"

The waitress looked confused. "Well, it's not a real school. Just do what everyone else is doing. No one will notice."

A man walked into the diner then, and we all turned to hear the little door bells jingle.

"I have to go in. When you get here, you'll need to know the code word."

"Okay," Brady said. "And what is that?"

She looked around again, making sure no one was listening.

"It's *Sage*," she said, before quickly retreating into the diner and closing the door behind her.

o o o

REBECCA PHELPS

The school, if it could be called that, was easy enough to find. It was one of the only structures still standing at the end of the road, surrounded by rows of half-built houses that sat like empty birdcages on either side. I couldn't tell by looking at them if they had been abandoned halfway through their construction, or if they had once been whole and later dismantled brick by brick until nothing was left but their skeletons.

But the school, which was swarming with people, still stood. Outside, vendors shouted that they had various goods—apples, diapers, even shoes, and long lines of people stood in front of them, waiting for what seemed like a very long time. The line for shoes had dozens of people in it, even though the booth that advertised them on a large sign seemed to be unmanned, and no shoes appeared to fill the empty stacked boxes behind it. I supposed that the people must have been hoping that whoever worked there would be back with an extra supply.

On the other side of the makeshift marketplace was a small outdoor area with a red cross above it. This seemed to be the clinic, and an even longer line of people were waiting there. As we drew closer to the school, I could see that there appeared to be only one woman working in the clinic. She was wearing a traditional nurse's outfit, complete with a triangular white hat. Nearby stood a small table with a handful of prefilled syringes lined up in a neat fashion and nothing else. As each person sat down, she tied a rubber band around their upper arm and gave them a shot.

I slowed down to watch for a moment before we went into the building, and realized that the woman didn't seem to be talking to any of the patients, nor did she have any other medicine. People simply sat down and she wordlessly gave them their shot.

"How does she know what's wrong with them?" I asked Brady, but he only shrugged.

"Don't stare," he whispered. "We can't call attention to ourselves."

I agreed, and we walked in side by side. I was relieved that we seemed to be dressed the same as everyone else.

A man in a uniform, with some sort of machine gun dangling over his shoulder, approached us. We both froze. He said something in Russian and I quickly glanced at Brady, who shook his head.

"Why are you late?" the man repeated, this time in English.

"Sorry, sir," Brady said.

"Go in, you'll miss the lesson."

Brady nodded and began to take my hand again.

"Eh-eh, none of that," the man said, grabbing my hand away from Brady's. He nodded in the direction of the end of the hallway. "Go, young man, or I'll have to report you."

He then quickly led me down a separate hall, and all I could do was stare back over my shoulder at Brady as we walked. He must have seen the sheer terror in my eyes as I was dragged farther and farther away.

"Meet you here after school, sis," he called, trying to keep his voice on an even keel.

I could only nod before the man opened a door and all but pushed me into a classroom.

The room was packed with about thirty to forty students, all sitting in cramped little desks and writing in notebooks. It honestly didn't look too different from a normal class, except that all the students were girls and there was no teacher in the front of the room. Instead, an old-fashioned tape recorder sat on a desk,

REBECCA PHELPS

reciting phrases in Russian and repeating them in English.

Nobody looked at me as I found a seat on the floor next to several other girls around my age. I pictured Brady being led into a similar room full of boys.

I didn't have a notebook, so I just sat and listened. A girl next to me saw that I wasn't writing and looked at me, confused.

"You'll get in trouble," she whispered, ripping several blank pages out of her notebook and handing them to me, along with an extra pencil.

"Thank you." I glanced at her paper and realized she was transcribing everything said on the voice recorder, first the Russian phrase and then the English translation.

I didn't know how to spell in Russian, of course, so I just scribbled the words phonetically. It was a weird assortment of information, mostly recipes. Apple pie, potato casserole, meatless lasagna, and all followed by details of what to substitute if you're missing any of the ingredients. Rhubarb for apples. Canned syrup for vanilla. Ketchup for tomato sauce.

I wrote as quickly as I could, but couldn't keep up with the pace of the recorder.

Another phrase in Russian was quickly etched by the girl to my side, followed by the English:

"*President Koenig will rule for one thousand years.*"

Everybody wrote this down, and I struggled to write faster.

"*The study of mathematics makes women infertile.*"

I almost laughed at this one, until I saw the room full of girls quickly copying it down. No one smiled, and no one looked up from their papers.

I leaned over to the girl next to me, whispering, "Isn't there a real teacher?"

She glanced over to me, then addressed her paper. "Are you new or something?"

I flinched. Brady had warned me not to give myself away. "I just transferred."

"Why bother?" she asked, dismissing me as an idiot. But then a second later, she added, "The real teacher comes on Fridays. Not that you could tell the difference."

The day wore on in this fashion, and the recordings never seemed to end. Every now and then, the old cassette tape would click as it reached its end, and a student would get up and switch it over to the other side. When that side had finished, the student selected another tape from a large stack and put that one in. Nobody moved while this happened.

I wanted to kick myself for leaving my father, the one family member I had left, all to go on this hopeless and ultimately futile journey. None of this had brought me any closer to the real goal, saving my brother. This was nothing but a nightmare flip side to our world, and I needed to find Brady and get out of here as quickly as possible.

"*Class dismissed*," the recording announced, with no warning or fanfare.

I looked up and realized that the sun had started to go down, and felt completely disoriented. Everyone around me began to pack up and leave, without saying a word to each other. They formed a neat single-file line and began to worm their way out of the room.

The line began to shuffle down the hall, and all the girls quietly and neatly took their turn entering a large women's bathroom and then filing back out, all while the others waited patiently. Again, no one spoke. The whole process took about half an hour before I could get back to the front of the building and wait for Brady.

Buses appeared, apparently to take the long line of girls off to some other place, but I couldn't leave because the boys were not yet out. Afraid that standing around and waiting would make me seem conspicuous, I quickly decided to get into the line for shoes. It was the same length as before, apparently because no shoes had arrived.

I waited about fifteen minutes before a guard came by, quickly grabbing everyone's arms and examining them briefly before moving on. When he got to me, I didn't know what I was supposed to do, so I simply let him take my arm.

"You haven't had your shot yet," he said in English.

"Not yet, sir."

He made a note in a notebook, and without looking up, he said, "You have to have your shot first. Do you want to spread the disease?"

The people in line before and after me seemed to hear this, and they all slowly stepped away from me.

"No, sir."

He then looked up at me expectantly, and I glanced over at the long line for shots at the clinic.

I nodded and left the shoe line to walk over there, all while staring desperately at the front door of the school and waiting for Brady to come out.

The line for the shots was longer than before, with the same single nurse administering them. I waited for half an hour, feeling so hungry that I was growing weak in the knees. I didn't dare ask anyone about eating, and nobody seemed to be in a hurry to do so.

At last, a long line of boys began to make their way out of the school, single file and neatly ordered. Head after head waltzed out, and I began to panic that Brady would not be among them. But finally, I saw him, his head down and walking in unison with the others.

I had only moved a few inches in the line, and I wasn't sure if he was going to see me. His eyes scanned as covertly as possible, and when they finally locked with mine, I saw a look on his face I hadn't seen before—complete relief.

He walked up to me slowly, casually, and despite every instinct inside of me to throw my arms around him, I knew I couldn't draw attention to us.

"I saved you a spot," I said, perhaps a bit too eagerly.

Brady stood next to me for a moment, subtly brushing my arm with one finger, so I would know that he was with me. And that was all I needed to feel an ocean of calm.

"Oh, I just remembered," he played along. "We told Mom we'd be home for dinner. We'll have to do this tomorrow."

He grabbed my hand and was about to lead me away when a guard, identical to all the others, appeared by our side.

"Where are you going?" he asked, again in English. It concerned me slightly that all the guards had begun speaking English with us, as though it were obvious that we didn't understand Russian. What was tipping them off?

"We have to be home for dinner," Brady answered.

"Home?" the guard said, a smile crossing his lips. "How nice for you. But you can't ride the bus until you've had your shot, now, can you?"

I tugged slightly on Brady's arm, pulling him back into line. I realized that if it were that easy to leave, there would probably be a lot of people doing it.

"Of course," Brady said, clearly arriving at the same thought. "Sorry, I wasn't thinking."

"Do you have your papers?" the guard asked.

"Of course." Brady searched his pockets, just like he had in the diner. And I wished he could somehow have magic pockets that would miraculously produce all the things he pretended to look for in them.

The guard looked distracted, surveying the line we were in and the two dozen or so people who waited ahead of us.

I realized we were caught and wondered how we would escape from wherever this guard was sure to lead us so we could go back to the lake. But I never had to finish the thought.

A guard from some distance away called to the man who had stopped us, saying something in Russian with a calmness that belied the urgent response he received.

"Carry on," the guard spat out at us, not even looking back in our direction, before walking over to meet the other man.

I let out a sigh that seemed to originate from somewhere deep inside my gut, and I felt myself shaking. I wasn't sure if it was fear or hunger, or something in between, but I couldn't seem to make it stop.

"I'm sorry," Brady whispered to me. "That was close."

I stared ahead, trying to control the shaking.

"We'll finish up here and then we can go. Don't worry, kiddo."

I nodded, still staring ahead. I could hear my teeth chattering, even though it wasn't cold.

Brady put his arm around me, and I could feel the warmth seeping through my shirt.

The line took another forty-five minutes, and Brady kept his arm around me the whole time. I was eventually able to stop shaking, and a numbness took its place. My mind became locked, unable to process any more of this horrible world. It drifted instead to other times, to watching TV with my brother when we were younger. To Kieren's hand, holding mine at the train station before we left.

The shot didn't hurt. I could barely feel it, in fact. I waited calmly while Brady got his. Nobody spoke. The nurse didn't even look at us.

Once we were done, it was clear that we were free to go, as those in line before us had been. We started walking away from the school, back down the road to the diner. It was fully dark now, and streetlights cast a cold yellow glare onto the tops of our heads.

A few people shuffled past, not paying us any mind.

"What time do you think it is?" I asked, not knowing how much longer I could go without food.

"There was a clock in the diner," he said. "We'll go peek in the window, then find a place to wait until midnight."

"Okay." I was too weak to offer any alternative. I felt I had no more great ideas. It had been my plan to come here, and so far it had been a disaster. And now we both had some kind of vaccine coursing through our veins—to prevent what, I had no idea.

Brady led me to the diner and looked in the window.

"It's almost eight," he said. "Come here, let's try something."

I walked with him around the building, down the alley, to the dumpster behind it.

"Bingo."

"What's that?" I asked, suddenly having to sit down. I found a

REBECCA PHELPS

couple of crates and pushed them together, letting my body plop down on one of them.

"I used to work in a restaurant. We'd put the day-old rolls and stuff out in the back for whoever wanted them."

He came and sat down next to me, a large grocery bag full of old bread in his hands.

I had to admit, I was a little put off by the idea that the bag had been on the dirty ground, but I was so hungry at that point that the thought quickly disintegrated.

"Sorry it's not more."

"I don't even care. I'm about to pass out."

We reached into the bag and devoured about three rolls each.

"Better?"

"Yes, thank you," I said, feeling very calm and very sleepy. And then out of nowhere, my stomach cramped up into a horrible knot. "Oh God." I leaped off the crate and looked for a more private corner in which to throw up. I held my hair back, falling down onto my knees and letting it all go.

I tried to sit up, and Brady came and sat next to me, taking my hair out of my hand and holding it back for me. Another wave hit me with no warning, and I had to lean over and throw up again.

I sat back from the disgusting mess, panting, wiping my mouth with the back of my hand, overcome by a flash of heat.

"Slowly, slowly," Brady said. "Just let it all go."

"That's so gross," I said, pulling my shirt away from my neck. The heat was still creeping up my face, but I also felt infinitely better. "I'm so sorry."

"Oh, please, that was nothing," Brady said, letting himself laugh. "Piper and I once got into her mom's wine coolers and she threw up for about two hours. Now *that* was gross. I mean, it got everywhere. And it was pink."

I couldn't help but laugh, feeling slightly better.

"And her mom was asleep in the next room, so we couldn't make any noise. Two hours of silent pink puking. Needless to say, I don't drink anymore."

Brady helped me back to the crates, and I sat for a moment with my head between my legs while he put one of his cool hands on my forehead.

"You must have eaten a bad roll or something," he continued.

"I don't know," I said, feeling a throbbing in my arm where the shot had gone in. "Does your arm hurt?"

"No."

"Brady, what was in those shots?"

"Nothing," he said, again sounding so confident that I couldn't help but believe him. "Don't worry about that."

But I continued to rub my arm, feeling a hot sting emanating from the injection point.

"In the morning, her mom found the empty bottles," Brady said, continuing his story as he kept his hand on my forehead. "I thought she was going to kill me." His voice sounded far away, and I could tell he was back in that room with Piper.

"You'll get her back," I promised him. "This isn't over."

He didn't say anything. I leaned my forehead against his arm, my body racked by a deep exhaustion. And the last thing I felt before drifting off to sleep was Brady kissing the top of my head.

CHAPTER 15

"It's midnight," Brady said, gently shaking me awake.

I shivered a bit as I came to, feeling a stiffness and a deep-seated cold work its way through my bones. The only part of me that was still warm was my head, where it had been lying on Brady's arm. He must have heard it in my breath as I sat up, and he gently rubbed his hands up and down my arms to warm me.

"You okay?"

"Yeah, yeah," I responded. "Just waking up. Are you sure it's time?"

"I saw that waitress walk by."

We stood up and slowly walked down the alley and back towards the front of the diner, ever vigilant about being watched. But when we got there, we looked into the front window and saw the waitress and four other people standing in a circle waiting for us.

My first instinct was to hide, but it was clearly too late. They were all staring at the front door, as if knowing that at any moment we would be walking in.

"Do you think it's safe?" I asked Brady.

He said nothing, but instead took my hand and guided me inside.

"You came," said the waitress, clearly relieved.

"Of course," Brady answered.

She fired off the names of the other people in the group, one other girl and two guys. Unfortunately, not one name stuck in my head, as I was still deciding privately whether to trust them. Everybody nodded and we stared at each other for a moment, not speaking. I could tell they were sizing us up, too, and I could only hope that we looked trustworthy, because I knew that these people were our only hope of escaping this little piece of hell.

Brady introduced himself. "And this is Marina."

"Do you have your scars?" asked the other girl, and I thought for a moment that I must have heard her wrong.

"They just got here, I told you," explained the waitress.

"They should get marked first," the girl continued, touching her arm. And I remembered that the waitress had shown us that mark, the three scars on her forearm.

"How are they supposed to do that when they're new?" asked the waitress. I again became aware of a throbbing in my arm where the injection had gone in earlier. Brady must have heard me groan in pain because he became very nervous.

"Marina?" he whispered to me.

"It's okay," I responded, but I knew it wasn't. The pain was getting worse and I felt queasy again.

"What's wrong with her?" asked the waitress, helping me to sit down at the nearest booth.

"Nothing," said Brady, sounding defensive. "Her arm just hurts."

"You didn't get the shot, did you?" she spat back at him.

Brady stood and stared at her. "You're the one who told us to go to the school all day!"

"So you would blend in. You were sticking out like sore thumbs walking around in the middle of the day. You weren't supposed to get in any of the lines."

"Well, you didn't say that, did you?" Brady almost shouted back at her.

"She looks green," said one of the boys. "Should we bring her downstairs?"

"No," insisted the girl who had spoken before. "Not until she's had her scars."

"This is stupid," said the waitress. "I told you, they're from the other side."

"We don't even know if there is another side," said the other girl, and I could tell this was not a new fight for them.

A wave of nausea came and went. I couldn't remember the last time I had felt this terrible. "Brady," I said, clutching his arm, "what do we do?"

He knelt down in front of me and started very tenderly rolling up my sleeve to see the injection point. "Can we get her some water, please?" he asked no one in particular. I could hear the waitress's bare feet pattering their way behind the diner counter.

I tried to catch my breath. I was deeply embarrassed to be

making such a scene in front of total strangers, especially when we were trying to impress them. But I was also very aware that something was wrong with me, and it was getting worse.

"What's all the screaming about?" came a calm voice from behind the group, and we all looked up towards the back of the diner. As the crowd parted a bit, I could see a very familiar face approaching. It was Sage, and for the first time, she wasn't wearing flowing white clothes and she didn't have her usual air of absentminded fluttering energy. She seemed quite calm and collected, and devoid of any real style. She looked older here, and a little more worn-down. And despite how sick I was feeling, I couldn't help but take a private moment to grieve that this place seemed to have gotten the best of her.

"They're from the other side," said the waitress, bringing us a glass of water, which I immediately gulped down only to feel it sitting poorly in my stomach.

"Mmm," Sage responded. "Well, they need to prove it."

"They already did," the waitress insisted. "They thought Paris was the capital of France and they had one of those dollars."

"Parlor tricks," Sage continued. She squatted down by my side, all but pushing Brady out of the way. "What's wrong with her?"

"She got some sort of shot," Brady explained, and his voice couldn't mask his concern any longer. Hearing that Brady sounded nervous completely destroyed any confidence I had left.

"Let me see," Sage said, a certain gentleness working its way back into her tone.

Brady finished rolling up my sleeve, and I could hear an audible gasp come out of some of the people in the group upon seeing my arm. But Sage remained calm. I tried to look down and see what they were all reacting to, but the rolled-up sleeve was in the way and I lacked the energy to even pull it aside to see it myself.

"It's infected," Sage explained. "The ball will have to be removed, and you'll need an antibiotic."

"What ball?" Brady asked. "You mean the vaccine?"

"That's what they tell us," Sage said, still staring at my arm. Then, probably realizing she was being vague, she looked up at Brady. "It's a tiny ball that releases a constant stream of vaccine. We have a lot of diseases here. But people from the other side often have a bad reaction. We don't know why."

Brady stood up and grabbed his upper arm, almost instinctively. "I feel fine."

Sage looked up at him. "Did you get one too?"

Brady looked at his arm, flustered. "I mean . . . ," he began. "They said we had to, so . . ."

"We should take yours out, too, just in case." Sage sighed. "Then we'll drop you back off at the high school."

"I told them we could help them," said the waitress.

"Well, you shouldn't have said that, Caryn," Sage said. "He's a ticking time bomb and she's already exploded."

I shivered again. Why did she say that? What the hell did they put in me? I tried to close my eyes and will it away, as though DW was a bad dream you could wake up from. But this was no dream. The pain stabbing out of my arm was real, and it was probably already too late to do anything about it. Still, I had to try.

"Sage," I said, and I could hear that my voice was barely a whisper, so I said it again. "Sage, please. Help us."

Sage looked down at me and then back at Brady, who still stood by my side.

"Did you tell them my name?" she asked Caryn.

"Not exactly. I told them the password," Caryn replied.

Sage sighed. "Well, it's the same thing, isn't it?"

"Your name is Sage," I said, finding all my remaining strength to continue talking. "On the other side, you were a friend of my mother's. You live in the hotel, on the top floor, with your husband, John. The bathroom is painted . . ."

I had to catch my breath and I could hear a wheezing sound when I inhaled. Whatever this infection was, it was spreading very quickly, and I could tell from the hot, dizzy feeling in my head that I was probably running a very high fever.

" . . . fire-engine red," I continued, feeling myself lose consciousness. Brady was there to catch me as I began to slump over, and then everything went black.

o o o

I woke up this time stretched out on a cot, in a darkened room. I couldn't tell how much time had passed, but it seemed like only minutes. A cool washcloth was on my forehead and it was the only thing giving me any relief.

I became aware that Sage was by my side, and then felt a stinging sensation in the bicep of my noninfected arm. I looked down to see she was giving me an injection.

"It's okay," Sage said. "It's an antibiotic. It should work quickly, and you'll feel better soon."

I nodded, realizing that the deep pain in my other arm had gone from a sharp pulsing to a dull thud. I looked down and saw that the entire sleeve had been ripped off my shirt and a bandage was wrapped tightly around the site where I had been given the shot.

"We took it out," Sage explained. "It's a good thing you were passed out, because it kills when it's embedded like yours was."

As she was saying it, I heard Brady grunt from a nearby corner of the room. His sleeve was rolled up, and Caryn the waitress was digging into his arm with a pair of tweezers.

"Sorry," she said, her face contorting a bit with a sympathetic pain.

"It's okay," Brady said, trying to sound tougher than I imagined he actually felt in the moment. "Do you need more light or something?"

"No, I can see it," she said. "I've almost got it. I'm sorry, I've only done this a few times before."

"And it hurts like hell every time," teased one of the boys from earlier, who was sitting at a table nearby playing cards with the others.

"You want to come over here and take over, Milo? I'll get you a pair of gloves."

"I'm no surgeon," replied the boy.

"Neither is she," said the other boy, and they all laughed at Caryn's expense.

I sat up a bit to watch the scene, relieved that the fever seemed to have broken. I was already feeling better, though still a bit woozy.

"Got it!" Caryn cried, removing the tweezers from Brady's arm. Whatever she'd taken out must have been almost microscopic in size, because the tweezers looked empty from where I was sitting.

"Run and flush it with the other," said Sage, and Caryn did as she was told, beelining for a nearby bathroom. "Can't have them finding those if they ever raid the place."

Sage left my side and went to start wrapping fresh gauze around Brady's injection site. "Keep this clean," she instructed him. "And change the bandage once a day for three days, you got it?"

Brady nodded, looking back at me.

I offered him a weak smile, wanting to let him know I was feeling better.

"If you need the vaccines so much," I began, turning to the boy at the table who was apparently named Milo, "why did you take yours out?"

Milo shrugged. "I had a reaction like yours. I think it's because I'm part Otherlander."

"Otherlander?" I asked, figuring he must have meant our plane.

"Oh, please," said Caryn, returning from the bathroom. "You're not Otherlander." She then turned her attention to me. "People here sometimes refer to the other side like being part Cherokee or something. It sounds cool, but it's probably not true."

"Won't you get busted if you don't have the vaccine?" Brady asked.

"You sound like one of them," said Milo. "You sure you're not a spy?"

I felt a surge of panic take over me. We couldn't lose the trust of these people. We needed them to get back to the lake. I started to stutter out a response, but I didn't know how to prove our innocence any more than I already had.

"He's messing with you," said Caryn. "We know you're not spies."

"Will you help us?" asked Brady, who continued to stand a slight distance from the others. "We need to get back to the lake."

"Here we go again," said Milo, throwing down his cards

and going to a small refrigerator for a drink. "We're not the Otherlander Underground Railroad, buddy. You got yourself over here, get yourself back."

I tried to stand then, but felt the weakness still lingering in my legs and had to immediately sit back down. Milo's reference to the Underground Railroad threw me, as it was something that existed in our plane too. I remembered what Sage had told me—the planes split off from each other when a different action occurred, causing different results. So this plane and ours had been the same once, a long time ago. When did they split? And why?

"Sage?" I asked, still unable to leave the cot. "What happened here?"

Sage looked to Milo, who was sulking by the fridge, drinking something out of a dark bottle. "It doesn't matter," she began. "We can take you to the lake, if that's what you want. But it needs to be tonight. If they've seen you at the high school, they'll be looking for you by tomorrow."

"You all keep saying 'they,'" I realized out loud. "Do you mean the—the Russian people?"

"What Russian people?" Milo asked. I could tell from his tone he was messing with me.

"Everyone speaks Russian here."

"They speak English too. What's the problem?"

I turned to Caryn, realizing I would never get a straight answer out of Milo. "Is this Russia or something?"

"No, nothing like that," she assured us, shaking her head. "It's not that bad."

"We saw a picture of a man," Brady said. "A man with black hair. It said he was the leader. His portrait was hanging over the door in the hotel."

"Of course," said Sage. "You're required to have at least one hanging in every building. We've got one here, don't we, Milo?"

"Sure do."

"Where did you put it again?"

"It's in the john," he replied, and the others all laughed. "On the back of the toilet lid." The others erupted with an even louder response, and finally it felt like the tension in the room might be dissipating. "What? Gotta have something to aim for."

"Who is he?" Brady asked, his voice still tense despite the others' laughter.

"President Koenig," Caryn answered.

"Did he do this?"

Caryn turned to Sage, clearly trying to determine how much she should say. "Yes."

"So vote him out," Brady continued. "I mean, you have elections here, don't you?"

"There are elections, yes. But we don't—they're not for us," Caryn continued.

"We have the wrong papers," Milo chimed in. "It's not a free-for-all here."

"Well, what happens when his term is up?" I asked.

Caryn just smiled, like she found me adorable. "What's a *term*?"

The room fell silent, everyone turning to their own thoughts.

"Collect yourself for a moment and then we'll take you," said Sage. She then went to sit on a small, neatly made bed in another part of the room. It was the first time I realized that this was where she lived, and we were all crashing it in the middle of the night. She looked tired, and I felt terrible for being such a burden.

214

"I have to ask," said Brady, his mouth clenching around the question. "Did a girl named Piper come through here? About this tall," he gestured, "with long brown hair."

"Jesus, he's with her," said Milo. "That figures."

"She went to the train," said Caryn. I thought Brady would leap across the room to her on hearing this, but he managed to steady himself. Finally a specific answer, and finally some proof that we were right about Piper. She did come through the lake portal, and she was here.

"The train?"

"Is she your girlfriend?" asked Caryn, who clearly already had a crush on Brady.

"Yes," he answered, anxious for her to continue. "What train? You mean the train station?"

"Of course."

"Don't say any more," said Sage, sitting up on her cot. "If you want to get back to the lake, we should go in about twenty minutes. They turn the perimeter lights at the hotel off at one, and that's the best time to sneak in."

"But wait," Brady insisted, getting more and more agitated. "I need to know why she went to the train station."

"She said she wanted to see how far it spread. I assumed she meant the disease. To see if it had gotten to your town, who else was affected. She said she wouldn't be able to rest until she knew. She was supposed to come back in a few days, but she never did."

I could feel Brady deflating like an old balloon. We were so close, but she was still lost to us. Why hadn't she come back? What happened to her when she got home? Did she get the disease?

I turned to Sage, who was sitting up on her cot looking some-how defeated and sad. She rubbed her graying hair, shaking her head slightly. "Over and over again," I heard her mutter.

"Sage?" Brady asked. "Do you know why she wouldn't come back?"

"How should I know?"

"Can you help us find her?" Brady continued, a pleading aspect to his voice denoting a new kind of fear.

"I didn't put a GPS in the girl," Sage spat at nobody in partic-ular. "I offered to take her back to the lake that night, but she insisted on going on this fool's errand first."

"There must be someone we can call?" asked Caryn. "Can't you see how worried he is?"

"I'm not your parents!" shouted Sage. "Start taking responsi-bility for your own horrible choices." Her newfound anger was short-lived, burning up inside her for a moment or two, before she too seemed to shrink before our eyes, lying back down and staring at the ceiling above her little cot. "I'm sorry," she mut-tered. "But I really don't know."

"So she's stuck," said Brady, almost to himself. "She's stuck here somewhere in this nightmare ass-backwards place."

"Watch it," said Milo, his forceful tone making me momen-tarily afraid that he might tackle Brady. And even though Brady was pretty tough, one look at Milo told me he could pummel just about anybody in his path. "You're no better than us."

"I didn't mean it like that," said Brady, trying to defuse the bomb he had lit.

"Let me rest," said Sage. "Everybody be quiet. Give me a few minutes of peace."

"Excuse me," Brady said, bolting out of the room and up the stairs.

I stood, finding my footing once again and feeling stronger already. But inside, I was falling apart, realizing how desperate this situation was becoming. Piper was slipping farther and farther away from Brady. I couldn't wait to get out of here, and away from these people.

"Sorry," I said to Milo, who didn't seem to care in the least what I thought. I followed Brady up the stairs.

Searching the diner, I finally found him sitting alone in the last booth. His head was buried in his arms and I realized that he was crying. My first instinct was to leave him alone, give him some privacy. But he was my friend, and I didn't want him to think that nobody cared what he was going through.

I sat down next to him and put my hand on his back. "It's okay," was all I could think of to say.

"I'm never going to see her again," he said, his voice muffled by his sleeve.

"Of course you are," I told him, wanting desperately to hug him. "You know where she is. She took the train back home. She just took it from here is all."

"We have to go back to the lake in a few minutes," Brady reminded me, looking up. "It's too late."

I nodded, trying to think of what choices we still had.

"Besides," Brady continued, "if she wanted to be with me, she wouldn't have left. It's like you said earlier, isn't it? If she loved me, she would have stayed."

"That's not necessarily true," I said, thinking of my mother's words. *You are my warrior.* My mother had stayed with me as long as she could before going in search of Robbie. It felt like an abandonment at first, but that's because I didn't know. Sometimes people do things for all sorts of hidden reasons.

"She probably really did think she'd be right back," I said. "And she knew you were strong enough to be on your own until then."

"But I'm not strong," Brady said. "And I'm so sick of having to act like I am all the time. This isn't fair. I should get to keep one thing." He started crying again, and I took his hand.

"Brady," I whispered, trying to calm him, although he was already collecting himself. "Look at me."

He turned his head. I took in his devastated eyes, realizing that if he listened to what I was about to say, I might never see them again.

"Piper needs you right now, do you hear me?"

He calmed himself and nodded, seeming to throw the emotion away from his face. I could hear him clear his throat as embarrassment crept in.

"You still love her?"

He stared at me for a moment, as if surprised by the question. His hand was still holding mine, and for a moment I wasn't sure if he was trying to decide the answer, or if he was thinking about me.

But then he pulled away from me. "Yes," he admitted. "I do."

"Go get her, then. Go to the train, go to our town, and find her. When you have her, you can both come back here together and come through the lake portal."

Brady exhaled slowly, thinking about what I was telling him. "It's too dangerous, Marina. We've already been down a day."

"You heard what George said. You can stay up to a week. It'll take you one day to get there and find her, and another to get back."

He nodded, seeming to visualize the journey.

"Just promise me—if you can't find her right away . . ."

"I'll come back." He smiled. "I promise. I won't stay too long."

I sighed, relieved to hear the confidence back in his voice.

"What about you?"

"I'll be fine. Sage and Caryn will take me back, and my father is waiting for me."

"No, I'll take you back to the lake first."

"Brady," I said, stopping him. "You and I both know that if you make it all the way to the lake, you're not going to get back out again."

Brady got up and started walking very slowly away from me, pacing to let his energy come back to him. "I don't have any money to buy a ticket."

"Wait," I said, checking the stairwell to make sure no one was listening. I went over to the cash register and started pressing buttons until the drawer opened. But when it did, the drawer was empty. I was about to close it again when I picked up the cash tray to be sure. And that's when I found a hundred-dollar bill hiding under some papers.

"We can't take that, Marina. She probably needs it."

"We'll pay her back," I said, knowing it was probably a lie. "I promise."

I handed the bill to Brady, whose hand lingered on mine for a moment.

"Are you sure you'll be okay?"

"I'm a big girl," I told him, knowing the confidence I was feigning was probably not convincing anyone. But at the same time, I knew I was doing the right thing. If Brady stayed with me, he would always wonder about Piper. Wonder if he could have done more to find her. He would resent me in the end.

"I feel like I'm never going to see you again," Brady told me then, not moving towards the door yet.

"I will see you," I declared, the words filling my heart as they escaped my lips, "when you and Piper come home."

Brady nodded, and there was nothing more to say. He leaned over and kissed my cheek, and I closed my eyes to feel the warmth of his lips on me, knowing that it was a memory that would probably return to me in the middle of the night for a very long time.

"Go," I whispered. And I watched him walk out the door. He didn't slow down, and he didn't look back at me. He walked out of the diner, turned the corner, and disappeared past the window.

And then he was gone.

o o o

It was a cold and silent walk back to the hotel. Only Sage, Caryn, and Milo came with me, and none of them had seemed too surprised when I told them that Brady had gone to the train station. "One less problem to worry about," Milo had said.

We walked normally and quite calmly until we reached the perimeter of the nicer part of town. It was a noticeable difference, with everything from the buildings to the sidewalks taking on a polish and style that was completely lacking back in the poorer quarters. Everything turned green, and little boxes with doggy waste bags were even set up every several feet so the rich society matrons could clean up after their Labradors and poodles.

Sage whispered to me. "Do what we do."

220   REBECCA PHELPS

She and the others bowed their heads, sticking out their hands slightly and shuffling past the pedestrians—of which there were many, despite the late hour—with a subservient air about them.

Every now and then, Sage would speak to a passerby in a low tone that I could barely make out. "Donation, citizen?"

The well-heeled people would invariably say no, or shake their heads and keep walking. As we got closer to the hotel, Sage stopped asking, and soon I realized people were avoiding us altogether. There was one couple, decked out for the evening in the most beautifully ornate clothes, who actually crossed the street when they saw us coming. That's when I realized that Sage didn't actually want donations. It was a ploy to scare people away from us.

And it seemed to be working. We were all but invisible as we approached the hotel. "Walk past it," Sage whispered, and we all did.

Once we'd gone several feet beyond the main gate, Sage and the others, as part of some secret plan that they seemed to have already worked out, slowly turned and started walking back again. Soon, just as Sage had said, all the perimeter lights surrounding the hotel, which had been illuminating the sidewalk and all the nearby foliage, turned off.

"Now," Milo whispered with urgency, and he grabbed my wrist and led me around the corner, down what had once been the alley that Brady and I had traversed to find the side door. But here, there was a fence that ran the length of the walkway. We continued down alongside it until we reached a different chain-link fence straight ahead with a row of thick trees behind it. I couldn't see anything past the trees, but I knew from where we were standing that we were probably near the lap pool I had seen earlier.

"Stand watch," said Sage, commanding Milo and Caryn, who both assumed sentinel-like positions facing outward. I quickly followed suit, relieved that I didn't see anyone coming. Sage got down on her knees and started feeling along the base of the chain-link. "Got it."

There was a very slight rip running up and down the intertwining links. Sage took a pair of pliers out of her bag and used them to peel the fence open along the slit, creating an opening just big enough for a person to worm through, lying flat on the ground. I immediately threw myself down to give it a shot.

"Wait," said Milo. "Do you want to cut yourself?"

"Boy, she is anxious," said Sage.

"Can you blame her?" asked Caryn, who had lost a bit of her earlier energy, ever since hearing that Brady wouldn't be joining us.

"Wrap yourself in this," instructed Sage, who took a thick wool blanket out of her bag. "Or you'll cut yourself on the edges."

I wrapped the blanket around myself tightly, then got down on my stomach and shuffled my way, quite awkwardly, through the opening, managing to snag the blanket only a couple of times. Once I was through, I handed the blanket to Milo, and he did the same, followed by Caryn, and lastly Sage.

Once on the other side, I wanted to run immediately.

"Wait," Sage whispered again, clearly losing patience with me. She took her pliers and carefully folded the fence back into place behind us. "They send someone to check the grounds every thirty minutes. If they find this, it's over."

I nodded, again feeling guilty that I was being such an imposition to them. But I couldn't help myself. We were so close to the lake, I was bubbling over inside. Just knowing that my father

222   REBECCA PHELPS

was there waiting for me, that soon I could throw myself into his arms and truly feel safe again, was enough to make me stop thinking clearly.

Still, I followed my three guides as quietly as possible, and tried to always stay a step behind as we made the long and silent journey down the winding path to the lake.

"Almost there," Sage said, and once again, she reached into her bag. Holding out one hand, she motioned for all of us to stop behind her. She pulled something out that looked like a small piece of metal, and soon she held it to her lips and blew out a perfect imitation of an owl call.

A moment later, another owl call responded from the woods by the lake. Sage blew hers one more time, and within seconds the other one echoed back. I realized, peering through the darkness in the direction of the water, that it was probably coming from George's cabin.

"We're clear," Sage whispered, and we all started walking towards the source of the other call. Something that George had said earlier came back to me then. He stayed by the lake to make sure the men in the uniforms never found out about the portal. He must have been the one who'd cut the slit in the fence so Sage and her friends could get through. And for that, I owed him a lot.

But as we approached his cabin, I thought of the pictures he kept of my mother in the closet. What if he had been in love with her, and not Sage? What if he still loved her, even the dark, twisted version of her that lived on this plane? Would he still be devoted to her?

My questions were answered before we reached the lip of the woods. A slight click came from nowhere, and suddenly the entire woods around us were drowned in a sea of bright lights, which had been rigged to the tops of dozens of trees, flooding the ground below like a football stadium. We were caught, and the four of us froze.

"Hide her, hide her," Sage hissed to Milo, who grabbed me by the waist and all but carried me off into the thickest part of the foliage to one side of the path. We ran only a few feet before I could hear the familiar dinging of a bicycle bell coming from the direction of George's cabin.

"This'll have to do," Milo whispered, practically hurling me to the ground and burying me in a pile of leaves. He quickly grabbed a handful of mud and smeared it over my face, then covered all but my nose in the leaves as well. "Stay still," I heard him add before he disappeared. I was lying under a fairly bright light from a nearby tree, and I could only hope the camouflage would hold.

I heard the little bell from the bicycle come to a chirping stop near the others on the path. "Found them," the man in the uniform called. And soon other footsteps approached, maybe three or four separate sets of feet. I kept my eyes closed and focused on their voices, trying not to even breathe.

"George, how could you?" Caryn said.

"I didn't . . . ," George began, his voice small and defeated.

"He's in love with her," Milo replied, rejoining the others. "I told you this would happen."

"Where were you just now?" the soldier on the bike asked Milo.

"Taking a leak," Milo replied, as casually as possible.

"Search the woods," the soldier called, and I heard two sets of footsteps start in my direction. I sealed my mouth and did everything I could not to move, but I knew it was a matter of seconds before I was discovered.

"She's not in the woods, Rain. She went to the hotel," said Sage, using the nickname that only people who went to high school with my mother seemed to know. So this version of Sage must have grown up with my mother, too, but in this reality.

Had they been friends? And if so, when did my mother change?

"Stop," my mother's voice responded, cutting off my thoughts. Miraculously, the footsteps stopped just short of me. I could feel my heart pounding in my rib cage, and wished I knew some magic trick to make it stop. "Why would she go to the hotel?"

"You didn't recognize her?" Sage continued. "She's your daughter."

The man with the bicycle laughed. "Ana doesn't have a daughter," he said. "Only a son."

I could feel the impulse to gasp hit my throat. What son? Did he mean Robbie? Was there a version of Robbie here in this plane? But not of me? Or was this some other son that only existed here? There were too many questions flooding my brain. I couldn't process them. And my shallow breathing was starting to make me dizzy.

The two men with the bicycles were chatting softly in Russian and clearly finding each other very amusing.

"Back to the hotel," my mother snapped. And like that, all the other chatter stopped. "George, you too."

"It's late, Rain. I'd like to get to bed."

My mother must have given him a sharp look, because after a second's pause, George corrected himself: "Sorry. *Ana*."

"We'd all prefer to be in bed, George. But you keep letting these vagrants into the woods."

"They just want to go swimming is all, Ana. What's wrong with that?"

"They'll spread their disease into the lake," my mother retorted, a tone of disgust in her voice I had grown all too familiar with during her long and declining depression in our house.

"Enough," said the guard with the bicycle. "They'll get away."

"The young man who came in with her?" my mother asked.

"He took off," I heard Caryn respond. "He didn't say where."

"Fine," my mother said. And the whole caravan started to walk away from me, back towards the hotel. I found my body paralyzed by fear. Was one of them lingering, waiting to catch me? I tried to count the number of different footfalls I heard receding, but it was impossible. Several minutes went by, and I lay there, listening to the slight rustling of leaves as animals paced by and bugs chirped their late-night songs. Rather than ebbing, the fear began to increase. My bones grew stiff with the anxiety of not moving. I thought I would scream from the tension of it.

And then the lights turned off.

I was alone in the dark. I could hear my breath coming out in rasps as I struggled to contain my nerves. Finally I couldn't stand it anymore. I didn't care if anyone caught me—I just couldn't stay there like that for one more second. I launched my body up off the ground, not daring to look in any direction but the lake.

Like a child trying to outrun a nightmare, I all but flew through the rest of the woods, not looking once at George's cabin, and dove headfirst into the water. Afraid that someone might hear me paddling, I instead gulped in a large mouthful of air and swam underwater in the direction of the box with

REBECCA PHELPS

the portal in it. I couldn't see anything in the bleak darkness, of course. So I swam as far as I could before coming up for air. When I did, I turned quickly to judge my location based on the shoreline, and found that I was probably over the box. George's cabin was to my left, its dark silhouette stark against the lightly glowing night air behind the woods.

I took a deep breath, and just before my eyes went under, I saw the lights in George's cabin snap on. This was it. Somebody was back at the cabin. I didn't know if they had seen me, but I knew that no matter what, I couldn't come up to the surface again. I either found the box, or I would be stuck here, possibly forever.

In the darkness at the bottom of the lake, I desperately felt along for the outline of wood. And all I felt was sand. I could feel my chest straining under the lack of air, and knew I had maybe half a minute left before I wouldn't be able to hold my breath anymore.

My fingers desperately groped the ground, my eyes straining to make out any form in the pitch-darkness. I was on the brink of giving up hope when I felt something. It was hard and metal, and I realized it was the clasp of the box.

My breath was all but gone, but it was now or never. With all my strength, I flung open the lid of the box and pulled myself through. The flash of light passed, followed by an even more profound darkness.

As with before, I had no idea which direction I was facing, and it was too dark to follow my air bubbles. I picked a direction and started swimming against the thick, murky water, only to bump my head against the lake floor.

I was upside-down. And I was out of breath.

Quickly, and with my last might, I pushed myself off the sandy wall beneath me and propelled my body upwards, opening my mouth and letting the last of my air escape. It seemed like an eternity of water around me, and for a moment I wondered if this time I really was going to drown.

But then the light started to seep into my vision, and soon the water's surface appeared before my eyes. My head burst through, and I gulped in a mouthful of air. For a moment, all I could do was breathe and be grateful. I had never been a religious person, despite the efforts of St. Joe's to make me one, but I found myself thanking God that I was alive and that air was filling my lungs.

Before me, I saw only the water and the far edge of the lake, and I realized I was facing away from the shore.

That's when I turned around, in the bright light of day, and saw them standing there waiting for me.

Sage and John looked like they had been standing vigil for hours, and both sighed deeply upon seeing me. And after a moment, I saw Kieren come to join them. I felt like I must be seeing things, and my brain couldn't reconcile the image of him on the shore with what I had been expecting to see. I searched left and right for my father, feeling I would burst if I didn't see him. But he wasn't there. Kieren bent over at the waist, as if catching his breath after a long run.

And somehow I knew, looking at Kieren, that my father wasn't coming.

CHAPTER 16

Back at the hotel, Sage was treating me like a wounded bird she had pulled in from the forest. A cup of tea. A warm blanket. And the smell of something savory she was cooking in the kitchen. We were all sitting in her apartment, on the throw pillows where Brady and I had been offered tea before.

The information was coming at me faster than I could comprehend it. My father had been taken into "detention," whatever that meant, at a processing center in town. Something had happened at the high school, something big that had changed everything.

"Slow down," I told Kieren, feeling more frustrated than ever. "Tell me what you're talking about."

"The police were at your house," Kieren began, clearly trying to check his pace and use phrases that would be clear to me.

"They had become suspicious about your mom's disappearance. Like, maybe your dad had something to do with it."

"What?"

"I know it's insane. But I guess they wanted to interview you, see if you knew more than you were saying."

"Oh God."

"So your dad called the camp, from the number on their website."

"And let me guess. They had never heard of me."

Kieren gave me a moment to process this before going on. "Your dad called your friend Christy, and asked if she knew where you were. And Christy told him everything."

I buried my face in my hands, imagining poor Christy on the phone with my father, panicking. I felt terrible for having put her in that position. It hadn't even occurred to me how selfish it was of me to ask such a big favor of her. And I couldn't wait to talk to her again so I could apologize.

"Don't be mad at her," Kieren said.

"No, no, I'm not," I insisted. "I just feel guilty. I should have never asked her to lie for me."

"Christy came to find me and asked if I could help. So I went to your house . . ."

"You what?" I asked. "Are you crazy? My dad could have seen you. He would have killed you."

"I didn't care about that anymore. I wanted to tell him that you were okay."

"What did he say when he saw you?"

Kieren was silent for a moment, and he stared down at the cup of tea that he had yet to sip. The quiet of the room echoed in my ears, chilling me to the bone.

"They were already taking him away," Kieren said. "I'm sorry, M. I was too late. I snuck in through the back door after they were gone. They took him so quickly, his phone and keys were still sitting on the counter."

"I don't understand. My father texted me that he was coming. That he knew where I was."

"That was me," Kieren explained. "I'm sorry. Somehow I thought that if you knew I was the one coming, you might not stick around till I got here."

"Why wouldn't I?"

Kieren shrugged, seeming to turn within himself. "Where's Brady?" he asked, still not meeting my eyes.

"He stayed down," I explained. "We think we found out where Piper went. So he followed her."

Kieren nodded, appearing somehow relieved. I heard him exhale, and a slight shuddering sound made his breath uneven.

"What is it?"

He shrugged again. "I'm so happy you're okay," he said, finally looking up at me.

Sage approached the table then, after what had been a long and whispered exchange with John in the kitchen. She carried a large tray, with several bowls wobbling on top of it.

"Okay, hot soup! Watch that your tongues don't get burned."

"We actually have to go," Kieren said, beginning to stand. "Thank you, though."

"You'll have some soup first."

Kieren looked to me, and I supposed my face couldn't hide the fact that I was starving. The last thing I had eaten was the stale bread that I had thrown up in the alley. I was finally feeling better, now that the antibiotic shot had completely kicked in.

We stayed and ate our soup, and I even went back for seconds. After a bit, Sage finally cleared her throat.

"About what's down there," Sage began, out of nowhere. "About what's under the lake . . . we wanted to warn you."

I sat back and listened. I was done eating, and didn't really want to think anymore about that horrible world down there.

"You went into the hotel, I presume?" she asked. John came over and joined her, and for the first time, a sympathetic expression came over his face.

"Yes."

Sage sighed. She turned to her husband. "John?"

John too cleared his throat, and for an awkward moment, this felt like one of those horrible movies where the parents sit the kids down to discuss the birds and the bees, and the children pretend that they don't already know about them. Besides, there was really nothing to say. The plane that existed under the lake was an anomaly. Something horrible had happened down there, and it didn't matter. Because it wasn't real.

"We made a mistake," John said, a deep sadness filling his voice. "We shouldn't have created that portal. We've regretted it since, but we can't undo it."

Kieren looked to me, obviously wanting some explanation of what I had seen down there.

"But you should know," John continued. "That's not your mother. Your mother is a kind and lovely woman." He exchanged a look with Sage, who nodded for him to continue. "She's our friend."

"She's our dear friend," Sage agreed.

"And our job now," John continued, "is to keep that plane separate from ours. You remember what we said? About your brother, and the crossing of the planes? Marina, that is why it is so important for him to come out."

"What are they talking about?" Kieren asked me.

"I'll tell you later," I promised. "Let's just go."

Kieren stood up and I joined him. "Thank you for the soup," I said to Sage, and we turned to leave the apartment. "You'll keep an eye out for Brady and Piper. They're going to be coming back through the lake."

Sage nodded. "Of course."

Kieren and I began to leave, but I could hear Sage shuffling behind me.

"Marina?" she said, standing to watch us go. "With your brother—with Robbie, I mean—it has to happen soon, dear."

"M? What's she saying?" Kieren whispered to me.

All I could do was shake my head. "Can we go home, please? I want to go home."

Kieren took my hand and guided me out the door. I could feel Sage's and John's eyes on our backs as we walked out, but I didn't turn to face them. We swung by the room where I had stayed and grabbed my suitcase, then headed out the front door.

On the road in front of the hotel, which was blissfully back to its run-down state, sat a car I didn't recognize.

"Where'd you get this?"

"It's Scott's," Kieren answered.

"Does he know you took it this far?"

"He does now." Kieren opened the door for me and I got in, the shadow of the tall, ugly hotel building falling like a cloak over the car and the road all around us.

As we drove off, I grabbed my phone out of my suitcase and turned it back on, waiting for it to find a signal. Then I sent a text to Christy: *I'm so sorry. We're on our way home.* I didn't know what else to say, and so I put the phone back in my bag.

I was asleep before we hit the edge of town.

o o o

I must have been more tired than I realized, because the day drifted by and slowly turned to night, the shadows growing longer and the sky turning pink, then purple, and finally black. I slipped in and out of awareness, vivid dreams of my mother's cold eyes haunting me into waking up, only to have the exhaustion overtake me again. All the while, Kieren drove in silence. At some point, I realized he had his earphones in so as to not wake me, and the realization that we must have been close to home filled me with a warmth that I hadn't even realized I was missing.

The peacefulness of that feeling was short-lived, however. Because when I woke up, we were stopped in a parking lot I didn't recognize.

"Kieren?" I asked, coming to and rubbing my eyes.

"We're here," he answered, taking out the earphones.

I looked up at a large, intimidating building that did not look familiar, and I sat up, trying to get my bearings.

"We're where?"

Kieren turned and looked at me, letting me put together the pieces by myself, I suppose. It was dark out by this point, and the parking lot was poorly lit.

The building was not tall, and it didn't seem to have too many windows. Yet something about it seemed oddly familiar, certain shapes and shadows striking me as though I had seen them

234   REBECCA PHELPS

hundreds of times—the way the trees formed along the skyline, and the curve of the road that led to the parking lot. I found myself spinning around in my seat, undoing my seat belt, and almost hurling myself out of the car.

And even when I started to put together the inevitable truth that was staring me in the face, I still couldn't quite process it. I knew that road, and I knew those trees. And now that I looked at the building, I realized that I knew its outline quite well.

We were at the high school. We were home, in the parking lot of our own school. But it was changed. And this wasn't some small thing like a brick wall covering a door. This time, no one could deny what was happening. The school had changed. It had become something dark and sinister over-night, and it didn't occur to me at first how that could possi-bly be.

"What is it?" I asked Kieren, who had also left the car.

"Don't you know?"

I shook my head.

"M, it's the base. The military base. Like it used to be."

I stared at him over the dark form of the car. "It can't be." My legs wobbled beneath me, my throat going dry. "Is it a different dimension? Did I come back to the wrong place?"

"No," he insisted, and I finally noticed the half-moon cir-cles under his eyes, the strain across his face, telling me that he hadn't slept. What if this wasn't even my Kieren?

"What's the last thing you remember saying to me?"

But Kieren just smiled, shaking his head. "At the train station. I told you I'd take Robbie's place."

I relaxed a bit, realizing that only my Kieren could have known that.

"You're in the right dimension, M. But it's changed."

I nodded dumbly, but I still didn't understand.

"The day after you and Brady left, we woke up and it was like this. There were guards driving around with MP written on their armbands. The school had changed, just overnight."

"MP?"

"Military police."

The breath expelled from my lungs with an audible hum. "Has anything else changed?"

"No, not that I know of."

Before Kieren could explain any further, a car pulled into the lot with bright lights mounted on its roof, shining in our direction.

"What are you doing there?" asked a man's voice, booming over a loudspeaker from the car.

"Nothing, sir," Kieren was quick to respond, holding up his hands. "Show him your hands," Kieren whispered to me, and I did as I was instructed.

The car stopped, and I saw that it was a security vehicle of some kind. It wasn't a traditional police car, but rather something similar with an intimidating-looking emblem on its side. The man who had been speaking to us got out of the car and approached, a flashlight in our eyes the whole time. As such, I couldn't really see a thing as he walked closer.

"This area is off-limits."

"Sorry, sir. We were lost," Kieren replied.

The man finally lowered the flashlight and stared me in the eyes, as though looking for some sign that we were telling the truth. His gaze was intense and cold, just like the Russian police in the plane under the lake.

"Get unlost," the man said, turning to Kieren. "Get back in your vehicle and go. Next time, I'll bring you in."

"Yes, sir," Kieren replied, curtly and with no hint of emotion. He waved me back into the car, and I knew better than to hesitate. I got in and put my seat belt back on.

Kieren drove out of the lot before the officer in the car had a chance to change his mind, and we traveled in silence for a moment until he could turn off the main road and park along a side street.

"I'm sorry," Kieren said. "I guess I shouldn't have taken you there at night, but I knew you'd want to see it." He looked to the dashboard clock to check the time. "We need to go. There's a curfew now. We have to be inside in fifteen minutes."

But I wasn't really listening. "What have we done?" I asked. I buried my head in my hands, trying to process it. "Who was that guard? Was he from here or from . . ." I let the sentence trail off. I couldn't bring myself to finish it.

I felt Kieren put his hand on my shoulder. "Do you want to go home?"

The thought of the dark, empty house was too horrible to even imagine. My family was gone. And I shook my head, too afraid to even think about the quiet rooms that awaited me there. "I've never slept in it alone."

"I could stay for a bit. My dad thinks I'm camping with Scott anyway. That's how I got away."

It seemed the only option. I offered a weak nod, and we drove silently through the empty streets.

O O O

The house was cold, and it felt like a million years since I'd been there. I walked through the vacant rooms like they were part of a museum or something. Like I had never lived in them.

"It's strange," was all I could say. "I'm the only one left."

"Don't say that," Kieren pleaded, following me past the kitchen and into the abandoned living room. "They'll be back."

I could only smile. "I'm so tired," I finally said.

Kieren stood awkwardly. "Listen, if you want some privacy, I can go crash at Scott's. I'll come back for you in the morning."

A voice in my head was screaming not to let him go. I walked up and gave him a small kiss, aiming for the lips, but missing the mark a bit. I felt a little ridiculous, trying to recapture the time his kiss had come so naturally. "Come upstairs for a minute?"

Kieren let out a small laugh, and for a moment, I felt I had made a terrible mistake. Maybe that night hadn't meant anything to him. Maybe he had completely forgotten about it. That made two kisses in a row with guys who clearly weren't into it. What was wrong with me?

"You don't want to?" I asked, dreading the answer.

"Of course I want to."

I almost thought I saw him blush in the darkness of the living room. I turned and headed upstairs. I could sense him following me, though I was too nervous to look back.

Once in my room, I sat on the edge of the mattress, waiting for him to do something. He took off his shoes and came to sit down beside me. We sat in uncomfortable silence for a moment, and to be honest, I didn't really know what was supposed to happen next. I just knew I didn't want him to go.

I lay down, and he did the same, tentatively at first, but then pressing up closer to me. He put his arm around my waist.

REBECCA PHELPS

I couldn't help but laugh, imagining the young boy he had been once. Remembering a time he and Robbie and I had played Twister in the basement, falling all over each other and laughing until our sides ached.

I didn't have my brother anymore. But I had Kieren. I realized that the feeling that overwhelmed me in that moment was probably something very close to love. And I found myself thanking God—if there was in fact a God—that he was with me.

"Kieren," I said, feeling his warm breath on my cheek, and holding him tight.

"Yes?"

"I forgive you."

He didn't say anything for a moment, his face buried below a tuft of hair, and I was beginning to wonder if he had heard me. But then I felt his whole body shudder. He was crying. I held him as closely as I could, putting my arms around him and letting him cry into my neck.

"Shh," I whispered, not sure how to comfort him. I kissed his forehead, and then the top of his head. I kissed his cheeks, and finally his lips again.

It should have felt strange, but it didn't. It seemed inevitable, somehow. Like this was something we had always had between us—we'd just been too young to know it. I could have kissed him all night.

After a moment, I felt his hand come up under my shirt, and I flinched away. "Sorry." I straightened my shirt, acting more by instinct than decision.

"No, I'm sorry," Kieren said, rolling away from me a bit.

We stayed that way, lying next to each other in silence for a moment. He didn't say anything, but he didn't seem to want to leave either.

"Are you mad?" I asked.

"No, no," he insisted, turning back towards me and kissing me gently on the lips again. "No, of course not."

He sat up on the mattress, and I watched his long back curve against the glow from the windows. A part of me felt like I was playing grown-up, and I'm sure he knew it. But in that moment, I would have done more with him if he'd asked. And so I was a bit relieved that he wasn't asking.

"Will you stay here with me?"

He turned and smiled down at me. "As long as you'll let me." He stroked my side with the back of his hand, almost absentmindedly.

I began to laugh, the gentle touch of his fingers hitting that part of my sides that always got me.

"Still ticklish?" he asked, a mischievous look coming over his face.

"Don't you dare," I giggled, pushing his hands away. The smile on my face must have lingered for quite a while after he stopped, because he just kept staring.

"What?"

"I'm happy," I said. For the first time in months, I felt safe and I felt right. More so even than I had when I was with Brady. More than I had since my mother got sick. Maybe even since Robbie left. "I just wish . . . ," I said, and the words were seeping out of my mouth of their own volition. But then my brain caught up with them and wanted to take them back.

"You wish?"

I shook my head. I didn't want to say it. But Kieren knew me, and he knew what I wished. He had always known.

"You wish Robbie was here," he finished my sentence for me. And I couldn't deny that that's what I was thinking. "M, I heard what that lady said. That Robbie needs to come out of DW."

I weighed my thoughts, not wanting to ruin this beautiful moment with Kieren, but knowing that he needed to know the truth.

"Tell me."

I shrugged a bit, not sure how he would take it. "It's like you said," I admitted. "He has to come out of the train portal. And there's no way . . ." I cleared my throat, which was suddenly quite dry. "There's no way he can do it alive."

He nodded, not seeming surprised, and put his head back down to be level with mine. We stared into each other's eyes for a bit.

"You promised me you wouldn't do anything crazy," I reminded him.

"I know," he said, as though he had already been expecting my protests. A smile crossed his lips, but I couldn't read what he was thinking. "Do you still have the penny I gave you?"

I laughed and took it out of my pocket. "Why did you make this for me, anyway?"

He shrugged, looking embarrassed. "I don't know. I had seen some older kids from the high school doing it once, and I thought it looked cool. I think I was trying to impress you." His face flushed pink with the confession.

I put the penny back in my pocket, my cheeks burning and probably turning the same color.

"It wasn't until . . . until Robbie went in . . . that I realized that that was a special part of the train track. Maybe those kids I had seen knew something about it. I don't know."

"You said it would protect me."

He nodded, finally looking sleepy. "I hope it will," he whispered, and I watched him in silence as his eyes closed and he drifted off to sleep.

o   o   o

I woke because I heard the engine start. My eyes flickered open to that cold, gray first-morning light, and once again I was alone. I rolled over, rubbing a crick out of my neck, and walked through the house looking for Kieren. I suppose I knew, however, that I wouldn't find him.

I looked out of the front window in time to see him driving off in Scott's car, and my gut twisted up inside of me. Somehow I knew immediately where he was going.

I grabbed my bike from the garage and pedaled standing up, going as fast as I possibly could.

My legs woke up quickly as they pedaled, and the early-morning air was like a splash of cold water to my face. My mind was racing, replaying last night's conversation and hoping, despite myself, that Kieren wasn't doing what I thought he was doing.

But when I pulled into the parking lot at the train station, I saw the car. I pedaled to the building and threw the bike down onto the sidewalk. Running up to the platform, I flicked my head from left to right, hoping to catch a glimpse of him. He wasn't there, or inside the station either. Before my mind caught up with my feet, I was running down the bike path towards the place where he had made me the penny.

I made out his figure on the track just around a slight bend, and I became aware of the rumbling from the train at the same time. It was only a few hundred feet away, and Kieren was standing to meet it, dead center on the tracks.

"Kieren!" I screamed, the shrill voice escaping from deep within me with such intensity that I almost didn't recognize it.

He was facing the train, and he didn't turn to look at me. "Go home, M!" he shouted.

I ran up beside him, waves of fear pulsing through my legs and almost making me trip. The train horn wailed so loudly that I couldn't hear myself think. I tried to shout his name again, but everything was drowned out by that desperate shriek from the train.

Kieren continued to look straight ahead as I stood by the side of the track, and I knew that it was too late to simply walk up and pull him out of danger. The train was almost upon us.

I heard, somewhere deep inside me, a voice screaming, "No, no, no," and I wasn't sure if it was actually coming out of my body or if it was just the echo of my mind. But nothing could make it stop as the train grew closer and closer.

I didn't think. I didn't decide. I didn't even breathe. My legs leaped on their own, onto the track, towards Kieren, and I remember using all my might to push him out of the way. The train came.

And the last thing I heard was the silence as my own screaming came to an end.

PART THREE

CHAPTER 17

I didn't notice the flash of light, though I'm sure it must have happened. All I noticed was the blackness. And the quiet. And slowly, very slowly, the rumbling. It was the train, humming its way down the track.

When I stood up, I saw that I was indeed on a train, but not the one I had taken west with Brady. The floor of the car I stood in was patched up and well worn, in some places nothing more than a few wooden boards hammered together haphazardly, the passing track visible below. Several of the windows were broken, or missing altogether, and the wind that blew in through them as the train rambled along stirred the few things that still existed inside—papers dancing in circles over the ripped-up seats; old train ticket stubs flipping over on their sides before eventually finding their way through the slits in the wood and disappearing onto the track.

It was a train car out of time and out of place, and for more than a moment, I was sure that I was dead. It made perfect sense to me, I suppose, that this would be my purgatory. A train. An empty train that I would inevitably ride forever.

But out the window, I recognized a few landmarks that told me perhaps I wasn't as far away as that. We weren't in my town, but the curve of the land, the feel of the trees, the architecture of the small passing houses, all conspired to assure me that we were close. It might just be that whatever dimension I had landed in wasn't too different from my own.

I walked the length of the car, and I reached for the door at the far end of it. I was relieved to see that it opened with very little effort, making a bit of a whooshing sound as the chilled air rushed in through the newly formed void. I stepped gingerly over the small platforms that connected this car to the next, completely exposed to the outside and with only a chain dangling along the sides to keep me from falling. Maybe this dimension wasn't so similar to my own, after all. I couldn't imagine a train in our world that would still let people cross from car to car by actually stepping outside while in motion.

The door to the next car opened easily as well, but I was disappointed to find that the car itself looked just like that last one. Was this whole train abandoned? Where was it going? And when would it stop?

The third car offered up some signs of life, at least. It was a sleeping car, with bunks lined up against both sides. It didn't look like anyone had slept in them for a while, but at least the mattresses and turned-down sheets gave the appearance that someone once had, and maybe not even that long ago.

I continued to make my way through the train, car to car. It looked like every car had once served a purpose—the dining car, the ladies' lounge car, even a library car. It was as if at one point, in some world long ago, this had been the luxury liner of train travel, the *Titanic* of railroads. But now, like the *Titanic* itself, it was nothing but a carved-out shadow, a bleak reminder of the destructiveness of time. The books in the library car were scattered and ripped, their pages torn out and blowing like oversized snowflakes in and out of the windows.

The train moved on, passing through tunnels and dark, towering woods. And it didn't stop. Time moved on, too, and I began to realize the sad truth that it probably never would. Maybe I was right the first time. Maybe I had died.

I thought of Catholic school. My teachers had never been the superstrict cliché of Catholic nuns, but they were true believers. My seventh grade math teacher, Sister Linda, had stopped class once when a group of boys was being too rowdy and reminded us that hell held a special place for bad children. I thought she was crazy. And I remember thinking that it was a perverted and warped thing to say to a group of twelve-year-olds.

Now I wondered if she was right. I thought back on the things I had done. I'd lied to my father. I'd tried to lure Brady away from his girlfriend. And I'd spent the night with Kieren. We hadn't done much. Just kissed. But was that enough? Was I condemned to ride this train for all eternity as a result? Could God really be that cruel?

Suddenly, I heard giggling. I didn't recognize it at first. It seemed like such an impossible thing on this train. But when it came again, riding a wave of sound from somewhere several cars away, I was sure that I hadn't been mistaken.

I made my way to the next car, and as I took the first step, I gasped. In this car, whole boards were missing from the floor, and the track passing beneath was only inches from my feet. One more step and that would have been the end of me. I caught my breath and walked more carefully, tiptoeing my way on the firmer boards to the other end.

The car after that was something I never would have expected. It had been carefully boarded up, from floor to ceiling, by someone who had taken great care to cover every opening. And in the absence of natural light, it had overhead bulbs hanging from electrical cords and buzzing with a soft glow. It hadn't occurred to me that this train would have electricity. The car was dedicated to one purpose: it seemed to be a large walk-in pantry. Piles of food were stacked, very carefully, in neat rows up and down the length of the car. Cans of soup on one side. Boxes of ramen on another. And even baskets of fresh fruit, arranged by size. Apples and nectarines in one basket. Grapes, berries, and walnuts in another. Bananas on their own, so as not to rot the neighboring fruit. Someone had given this car a lot of thought. Or else they just had a lot of time on their hands.

And then I heard another giggle.

The next car was an actual living area, complete with floral wallpaper and curtains made from a patchwork of dark fabrics hanging by the windows, tied back with ribbons. A plush-looking couch was half covered in what appeared to be books from the library car, some clearly taped together with whatever tape was available, and in some cases tied together with string like Christmas presents waiting to be unwrapped.

The giggling came from the next car up. I tried to think of how many doors I had already passed through. Maybe a dozen?

So was I nearing the front of the train, then? Or did this train have no front?

I tentatively pushed open the door at the end of the car and stepped onto the platform, seeing that I no longer recognized any of the scenery around me. I wasn't sure if I should push open the next door, as it seemed that someone was probably living in there. In the end, I decided to knock, not wanting to be rude.

The giggling stopped. I stood in the chill of the wind blowing between the cars, starting to feel a sense of vertigo at the passing of the track beneath me and grasping the flimsy chain that kept me from falling out. I started to feel that if the door didn't open soon, I would have to push it open and let myself in, because I couldn't stand to remain there on that exposed platform for too much longer.

Then the door opened. The girl who stood before me, a look of complete shock and even fear in her eyes, was at once a total stranger to me and at the same time had a face that had been haunting me for months.

It was Piper McMahon. Beautiful, lost, and tortured Piper McMahon was living on this train. And an awkward glance at her feet and back up revealed that she wasn't wearing very much, but was instead covering herself with some sort of tapestry. She looked like a movie star, as though her hair had been styled to fall over her shoulders just so.

"Baby, who is it?" came a man's voice behind her.

"I don't know," she called over her shoulder. "It's a girl."

I started to wobble, and for one horrific moment, I thought I might actually fall. I grabbed for the chain to my right, but its swinging motion hardly helped to steady me.

"Whoa, whoa," Piper said, tucking the tapestry into itself like a towel after a shower and putting her hand on my shoulder. "Don't fall off now. You just got here." She helped guide me into the car and closed the door behind us.

Inside was a quaint little bedroom, complete with a small kitchenette. Standing in front of the little makeshift stovetop, a large wooden cooking spoon in his hand, was a young man with a beard, wearing an old tattered pair of sweatpants that cut off at his shins. And I almost didn't recognize him until I looked into his eyes, and saw that they hadn't changed a bit in four years.

My brother looked at me, and it took him a moment to process what he was seeing. When he did, the look that came over his handsome new face was probably somewhat akin to my expression when I heard that he had died.

"No," was all he said. His shoulders slumped and he turned away from me, throwing the spoon down on the floor.

"Baby?" Piper asked, her voice tentative, obviously aware that something was very wrong.

Robbie seemed to go a bit crazy then, and all Piper and I could do was stand and watch as he began to kick the wall of the train car with all his might. He kicked and kicked until he managed to splinter the wood by his side. And when he was done, he collapsed down into a heap on the ground. I watched as he buried his head against the wall and began to mutter. For a horrible moment, I wondered if his years on this train had made him completely lose his mind.

"Robbie?" I asked, hearing the crack in my own voice.

He turned and pressed his back against the wall, looking at me and flinching from what I imagine was the splintered wood scraping his back. Then he suddenly laughed.

"Sorry," he said. "That was dramatic, huh?"

Piper laughed a bit, covering her mouth immediately.

"It's just this damn train. It claims another."

Piper offered me a half smile. She reached out her hand, urging me to come and meet her in the middle of the car. "It's okay," she said. "He's better now."

I approached Piper slowly, my eyes on my brother, who had yet to actually say anything to me.

When I reached her by the bed, she put her arm around my shoulder. She had a warmer and more generous energy about her than I had expected, and I understood at once what Brady must have missed about her, aside from her obvious beauty.

Brady. He went home to find Piper. But he wouldn't find her there.

"Sorry," Robbie said, still sitting on the floor. "How rude. Piper, this is my sister, Marina. M, this is Piper. Or do you two already know each other?"

Piper looked at me and shook her head. "No, I don't think so."

I shook my head as well. We had never met.

"Robbie?" I asked again, waiting for him to acknowledge me.

Robbie stared dead-eyed for a moment, still processing that I was there on the train with him, I imagine. And most likely thinking—as I was, of course—that now our parents had lost two children.

He held out his hands to me at last, and it was only a flash before I threw myself down to the floor and into his arms. Before I knew it, I felt Piper next to us, wrapping us both up into what had become a big group hug.

"This is beautiful," she said. "I always wanted a sister."

○ ○ ○

When Robbie and I were very little, our parents took us to explore a coal mine. It was part of some tourist trap on the road to something else, a novelty my father had read about in the back of a magazine. He had always been a scientist at heart, and I suspect he thought it would be one of those fabulously educational pit stops that peppered our childhood. *Children, this is where coal comes from. This is how we power the oven.*

I was probably about six at the time, which would have made Robbie eight. I don't remember much about it, of course—part of the seamless blur of childhood. But I remember how it felt.

It was dark, naturally. Very dark. And the company that led the tours had purposely kept it that way in an apparent effort to recreate the experience of the first miners who had ventured into it. Only a few lamps hanging from chains lit the way down, down, down, into the depths of the place.

People giggled, and people talked. And their voices echoed, and reverberated, and eventually died down, swallowed by the giant darkness around us. And I remember thinking, even then, that they were only talking to cover the void. Because the silence as we went deeper and deeper started to make the skin crawl.

It grew cold, and the air grew still. But we kept going down. I held my father's hand, and he rattled on at first about stalactites and stalagmites and the process of mining coal and converting it to energy. But after a while, even he grew silent.

I stopped to watch some water trickle over the black rock. In the dim light, it was only visible as an occasional flash of yellow,

REBECCA PHELPS

pulsating its way downward. And when I looked up, somehow and in some way, I was alone.

The group had moved on and I hadn't noticed. I guess my father, wrapped up in the experience, playing explorer, had assumed I was still by his side. And my mother, who I'm sure had only taken the trip to humor my father, was obliviously walking, probably swirling in a sea of thoughts.

The silence was deafening. The quiet of it, the hum of nothing, made the eardrums ache. It was a feeling I wouldn't experience again until almost a decade later, following Brady into the boiler room.

Silence creates a void. Silence begs to be filled.

I stood in the dark, feeling the great chill of solitude take over my bones, letting the silence claim me. I was scared, of course. I was terrified. But I was fascinated too. It was the first time I felt the enormity of how very alone we are in the universe. In that darkness, I was suspended, as if floating in space. I held my breath and listened to the absence of sound, aching to run and yet unable to move.

And then I felt my brother's hand. Robbie had been sent back by my father to find me. They must not have been far, just around the next bend, but in the absorbency of the walls, all sound had been wiped out. And yet Robbie had found me, and he led me back.

Robbie always found me. Even in my dreams. Even after he died.

I had been alone in a cave for four years. And now Robbie had come back to me. Any thoughts I had that someday I would come into DW and find him, take him, save him, they vanished now that we were actually together. Because as always, it was the other way around. I was the one who felt saved.

I would not push my brother back through the portal. I would not lose him again. We would find another way, or we would stay here forever. That was the deal.

o o o

Piper McMahon was not much of a cook. Her great addition to the ramen Robbie had prepared was to add a handful of raw walnuts to it.

"Now it has protein," she said.

Robbie smiled, and I could see that he was in love with her. I wondered if he would have loved her in the real world, or if his great affection was more a result of the years he had spent on this train alone before she showed up. But when I saw her laugh, her perfect teeth almost reflexively biting her lower lip, I knew that girls like Piper would always have men falling in love with them, no matter where they were.

"I'm a little confused, Piper," I had to say. "How did you get here? What happened?"

"Oh, it's a crazy story," she began, stirring her ramen. She turned to Robbie. "Isn't it crazy, baby?"

"Mm-hmm."

The "baby" stuff was starting to get under my skin, and I felt like I had to say something. I couldn't stop thinking of everything Brady had done to find her, how heartbroken he was about her disappearing. Had she been here on this train calling my brother "baby" the whole time?

"Because Brady and I went to find you, you know," I said.

Piper put her fork down, and I saw her flinch. "You know Brady?" she asked quietly.

"He's . . . ," I began, hesitating for a moment over the word. "He's my friend." I glanced at Robbie, who didn't seem fazed by the mention of anyone named Brady, and I couldn't help but add, "He really loves you."

She nodded. "How is he?" she asked, sincerely concerned.

"He's worried about you. We went to see the Mystics, Piper. And we went into the portal under the lake."

"Oh God," she said. "I was afraid he might do something like that. Didn't I say he might do that, Robbie?"

"You did," he agreed, biting into an apple. I got the feeling he had heard this story before and wasn't really interested in it.

"Is he back home now?"

"No, Piper," I said, trying to be gentle since she at least seemed to be genuinely worried about him. "He stayed down in the world under the lake. He took the train home from there to find you. Since that's what we heard you had done."

"He's still down there?" she asked, a film of horror covering her face. "Oh God, of course. You have to believe me, I really was going to stay in that dimension. I was going home."

"I believe you."

"I had no idea I'd end up . . . wherever we are. On this train. Not really anywhere, I guess." A new thought jostled her almost out of her seat. "Was Brady okay when you saw him?"

"He's fine. He promised he wouldn't stay more than a couple of days. I'm sure when he didn't find you, he came straight home. He's probably back by now."

"But did he have his shot?"

"We both . . . ," I began, remembering that our vaccine pellets had been removed. "We both got the shot, but then I had a bad reaction to it. So Sage took them out."

Piper sighed, slumping down on the bed. "What if he gets the disease now?"

Robbie, seeing that Piper was upset, finally seemed stirred by this conversation and went to sit next to her on the bed. "He'll be fine," he whispered to her.

"Piper?" I said, growing annoyed with my brother's affection for this girl and his complete ignoring of me. "Can you tell me what happened, please?"

"Well, I guess I need to start from the beginning, huh?" she asked. "Yeah, that's the only way the story makes any sense."

I nodded.

"I hadn't really thought it out, you know. I'm sure Brady told you what I did—that I took my parents out of DW and brought them into our world. I snuck them out in the middle of the night, I couldn't explain to them why. That on another plane they had been in an accident, a horrible accident."

"Were you there when it happened?" I asked.

She nodded. "My dad had taken us camping. *One more time before summer's over*, he had said. He liked to surprise us with things like that. We were driving late at night, way up in the mountains. It was dark and . . ."

Robbie scooched even closer to her, so their thighs were touching. She reached down, almost instinctively, and put her hand on his leg as though it was her own.

"The car came out of nowhere. He crossed over the dividing line, into our lane. I don't know, maybe he was drunk or something. Next thing I knew, our car was flipping over and over. Again and again."

A single tear fell down her cheek. Robbie looked away, like it was too much for him to hear the pain in her voice.

"When it stopped, we were upright again. I had been in the back seat, which hadn't really been crushed. But the front seat . . ."

"You don't have to tell me, Piper. I'm sorry," I said. "I didn't mean to make you live through it again."

But my words slid right over her head like they were made of air.

"My mother always had the most beautiful legs. Like a dancer's. They were crushed. She looked like she was asleep. My father's neck was bent at a weird angle. I crawled out of the window. I didn't have my cell phone. That was one of Dad's rules for camping. I thought I could find a car, call for help."

"Baby . . ." Robbie nestled his nose into her neck, like he was trying to give her his warmth.

"I had made it back up to the road before the car exploded behind me. I had never felt heat like that before. It knocked me over." Piper cleared her throat, trying to breathe away all the horrible memories.

"I'm so sorry, Piper. I can't even imagine."

"I hitched a ride in a station wagon. A mom driving her two kids somewhere, with me sandwiched in between. She didn't ask why I had been crying, why I was so dirty. Guess she figured it was none of her business. I was halfway back to town when I decided what to do."

I nodded for her to continue, my heart breaking for her.

"I realized that no one in town knew they were dead. The police might find the car eventually, but we were in the middle of nowhere. The car might not be found for years. No one else at home knew. What if I kept it that way? If my parents were back at home in the morning, nobody would know the difference."

I looked to Robbie to see how he was taking all this, but he'd clearly heard it before. His eyes were glassy and vague, focused somewhere on the floor.

"I snuck into the school through a back door we had made a key to last year. I went through the portal, and the whole time I was thinking: *What if they're dead there too? What if this doesn't work?* I was really prepared to come home empty-handed. But then I got to our house on the other side, and I found them sleeping peacefully in their beds. I woke them up and told them they had to come with me, that it was an emergency."

"They believed you?" I asked, thinking that in the middle of the night, my parents would have probably just told me to go back to bed and leave them alone.

"No, not at all." She laughed. "At first, they thought I had made a mess in the kitchen or something. They finally agreed to follow me downstairs. Then I told them the problem wasn't at home, it was at the school. After more fighting, I convinced them to walk with me towards the school. My mother was angry at me," she said with a chuckle, but there was a bitter sadness behind it. "And my father was too tired to argue, which is how you know when he's really mad."

Robbie's eyes were still fixed on the floor, though he appeared to be listening in his own way.

"Finally I got them to the school and down into the boiler room. The whole time they kept asking, 'Piper, what are we doing? What is this?' They finally said they wouldn't follow me another step. So I told them about the accident, that in another dimension somewhere they were dead. I told them everything about DW. They didn't believe me, of course, until they were through the door. Nobody ever believes it until they're through the door.

"Once we had crossed over, we walked the few blocks back home in silence. The whole time I kept praying they wouldn't ask any more questions that might make them decide to turn around and go back. Thankfully, they didn't. Maybe they were just too tired. Maybe they thought I was having some teenage drama that they didn't understand. For whatever reason, they let it lie. We all went to bed, and in the morning we acted like it was just another day."

She shook her head to get the tears out of her eyes, and let out a bit of a giggle, which I had begun to realize was a nervous habit.

"And it was," she continued. "It was a new and beautiful day. Until it wasn't."

"What happened?"

"After a few months, things started to shift. Things around me. The trees. The sidewalk."

"They disappeared?" I asked her, remembering what Brady had told me.

"One day the whole house wasn't a house. It was—it's hard to explain. It was like a military barracks or something. There were soldiers in it, sitting around a big table eating breakfast. I screamed at them, 'Get out of my house!' But they just stared at me, and then . . . and then they weren't soldiers. They were my parents. Eating at our table. Staring at me. And it was my house again, just like that."

I took a deep breath and looked out the window for a moment. A field was passing outside, the long grains of wheat blending into a seamless flurry of yellow, zipping by too quickly to take form.

"I knew I had to fix it," Piper concluded. "I had to make it right. And I knew the way to do it was to put them back, of course—to take them back through the portal. But I couldn't bring myself to do it.

"So I went to the Mystics to see if they could help. I liked them. I liked Sage a lot, she was so warm. But they couldn't help me. They told me that my parents had to go back, that I had thrown off the balance of energy between the planes. And that my parents belonged in DW . . . with their own daughter.

"It was the first time I had thought about it. That somewhere there was another version of me, sitting around with no parents. I called my DW parents and told them the truth: I wasn't their real daughter. They had another daughter waiting for them on the other side, and they should go back to her. They shouldn't wait for me. After I hung up, I was going to come home myself, to that empty house."

"Why didn't you?"

"I overheard Sage and John talking about the portal under the lake. About trying to keep me away from it. And of course, like a fly to honey, I had to see for myself." She laughed, shaking her head. "Isn't that right, baby? I'm always getting myself into trouble."

"Always," Robbie agreed, smiling at her with a newfound attention. "It's how you got here," he joked, and they both laughed.

"I had this idea that maybe I could go visit DW sometimes. That my other self and I—maybe we could share those parents. Take turns, maybe. I know it was stupid. I just wasn't ready to say good-bye."

I nodded, and my eyes flitted to Robbie.

"So I went to the lake and found that portal under the water. Isn't it terrible under there? So depressing, all those Russians.

The folks at Sage's diner told me I had to go back through the lake immediately. And I was going to. But the idea—the idea that our town was awful, like that place. That we were suffering. I don't know, I just had to see. Like, maybe there was something I could do. Maybe that was the reason for the whole trip, even. I never felt like I had a purpose before. Suddenly I did—what if I could help people? What if I could save our whole town somehow?"

Robbie sat and listened, his eyes still haunted with a distance that kept him somewhere far away from me.

"Okay," I said. "So how did you end up on this train with Robbie?"

"I went to the station in the world with the Russians," she began, "like I said I would. Sage had loaned me some money for a ticket. A train came. And when the door opened, I handed the ticket to the conductor and got on."

"And?" I asked. "Was it the wrong train?"

She smiled and shrugged. "It was *this* train. Once I was on, the conductor was nowhere to be found. I walked through the cars until I reached the front. And that's when I met your brother."

My mind was spinning. "You just got on?"

"Yes," she said. "Your brother was sitting right here, where I am now, working on some little thing." She smiled, like she was telling an adorable story about a toddler she used to babysit for. She continued to talk about him like he wasn't even there, which he might as well not have been. He had tuned us out completely and was staring out the window. "He had a bunch of wires laid out in front of him. You took them out of the lamps, didn't you, baby? And he was connecting them together with a bunch of circuits from the train engine. Like he was making a little computer or something."

"A motherboard," I said. "Is that it, Robbie?" I thought of the long hours we'd spent helping our father in his workshop.

"He's always doing stuff like that," she said fondly. "Has he always been so smart?"

I stood up and looked out the window at the passing landscape, which was now a deeply wooded area, growing dark as the long day had finally come to a close. If what Piper was saying was true, it meant getting hit wasn't the only way onto this train. And so maybe it wasn't the only way off it either.

"It was a coincidence," Robbie finally said.

"What's that?" I asked.

"This train, the one we're on, it goes between all the dimensions and stops for a bit wherever it happens to be. It doesn't stay long. Piper just happened to be in the wrong station at the wrong time."

"It was the right station," Piper corrected him, a warm crinkle forming on the side of her eyes as she smiled at him. "At the right time."

"So the train does stop," I realized out loud.

"Yes," she said. "But we never know when, and we never know for how long. So we're always afraid to go too far. We don't want to get stranded somewhere. That's why we have such a random assortment of food," she said with a chuckle. "We grab whatever is nearby, or in the station where we've stopped, and then jump back on."

"And the conductor?" I asked. "Can you ask him where we're going?"

"Can I tell you something scary?" she asked, and I had to laugh. As though this whole thing didn't already count as "something scary."

"Yes."

"I don't think there is a conductor," she told me. "We never see him, except when the train is about to leave the stations. He peeks out his head and shouts, 'All aboard,' and when we get back on, he's just gone. It's like he's a ghost or something."

I thought about this, trying to figure out where this train fit into the intersecting mesh of planes and dimensions that Sage had told me about. And trying to figure out who the conductor in charge of it might be.

o o o

That night, I caught Robbie up on everything that had happened since he'd left, including the fact that Mom had disappeared and Dad was in some sort of detainment center. I didn't want to worry him, but I didn't want to lie to him either.

After a while, he said he was too tired to keep talking. Piper insisted on giving me their bed, and went next door to share the couch with Robbie.

The night passed slowly, trickling by as the chugging sound of the train kept a steady beat, both in and out of my dreams. I woke up several times to look through the rear window into the other car, just to make sure Robbie was still there.

At last, I fell into a deep sleep, making a cocoon out of the sheets like I used to do at home. I was on another planet when a sound woke me—or rather, the absence of sound. It took me a minute to realize what was wrong, and then finally it occurred to me. The train had stopped.

I whipped my head out from under the blankets to find that the sun had come up. Birds were singing in a nearby tree. Piper and Robbie came back into the car before I even had a chance to take stock of what was outside the windows.

"It's happening," Piper said.

"Do you want to wait here?" Robbie asked me. "We might not have much time."

"What's happening? Where are we?" I asked, still rubbing sleep out of my eyes.

"We're at a station," Robbie explained. "We have to try to grab some food while we can."

"It's like I told you," Piper added, clearly excited.

I nodded, everything coming back to me now that I was really awake. "I'm coming," I said, quickly pulling on my shoes. There was no way I was staying on this train, knowing that there was a chance Robbie might not come back in time.

We walked through the door and out onto the little metal platforms that divided the cars, and Robbie unhooked the chain that dangled along the side so we could hop off.

"Won't it look suspicious?" I asked. "If we hop off the train like this?"

"Didn't I tell you?" Piper asked, jumping off after Robbie and then waiting for me to do the same. "They usually can't see us."

"How do you think we take the food?" Robbie asked, turning to me with a comforting smile. It was the old smile that I remembered, probably the first time he had really looked like himself to me. "Don't worry, M. Nothing bad will happen."

I nodded, believing him as I always had, and followed them into the station.

Sure enough, nobody seemed to notice we were there. We walked right in, past a crowd of bustling passengers, the signs overhead listing dozens of different destinations. I didn't recognize any of them, except for San Francisco and Alberta.

We walked over to the food kiosks, of which there were several, and I tried to follow Piper and Robbie's lead of acting casual while eyeing the potential assortments of fruit, snack bars, and gum offered up in baskets in front of the ordering counters. Of course, the act didn't really seem necessary, as even more people were walking by us without seeming to see us. But I could see them, and what I noticed most of all made me do a double take.

They were all dressed like it was the '50s, just like under the lake portal. So was this another plane like that one had been, where some sort of retro style was in vogue? Or was it actually the '50s here? Or maybe . . . was it possible that this was the same plane as the one under the lake? And if so, could we get home from here?

A rush of adrenaline filled my veins. Could it be that simple? But before I suggested it, I had to be sure it was the same place.

I tried to listen to the conversations of passersby, to see if they were speaking Russian. I heard several languages being spoken, but mostly English. In that way, it seemed like any train station in the country, and I couldn't be sure. I needed to find a newspaper. Maybe something in it could tip me off as to where we were.

"So I'll meet you right back here," Robbie said to Piper. "Keep her close, okay?"

"Of course, baby," Piper said, giving him a little kiss. "Come on," she said to me.

"Where are we going?"

"To use the facilities," she answered, and I must have looked confused, wondering if that was code for something. "The little girls' room," she explained, motioning to a nearby sign hanging over a door that said WOMEN.

In the restroom, I did hear two women speaking Russian, but then they switched to English when I came out of the stall to wash my hands. Was that a coincidence? Or, despite what Piper had said, could they see me?

Piper and I made our way back to the food kiosks, and I was relieved to see that Robbie was already there. Robbie and Piper stood with their backs to the food baskets, and subtly shifted some things into their pockets without even looking behind them to see what they were grabbing. I did the same.

"Okay, we better get back," Robbie said, and then he turned to me. "The stops usually only last about fifteen minutes."

My voice caught in my throat. I still wasn't sure this was the right dimension, and I didn't want to suggest staying if it meant we'd be trapped in the wrong place.

I glanced quickly left and right for a newspaper, and found one in a stack by one of the food vendors. I grabbed it off the top, but I didn't have a chance to read it as Piper was pulling my hand, all but dragging me behind her. I kept it pressed close to me as we wove through the passing crowds.

We made it back to the area outside the station, and found that at least six trains were pulled up to the various platforms, with others on their way in and out. I had no idea, of course, what our train looked like, having never seen the outside of it. And for a moment, with Robbie and Piper both scanning the possible trains and looking quite anxious as they did so, I began to panic that the train had left without us.

Maybe that was for the best. I cleared my throat before I

spoke. "Robbie," I began, "I think this might be the dimension under the lake."

"What's that?" Robbie asked, his eyes still scanning past various trains that were pulling in and out of the station as if in a choreographed dance.

"I said I think maybe we should stay—"

"There it is!" Robbie said, pointing, and he wasn't able to hide the relief in his voice. Piper sighed, her breath catching in her throat. I wondered how often this happened.

Robbie and Piper hadn't heard me. Instead, Piper continued to drag me by the hand across two empty platforms to a very shiny old-fashioned train. It didn't seem possible to me that this was the right one. On the outside, it looked as clean and polished as could be. I thought of the dilapidated library car and the abandoned dining car I had passed through, and I realized that this must have been what the train originally looked like. It had been gorgeous once.

Robbie and Piper both stood by the doors, as if waiting for them to open.

"Come on," Robbie whispered under his breath. Piper took his hand.

My hands now free, I began furiously flipping through the newspaper pages, trying to find any evidence as to which dimension we were in. But it seemed hopeless. The stories were about people I didn't know, sporting events with stars I'd never heard of, fashion pages full of people doing their best imitation of Elizabeth Taylor.

Should I suggest that we stay? What if I was wrong?

But then the doors opened. And out popped the head of a man in a faded red cap, wearing a jacket that almost looked like something from an old Confederate Army costume I had seen in textbooks when we'd studied the Civil War.

He looked worn and skeletal, his sharp cheekbones protruding beneath tired, somewhat haunted eyes. He didn't even seem human, but almost like a CGI character in a movie. I was shocked when he looked right at me, seeing through me, it seemed, with an accusatory glare that made me shiver as I stood there.

I dropped the newspaper, my hands losing all control at the chill that ran through me from the conductor's glare. His ageless eyes trailed from my head down to my feet.

"Your paper, miss."

I swallowed the fear down into my throat. "Thank you," I whispered, leaning down to pick it up.

"Do you have your tickets?"

"You have mine already," Piper told him politely.

Robbie averted his eyes, looking down at his shoes. "I'll pay on the train," he said.

The conductor nodded, and stepped back to allow us to enter. Robbie took both of our hands and we all boarded the train together. My mind had gone blank by that point.

Once we were aboard, as Piper had promised, the train reverted to its former self. We were in the lounge car, where the books were scattered out across the couch. And the train began to lurch out of the station.

I looked down at the now-jumbled newspaper I held under my arm, the front page of the National section now on top. And the headline, in bold text, proclaimed, "New Minister of Treasury Appointed." And underneath that, shaking hands with a blond man in a sharp military suit, was my mother—looking as she had in the hotel under the lake portal.

"Robbie," I said, an urgency now making my voice loud and vivid. "It's the world under the lake! Get off the train. We have to get off the train."

"We can't."

"But we can get home from here," I insisted.

"No, Marina, we can't," said Piper, her voice resigned and tender. She held my arm tightly as the train rumbled beneath our feet.

I looked desperately from her eyes to his, and then back again. They both had the same pitying but firm expression. Piper looked at Robbie, as if trying to decide whether to say what she was thinking.

Then his eyes fell down to the newspaper in my hands, to our mother's picture, clear as day, staring back at him. But his stone face didn't even flinch at the sight.

"You've both been here before," I realized as the train began to pull away from the station. My shoulders slumped in despair. "And why can't we stay?" I asked, though I dreaded the answer.

"Because," Robbie explained, looking to Piper again for courage. "We're not really here."

CHAPTER 18

"What do you mean, we're not really here?" I asked once we'd made it back to the little bedroom car.

Once again, Robbie glanced at Piper before he spoke, and she offered him a loving smile. It scared me how much he needed her. How lost he was without her.

"The train portal isn't like the others," Piper finally answered me. "You don't take over your other self. You can't interact with people. Like I said, most of them can't even see you. It's like you're just . . ."

"A ghost," Robbie finished her thought. An eerie silence fell between us all, and I could feel the weight of Robbie's pain in every breath that escaped his lips, in the deep, haunted look that had taken over his beautiful brown eyes—the same shade as our mother's.

"You've tried to stay somewhere before?" I prodded.

"When I was first on the train," he nodded. "The first time it stopped. I didn't know where I was. I just knew I had to get off the damn train."

I bit my lip, not wanting to interrupt. I could see him as clear as day. Fourteen years old, skinny and alone. Scared to death. In some strange train station somewhere. "What happened, Robbie?"

"I stood on the platform, watching the train pull out of the station. I was just gonna let it go."

Piper scooted closer to him on the bed, placing a careful hand on his knee, which he didn't seem to notice.

"The walls started melting. The people..." His voice trailed off for a moment, not betraying a hint of emotion. "It was like they were painted there, and the paint was dripping. It was like the hands that hold the world up around you had decided to let it all drop."

"My God," I whispered.

"I ran for the train," Robbie explained. "And I hopped back on. The conductor was there. It was the first time I saw him. He wasn't there when I first got hit. And he asked me for my ticket, like he has every time since."

"I'm gonna make some coffee," Piper declared, apropos of nothing. I couldn't tell if her cheeriness was real, or if it was her way of coping with stress. Either way, it made her seem impossible to know, like a Barbie doll on happy pills.

"Thanks, baby," Robbie called to her, a smile finally cracking across his lips.

"And then?" I asked, trying to get Robbie focused back on his story.

"That's it," Robbie said. "I never tried it again. I assume the same thing would happen."

I nodded. It made sense, of course, given what Sage had told me. The train connects all the planes that ever existed. So when the train pulled into a station, it was like it was visiting a certain plane. But then when it pulled out, that plane disappeared. Or at least, it disappeared as far as the train and its reluctant inhabitants were concerned.

"But you've seen Mom before," I realized aloud, nodding to the newspaper, which had made its way to the floor.

"Yeah, I've been to that station a few times," he conceded. "It's always the same. Everyone dressed like it's an old movie or something. And Mom is always in the paper for something different."

"Piper?" I looked up to her as she was making the coffee. "Is that the same station where you got on?"

"No." She sighed, looking like she was growing tired of this conversation. Or maybe she just didn't like how it was affecting Robbie. "Different station, same dimension."

"But why?" I couldn't help but wonder out loud. "There are billions of dimensions. Why does the train keep getting sucked back to that one? It's like it has some sort of pull or something . . ."

"I don't know." My brother shrugged. "We started showing up there a lot after Piper came. To be honest, I'm sick of trying to figure out how any of this works."

"But maybe Piper connects you to it somehow since it's where she got on—"

"Time for your lesson, baby," Piper said, returning with three cups of coffee and handing me one. "Pick a subject."

Robbie got up and started rifling through some of the books that they kept by the bed. I must have looked confused when he glanced up and caught my eye.

"Piper teaches me something new every day," he said, smiling at her like she was the damn Mona Lisa.

"You can't go through life with an eighth-grade education," she said to me, clearly waiting for me to agree.

But this isn't life, I thought to myself as he continued to scan the books.

I didn't say it out loud. I just watched Robbie from a slight distance, as though he was a painting to be examined. I was still trying to gauge how four years on this train had affected my brother. He'd grown strangely quiet, like he had left the room but his body remained. Robbie had always been melancholy at times, so in some ways this gloomy air was a welcome reminder that I truly had him back.

But he never seemed to shake it off anymore.

I pictured myself on this train. All alone, for years, waiting for an end to a nightmare that might never come. And I knew that, had it been me, I wouldn't have been strong enough. I would have gone crazy long ago.

This is no life, I repeated to myself. *I have to get him out of here.*

"Mmm, how about graphing?" Robbie asked, handing her a math textbook that looked like it was about forty years old.

"Oh, wow," Piper said. "Okay, let's see what I remember. Not my best subject." She turned to me then. "Do you know a lot about graphing?"

"Make an x and a y line," I stated, my mind already racing to another place, trying to connect the dots of the thoughts that were swirling around in my head. "And once you solve for where x and y intersect," I continued, following my brother's gaze out the window, "then you can chart the location."

Piper nodded. "Yeah, that's it." She opened the book and

reached into a tin cup on the windowsill for some pencils. "So let's get started."

"Excuse me," I said, standing with no real idea where I wanted to go. "I'm gonna just . . . I'm gonna lie down." I headed next door into the lounge car, and once alone, I plopped myself down on the sofa. My eyes scanned over the books, with their obscure titles and worn print. Some of them must have been from the original train library, maybe one hundred years old. Someone bought those books once. And that someone was no longer here.

There was a way off this train. I knew it—x and y always intersected somewhere. You just had to chart the right point. And find a way to get there. My mind kept returning to the idea that Piper's presence was somehow luring the train back to the dimension where she had boarded. Was it possible that the conductor was trying to take her back to where she had come from, as if to say, "You can stay here, it's where you belong"? So then why wasn't the same happening for the place where my brother and I had boarded?

Was it because we had never really "boarded" at all? We'd been hit.

Robbie never saw the conductor until the first time the train stopped. And so he wasn't a real passenger. Passengers have to be admitted. Passengers have to buy tickets. "Wait a second," I said to no one. "Wait a second."

I got up and crossed the little platform between cars, coming back into the bedroom car and closing the door behind me. "You've never bought a ticket," I declared, looking at Robbie.

He shrugged. "I don't have any money."

"Of course the train won't take you where you want to go. You have to buy a ticket first."

"Do you have any money?" asked Robbie.

I bowed my head, thinking of the time I had stolen the hundred-dollar bill from the cash register for Brady. But something told me that the kind of tickets they sold in the stations weren't what we needed. This wasn't a normal train, and it didn't need normal currency.

I checked my pockets, and of course all I found there was Kieren's flattened penny.

"Not really."

That's when the train did something odd. It sped up, taking the next curve at such velocity that the whole car tilted to the side and for a moment I thought we might tip over. I grabbed the wall, bracing myself, but we made the turn and straightened up again.

Then we entered a tunnel and everything grew very dark. Only intermittent flashes of light speared their way into the car through the windows as we would occasionally pass openings in the tunnel, only to be plunged into the darkness again.

"What's happening?" Piper asked, and for the first time, I actually heard fear in her voice.

"I don't know," Robbie said.

We all stood frozen in our spots, not sure what we were supposed to do. Something was happening, but clearly none of us knew what.

The train continued to chug along, its rhythms steadily increasing and the tunnel seeming to never end.

And then we heard the footsteps. At first, I thought it was more banging from the train itself as it shot its way through the tunnel, but then the *pat-pat*, *pat-pat* of heavy boots hitting the wood planks of the floors became undeniable.

Someone was coming this way, and getting closer.

I moved towards the bed, away from the lounge car where the footsteps were growing louder. And finally, with nowhere left to go, I sat next to my brother, feeling his hand on my shoulder. My heart was pounding out of my chest as the door to the car opened.

The conductor stood there, staring down at us with his skeletal eyes and a face completely devoid of emotion. An eternity seemed to pass while we all sat there, and I could hear the breath catching in Piper's throat. Out of the corner of my eye, I saw her bury her head in Robbie's arm. I felt like the Angel of Death had come to claim us, but I knew I had to stay strong.

"Tickets, please," was all he said.

Robbie gulped in a deep breath, and I looked to him to judge by his reaction if this had ever happened before. The answer, clearly, was no.

"We don't have any . . . ," he began.

"Here," I said, standing and thrusting out my hand. "Here you go." I held out Kieren's penny, and the conductor's eyes fell to meet it.

He took another step towards me, and I wasn't sure if my legs would be able to hold me up. But my knees stayed locked, and I held my ground.

The conductor reached out one of his bony hands, and I could see the coin shaking in my palm at the sight of his long stick-like fingers touching mine.

He took the penny out of my hand and put it in his pocket.

"Where do you want to go?"

I looked back at Robbie and Piper, sitting together on the bed, their eyes glued on me and clearly having no idea what was happening.

"Home," I said. "Take us home."

The conductor continued to stare at me for a moment, his deeply set eyes almost hollow in their emptiness.

And then he nodded, and he left the car. A moment passed in which none of us spoke.

But after that moment, the train slowed down, and it left the tunnel, shedding a burst of light into the car.

o o o

The train pulled through many more stations that day, and it would slow down as it passed through, but it didn't stop. I began to realize, after a while, that most of the places we pulled through were indistinguishable from each other. Most planes, I suspected, weren't really that different from one another. People went to work, they took their kids to school. College kids with large backpacks would wait together in clumps, off on some summer camping trip or on their way to study abroad somewhere.

Sometimes we would pass through stations where the fashions were different, like in the strange 1950s-inspired world where my mother was, apparently, some sort of political figure who ran a fancy hotel.

We passed through a place where half the women were wearing corsets outside their clothes, and another where the men all had their heads shaved, while the women had very long hair that they seemed not to have cut in years.

We passed through an empty station. Not even an alley cat was waiting for the train there, and I wondered if the station was closed, or something horrible had happened to all the people.

And finally, after the long day and another night had passed, the train chugged its way onto a small platform with a little run-down station next to it, covered almost completely in ivy.

None of us recognized it at first, and probably wouldn't have thought much of it had the train not pulled to a stop.

I looked at Robbie, whose blank eyes were staring out the window like a child seeing a distant uncle that he had no memory of and didn't want to hug. Piper seemed distracted, reading something in a large book, and barely even looked up.

"Guys," I said, standing to get a better look and finally recognizing small things, like the way the awning that hung overhead had a small crack in it, and the way the shadows fell on the stairs leading to the platform. "I think we're here."

We all stood and looked out together, Robbie beginning to shake his head. "No, this can't be it."

"It *is* it," I insisted. "Can't you tell?"

"It's too small," he almost muttered, and I could see him regressing back into himself, becoming once again the child he had been when the accident happened.

"Robbie, it's okay," I told him, trying to catch his eyes. "We're home." But he didn't budge. I looked to Piper, who had finally put down the book. "Help me convince him." She took a better look at the station, and was clearly seeing what I had.

"I think she's right, baby. I think we should get off and look around."

"I'll wait here," he said, planting himself down on the bed. "You girls go."

I sat next to him again, trying to face him head-on so that he'd have to look at me. "Robbie," I began. "Are you afraid?"

He didn't move a muscle at first, his eyes landing somewhere in the space between us. But then he nodded.

"What are you afraid of?"

He shrugged. "It'll disappear when the train leaves. Just like the others."

I nodded, understanding how traumatized he must have been from his years on this train, from watching everything that seemed real melt away. But I just had a feeling in my gut. Those other dimensions disappeared because we weren't supposed to be there. But that wouldn't happen now that we were home.

I had to believe it was true.

"I won't disappear," I promised him. And I reached out a hand for Piper, who joined us. "And neither will Piper."

"That's right," she insisted, seeming to get more excited about the idea of finally being home. "Robbie, we have to at least look. What if she's right?" Piper was already standing as she said this, combing her fingers through her hair.

Robbie watched her, and the sadness that came over his face revealed everything. He was afraid he'd lose her here. That somehow she'd go back to Brady now that she could. But I knew that it was possible Brady wasn't even back yet. And I knew that, in any event, it was time to go.

"Dad is here," I reminded him, trying to reel him back in to the positive, to convince him that this wasn't an illusion. "Robbie, come with me. Let's go see Dad."

Robbie finally looked back at me, and the slight nod of his head was all the encouragement I needed to know that he was finally ready to go. He stood next to me, and I took his hand.

When we first stepped off the train and onto the platform— the three of us, with our eyes blinking at the light of day—I thought for a second that maybe Robbie was right and that this wasn't our home. It really did look so different, not just because of the ivy once again covering the building or the extra cracks in the pavement.

Even though I had been here quite recently, it was like I was finally seeing it for what it really was. The station was small, like a little hutch almost. And it took a full moment for it to really sink in that it was the exact same size it had always been. We were just bigger now. Everything that had seemed so giant growing up in this town was finally reduced to its true scale.

We started to walk down the stairs, into the deserted parking lot.

Robbie was nervous, and I felt his hand shaking in mine and his legs falter more than once. We made it all the way to the edge of the parking lot before he stopped walking and started shaking his head.

"No, no, no, no, back on the train, back on the train."

"It's okay, Robbie. Let's keep walking," I pleaded.

"It really is okay, baby. We're home. Can't you see it?"

"Back on the train," he muttered, sitting down on a nearby curb. "It's all going to melt. It's all going to melt."

"It won't melt, Robbie. Look!" I all but shouted. I sat down next to him and started pointing out things we could see across the street. "Look, there's the pharmacy. And the diner. Do you see it?"

He looked up, but his expression didn't change.

"And the stoplight that's always broken. Robbie, are you looking?"

His eyes bulged out and glazed with tears, but I could tell he didn't really believe me yet.

Piper looked scared and frustrated. She kept taking deep breaths. "I want to go home," she finally said.

"Come here," I insisted, pulling Robbie up and crossing the empty street, all but dragging him behind me. Piper ran to catch us.

We made it to the pharmacy, and I searched the wall for the place where the sign had been, although someone had clearly tried to paint over it again since we'd left. Finally, though, I found it.

"There!" I said, pointing to the wall. The letters were more faint than ever, but they were there. DANCE HALL GIRLS. The *D* in DANCE was very clear, and I gestured for Robbie to lean in even closer.

It wasn't like in DW, where the colors had been too bright, where everything was Technicolor. It was real and it was right. We were home.

"Nothing is melting, Robbie," I said, desperately trying to see that flash of recognition in his eyes, that comfort of belief. "It's real. It's all real." I grabbed his hand and made him touch the brick wall.

Finally he turned his head to his new girlfriend, and I realized that my word was not going to be enough.

"Piper?" he asked her. She was crying, and she simply nodded her head. He threw himself into her arms, letting her hold him. And as she whispered into his ear something that I couldn't hear, I touched the wall myself, letting its hard, scratchy surface tickle my fingertips.

We were home. Thank God. We were home.

That's when we heard the first siren.

It was a fire truck, and we all stood back to watch it go by. The man in the driver's seat was wearing a strange uniform.

The truck passed, leaving us all still standing on the deserted sidewalk. I knew that we were home, but I would feel more comfortable if some people were around—anyone dressed in normal clothing to seal the fact in my mind.

"Where is everyone?" Piper asked, echoing my thoughts.

I shook my head at first, muttering to myself. "It's too early for the curfew."

"What curfew?" Robbie asked.

I hesitated for a moment, not wanting to upset him when he was already so uneasy. But I also knew that there was no way to keep things from him at this point.

"Some things have changed."

Piper, still holding Robbie's hand, looked frustrated. "What things?"

We all turned as our train tooted its last puff of resistance before chugging away from us, and it was too late to get back on now even if we wanted to.

"Come on," I told them. "I'll show you."

o o o

It took about twenty minutes to walk to the high school, and nobody said much along the way. We were too busy looking around our town, letting the sunlight stream down through familiar leaves and imprint its warmth on our faces. Even the air smelled right, and for a moment I thought maybe I should just take Robbie home so we could both sleep in our own beds.

But then I remembered there would be nobody there to greet us.

About half a block from the high school, I realized things had gotten worse, because that was when we finally started to see people. Lots of people. And they were all barefoot.

The whole town, it seemed, was lined up in front of the school, which still took the form of the military building it had been when Kieren had shown it to me. The eerie familiarity of this scene was so chilling that for a moment I couldn't walk any farther. Robbie and Piper, mouths agape with no context to understand what they were seeing, stopped next to me. People of all ages waited in long lines at various kiosks.

It was exactly the same as the underwater world. I began to doubt that we were really home. Had I made a huge mistake? And had I trapped Robbie and Piper here with my error?

"Marina?" I heard a familiar voice cry, and I spun to see Christy waiting in one of the lines, wearing the same plain jeans and T-shirt as everyone else, and also barefoot.

Every muscle in my body relaxed a bit with relief. "Oh, thank God," I said, throwing my arms around her. "Are you real?"

"Of course I'm real," she said, looking confused. "But I thought . . . they said you fell in front of the train. That Kieren . . ."

"Where's Kieren?"

She didn't say anything at first, and my heart sank. Did he do something crazy after I left?

"They questioned him for hours," Christy said, lowering her voice so others couldn't hear. "They thought he pushed you too. Now he never leaves his house."

"M," Robbie said, his voice oddly steady and deep, a tone that I hadn't heard from him much. "What is she talking about?"

"Nothing," I insisted. "Nobody pushed me."

"You were with Kieren?" he asked, his throat choking out the name.

"It wasn't like that," I said. "You don't understand, Robbie. It's okay."

"Robbie?" Christy asked, and her eyes finally took in the two people standing next to me. She didn't know what Robbie looked like, of course—only his name—so her reaction to seeing him was merely confusion. But when her eyes fell on Piper, the beautiful face that had haunted us from hundreds of flyers for months, and then took in the fact that Robbie and Piper were together, she seemed to do the math.

She looked back to me, and very quietly whispered, "Marina? Is this your brother?"

I nodded and looked around, following her lead to make sure no one was listening to us. "Christy, what is going on here?"

She shrugged. "The president is visiting or something. So they need to make sure we're all clean."

"Clean?"

"Of the disease," she answered, her eyes on the front of the line. "The MPs came around a week ago and told us we had to turn in our shoes. They said the disease starts on the toes, and they need to be able to see them."

"Christy," I said, shaking my head to keep my thoughts clear, "when you say 'the president,' which one do you mean?"

She looked at me like I was insane, and I might very well have been. "Koenig." She laughed. "Who do you think I mean?"

Dear God, I almost said out loud. *The planes have merged.*

Just then, a large screen above the parking lot beeped a couple of times, then burst to life. On it, a woman appeared, standing in front of an exotic jungle, a smile plastered on her face. She began to speak. It took me a moment to realize why she seemed so odd: she wasn't real. Something about the eyes gave it away. She

REBECCA PHELPS

was computer generated. She talked about cleanliness, about protecting our fellow citizens.

"Let's show President Koenig our best selves, shall we? To make a better future, we all must do our part . . . today."

I felt a tiny explosion inside my gut. The world seemed to be spinning out of control. I was so sure using Kieren's penny would work, that the train would take us back home. But somehow it had taken us to this hybrid dimension instead.

Why did the worlds cross? And when?

"C-Christy," I stuttered. "When did you last see me?"

She looked at me, confused.

"When did we last talk? I mean, you and me?"

She thought about it for a second, shuffling up in the line a bit. "Well, you texted me from Portland. But I don't think I've seen you since the graduation ceremony . . . so, four months ago."

The words sank slowly into my mind. So this was the real Christy. But *four months* ago? Is that how long I was on that train?

I didn't have much time to figure it out, because I now saw what we were in line for—a nurse in a traditional 1950s outfit was dispensing shots into people's arms.

I pushed my brother and Piper back a bit. "Come on," I whispered to Christy. "Don't do this, come with us."

"I can't," she said, turning back. "I've already got my number. If I sneak out of line, they'll know." In her hand, she was holding a small yellow card with a number printed on it.

"I'm cold," Piper said, starting to shuffle her feet. "Can we go home? I want to go home."

"We're going," I assured her.

I leaned in to Christy to say one more thing. "Can you text

Kieren and tell him I'm okay? That he should meet me at the pyramid house tonight."

"No," Robbie interjected. "Not him."

"We need him, Robbie. Trust me." I turned back to Christy.

"I'll tell him," Christy whispered. "But he won't be able to get out after curfew."

"Please," I begged again. "Tell him to find a way."

Christy nodded reluctantly. We had reached the front of the line, and I knew we should walk away. But I needed to ask. "Hey, you haven't seen that guy Brady around, have you?"

"No," she said, distracted, as it was almost her turn. When she saw the worry in my face, however, she offered a weak smile. "But that doesn't mean anything. I never saw him before except at school. And he graduated, right?"

"Right," I agreed.

As Christy offered her number card to the nurse, Robbie and Piper and I snuck away. We walked in unison, silently praying not to get stopped, out of the parking lot and down the street, as far away from that hellish place as our feet could take us.

"Now what do we do?" Robbie asked me.

I smiled at my brother. "Now we see Dad."

CHAPTER 19

The detention center looked more like a power station than a prison. Piper waited in the lobby, awkwardly trying to make a bed out of the molded plastic chairs. We had offered to take her to her house, but upon remembering that she would find it as empty as ours, she was reluctant to leave our side.

My hand felt clammy as I reached for Robbie's, but his was cold. I couldn't read his expression. Only a slowness in his gait, a halting in his breath, revealed the tension he felt. We were being ushered into a small beige-colored room, devoid of any furnishings save two chairs facing a table, with a third on the other side.

Robbie and I stood together, too nervous to sit, while the guard who had escorted us in retreated to a corner and stood at attention, his eyes distant. I noticed he was wearing the same uniform as the guards at the high school. I swallowed hard, trying to keep the well of emotions from overflowing.

Finally the door opened, and my father walked through. He was wearing dark pants and a dark blue shirt, which were not his own. His hands were free, but I realized he was a prisoner here. He walked slowly, like someone who had been broken down somehow. But when he looked up and saw Robbie, his eyes all but exploded out of his head.

And then something happened that I wasn't expecting. I thought Dad would scream or flail, or maybe even deny that it was really Robbie standing in front of him. After all, he'd had no preparation for this moment.

But Dad didn't do any of those things. Instead he turned white, and then red, and finally, with eyes rimmed with tears, he simply mumbled to himself in the faintest voice, "She was right."

"Dad?" Robbie asked. Or maybe it was more of a begging. A begging to be believed, accepted, and loved still.

"She was right," Dad repeated, more to himself than to us. "I should have believed her."

Then Dad ran to Robbie and held him. The guard in the corner shuffled a bit; there wasn't supposed to be any contact. But even he seemed to sense that he should let them be.

The tears fell hot and heavy down my cheeks, burning their way past my chin and falling freely until they landed with tiny thuds on my shoes. I wiped my face and felt the wetness coat my fingers.

Robbie was taller than Dad now, but he fell into him like a baby nonetheless. When they separated, a smile cracked over Robbie's face that lightened the room and seemed to surround us, temporarily at least, with warmth.

REBECCA PHELPS

Nobody spoke for a moment.

"Are you okay?" Dad finally asked. "Are you whole? Are you hurt?"

"I'm okay, Dad," Robbie said, keeping his voice steady and his head straight.

"You're so tall. You look . . ." Dad's voice cracked, but he pulled it back together. "You look like your mother."

I stood next to Robbie, placing a gentle hand on his back. Dad leaned in and embraced me as well. "I knew you'd find a way back to me, kiddo. I just never believed you'd really find your brother."

"I'm sorry I scared you, Dad," I whispered in his ear, but he only shook his head and smiled.

The guard cleared his throat, and we all shuffled to the chairs.

"They're not going to keep me here much longer," Dad said. "They're transferring me. There will be a trial, but I don't think . . . I don't think I'm going to win. They think I did something to your mother."

"Dad, we're going to fix this," I promised him. "We'll figure it out. We'll put everything back the way it was."

"The way it was when?" my dad asked, looking at Robbie. "Before she went missing? No, Robbie is back now. Let's let it lie."

"You don't know what it's like out there, Dad. What's been happening."

"Honey, I know you mean well," Dad said, cutting me off. "But there was a reason your mother left. We didn't want you to know, but I guess you did. We weren't happy. Your mother—she was never the same after."

"But Dad, this isn't just about Mom anymore."

I stopped myself before I could say anything else. Maybe it was for the best that Dad didn't know what was happening outside, how the world was changing. There was nothing he could do about it from in here anyway.

But gauging his reaction to seeing Robbie led me to realize something new about my father. I leaned in close so the guard couldn't hear us. "You don't seem too surprised that Robbie is alive," I continued. "Did Mom tell you, Dad? About DW? Is that what you meant by 'she was right'?"

"No," he insisted. "All I know . . ."

He trailed off, seeming to weigh how much to reveal.

"Dad?"

"When Robbie . . . was hit . . . your mother said she should go get him. And I asked her what she was talking about. She wouldn't tell me. But then later she said that if she ever disappeared, if anything happened to her, that I should know she was okay. That I shouldn't try to find her."

"When did she say this?"

"Years ago, right after the accident. I thought she was just rambling. A depressed woman, in shock." Dad buried his head in his hands. As brilliant as he was, I knew none of this made any sense to him.

So my mother had been planning this trip for a while, apparently. And she told my father that she'd be somewhere safe. That he shouldn't go look for her.

But where? Where would she go?

And did her leaving cause the world beneath the lake to penetrate our own?

"And you really didn't know about the portals beneath the school?"

Dad sighed heavily, looking quite tired and worn down. "No," he whispered. "I mean, you live in this town long enough, you hear rumors. But no, I never believed them. I asked your mother once if they were true, since she'd gone to high school here. She just laughed. Said it was 'kids playing games.' I felt like a fool for even asking."

"Ten minutes," the guard announced from the corner of the room. There was so much more to say, but there was no way to fit it in.

"You're going to get out of here soon, Dad," I said.

"Don't get in trouble, please," my father pleaded. "Just stay together, you two. You have each other again."

I looked at Robbie. "Yes, we do. But we're not done, not until we're all together."

Robbie dipped his head for a moment, and my father kissed it. "My boy," Dad whispered. "My sweet boy."

o o o

Later that night, we didn't even make it to the perimeter of Money Row or to the street that held the pyramid house before we realized that something was wrong. There was too much commotion, too many cars going back and forth, which would have been odd even if there hadn't been a curfew in place keeping most people confined to their homes after dark.

Music was playing from somewhere, upbeat old songs. The people zipping by our bikes in their sedans and SUVs were all dressed up, completely oblivious to us. But still, we pulled over so we wouldn't be spotted.

"What's going on?" Robbie asked me. "Who are all these people?"

"I have no idea," I told him. "Last time I was here, the whole neighborhood was abandoned, and the pyramid house was empty. That's why they had the meetings there."

"Who did?"

I hesitated for a moment. "Kieren," I told him, "and some of your old friends."

"I don't want to hear anymore."

"Robbie, they were trying to figure out how to save you."

"Those guys couldn't save a parking spot," Robbie said flatly. "They're idiots." He turned to Piper, who had ridden our mother's old bike. "You doing okay?"

"Yeah," she said, smiling and catching her breath a bit. "It's great to ride a bike again, huh?"

I was struck by Piper's undying optimism. She may have been the happiest person I'd ever met. Normally I might have found it annoying, but Piper had a natural grace and honesty to her that made it all seem effortless, impossible to fault.

"People change," I said to Robbie, even though he was no longer listening to me. "You haven't seen them since you were fourteen."

A pair of headlights whizzed by us and we all instinctively shielded our faces. The lights passed, and we decided it would be better to ditch the bikes by the side of the road and go the rest of the way on foot. Heading off the pavement, we made our way through a marsh, which was one of the few parts of town apparently unaffected by the changes DW had brought. Still cold, still wet, still abandoned.

Approaching the house from the side, we gathered at its low garden wall and saw through the window that a party was happening in the living room. About fifty people were scattered

REBECCA PHELPS

around, wearing fashions that were at once familiar and oddly dated. They were sipping champagne and laughing so loudly I doubted they would notice us even if we screamed.

I was staring at a woman in a large diamond necklace, sensing Piper shifting from foot to foot impatiently beside me, when another woman entered the room.

I had seen our mother three times since her disappearance— the first time in the hotel, when she'd looked right through me, then in the woods late that night, and finally in the newspaper announcing her new government position. And yet every time I glimpsed her, my heart leaped at the shock.

She was more beautiful than ever, her hair pulled back into a tight bun and her flawless face devoid of any wrinkles. Her dress was simple but very flattering. Long and black, cut perfectly to show off her tiny waist. She didn't seem like herself, but instead like an actress who had been cast to play our mother in this strange movie. And she was surrounded by men in fancy suits, all jockeying for a chance to get closer to her.

I turned to Robbie to see if he had noticed her, but I didn't have to ask. His face said it all. He looked like a little boy again, watching her walk through the room. After a moment, he couldn't take it anymore, and he turned his back to the window, slumping down along the wall and sliding to the ground so he could sit.

I crouched down to check on him. "You okay?"

"It's just actually seeing her," he muttered, and his eyes took on that distant look they had had on the train, when I was afraid he was losing his mind. "She's right there."

"Baby?" Piper asked, coming down to sit with him. "Is that her?"

Robbie nodded, and she put her arms around him.

"She's so beautiful," Piper said, meaning it as a form of comfort. Like my mother's beauty would be a consolation of some kind.

I shimmied up the wall a bit to peek back in, and I realized that our mother—or rather, her DW doppelgänger—seemed to be the guest of honor at this party. She was holding court in the center of the room as people came up to greet her and shake her hand.

"I think this is it," I told them. "What we saw in the paper, she's being presented with something."

"I don't want to look," Robbie said. "I don't want to see her like that."

"We should go," Piper said. "This isn't what we thought it would be. We should go."

"I just don't understand it," I said, talking more to myself than anyone else.

"What?" Robbie asked.

"Sage said the planes were crossing because you were stuck in the train portal. That when I took you out, things would go back to normal. Why is it like this?"

I didn't have much time to sit with that question before something quite chilling happened in the room. Robbie and Piper weren't looking in the window anymore, and I was glad, because at that moment another person walked in, shaking hands and looking very much at home. And that person was Robbie.

Of course, it wasn't really Robbie. It was some sort of cruel twin, the one who belonged here with this version of our mother. *Ana doesn't have a daughter. She only has a son.*

I was confused for a moment. Kieren had told me once that

when you cross into Down World, you take over the other version of yourself. That way, there are never two of the same person at the same time. But then I thought about it. We weren't in Down World. Down World was in us. And my real brother, the one crouching by my feet, was the one who belonged here. So the young man standing next to my mother—he was Down World Robbie. And he wasn't supposed to be here.

I was relieved when a whistling came from the woods, giving me an excuse to turn my attention elsewhere. At first, I couldn't see anyone out there, but when the whistling came again, I got excited, thinking it was probably Kieren.

"He found us," I said, grabbing Robbie's hand and leading him into the marsh as quickly as possible, making sure he didn't have a moment to look back in the window. We'd made it just beyond the glow of light from the house when a figure became clear in front of us.

"Come on," the voice said. "Hurry."

We followed the shadowy figure through a small patch of marsh and back to the main road, around a bend from the pyramid house. A car was idling there, and I recognized it as Scott's. The boy who stood before us wasn't Kieren; it was Scott himself.

"Where's Kieren?" I asked.

"They're waiting for you. It's not safe here anymore. Get in."

Scott seemed to be making a concerted effort not to look at Robbie, but Robbie was looking right at him and seemed almost frozen as a result.

"Scott," Robbie whispered. It seeped out of his mouth, almost like a question. They hadn't seen each other in so long, I wondered if Robbie wasn't sure it was the same boy he had grown up with.

"Hey," Scott said, still not looking Robbie in the eyes. "You should get in the car."

"Scott, it's me," Robbie said, a desperation creeping into his tone. "Look at me."

But it was asking the impossible. Scott simply couldn't do it. He kept nodding and motioning to the car, his eyes eager to land on anything but his old friend.

I had begun to understand something since my mother went missing. When faced with the impossible, most people shut down. You may think you'll be brave, or that you'll scream or cry or fight. You may think you know yourself, know how you'll react. But when the unthinkable happens, when your old friend who's been dead for four years is suddenly staring you in the eyes, you don't know what you'll do. You don't know who you'll be.

Scott couldn't look at Robbie. And I didn't blame him.

We got in the car, and nobody said a word.

○ ○ ○

The new meeting place was Kieren's rec room. There were two reasons for this—one, of course, was that the pyramid house and all its neighbors had been taken over by the new elite. Somehow our town, I gathered, had once again become an important military base. And that meant that "important" people needed somewhere fancy to live again.

The second reason, I discovered as soon as we arrived at the house and snuck around the back to enter through the sliding door, was that Kieren's father had at some point been brought into the fold about the portals, and was now leading the meetings.

REBECCA PHELPS

When I saw him at first, I panicked. I had only met the man a handful of times, and that was many years ago. He had always been an intimidating figure, cold and very tall, with closely cropped hair that gave him the appearance of a drill sergeant. And I knew that in some ways that was how Kieren had always seen him—a man barking orders that he was inadequate to follow.

Now he stood in front of us, almost blocking the door with his imposing shoulders, and I didn't know what to say. Should I explain why we were here? Should I call him by his name, Mr. Protsky? It sounded weird in my head, because I had never used it before. As a child, I was always too scared to talk to him.

And yet he didn't seem surprised to see us. Of course, he wasn't looking at me. He was looking at Robbie. I had grown accustomed to having Robbie by my side again. Somehow, in some way, I guess I had never really accepted him as dead. And so it didn't take long for my brain to adjust to him being alive again. It was like he was always with me, and now it was just literal.

But of course, it wasn't like that for everyone. And the reality of what must have happened in this house—the years of grief after the accident that must have rivaled only those in my own home, the self-blame, the heartbreak, and now the worry for Kieren, who according to Christy never left the house anymore—came into clear light the moment I glanced past Mr. Protsky and saw Kieren slumped on the couch.

My family had destroyed this one, just as they had destroyed ours. That one moment in time, the accident, the thing we didn't talk about anymore, had set us all off into some kind of hellish spiral. And even here in this plane, in whatever pocket of DW we had fallen into, we were still in it. We could never escape it.

"Mr. Protsky . . . ," I began, because no one was speaking.

"Is it real?" he said, cutting me off. "Are you real?" He was talking to Robbie.

Robbie had retreated somewhere deep inside himself, although he still had the presence of mind to hold Piper's hand. He nodded, probably growing sick of being asked that question.

Mr. Protsky did something then that I didn't know he was capable of. He began to cry, but in that way that men do when they've been hardwired to know they can't let anyone see it. His crying manifested itself in coughing and even gasping. It was terrifying to hear, and quickly devolved into a full-on coughing fit from somewhere deep inside his lungs.

"Dad, let them in," Kieren said. "They're standing in the doorway. Someone will see them."

Mr. Protsky still couldn't speak, but he stood back a bit and let Robbie, Scott, Piper, and me inside.

The door closed and our eyes adjusted to the dim light. Kieren had stood up beside the couch. He looked pale and very tired. I had never seen him like that before, and it took me aback for a moment. I had been worried that he would do something horrible to himself. For years, he had been ready to sacrifice himself to save Robbie, and just when he was about to do it, I had ruined it. He'd probably assumed that I would be trapped in DW forever too.

The relief on his face told me I was right about everything. He smiled when he saw me, and it was like a man trapped in a desert coming upon an oasis—not ready to believe that it was real.

I forgot everything else for a moment and rushed to him. "I'm sorry," I whispered. "I didn't mean to push you. I just couldn't let you do it."

"I was coming in after you," Kieren said very softly, his mouth by my ear. I doubted anyone else could hear him. "But my dad found out and stopped me."

"Let's all sit down, shall we?" Mr. Protsky said, having recovered from his coughing fit. Robbie finally turned away from Piper, with whom he had been whispering by the door, and he saw me with Kieren.

"What the hell is this?" he asked.

Robbie was looking at us in disgust, and I instinctively stepped away from Kieren. I felt once again like a little girl, like I had tried to cross the street without waiting for Robbie and he was reprimanding me in front of everyone.

"Hi, I'm Piper," Piper said to Mr. Protsky, her voice taking on its naturally light and infectiously happy tone.

Kieren looked confused, knowing who she was, of course, but having no idea how she'd got there. "Hi."

"Piper and Robbie . . . ," I began, not knowing how to explain it. "They're friends now." It was an awkward way to sum up something so complicated, but it seemed to suffice for everyone in the room, who had better things to think about.

"M, get over here," Robbie said, not interested in any of these pleasantries. I did as I was told, walking over to stand near him and Piper.

"Hello, brother," Kieren said, a smile the size of Texas cracking over his dry lips. "I knew it," he continued. "I knew I'd see you again. I knew we'd get you back."

"I'm not your brother," Robbie said, his eyes boring into Kieren's.

Kieren didn't seem surprised that Robbie was angry. It was like he had been expecting it. But there was something otherworldly happening in Kieren's gaze, like he was a preacher addressing a flock of doubters, certain that with time he could convince them something divine was happening amongst them.

"I understand," Kieren said, his eyes not wavering. "But that doesn't change anything."

"Let's sit down," Mr. Protsky said again. "We'll make a plan."

"I have to use the bathroom," Scott said, breaking up the quiet reverence in the room, and relaxing everyone a little.

"I'm hungry," I heard Piper whisper to Robbie, and Robbie immediately snapped to attention.

"Do you have anything to eat?" Robbie asked, helping Piper sit down.

"It's okay." Kieren addressed his dad. The spiritual awakening that had begun when he'd seen Robbie continued to flood his features. "They're all tired. It's late."

"Oh God, I'm sorry," I said, having completely lost track of time. I turned to Mr. Protsky. "It must be one in the morning. We didn't mean to bother you."

"We stay up late here."

"But I don't want to wake Mrs. Protsky. We can come back in the morning."

"We're divorced," Mr. Protsky stated, still obviously harboring a grudge over the fact and not making any effort to hide it.

I turned to Kieren, and I felt quite ashamed that I hadn't known that. Kieren never talked about his home life. In fact, for quite a while all we had talked about was DW and getting Robbie back.

When did his parents divorce? Did his mom live nearby? What kind of a friend had I been for him, not even knowing these basic things about his life?

"I didn't know," was all I said, talking to Kieren. "I'm sorry."

I realized that I kept apologizing, and I didn't even know what for anymore. I was just sorry. I was sorry for everything that was happening.

"I'll make some sandwiches," Mr. Protsky said. "Then why doesn't everyone lie down for a bit? We can talk in the morning. Kieren, unfold the cot."

"Yes, sir," Kieren responded, springing into action. He still seemed lighter somehow, as if none of the talk of divorce or anything else was affecting him. Robbie was alive, and I realized that, even if Robbie never forgave him, that was all Kieren needed to know.

Mr. Protsky left the room and Scott came back from the bathroom.

I felt a bit lost. Everyone seemed to have found their station in the room. Scott helped Kieren unfold the cot, where he had clearly crashed many times before. Robbie and Piper sat together on the couch, exchanging more of their secret whispers. But I had no place here.

I wanted to run and hide, but there was nowhere to go.

After a minute, Mr. Protsky came back with sandwiches and everyone began to devour them. Robbie still didn't talk to Kieren, or even look at him, but seeing the two of them silently stuff their mouths, both leaning over the same little coffee table, brought at least a sense of peace to quiet me.

"Aren't you hungry?" Kieren asked me.

I shook my head. I couldn't think of food. I just wanted to watch this scene and pretend it was the whole truth, that we were together again and that everything was back to normal.

But it wasn't. Outside that door, everything in our town had turned upside down. My real mother was gone, and that hideous mannequin had taken her place.

"Listen, Dad's right," Kieren said, nodding to his father. "Everyone should crash here. You've already risked too much being out this late. Um, Scott, take the cot. Robbie, we can fold out the couch bed for you and Piper."

"Not in my house," stated Mr. Protsky, steely and forceful once again.

"Right," Kieren said. "Okay, um . . ."

"It's fine," Piper said, taking my hand. "Marina and I can share a bed. It'll be like a slumber party. Where should we go?"

Kieren looked to his dad to make sure it was okay with him, and apparently it was.

"Come on," Kieren said. "You can have my room."

"Just a sec," I said, kneeling down for a moment by Robbie. "You okay?" I asked, keeping my voice low.

His big vacant eyes fell on me, then focused for a moment. He smiled a bit, looking for all the world like our mother. I gave him another hug, and stood to follow Kieren and Piper up the stairs.

I was struck by how everything in the house was just as I remembered it, although blanketed under a layer of dust. The dining room didn't seem used anymore, and the lumpy living-room couch seemed relegated to a cat's bed. It was like time had left the house behind.

When we got into Kieren's room, he quickly started pushing dirty clothes out of the way, and I was reminded of the time I had walked into Brady's room and he had done the same thing. Boys were funny to me, always conscious of how they were being perceived, assuming they were being judged. I didn't care if his room was messy.

"I'm going to find the little girls' room," Piper said. "Do you have an extra toothbrush?"

"Um . . . ," Kieren began.

"Never mind. That's why God gave us fingers, I guess." She went into the hallway, and we both watched her go.

I turned and examined Kieren's shelves. I had never actually been in his room before. We always used to play in the rec room when we were kids. On one shelf were two pictures—one of me, him, and Robbie that one of our mothers must have taken at a park somewhere, all hanging from some monkey bars and smiling for miles, and the other of just me. I didn't recognize myself at first, but then I remembered it. It was the one Robbie had taken of me at the pyramid house.

"You kept this?" I asked.

"I love that picture," Kieren said, walking closer.

I flinched, embarrassed to know I had been living on his shelf all these years. "I didn't recognize myself," I said. I wondered how much of that child was left in me now. What would she think, if she were looking at a picture of me?

In this brief moment of privacy, we both grew shy, but finally Kieren came up behind me and put his arms around my waist. We stood there together a moment, looking at the picture and holding each other.

"Why isn't it back to normal, Kieren?"

"I don't know. We'll figure it out in the morning," he said. "I'll take you to the old grounds. There's someone there who might be able to help."

"The old grounds?"

"All done!" Piper exclaimed, coming back into the room. "You know you're almost out of toothpaste," she said to Kieren, pushing some books off his bed and climbing in like she owned the place.

I laughed, breaking away from Kieren. "I guess it's my turn."

"I'll explain in the morning," Kieren said, nodding to Piper and excusing himself from the room.

"Is Kieren your boyfriend now?" Piper asked after he had left.

I didn't know what to say, so I went to brush my teeth. I almost didn't recognize my image in the mirror, I looked so tired and so changed. For a moment, I actually thought I looked like my mother. The real one, not the lady in the pyramid house.

When I was done, I climbed into Kieren's bed, trying to smell some trace of him in the sheets, but they didn't smell like anything. Piper rolled to face me.

"I miss talking to girls," she said. "Do you have a lot of girlfriends?"

I thought of Christy, and the girls I had known at St. Joe's. I felt so far away from all of them, but I did miss them. "Not really. You must have a lot, huh?"

"I guess," she said, seeming disinterested. "They don't know me. No one knew me, until Robbie."

"Not even Brady?" I asked. I hadn't meant to bring him up, but I couldn't help it. She hadn't mentioned him at all, really. Didn't she miss him? Didn't she love him anymore?

She was quiet for so long, I wondered if she had heard me. "Brady and I were together for a long time," she finally said. "And I think, in some ways, he was always going to see me as fourteen. I think he thought of me as this pretty child who got lost somewhere in a field or something, and it was his job to make sure I didn't get lost again."

"What's wrong with that?" It sounded lovely to me, to have a protector, to have a guardian who would never let anything bad happen to me.

"We're not children," Piper said, referring to herself and me. "It's easy to play the part. Especially when you're pretty. Like we are."

I must have blushed. I had never heard anyone talk like her before. Piper didn't seem to have an ounce of insecurity in her body.

"But we can't do that to ourselves," she continued. And then she smiled at me, starting to look sleepy.

"You didn't want to go to Colorado?"

"God no," she said. "I like the beach. Your brother and I were talking about living by the ocean someday. In a little house, you know?"

I nodded. I had never known that my brother liked the ocean. He had only seen it once, when we visited my aunt in Boston. And it didn't occur to me that he had noticed it at all.

"Would you like that?" Piper asked me. "To live with us by the beach?"

"I don't know," I said. "I don't know where I want to live."

Piper grew quiet then, drifting away. I thought of my dream apartment, and my fire-engine-red bathroom. They weren't mine. They were Sage's. And now, my fantasies stripped away, I was left with no imaginary escape to dream of.

CHAPTER 20

The old grounds, as they apparently used to be called, were completely altered when we all arrived there in the morning. The gas station that had occupied most of the lot for as long as I could remember was gone, and the few scattered skeletons of old carnival games were no longer abandoned and ravaged by time, but rather freshly scrubbed, apparently once again being used by the children of the local diplomats who had settled here.

Of course, this early in the morning, the place was abandoned yet again, a filmy layer of dew having settled over the cool night onto the empty bucket seats of the Ferris wheel and the shuttered-up vendor stalls boasting funnel cake and fresh cups of hot cocoa.

We were all there, everyone from the night before, with Mr. Protsky leading the charge.

"Where do we go?" I asked Kieren, although anyone could have heard me.

"The fun house," answered Mr. Protsky, walking across the grounds to a large structure looming over the back of the field.

We all followed silently. Scott continued to trail behind Kieren and me like a nefarious shadow, silently boring his eyes into my back with a heated anger.

I began to wonder if Scott was in love with Kieren, or if he just blamed me for everything that had gone wrong. And despite my resentment of being viewed in that way, I couldn't exactly argue that it wasn't true.

"Kieren," I whispered. "Why are we meeting here in the open? Wouldn't it be better at your dad's house?"

"It's okay," he answered. "No one will see us." He looked around the grounds, his face seeming to assess how much they'd changed. "I guess this place used to have some significance for them."

"For who?"

But he only put a hand on my back and led me inside, trusting that the question was about to answer itself.

We had to enter the fun house through the rotating cylinder that normally served as an exit; at the moment it wasn't moving. I expected it to be dark inside, but instead found it well lit with camping lanterns, which illuminated, in grotesque silhouettes, the fun-house mirrors and distorted walls.

I was surprised to find a small breakfast party already assembled inside the fun house, and even more surprised to discover who was in the group.

Sage was there, having a morning cup of coffee, which she sipped gently out of a small tin cup, and she was joined by John and George. Sage's white flowing dress and John's dirty fingernails revealed that these were the real people from Portland, and not the altered personas that lived in that bitter land under the lake.

"Hello, dear," Sage said when she saw me, not seeming the least bit thrown by my presence.

"Sage," I said, taking a moment to process it all. "What are you doing here?"

Sage and John both laughed at my tone, and I realized that my words had come out sounding a bit harsher than I had meant.

"Sorry," I muttered.

"No, it's all right."

"Is that him?" John cut in, addressing Mr. Protsky and cutting to the chase in his usual brusque manner. He clearly meant Robbie. This was becoming a pattern. Nobody wanted to address Robbie directly, as though he was merely a ghost floating through the room and the only way to confirm his presence was to ask one of the living.

"It is," Mr. Protsky confirmed.

"Oh, boy," Sage said, taking in Robbie with a sweet twinkle in her eye. "He's so tall."

"I can hear you," Robbie said, but nobody paid him any mind. Piper whispered something in his ear and he nodded.

"Hello, Piper," said Sage, finally standing and approaching to give Robbie's beautiful new girlfriend a hug. Piper, in turn, was warm and overjoyed to see Sage, hugging her back with an intense sincerity. "You made it home," Sage said, clearly relieved.

"I did. Marina told me what you did for her . . . and for Brady."

"Have you seen him?" I asked Sage. "Did he come back?"

Sage shook her head gently. "I don't know. If he did, he didn't stop to say hi."

A flash of worry passed over Piper's face, but then she turned back to Robbie, who offered her an encouraging embrace.

"Why are you here then, Sage?" I asked again, not caring this time if I sounded rude.

"The highway runs both ways, doesn't it?" asked Sage, not the least bit perturbed by my tone. "We heard what was happening in the town."

"Who told you?"

"I did," said Mr. Protsky, sitting down and helping himself to a cup of coffee from the nearby pot.

Seeing him sit down with such familiarity next to Sage and John, I realized something that I had never put together before. And I felt like an idiot for not seeing it sooner.

"You know each other," I said, quite dumbly.

"Can we get some breakfast, Dad?" Kieren asked. "M and I could run and get something . . ."

"I'm not going," I said, finally doing the math. "You went to the high school too," I said to Mr. Protsky. And then I looked at Sage and John, and even at sullen George, who sat like a log the whole time, sipping his coffee, deeply immersed in whatever thoughts occupied that sad old brain of his.

"I did," Mr. Protsky admitted.

"So you know," I began. "You know about DW." I replayed the last four years of my life, the rift between our families after the accident. The way my mother hated Kieren and hated his whole family. "You always knew about it."

"I knew that there was a group of kids messing around with something in the basement," he said, nodding to Sage and the others. "We didn't exactly run in the same circles, though, and I figured it had nothing to do with me."

"But you knew that our mom was part of the group," I insisted, still reeling from the fact that I'd never put this together. I looked to Robbie, who seemed to be processing this information as well. How could we have not known this growing up?

"Have you known this whole time that Robbie was in DW? Since the start? And that our mother would try to go in after him?"

"Your mother called me, right after the accident. She said she suspected it, and she told me about the portal on the tracks. But I told her not to try to follow him, that it was too dangerous. At that time, it was soon enough after he had entered . . ."

"Go on," Robbie prodded, hearing for the first time what had been happening on the other side of reality from his imprisonment on that train.

Mr. Protsky finally turned to Robbie, and his voice shifted. A sadness entered it, a weakness. His eyes kept blinking, like Robbie was the sun and he couldn't stand to stare straight at him. Yet he continued.

"I was hoping you'd find your own way out. I knew if we sent anyone in after you, they would just . . ."

"Be stuck on the train too," finished Piper, taking Robbie's hand. "And you were right—we would have been stuck there forever," she added, turning to me. "But we were saved."

"So why aren't things back to normal?" I asked. Sage and John exchanged a look, and I turned to confront them both. "You said when I took Robbie out, that things would go back to normal."

"That's not exactly what I said," Sage explained.

"Yes, it is," I almost shouted. "You said he was trapped between the planes, that that was the problem. Well, he's not trapped anymore! I saved him."

Robbie put his hand on my back, and Kieren had begun to pace. I was upsetting everyone in the room, but I didn't care anymore. I had done everything I was told. Why wasn't it enough?

"Why isn't everything okay now?" I asked, hearing the hysteria in my own voice. "Why have the planes crossed like this?"

"You were supposed to push him," came the calm, otherworldly voice of George, who still sat in a trance next to his friends, not looking up to meet my eyes.

"What?" I asked, my head spinning. Robbie had to steady me for a moment as I tried to gain my balance.

"Push him off the train," George explained. "Back through the portal. That was the way."

"You're wrong," I said, looking at John. "You said that was the only way off the train, but you were wrong. You don't need to go back out through the portal. You just need to pay for your ticket. That's how we got here. You just need . . ."

"A special coin," John finished my sentence. "A coin made on the rails at the portal site."

I felt like a dead weight had come from nowhere and collapsed on the building. Nobody spoke for a moment.

"You knew," I said, realizing the gravity of what John had tried to do. He had commanded me to kill my brother, knowing that it wasn't necessary. "You knew about the coin, and you still told me pushing him was the only way off the train."

"I didn't say it was the only way off the train," John explained, trying to remain calm. "I said it was the only way that would work."

"He's not supposed to be here, not like this," said Sage, trying, as she always seemed to be doing, to soften the blow of her husband's words. "Your mother and her son—the other Robbie—they've taken the place of the ones who were here."

"No," I immediately countered. "Mom went into DW. She's probably trying to make her way back right now."

"Your mother is gone," Sage said, her voice oddly calm. "She's been in too long. That other woman, the one you saw under the lake—she's all that's left now."

The words fell over the crowd, and I finally grew silent, trying to understand.

"That's why you're never supposed to stay on the other side for too long," she continued. "It doesn't make much difference if you take your other self's place for a few minutes or even a few days. But if you stay for too long, you officially fill their place in the world. And the other version—the one that was supposed to be there—can never come back. Matter cannot be created or destroyed."

If you and your other self diverge too much from each other, it can be too late to go back. That's what George had said. He had been right—it was too late.

"So the other Robbie," I continued. "The one I saw last night at the pyramid house . . ."

I let the sentence trail off, and I could tell the others were staring at me. Robbie and Piper hadn't been looking in the window the night before; they had never seen the other Robbie.

"He's the only one who's supposed to exist now," explained Sage. "Your brother no longer has a place. That is why the planes were able to cross. Robbie's defying the laws of physics by existing here, and these are the consequences."

I felt the whole room turn and look at my brother, standing by my side. His face was stone, as it so often was lately. He didn't even seem sad, just lost.

"What if I die?" Robbie asked. I fiercely shook my head,

refusing to even hear it. But Robbie simply pulled me into his chest. I stood there, trembling. "If I die, will that make everything go back to the way it was?"

John shrugged. "If you weren't here, it might make the planes uncross. Make this dimension go back to the way it was."

"No, no," was all I could say. I broke away from Robbie, glaring at the empty faces of the people before us, casually discussing his death as though it meant nothing to them. But it meant everything to me.

I turned to run, knowing I had to get far away from all these people, but having no idea where I was supposed to go next.

I stepped onto the rotating cylinder, which began to spin as soon as my foot was on it. I was thrown to the ground and struggled to right myself as carnival music started up, pumping through the speakers all around me. Its warped and tinny notes seemed to mock me as I found my footing, wobbled my way out of the spinning wheel, and ran across the grounds. All the rides started to move of their own volition, as though they were on a timer.

It wasn't long before others began to appear—the well-heeled children of the new rulers of the town, hands clutching shiny new balloons or powdered pieces of funnel cake while harried nannies chased not far behind. I had no idea what time it was, or even what day it was. But since none of the children were in school, I had to assume it was a weekend. Christy said I had been gone for four months. When I left, it was June. So it must be October by now. That explained the chill in the air, the lingering gray of the morning.

Kieren came up behind me, not saying anything. I guess he realized I needed a moment to process. But I had run out of answers.

Think, Marina, I scolded myself. *There's always a solution.*

Kieren, clearly struggling with all the information as well, stood silently beside me. Nobody seemed to be watching us. The children were too preoccupied with their rides and their candies. There were goldfish to be won, roller coasters to ride.

"Are the others still in the fun house?" I asked.

"No. They snuck out the back when the carnival started up."

I nodded, not sure why I had asked. I didn't really care if they got caught, sipping their coffees in the glow of their own warped reflections.

Mirrors. They do it with mirrors.

"Kieren, what is DW?" I asked, the pieces of the puzzle all floating before me—my first trip down; the stolen egg timer; Piper McMahon, who got on Robbie's train at the station; the train with its ghastly conductor, his eyes piercing through mine, seeing through me. My mother's eyes in the hotel. She didn't know me. Or did she?

"I don't know," he answered. "It's like a shadow, I guess. Like the echo of somebody screaming. But there's no way to stop hearing it."

I shook my head. "There must be a way."

The planes intersected like a network, like a web. We had taken a wrong turn on our way home, and we had ended up on the wrong string. That was all. It was like a computer. Like a motherboard, the circuits wired together just so.

"And if we rewire it?" I asked of nobody, although Kieren was still there listening. "If we break down the pieces, put them back together?"

"What are you talking about, M?"

Robbie and Piper had come up next to us, with Scott trailing behind, but I wasn't looking at them.

"Yesterday, Kieren," I said, feeling a flood of adrenaline overtake me. The great high of solving a mystery, of being so close to a goal that you can smell it. "We go into Yesterday. We change the past."

"You can't go into Yesterday," he reminded me. "It's bricked up."

Something John had said was stuck in my mind. It was about the coin made on the tracks, the one that I used to pay the conductor. He had already known about it. They all had. Which means my mother knew about it too.

And she was on the tracks the night she disappeared.

"She made a key," I realized. "That's why she was on the tracks that night." I turned back to the others. "We assumed she was trying to go through the train portal—to find you, Robbie. But if she did that, she would have been trapped on that train with you. No, she wasn't there for the train portal. She was there to make a key."

"You mean, like the coin I made you?" asked Kieren.

"Yes. You made it on the tracks where the portal is. And somehow, for some reason, maybe some of that energy got trapped in that coin. Because it has a special power. You can use it to control DW—to go wherever you want to go. That's how we got here," I explained, nodding to Robbie and Piper.

"Marina handed the coin to the conductor," Piper explained. "And he took us home. Or wherever we are."

"And you think that coin could also open the Yesterday door?" Kieren asked, following my reasoning.

"I do," I explained, my thoughts returning to those doors

under the school, the brick walls, the little peepholes with nothing but blackness inside. "They aren't peepholes," I realized. "They're coin slots."

Kieren exhaled and cradled his head in his hands. We all fell silent for a moment, letting the ideas settle over us. The more I thought about it, the surer I was that I was right. All the pieces seemed to fit—why Mom was on the tracks that night, why she then went into the high school.

She must have realized it was too late to get Robbie off the train, too late to prevent what was inevitably going to happen as a result of him being there—namely, that the world she had built under the lake and ours would cross.

But what if the world under the lake had never existed in the first place?

What if Robbie had never been hit by that train?

A guard walked by then, wearing that same uniform that the man driving the fire truck and the one at the jail had been wearing. He eyed us unevenly for a moment, making me realize how suspicious we must have seemed, standing in a cluster, wearing shoes, which no one who wasn't part of the town's elite was still allowed to do.

We bowed our heads and started walking, pretending to take an interest in a carnival game where you shoot water pistols into a clown's mouth, trying to blow up the balloon on top. We all picked up a water gun, and Kieren handed the barker some money.

The guard finally moved on, convinced, I suppose, that we were the teenage children of some important colonel or general, and that we were enjoying the carnival like everyone else.

"She went into Yesterday," I concluded, knowing now that it must have been true. "But whatever she tried to do didn't work.

If it had, the world wouldn't be like this now. We have to follow her . . . and find out what went wrong."

Piper took aim at the clown's mouth, waiting for the game to start. "How do you know you'll go to the same place as her, though?"

"Why wouldn't I?"

"I mean," she began, "the door to Today leads to all sorts of places. I usually end up in town, by the drugstore."

It was Kieren who spoke up this time. "And I used to land in my bedroom, holding the wrench I use to fix my skateboard wheels when they come loose."

I looked down at my hand, gripping the water gun. I was wearing the ruby ring my parents had given me for my tenth birthday. They'd handed it to me in the kitchen, while we were eating breakfast.

"Where did you get those earrings?" I asked, turning to Piper.

She touched the fake diamond studs in her ears, smiling at me. "Groussman's, I think. Years ago."

The man behind the counter rang a small bell, and the water guns began to vibrate. We shot the water into the clowns' mouths, and Piper's balloon popped first.

"I win," she squealed.

Kieren turned to me. "I had my skateboard in my backpack the first time I went through."

I smiled. We had solved another part of the mystery: whatever token you had on you at the time you crossed determined where you ended up.

I thought of my mother's little dangling blue earrings from the night I'd last seen her. They were the same ones she was wearing in the old photos in her closet, from the beach in Portland.

The night she built the portal under the lake.

"None of that matters if we don't have the coins," Robbie said, coming back to the conversation after being distracted by the carnival game.

He was right, of course.

"I'll go to the track and make another coin," Kieren offered, as Piper gleefully collected her stuffed bear. "I'll meet you back at my house tonight."

"Make two," I said. "In case we need it to come back after."

"I'll help you, man," Scott offered, and the two of them ran off.

I watched them go for a minute, until they disappeared into the crowd, and then Robbie and Piper and I left in the other direction.

CHAPTER 21

I thought I would lose my mind sitting on the couch in Kieren's rec room, waiting for him to come back with the flattened pennies.

"What do you think it is?" Piper asked, sitting next to Robbie on the floor. "The thing that your mother changed?"

"Well, we know what she did in real life—*our* real life, anyway," I said, nodding to Robbie. "About ten years ago, she went to Portland to visit her old friends, the Mystics. She brought me with her but, Robbie, you stayed home with Dad." Robbie looked confused by this, as though straining to remember it, but he said nothing. "While she was there, she gave John a key, and he used it to build the lake portal. It's not like the doors under the school, though. It leads to only one place: the world we saw, Robbie, the one where Mom was in the paper."

"It's awful," Piper said.

"The world from that train station." Robbie nodded.

"I think what she's done now is gone back to that day, at the beach in Portland, ten years ago."

"Why?"

"Because of the lake portal. Maybe—I don't know, maybe she figured if she didn't build the portal, there would be no dark world to mix with ours."

Robbie nodded.

"Except . . . except that wouldn't save you. Her whole plan was to save you from being hit by the train. She must have changed something else too. But what?" I wracked my brain, trying to remember details from that beach. But suddenly it was like every image I had retained from that trip all those years ago started to fade. One second I could vividly recall the white billowing curtains, the red bathroom, then suddenly the memories were gone. I shook my head. More of the pictures disappeared. It was almost like they were being . . . erased.

"I loved that trip," Robbie said wistfully. "That woman Sage gave me chocolate ice cream every day while we were there."

Piper smiled at Robbie's memory, but I felt a chill run down my spine. "No, Robbie, you weren't there, remember? You stayed home. You had Little League or something."

"No, *you* stayed home, M. I was there with Mom, but you stayed with Dad."

I got up and started pacing. "Oh my God," I mumbled to myself, my breaths coming faster as I walked. "She brought you instead."

"What are you talking about?"

"She brought you to Portland. Instead of me. Because you'd be safe there."

"What do you mean, safe?" Robbie asked. "It was years before the accident."

"She wasn't planning on bringing you back," I explained gently.

"You mean, keep me in Portland? Raise me there?"

"It would keep you away from the train track." I nodded. "And that way you'd never have had your accident."

Suddenly all those images in my brain of the trip to the hotel were replaced with new ones: Dad and I playing with puzzles; Dad tucking me in, my heart beating too fast. The house feeling too empty with just the two of us left behind.

Robbie nodded slightly, weighing the repercussions of what I was saying. "If I was raised in Portland, I wouldn't have grown up with you."

"And we never would have met," Piper added, her hand clutching Robbie's.

"But I do remember growing up with you," Robbie continued. "Mom and I came back from that trip."

"That's how I remember it too," I said. "So then she must not have gone through with raising you there. If she had, we'd both remember it that way. Something must have gone wrong with her plan."

"What?" Piper asked.

I looked towards the window, to the world that was now overrun with the deranged reality from under the lake. "I don't know."

"So what can we do?" Piper asked.

"We'll follow her, all of us. We'll stop her from building the lake portal. And we'll make sure that . . ."

"Marina?" Robbie asked, his voice timid.

"That she *does* raise you there, Robbie. That you are kept away from the train tracks."

"No."

"The world we come back to should look just like our old one, but with Robbie alive in Portland."

"I said no. Not if I won't remember you," Robbie insisted.

"It'll be okay," I said. "We'll all go in together. When you leave DW, you always remember everything from before, right? As long as we're together, we'll remember each other."

Piper and Robbie sat with my words for a moment. Piper smiled, but her bottom lip was trembling.

"When we get back, you two can go. You can live wherever you want."

Robbie looked at me, a question lingering on his face. "Wherever we want?"

I smiled. "Piper said you wanted to live by the beach."

"We'll get a little place with an extra room," Piper said with a nod, the plan all set in her mind. "Marina will live with us."

"Yes," Robbie agreed. "When she finishes high school."

"Hold up," I said, trying not to laugh. "Don't plan my whole life for me. I'd like to do a few things first. I'm still learning how to drive."

"I'll teach you," Piper said. "I guess I'd better teach you both, huh?" she added, turning to Robbie. "I don't want to be the chauffeur for you two forever."

Robbie laughed, always seeming a bit lighter when Piper tried to cheer him up.

Kieren and Scott returned a moment later, their faces flushed red and their hair windblown. They had clearly biked back at full speed, still a bit out of breath.

"Did you get them?" I asked.

Kieren opened his hand and showed me two flattened pennies, which I tucked securely into my pocket. "Don't lose those now," he joked.

"Promise."

"Do you know where we're going?"

"Yes," I said. "I just need to run to my house and get something."

"I'll go with you," Kieren immediately offered.

"Stay," I insisted. "I'll be fine. Why don't you help your dad upstairs? I get the feeling he wants to talk to you."

Robbie looked up from the floor where he had been whispering with Piper. "You sure you're okay on your own?"

I smiled. "I promise to look both ways before crossing the street," I said, and I finally got a bit of a smile out of Robbie. "I'll be right back."

o o o

Outside I hopped on a bike and started pedaling for home. It was close to noon. Scott had explained to us that the front part of the school was still being used for lessons during the week, and sports events were still being hosted in the auditorium on weekends, though the place would be heavily guarded. They always ended by 4:30 so that everyone could be home by the curfew of 5 p.m. There was a basketball game that afternoon, in fact.

Of course, the boiler room was in the military part of the building.

The plan was to go to the basketball game with everyone else. As it was a Saturday and most of the military staff were off for the weekend, we figured this was our best bet to sneak down the hall towards the boiler room. There was a locked door in place now between the school part of the building and the military section, but Scott knew where they hid the keys.

We had to be careful, Scott had warned. Instead of a hall monitor asking to see a pass, if you got caught in the wrong hallway, the MPs simply took you away. Nobody really knew where they brought you, but it was somewhere you didn't want to go.

I got to my house and pulled the bike around the back, entering the quiet, empty kitchen like it belonged to someone else. Nothing about it felt normal anymore. Not even a scent of my mother's fragrance, or a stray wire or memory stick from my father's constant fiddling with computers remained. The house was clean and empty, a musky smell having taken over the rooms. The smell of abandonment, of isolation. I felt my palms sweating, the anticipation of tonight's plan making me shake.

Upstairs, on a shelf in my parents' room, I found the album I was looking for. I quickly flipped through until I found my mother's copies of those photos from the lake that George had kept in his closet. I hadn't looked at them in years.

There was Sage, about a decade younger. She was pretty, but somehow never had a real glow of youth about her. And a couple I didn't recognize was lounging by the lake with them, sipping something pink out of plastic cups. This must have been Jenny and Dave, I figured. They were clearly a couple. Jenny was a real beauty—blond hair and a tiny little polka-dot bikini. And Dave had the chiseled chin of an old movie star. I remembered what Sage had told me—that she'd had an affair with Dave when they were in DW. I could see the whole story. She had always been jealous of the prettier girls and their handsome young boyfriends. When she'd had the opportunity to be with Dave, and the prospect of no consequences to haunt them afterwards, of course she'd taken it.

Another photo was just of my mother, smiling with her hair pulled back, the little blue earrings from the night of her disappearance dangling from her earlobes.

And below that, in a place where I could have sworn there had been a picture of me and Mom together, there was now a picture of Mom and young Robbie.

So I was right.

I grabbed the photo of my mother with the earrings and put it in my back pocket. I felt a knot in my stomach and a dryness in my mouth. Could this plan really work? Would we make it to the school on time, and would Scott find the keys?

I was downstairs and about to go out the back door to grab the bike when I heard the revving on the driveway outside. At first, I thought I must have been hearing it wrong. It couldn't have been from the driveway, but instead must have been on the street.

Then I heard it again. I slowly walked through the house and peeked out the front window. I recognized the car immediately, and my heart leaped. I never thought I would see it again, or its driver. I ran out the front door and got into the passenger side of Brady's Pontiac, practically throwing myself at him.

His long arms wrapped tightly around me, and I could feel the tension seep from my muscles. *He was alive. Thank God.*

"You scared me so much," I whispered. "When you didn't come back—"

"I did come back," he interrupted.

I pulled back to see his face. His eyes looked sad and tired, but he offered me a weak grin.

"When?"

"Just a couple days after I left you. I took the train all the way home and back to Portland again, like we planned. When I couldn't find Piper anywhere, I snuck back to the lake and through the portal."

"But that was months ago."

He smiled and looked away.

"You've been here the whole time?" I asked softly.

His big brown eyes turned to the windshield, as if he was looking for answers in the clouds above our heads. "It gets worse here every day, doesn't it?"

"Brady, I have to tell you something. I found Piper. She's safe. But she's . . ."

"I know."

"You know?" I swallowed hard. "How?"

"I went to Kieren's earlier to see if he'd heard anything. I saw her holding hands with that guy. And I saw you too. Did any of you even think to come tell me that she was alive?"

"I didn't know you were back."

But he just shook his head.

"Brady, look at me. I would have gone straight to your place if I'd known."

He finally did turn to look at me, his marble eyes glassed over.

"I never should have told you to get on that train under the lake," I said. "I'm sorry. You were too late. She was already . . . she was with him already."

"Who is he?"

"He's . . ." I hesitated for a moment. How could I explain this to him? "He's my brother, Robbie. I saved him, Brady. I got him out. And she was with him. They were both trapped together in DW. And now they're both out."

He let all that information flood over him for a moment. "And she fell in love with him, of course. That's what she does. Rescuing lost kittens."

"Brady, don't," I said. I couldn't stand to have him talking about Robbie that way. I didn't want to think of my brother as being that vulnerable. But of course, part of the reason it hurt so much was because it was true. My brother was like a shell of himself since he'd returned. And without Piper, I shuddered to think what would become of him.

"I'm sorry," he offered, shaking his head. "That was mean. I shouldn't have said it."

I sat back for a moment, not sure what to say.

"Do you know what's happening here?" Brady asked. "Why it's like this?"

"We're going to fix it. We have a plan. We're going tonight."

He nodded. "The girl with a plan," he said with a smile.

"What does that mean?" It hadn't sounded cruel, but I could recognize the irony in it. My plans hadn't worked out so well up to then.

"Nothing," he said, turning away again.

"I can't just leave it like this."

"No, of course not."

He took a deep breath, massaging his temples. It seemed like something an older man would do, someone who was perpetually tired.

"What will you do now?" I asked.

He shook his head. "I honestly don't know. I was going to go to Colorado without her, you know? But I don't want to go if it's like this."

"It won't be," I promised. "Go, drive to Colorado. I promise, by the time you get there, it will be back to normal."

He laughed then, the distant laugh I had first heard in his room all those months ago.

"What?"

"I'm remembering the last time you told me to go somewhere," he teased me.

"This will be different. This time I know."

He looked at me again and offered me a very sincere smile, and I wasn't sure if he believed me or was simply humoring me. "I should have kissed you back when we were in the lake."

I could feel the blush taking over my cheeks.

"Sorry," he immediately offered. "That was probably creepy."

"No," I said, too embarrassed to say anything else. A thought of Kieren flashed through my mind. "I need to get back."

"Can I drive you?"

"No, I should take the bike," I said, realizing that it would be best if the others never knew that Brady was back. It would just cause an ugly scene between him and Piper, and I didn't want to put my brother through that.

"Be careful," he said, a seriousness settling over him.

We both knew, I suppose, that this was a real good-bye. I couldn't say the words, so I just nodded and got out of the car.

I heard a song playing as he drove off, something I didn't know the name of, but I felt like I had heard it before—a man begging over and over again to get what he wanted for the first time in his life.

I watched him pull away, heading out towards the highway.

The song faded, and then it was gone. And I imagined him driving to Colorado, all alone. My heart was breaking as he went, but I knew I had to shake it off. I had a lot of work to do.

o o o

A bitter wind blew through our clothes as we approached the school that afternoon. It seemed like all the kids in town were gathering to head inside for the basketball game, a fact that didn't surprise me, as there wasn't much else to do since the military had taken over.

The boys and I entered the auditorium together—Scott and Kieren sat by the exit doors, acting as lookouts to let us know when the coast was clear of guards and we could make our way down the hall. Meanwhile, I sat down nearby with Robbie, awaiting the signal. He kept a cap hung low on his head due to an unwavering paranoia that someone might recognize him from when he was a child. I didn't think that was likely, but he didn't want to take any chances. And Piper was waiting for us in the bathroom not far away, crouching in the farthest stall, since everyone here actually did know what she looked like and would ask a million questions if they saw her.

The game began and I half pretended to watch. We were all trying to act natural, although if anyone had actually noticed us, I'm sure they wouldn't have been fooled. I glanced over to Kieren, who was eyeing the hallway through the glass windows in the double doors. Every now and then, Scott would elbow him to pretend to watch the game, and they would both start cheering a little too enthusiastically. I buried my head, trying not to call any extra attention to them.

The guards paced the perimeter of the auditorium, taking no interest in the game. They were watching us. They weren't dressed as guards—they were wearing the same plain shirts and khaki shorts that the Russians in the woods back in Portland had been wearing. Trying to blend in, I suppose. But they couldn't have stood out more. They were here to corral us, to imprison us. And everybody knew it.

It was close to halfway through the game when I glanced over to Kieren and saw him give me the signal—two fingers scraped over his forehead, followed by a slight pointing gesture down the hall. It meant that there were two guards, but they had just turned a corner.

"I'm going," I whispered to Robbie. He was supposed to wait one minute, then get up and meet us by the bathroom. If the guards had returned by then, he would simply go into the men's room and wait until he heard them walk away.

I walked past Kieren and Scott and made my way to the bathroom where Piper was waiting. As planned, she had her feet on the toilet in the last stall, crouching down low. Somehow, that girl managed to make hovering over a toilet look like a modeling shoot.

"It's time," I told her, and she nodded and followed me.

I peeked my head out of the door to see Kieren and Scott standing on opposite ends of the hallway, looking out for guards. Kieren turned and started walking towards me, his eyes motioning to me to head back inside.

I closed the bathroom door, and Piper and I waited until we heard two sets of footsteps pass by. After a moment, the hall grew quite silent again. I knew the game was almost at the half, and lots of people would soon be filing out to use the bathrooms

REBECCA PHELPS

and hit the concession stand. We had to make our move before that happened, or there would be too many witnesses.

Slowly, I opened the door and peeked out again. I looked to the right and saw nothing, then to the left, where Kieren was standing with Robbie and Scott, waiting for us. "They're gone," Kieren whispered. "It's now or never."

Piper and I came out, and saw that Scott was holding the map they had prepared earlier. And in his hands, sure enough, was a large ring of keys. The plan was actually working.

"It's down the blue hall," Scott said. "This way."

We all tried to find a balance between walking quickly and walking naturally. At first, we were trying to go slow—just a few kids heading to their lockers or something. But soon we all began to realize that if we got caught, there was no longer any reasonable explanation for what we were doing in the hallway. The adrenaline of the ruse began to course through our blood, the impending fear of being seen. And before we knew it, we were all practically running down the blue hall.

At the end was the first door—one of those heavy metal doors that peppered the whole school and that we had all walked past hundreds of times without noticing. Kieren and Robbie faced out, practically blocking us with their bodies while Scott began trying keys.

I tried to breathe. I didn't want to rush Scott, but I knew it was a matter of minutes before the guards would make their rounds this way. We were so quiet, I could hear the slightest scuff of someone's shoe against the tile. I closed my lips so my breathing wouldn't be audible.

Kieren reached his hand back behind him, looking for mine. I took it, and I could feel the dampness in his palm. He was as nervous as the rest of us, though he was trying not to show it.

Robbie saw our hands holding, and he turned away. He still hadn't forgiven Kieren. Maybe once this dimension returned to normal they would have a chance to be friends again. I could only hope.

"Wrong one," I heard Scott mutter.

"What?" I whispered, trying not to sound too stressed out. I didn't want him to panic.

"Hold on," he said, trying another one.

I swallowed down my nerves, and tried to keep a calm energy about me.

I thought I heard something down the hallway then. Some sort of footsteps. It might have been the guards, or it might have been someone else. Scott was still working next to me, and I wanted to cry from the tension.

The footsteps receded a bit, and I could make out muffled laughter from that direction. It wasn't guards. Probably just some kids looking for a place to make out. I let out the faintest sigh, and then I heard the door click.

"Got it," Scott said, not making any effort to mask his own relief. We all went through the door and closed it very gently behind us.

For a moment, I wondered if we had walked through a portal. Instead of the dark, long-abandoned hallway I had been expecting, it was a clean, brick-walled corridor with bright fluorescent lights hanging overhead. They made a very slight buzzing sound, like miniature bees hovering nearby, waiting to strike.

I looked around for surveillance cameras, but thankfully didn't see any. Even if there were some, there was nothing we could do about it now. We simply had to get to the science room before anybody noticed.

REBECCA PHELPS

"Walk quickly," I instructed, and Kieren nodded.

"She's right. It's this way."

We all began to walk, with Scott still holding the map out in front of him. "There should be another door on the right, with a stairwell."

We made it another twenty feet or so without seeing anything, until I began to be convinced we had entered the wrong door. But then I spotted it.

"There," I almost shouted, immediately covering my mouth. "Sorry." I stepped back a bit to let Scott find the right key.

Once again, Kieren turned to face out, watching. I looked at Robbie, whose eyes revealed not a hint of emotion.

"Baby," Piper whispered to him, and he looked at her. As always, her face was all he needed to wake up a bit, to become present once more. "I love you."

Robbie smiled. "I love you too."

The door opened, and before I knew it, we were making our way down a stairwell, deep into the bowels of the building. Soon we were connecting with another hallway, the doors to several empty offices popping up from time to time on either side. It took me a moment to realize we were in the hallway that led to the science lab with the portals. They had cleaned it up. And the offices had been bricked up before. Now they were clearly in use, even though for the moment nobody was in them.

We finally got to the science lab at the end of the hall. My heart was racing so fast, I thought I might pass out. I could feel the desire to run down that little spiral staircase, open up the Yesterday door, and bolt through it before anything could go wrong. But I knew I had to be patient for a few minutes more.

We tried the knob, and of course it was locked. "Just one more," I whispered to Scott. "You're doing great."

Scott didn't seem to care about my compliments, however, and got to work without acknowledging me. Soon he got the door open and we all filed inside. The room was very dark, and I searched the wall for the light. But I couldn't find the switch.

As it turned out, I didn't need to. The lights turned on by themselves, a fact that shocked me so much I almost screamed.

And that's when we all froze. Because we weren't alone in the room.

Every time I saw my mother in this world—this dark and twisted world—it took me a moment to register what I was seeing. She was her, of course, but she wasn't her at all. In a way, it was like seeing the evil twin of a television character you had grown to love. And it was surprising how quickly your love of that character could turn to sheer hatred of the twin. Because the twin is the worst kind of imposter. The twin takes everything, even the face, even the voice, and corrupts it.

Was it really possible that this twisted image of my mother was just a different version of her? The same woman, simply on a different path? A path without me. A path without my father. A path, apparently, that made her happier than we ever could.

We had billions of universes, according to Sage. There were billions of me's too. Somewhere. Somehow. Were they happy? Were they scared? Would they ever be free?

"Keep them away from the tent," my mother instructed. And I recognized the man she was talking to—it was her lover from the hotel, the Russian guard. He came and grabbed Kieren and started to put him in handcuffs.

There were other guards there as well, three of them. They

began to restrain Robbie and Piper. Scott simply stood nearby and watched.

The woman with my mother's face approached me. "I'm sorry. But I can't let you go in."

"How did you know?" I asked. "How did you get here in time?"

She smiled. "I saw you last night, outside the window of the pyramid house. I knew you would try."

I felt my shoulders droop in despair. We had been so close. And now it was all for nothing. We were too late. There was nothing we could do to stop her.

"You have to understand," she said, "things end up the way they're meant to. We always think we can change them. That if we just did one thing differently, made another choice in a key moment . . . But nature finds a way."

"This isn't nature," I said, looking around me at the science lab. "This isn't right. You're not right. You have to let us go."

"Let's head upstairs," my mother said. "It's almost curfew."

They began to walk back out the door, two of the guards prodding the others along, and my mother's boyfriend coming to take my arm. I began to really panic. If I left this room, it was all over. They'd never let us sneak down here again. And we'd be trapped in this terrible reality forever.

I didn't have time to form a plan. We were walking out the door, the others already in the hall before us, when I swung around and poked my fingers into the man's eyes. I don't know what made me think to do that. I must have seen it in a movie once, or in some online defense video.

He doubled over in pain, grabbing his eyes, and my mother whipped around to see what had happened. I shoved the man away from me and ran back into the room, slamming the door before the others could get back to me, and turning the bolt lock.

I was alone in the science lab, but I knew it was only a matter of moments before they got the door open. So I spun and ran into the tent and down the spiral staircase.

This was it. If this didn't work, there was no plan B. I took one of the coins Kieren had handed me out of my pocket, walked up to the door to Yesterday, and slid it into the opening that I had thought was a peephole. At first, nothing happened, and I was crushed by the feeling that I had been wrong.

"Come on," I whispered. It was practically a prayer, and I thought of the masses I used to attend at St. Joe's. I never took Communion because we weren't religious, but I would watch the row of kids who did go up to take the wafers. On their knees, their eyes closed, waiting and waiting for something close to God to come to them.

"Please," I said. "Please work."

And then the brick faded away, and only a bright light remained.

I took a deep breath, hearing the guards banging on the door above me. Reaching into my back pocket, I took out the photo from Mom's album and held it in my hands, concentrating on the tan, happy people on that beach. And then I walked through the door.

CHAPTER 22

Once the yellow glow had subsided, the first thing I became aware of was sunlight. It surrounded me so completely, blanketing my whole body, that I thought at first I must have been trapped in some ongoing state of transition. The yellow light simply wouldn't fade.

But then I blinked and I heard splashing.

Taking a step away, I saw that I had come out of the back of the boathouse—the one that George had converted into his cabin on the other side. I was facing the woods, the sun piercing through the leaves onto my face. The splashing and laughing grew louder, coming from the beach on the other side of the small building.

Turning around, I could still see the yellow outline of the Yesterday door scorched into the wall itself, like the faded image of a screen saver burned into a computer screen. But even as I stood and looked at it, the yellow began to fade even further, and the red outline of bricks began to appear in its place.

The door was sealing itself.

I instinctively thrust a hand forward to try to stop it, even though I knew that wasn't possible. The faintest dark horizontal line in the upper-right corner of the brick indicated where the coin slot remained. My hand whipped to my pocket, feeling the flattened penny lodged there. I had one chance. A one-way ticket back.

At least one key fear was allayed as soon as I looked down at my body: I had been slightly afraid that I would be five years old again in this portal, but I seemed to be intact. Did that mean that my five-year-old self would be missing somewhere? If so, I needed to act quickly.

Peeking around George's small cabin, I saw about a dozen people laughing and splashing in the water. It was like the picture I still held in my hand. The same sunny day, the same people. I spied the young couple I had assumed were Jenny and Dave, kissing on the sand. Jenny wore the same polka-dot bikini. She turned in my direction, and I froze, although she didn't seem to notice me.

The other people on the beach were all sunbathing and swimming. I assumed they were guests of the hotel. It occurred to me that nobody here would recognize me—assuming they could see me at all, that is—and I could probably just blend in.

I sat down by the water, passing myself off as a guest.

After a minute, I heard a familiar voice shouting, "Look who finally showed up!" It was Sage, approaching the beach from the wooded trail. John, Jenny, and Dave all turned to face her.

I subtly looked up, my feet gently nuzzled by the lapping water of the lake.

Sage looked just as she had in the picture, which I carefully shielded from view—younger and prettier than when I had met her. She wore a large Indian tunic in a bright orange color that billowed in the lake breeze. The camera, which had probably taken the picture in my hand, dangled around her neck.

And following behind her on the trail, still in their travel clothes and carrying their suitcases, were my mother and her young son, little seven-year-old Robbie. Despite knowing better, I couldn't help but look behind them for a little five-year-old Marina chasing after.

But I wasn't there.

I knew this would happen, of course, but it still caused a pit of anger to form in my stomach. She had really left me behind.

Little Robbie looked so innocent in his blue jacket, with his little brown suitcase covered in dinosaur stickers. My mother wore the red sun hat I hadn't seen in years, a large wooden bangle dangling from her wrist. In fact, she looked younger, too, and not just because she seemed so relaxed with her son by her side. I could only assume that she had been able to take over her younger self's body somehow.

The fountain of youth. Another one of DW's dangerous powers.

As I watched her with Robbie, I struggled to recall some of my own memories of being on this trip when I was a child. But they were gone. I could no longer even picture those flowing white curtains and the red bathroom that had echoed in my brain for so many years. The only images that remained were the ones recently formed when I had been here with Brady.

It had all been so important to me once. How could it just be gone?

I shook my frustration away. There were more important things to think about now, and my real question was still not answered: If Mom's plan had been to stay here and raise Robbie in Portland, why did Robbie and I both remember her coming back?

What had gone wrong with the plan?

I watched as my mother gave John a kiss on the cheek, sparking a flash of jealousy to pass over Sage's eyes, which she tried, not too successfully, to hide. Once Sage had turned away, my mother nodded towards her suitcase, showing it to John. He got very excited then, practically licking his lips. But my mother kept eyeing Robbie.

John suddenly became very animated, teasing Robbie and throwing him up in the air. Robbie was clearly annoyed by it, as he was too old to be tossed around like a human Frisbee.

I could only make out bits and pieces of what they were saying, but I caught something about heading back to the hotel so the newcomers could settle in. I pretended to watch the water, waiting until I sensed they were gone.

When I turned around, they had all abandoned the beach. Only a few stragglers remained, catching the last afternoon rays before packing up their sun umbrellas and towels. The shadows were growing longer up and down the sand, so I slowly stood and made my way down the trail back to the hotel, blending into a small group of other guests. Nobody acknowledged me.

The hotel was very much like it had been when Brady and I first found it. Maybe a little cleaner, a little fresher somehow. There were a few people milling about in the lobby, sitting in old lounge chairs and sipping drinks. Talking on old-model cell phones.

I walked towards the stairs, like I was any other guest of the hotel, and nobody stopped me to ask if I had a room key, or even what room I was staying in.

Again, I wondered if anyone here could even see me, but my question was answered soon enough when a man bumped my arm by accident, on the stairs.

"Excuse me," he said as he passed.

I nodded, staring at the floor. Okay, so I was definitely not invisible, just as Brady and I hadn't been in the plane under the lake. That was good to know.

I reached the very top of the stairs and found that the door to Sage and John's apartment was slightly ajar. I could hear voices inside, and I tiptoed a bit closer to peek through the opening.

A strong scent of fresh paint and sawdust wafted to my nose. I could hear Sage's voice: "And over here I'm going to do, like, an Indian sitting area, with throw pillows on the floor."

"The bathroom is so bright," said my mother. "How did you pick that color?"

"It just came to me," Sage said, "like in a dream. Suddenly, I thought to myself: fire-engine red! And that was it."

"I tried to talk her out of it," I heard John say. "But you know how she is . . ."

"It's perfect," Sage countered. "Red is a powerful color."

"Robbie, go in and change for dinner," my mother said, and I heard Robbie's little footsteps making their way to the bathroom, followed by the door closing.

After a moment of silence, John's voice resumed, a bit closer to my mom this time, so he didn't have to speak as loudly.

"I'm so glad you brought him," he whispered, and I could only assume he meant Robbie.

"I told you I would," my mother replied.

"I'll put on a pot of tea," Sage said, her voice distracted somehow, and a bit too loud. It struck me that she was making a big show of the homey atmosphere she was building with John, as if she were trying to prove something to my mother.

He whispered something that I didn't quite catch. But the word *beautiful* stuck out to me. Was he hitting on my mother with Sage right there in the next room?

I heard her protesting slightly, her voice coy and almost girlish, but she was clearly flirting back. Then they walked a bit closer to the door. I panicked, having nowhere to go. And so I simply froze by the wall. If they came out, I'd have to bury my face and run for it before my mother saw me. Despite her younger body, she was the same woman who had left me all those months ago, the night she had called me her warrior.

But thankfully, it didn't come to that. They were simply moving closer to the door so that Robbie and Sage couldn't hear them.

"Did you really bring the key?" I heard John ask.

"Yes," Mom answered. "I told you I would. But John, I've been thinking . . ."

"Chamomile or jasmine?" Sage called from her kitchen area.

"Um, jasmine, please," my mother responded, and then she lowered her voice again. "We don't have to go through with it," she said. "There's nothing down there for us now. And we don't even know what kind of portal this would end up being. We've been lucky so far."

"We'll be lucky again," he insisted. "I already told my investor that it would be ready tonight. He's meeting us here in a few minutes."

"What investor?" my mother asked.

"Some Russian kid. His dad's worth billions in real estate or something. They want to put money into the hotel. Didn't I tell you?"

"No," my mother said, her voice faltering. "I mean, I don't think so. I would have remembered." She paused for a moment. "I don't remember."

"I told him he could go for a joyride or two through the portal. That's all. Just for fun. These guys love their thrills, you know."

"Are you crazy?"

"It's no big deal. Just for fun."

"Listen to me," my mother commanded, a certain hardness in her voice finally making her seem real to me. It was a tone I had heard many times, whenever Robbie and I were bad, or refused to brush our teeth or eat our dinner. "I don't want a portal near my son. Do you understand me? Otherwise our deal is off. I only brought the key so you could help me dispose of it. For good this time."

"You're being paranoid," John insisted.

"Yes, I am."

"I wouldn't let anything happen to Robbie."

"You can't promise that."

A tense silence fell over them, and for a moment I wondered if they had silently walked away. But then John spoke, a vulnerability in his voice I hadn't heard before.

"Is he really mine, Rain?"

Light years seemed to pass before my mother answered, and I could feel the walls of the hallway start to close in on me as the silence expanded and reverberated.

What did he mean, mine? *That Robbie was . . . No. It couldn't be that. Sage had told me that Mom had left John when she was nineteen. She moved back to town and met Dad. And Robbie was born the following year.*

"I don't know," my mother finally returned. I clasped a hand over my mouth, knowing I couldn't make a sound, even as the tears coated my cheeks.

"This was a mistake," my mother continued. "I should have known better. You'll never change. I need to get back to my daughter."

"Rain, don't. I still love y—"

"Stop it. Don't touch me. Sage is coming back."

"What can I do?" John asked, even more urgency in his voice. "What would make you stay?"

"Tea!" Sage shouted from the other room, and I could hear the bead curtain jangling as she approached.

My mother whispered intently, "If there's no portal, I'll stay. Otherwise Robbie and I are going home. I'll find another way to protect him."

As the footsteps headed away from the door, I stumbled backwards and staggered down half a flight of stairs before I couldn't walk anymore. I plopped down onto a step, my head in my hands, trying to collect my thoughts in the quiet stairwell.

How could I not have known about Robbie? Did my father know? Or at least suspect? And is this why my mother brought Robbie but not me this time? Because John was willing to raise her son—*their* son—but not some daughter she'd had with another man? Maybe the whole reason Robbie had skipped this trip when I was five was because my mom didn't want to be tempted to stay.

But did she mean what she said just now? Would she really stay if the portal was never built?

I remembered suddenly that Sage had said something else to me when Brady and I were here. The different dimensions were just different paths, formed when a decisive event caused life to veer into a new direction.

This trip had been my mother's decisive event—the moment when she'd made a decision that would affect the rest of her life. I could see the two potential realities forming in front of my eyes. In the first, she and Robbie went back home to Dad and me, and her son was killed at fourteen. In the other, she stayed, abandoning Dad and me, and her son was saved.

It was that simple: Go and he dies. Stay and he lives.

I knew that if it was up to John, he would build the portal no matter what. He was too addicted to DW, to the power of it. And besides, there was some "investor" to consider now—a Russian investor. That could only mean one thing.

I wanted to be generous and consider that maybe John and my mother had never meant the world under the lake to be so corrupted. Maybe it was just supposed to be a clean slate. But then John let the Russian in—a "joyride," he'd called it—and the man had clearly never left. Instead, he'd warped it into something sinister and twisted.

I wasn't sure how my mother factored into that world. Maybe the version of her I'd met under the lake was a completely different person. Maybe my real mother had gone down at some point in the ten years between this beach visit and the present to try to stop her evil doppelgänger from becoming too powerful, and had accidentally stayed too long and been eaten up by her.

Swallowing down these thoughts, I took a deep breath and

tried to focus. The truth was, I might never know what had gone wrong under the lake. But I did know this: I needed to stop it from ever happening, both to protect the world below from the Russian investor and to save my brother's life.

I stood and started heading down the stairs, not sure what my plan was but knowing I had to make one, when I almost walked right into a man heading up to the apartment. He was young and barrel-chested, smelling of expensive cologne, and wore a neatly pressed suit. It took me a moment to recognize him, but when I did, I felt my whole body shudder.

He was my mom's Russian boyfriend from the world beneath the lake. Alexei. That was his name.

"Excuse me," he said, the slightest bit of an accent apparent in his speech. He looked about twenty-five years old, and was very handsome, but in a cold and menacing way.

"S-sorry," I stuttered.

"Are you a friend of John's?" he asked, nodding to the stairs I had just descended. They only led to one place.

"No," I answered, perhaps a bit too quickly. "I mean . . . I'm just lost. I was looking for my room."

"Ah, what's the number?"

"Four. Fourth floor. I had the wrong one." I laughed, trying to sound casual. "I know where it is now. Excuse me."

I edged past him, heading down another flight of stairs and trying to walk at a measured pace.

Once I got to the lobby, I sat down and pretended to read a newspaper someone had left on a coffee table. I was right about the Russian investor, it seemed. It was, in fact, Alexei. And if he was here, was I already too late to stop the portal from being built?

o o o

It was very late when the group from the upstairs apartment finally came down, dressed for dinner. My brother looked tired, and a glance at the clock over the reception desk told me it was after eight. But my mother pulled him along in a possessive way. John was deep in conversation with Alexei, but even from a distance, I could see Alexei's eyes drifting over to my mother.

They all joined a stream of other guests headed to the dining room. None of them had the suitcase. At the last moment, Sage turned back, muttered something to the others like "just a moment," and then strode over to the front desk. I watched from over my newspaper as she plopped her purse down on the counter, asking the front-desk girl for something or other.

The girl nodded, and Sage followed her into the office, leaving her purse behind.

This was my only chance. That suitcase was somewhere in the apartment upstairs, and Sage's keys were surely in her purse. I ran up and grabbed the whole clunky, heavy bag, bolting up the stairs while I frantically searched through her collection of tissues, receipts, and lipsticks.

I found the keys jangling together at the bottom of the bag and got lucky on the first try as I heard the lock click open.

Bounding into their apartment, I discovered the suitcase by the bathroom. I knelt down to open it, all while glancing intermittently at the door. How much time before Sage discovered her purse was missing? One minute? Maybe two?

I opened the suitcase and let the top of it fall back. Inside was a small glass jar, like a beaker, narrow at the top and plugged with a cork, wedged into some Styrofoam padding that had been cut specifically to fit it. A pink solution sloshed around inside. It had a glow about it, an iridescence. I picked it up and stared at it, and I could see the liquid splash against the glass enclosure as my nervous hands shook.

The footsteps on the stairs were muffled at first, but then I could hear Sage's bracelets clinking together. She was humming to herself, obviously convinced that she had left her purse upstairs.

I stood, clutching the beaker to me, and ran for the front of the apartment. There was nowhere to hide, as it was all one large room. I eyed the bathroom furtively, but I knew I'd never get there in time. Instead, I pressed myself against the wall by the door. If she opened it all the way, I would be hidden behind it.

But when Sage came in, she only opened the door enough to pass through. I was completely exposed behind her. She was distracted, at least, looking around for her purse. So once she was a few feet into the room, I turned and ran out the door. I could sense her spinning to see me.

"What the—" she started. "Stop! Someone's in here! Thief! Someone stop her!"

Luckily, as Sage's apartment occupied the whole top of the building, there were no other guests nearby to hear her. I flung myself down the stairs, hearing her jewelry clucking like a scared hen behind me.

I knew she wouldn't be able to catch me. I ran so fast, the world turned into a blurred soup, and I didn't stop until I was deep in the woods, halfway to the lake.

There was only one person who could help me now. One person who might know how to destroy the solution inside the beaker, and that was George. I had no idea if he would do it or not.

As I ran, the weight of my actions hit me with full force. In a world where Robbie grew up in Portland, thousands of miles away from me, I wouldn't know Kieren. We were only friends because of Robbie. Without him in our lives, would we have ever even met?

I wouldn't have gone to St. Joe's, which I only did as a reaction to Robbie's death. Those three years on the hill, my friendship with Lana, reading books under the cypress trees, all gone in a flash.

I might have still been lost on my first day of sophomore year. After all, the second-year classes were in a completely different part of the school than the first-year ones. So it's possible Brady still would have helped me find my class, that I would have followed him to the train station that day and that we would have eventually become friends.

But our trip to Portland? I only went on that trip because of Robbie and my mother's disappearance. And Brady went because Piper didn't come back from seeing the Mystics. But with no lake portal to go into, Piper would have come back. She never would have met my brother on that timeless DW train, which he wouldn't have been on in any event. She and Brady would have gotten back together. They'd be in Colorado by now.

My whole life transformed before my eyes like a photograph left out in the sun, fading into oblivion. Had I been completely defined by my brother's death? Who would I be without it? Without Kieren? Games of Monopoly in Kieren's rec room. Robbie and I breaking into the pyramid house. M&M's swiped from a vending machine.

Kieren once said that DW demands a balance. No two versions of the same person can exist at once. A life for a life. He was willing, at one point, to sacrifice himself if it meant saving Robbie.

Was I willing too?

"You don't belong here," came a man's voice behind me. I whipped around and saw George approaching from the beach. I stood, clutching the beaker in my arms like a wounded baby.

George came up and took a closer look at me, seeming to be confused. "Rain?"

I shook my head. "I'm her daughter. My name is Marina."

George seemed to understand immediately. A profound sorrow took over his face. "Why are you here?"

I held out the beaker, delicately, like an offering in my palms. "Can you help me destroy this?"

He looked down at the beaker, nodding to himself in a knowing way, and let a silent whistle escape from between his dry lips.

"Yes," he said at last.

○ ○ ○

"The truth is," George began, as we sat on log stumps surrounded by a circle of lanterns, "it's already destroying itself."

"How's that?" I asked.

"It's a natural process with radioactive material." He shrugged, gesturing vaguely to the air. "The nuclei are unstable. Proteins escaping and being repelled. There's nothing you or I can do about it, really."

"But . . . can it still make a portal?"

"For now, it can. But eventually, as it degrades . . . no."

"How long will it take?"

"A long time," he said, placing the beaker gently by his feet.

"So what do we do?" I asked.

He scratched his head, letting out a deep sigh. "We dig a hole."

George popped into his would-be cabin and emerged with two shovels, handing one to me. "Not here," he said. "In the woods."

It took over an hour of digging through moss-covered ground and gnarled tree roots before George considered the hole satisfactory. It was maybe ten-feet deep by then. A bone-chilling cold seeped out of the rock-hard earth that surrounded it. When George finally let his shovel fall to the ground, and indicated to me that I should do the same, I couldn't hide my relief.

He gently lowered the beaker, wrapped in a blanket with a long rope tied around it, into the deep hole. He then threw the whole length of cord in after it, and motioned to me to pick my shovel back up. We filled the opening in silence, and George gently patted some ivy back on top of the upturned soil.

"And now?" I asked.

"Now I stay, and I watch, to be sure."

I nodded, my body all but collapsing with exhaustion.

"You can go home now, child," he continued.

"Home," I repeated. The word sat like a death sentence, floating in the space between us. There was an old saying: *You can't go home again.*

I started to walk towards the boathouse, but I turned back before I had gone too far. "Do you believe in heaven, George?"

He continued to stare at the ground, his eyes unwavering. "Depends on your definition of the word, I guess."

"A place where we all see each other again."

He nodded. "Maybe," he conceded. "There might be a heaven and there might be a hell. But on this earth, there's just the choices we make, and the way we live with them."

I took a deep breath, steeling myself for what I had to do.

Leaving George sitting there by the freshly buried beaker, I walked around the back of the boathouse. The brick door was waiting there for me. I slid the coin into the slot and waited for the bricks to melt away into yellow light. And then I walked forward, back into Today.

EPILOGUE

Six months passed, and another spring was upon us. I biked to school early every morning so I could feel the cool air tickling my forehead and waking me up to each new day.

I still didn't have my license, as I had never gotten around to taking the test again. So every day after school, Dad would take me to the abandoned field where the old grounds used to be, out by the gas station, to drive the car in loops. I had no trouble mastering parallel parking, but he would often call me out for stopping too suddenly at the makeshift stop signs he had set up.

"I know you're anxious to get your license," he told me one day. "But I think you should practice for a while longer."

"No problem, Dad. I'm not in any hurry."

"Hey, let's stop by the drugstore on the way home. I want to get your stepmother an anniversary card."

"Okay," I said, careful to put on the turn signal and look both ways before leaving the lot.

The town was somehow quieter since I'd gotten back, or maybe it just seemed that way to me. There had never been curfews in this reality, but still the streets felt empty at night. The only exceptions were game nights at the school, when people would hang out in the parking lot until about ten—parents and children—eating takeout and talking about what kind of season the teams were having.

I would sit with Christy, who was still my best friend. The portals under the school had been bricked up since the previous year, and nobody went down there anymore. It started to seem like a dream I had once had, and sometimes I wondered if I was the only one who had dreamed it.

But then I'd see a little something, hidden on the bottom of a school desk or etched on the door of a bathroom stall: "Where'd you go, DW?" "I've been Down. Have U?"

We pulled up to the drugstore so my father could pick out a card for my stepmother, Laura. In this reality, they had been married for five years. I was getting to know her slowly, and despite myself, I found that I actually liked her.

"We should get one for your brother too," my father said. "He got straight As his first semester at U of Oregon."

"I heard. You pick it out, okay?"

I headed for the magazine rack and I was flipping through something about "miracle skin" when I heard the skateboard scrape across the floor nearby.

"Not in here, kid!" came the manager's angry shout.

"Sorry," was all the kid said in return.

I peeked over the magazines to see the top of a head, and I

knew it was him. Kieren didn't know me, of course. I had wanted to tell him a million times about us. *We were friends*, I wanted to say. *We were more than friends. We were almost in love once.*

He caught my eye, and I realized I was staring. I looked away for a moment, embarrassed. He was done with high school now, and I had seen him working at his dad's cell phone store.

Where would he go next? To college, maybe? Or to join the military like his father had before him? His parents had never divorced in this reality, the stress of Robbie's death having never befallen their house. I had seen the whole family together at the high school football games.

When I looked up from the magazines again, Kieren was gone.

That night I was on my laptop doing some homework when I heard the beep of a new email. I scrolled over to see it, and I couldn't help but smile when I saw the name.

It was from Brady. We'd swapped email addresses after he arrived in Colorado, but I hadn't heard from him in a while.

Hey, kiddo.

Just wanted to see how junior year was treating you. You find your math lab yet? Just kidding.

Piper and I are loving Colorado. She's taking some classes. I haven't found a job yet, but I'm sure I will. I've got some leads. The mountains are beautiful. You can see them from our balcony.

If you're ever around this way, you should stop by and see us. I think you'd really like

Piper. Here's a pic of us up at a place called
Pike's Peak. It's amazing up there. You feel like
you can fly.

A picture of Piper and Brady followed, as promised, and
they both looked beautiful. Fresh faced and rosy cheeked. The
atmosphere up there really agreed with them.

And here's a postcard I found at the gift shop. I
don't know why, but it made me think of you, so
I wanted to show you the picture. I hope you're
doing good in school. Take care of yourself.

XO, Brady.

The picture he'd scanned was one of those postcards I'm sure
they sell at every ski resort in the world. It showed a woman
standing on a mountain late in the day, her back to the camera, the sun setting before her. She had her arms raised up high
above her, the last pink streams of sunlight glowing through her
fingers, like she was on fire.

And just as Brady promised, she looked like she could fly off
the mountain. She looked strong. She looked like a warrior.

ACKNOWLEDGMENTS

This book would not exist without the extraordinary community of writers and readers at Wattpad. You discovered my book, you voted for it, you left me thousands of supportive and encouraging messages, and you made me believe in myself and my story. I am profoundly grateful.

To the nicest group of Canadians a girl could ever hope to meet, the entire team at Wattpad HQ. You plucked my book out of obscurity and selected it as a 2019 Young Adult Watty winner. My wildest dreams have been coming true ever since. I am especially indebted to Deanna McFadden for selecting *Down World* for publication, and to my brilliant editor, Jen Hale, and copy editor, Sarah Howden. You asked all the right questions and didn't quit until I found the right answers. The book is infinitely better as a result.

I wrote *Down World* in thirty-minute spurts at 6 a.m., while my husband watched over our two kids. Every morning for a year, I'd trudge down the street to the coffee shop, laptop firmly wedged beneath one arm, not sure if anyone would ever read the words I was typing. Thank you to the Aroma Café for making the best muffins—and the strongest coffee—in the world. Thank you, Mom and Dad, for never missing a performance (even when you were the only ones in the theater). And thank you, Steffen, Luna, Levon, and Frenchie, for always believing I could do this.

ABOUT THE AUTHOR

Rebecca Phelps is an actress, screenwriter, novelist, and mom based in Los Angeles. She is the cocreator of the website novel2screen.net, which analyzes film and television adapted from other material. *Down World*, the recipient of a Watty Award for Best Young Adult Fiction, is her first novel. To hear more about the Down World trilogy, follow Rebecca on Instagram @geminirosey, or on Twitter @DownWorldNovel. Happy reading!

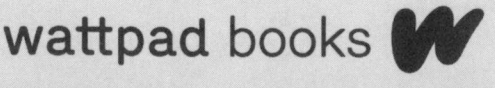

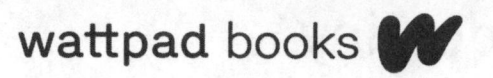

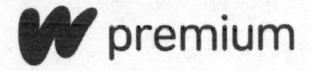

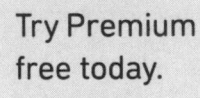